COMING
APART

COMING APART

APART

Jean Renvoize

STEIN AND DAY/Publishers/New York

First published in 1981
Copyright © 1981 by Jean Renvoize
All rights reserved
Designed by Louis A. Ditizio
Printed in the United States of America
STEIN AND DAY/*Publishers*
Scarborough House
Briarcliff Manor, N.Y. 10510

Library of Congress Cataloging in Publication Data

Renvoize, Jean.
  Coming apart.

  I. Title.
PR6068.E7C6   1981   823'.914   80-6202
ISBN 0-8128-2780-5   AACR2

For Bruce Hunter

COMING APART

DAY 1

---

*The story broke so late only the final evening editions were able to carry it.
It had been a poor day for news—an unimportant massacre in some
African state, a couple of small explosions in the holy cities of Belfast and
Jerusalem, union trouble at British Leyland—and the editors were cursing
because the story hadn't broken earlier. Since no one knew where Jess was
and the nanny had refused to open her mouth until her employer came
home, they had only the barest facts to go on, not enough to make it
worthwhile doing over the entire front page. So although the newsboys'
posters blared out* FAMOUS TV PERSONALITY'S BABY SNATCHED! TV STAR'S
BABY STOLEN! TRAGEDY HITS JESS BENNETT! *and other such, when home-
bound commuters eagerly sought to read all about it they searched in vain
until they reached the Stop Press at the back of the paper, only to find
their endless appetite for the life events of the famous whetted rather
than satisfied by the brief tale.*

  The syndicated story ran:

Jess Bennett, famous TV critic and personality, was at the BBC studios this
afternoon when Mathew, her 5-month-old son, was snatched from his
pram. Mathew's nanny had left him for two minutes outside their house to
make a phone call, and when she came out the baby had disappeared. Police are making inquiries.

Apart from spelling Matthew with only one "t"; truncating his age by two months; saying Jess was at the studios when in fact she was interviewing a geriatric playwright in his nursing home; reporting that the nanny made a phone call whereas the truth was she took a call and, most crucial of all, that the call lasted two minutes when it actually lasted eight, they got the story right. In the days that followed, that was not always to be the case.

WITH the exception of her father's "attack" upon her, Carrie grew up in a world entirely free of headlines. It was that most enervating of worlds, lower suburbia, where the opinion of neighbors matters far more than principles, moral or spiritual. Although the attack split her youth into two separate halves, her mother saw to it (as best she could under the appalling circumstances) that their exposure to notoriety should be brief and all the unpleasantness buried not only out of common view but so deep in their own unconscious that eventually weeks could go by without either of them recalling it.

This was not easy to achieve, but Agatha Warren was a determined woman. Her first move was to restore her tribal identity. A few weeks after her husband had been tried and sentenced, she reverted to her maiden name of Lowes and soon felt so comfortable with it it was almost as though Gerald Warren had never entered her life at all.

For Carrie it was more difficult. Born a Warren, she felt denatured by the change. Who was Caroline Lowes? Looking at the embarrassed scrawl on the covers of her new school books (her mother had done the job properly: change of name, change of address, change of school—the shameful past was cremated and the ashes thrown out with the garbage), Carrie would sometimes sit, hand half obscuring her face, reading and rereading her new name, trying to absorb it. She half expected that one day perception of her self would burst on her like a flash of magnesium lightning—boom! the miracle achieved!—she was Caroline Lowes indeed. Only it never happened. She stopped being Carrie Warren at fourteen, but she never really began being Carrie Lowes.

Anyone but her mother would have seen the danger in that state of affairs, but Agatha Lowes was a single-minded woman of no sensitivity. She didn't believe in psychology, psychiatry, and all that nonsense. Common sense, decency, and the respect of your neighbors, they were what really mattered in this world. Just once in a while, as she stuffed her large bosom into the elasticated undergarment that transformed her heavy flesh into a formidable pillar of rectitude, she would recall with momentary tenderness the baby her growing daughter once was. Then the bitterness that was the unacknowledged prime emotion she now felt toward Carrie was diluted long enough for her to wonder whether—in spite of all her care and wisdom—the child was doing all right, but her invariable conclusion was, yes, she was doing fine. Hadn't Carrie's new headteacher said she was quite pleased with her, considering not only the problems of adjustment to a new school, but above all the terrible shock she had undergone (poor little Carrie, to lose your father so unexpectedly, my dear Carrie, we *do* sympathize); and she seemed to have made lots of friends already, so obviously she was doing all right.

Only it took time for Carrie to take in the lie that her father had been felled by a heart attack. At first she kept wanting to cry out, he's not dead! he's not dead! But, as her mother kept reminding her, the whole point about the move halfway across London was to expel all memory of him from their lives, and, what with her mother's insistence and the guilt she carried inside her, it wasn't too long before she almost came to believe he really was dead.

He might as well have been dead as far as she was concerned anyway. At first she had written letters to him, but he never wrote back. When she cried about that her mother said jailbirds weren't allowed to write letters from prison, or just shrugged her shoulders and said what did she expect from someone like *him* (the venom in her voice when Agatha spoke of him hurt worse than her words). Carrie never asked outright to see him, of course, although she knew prisoners were allowed visitors. She quite understood that considering what he had done there was never any question of their meeting together. Just once—not long afterward when she still remembered clearly how it had all happened—she asked her mother, very tentatively, if it might be possible for her to visit him, but her mother had looked at her with her narrow stare, then said tightly, "He raped you, have you forgotten!" So she had never mentioned it again, and quite soon she had wrapped up the memory of all that had happened—of him, and of their love, and of the horror and the shame of it all—and buried the neat little parcel of phased-out Warren memorabilia deep down in the blood-black cavern of her wounded center. But she never quite managed to become Carrie Lowes, all the same.

Of course, if you are a normal person, with the normal ties of family and relations, it is almost impossible to cut yourself off entirely from your past.

6

And Agatha Lowes considered herself the essence of normality. Therefore she continued to keep in touch with the other members of the Lowes tribe (Warrens had ceased to exist). At the appropriate times, Agatha and Carrie received and sent birthday cards and Christmas presents were exchanged. But at family gatherings the mutual embarrassment was awful.

It was the first Christmas without Gerald. Christmas was a time when all Loweses came together, regardless of any conflicting claims of spouses' families. To an outsider it would not have been easy to spot which were natal Lowes and which were spousal Lowes, for most Lowes unerringly selected partners who were by nature so Lowes-like that the putting-on of a wedding ring seemed merely a formal ritual acknowledging a fate foretold from birth. Mostly they were large solid people, heavy in flesh and in mind. The occasional exceptionally large man invariably mated with a small woman so that the offspring reverted to norm, but even these little women had the true Lowes toughness and insensibility. Loweses were rarely ill and despised people who were. They would have made splendid settlers, stoically breaking in new land to the plough—not for them the restless onward and outward push of the curious-minded. But theirs was an untapped talent. Inhabiting a faceless suburb in South London undistinguishable from a dozen other suburbs, their only territorial ventures were, for the more successful Loweses, to move from small terrace houses with three up and two down to grander semi-detached ones with two baths and a garage.

The house this year's Christmas party was being held at was the finest achievement of all. Fully detached, it even had a drive so that you could deposit passengers at the front door and then take the car on a dozen yards or so to a separate garage. Nancy Pringle (née Lowes), whose husband George had recently been promoted to headmaster of the local comprehensive school, glowed with clan pride. She saw herself as being an advance guide, a pointer to where the whole Lowes clan was heading.

The only shadow was the expected arrival of Agatha and Carrie. There had been no question of not asking them. You never *asked* a Lowes for Christmas Day—Christmas involved a right and a duty. Every Lowes had a right and a duty to go to whoever was holding Christmas that year. It was unavoidable. But more than one Lowes hoped in his or her heart that Agatha would have a nasty attack of flu and be unable to come.

The older Lowes reminded each other of their unease the day Agatha had first brought Gerald Warren home. It was not that they sensed the rapist in him. Far from it. The policeman father of Carrie's favorite cousin, Richard, came closest to articulating their distrust: "He's not what you'd call a man's man, is he?" Gentle Gerald, slimly handsome with his shining fair hair and clear blue eyes, was not, and clearly never could be, of basic "Lowes" stock.

Like farmers faced with a maverick, their instinct was to weed out the stranger with delicate hands and blond locks. To the hints about his possible lack of manliness the young Agatha had responded with blushes. Lowes cannot talk openly about sex; it is one of their most clearly distinguishing features—and the family concern soon became reversed, that she should disgrace herself in a way no Lowes ever had before. Their marriage, then, was received with mixed relief and nervousness. It was inevitable that Agatha should soon be disillusioned—Gerald did not change, but her perception of him did—and the poetry in her soul, a tenuous throwback to some forgotten ancestor, withered and died. Carrie, her father's double, was born, but the romance was already ended. Agatha had reverted, and though once in a while Gerald timidly persisted, no more children were born. (Thank God, they all cried later when IT happened, thank God there was only one child!)

Agatha, entering the room that Christmas Day, did not have to be told what everyone was thinking. For all their sakes she had, of course, removed herself from the district—it had been expected, any of them would have done the same—but she still belonged. She could never cease to be a Lowes. Returning among them, she looked them straight in the eye, only a slight redness about her ears betraying any embarrassment.

Carrie was another matter. She was as at home in that room as a roe deer in a pen of bullocks. But she had grown up among them, she knew their ways and automatically accepted their own pleased estimate of themselves. If, after an hour or two of clan company, she had to slip away to an empty room for a few minutes to recover her spirits, she was still young and unsure enough to put her need down to her own lack, not theirs.

Today was the first time she had been exposed to Lowes *en masse* since her disgrace. She saw them as strangers. "Of course," she'd once overheard an aunt say, "if she'd been more of a Lowes she'd never have let it happen. Not that I'm saying it was her fault, poor child, but . . ." and the voice trailed away. At the time she hadn't known what her aunt meant: now, looking at all these faces examining her, she understood. Color flared in her face. Within seconds they all looked away, began to chat furiously among themselves to annihilate the moment of embarrassment, but she knew their inner eyes were still watching her. Although they looked anywhere but at her, from her alien kin there exuded the prurient curiosity of the chaste: she sensed every pore, every quivering Lowes cell focusing on her—all around the room banks of radar receivers were beaming in on her to see if IT showed.

She felt herself shrinking. Pride kept tears out of her eyes, but her body crawled with awareness of the revulsion they and she felt for it. Her shoulders slumped forward to disguise the sprouting breasts that these last few months had added to her problems. There had been times when a tough core of sense within her made her thrill to her new shape. When she looked at herself floating in the bath, at the long creamy thighs and the dark tuft of hair and now at the high breasts swelling more outrageously every day, she could not help for a moment or two adoring her new body. But the adoration was always short-lived, a private joy that withered almost instantly into disgust. (Though there remained a relief that her body was not growing askew as she had feared, scarred by the monstrous sin she had committed.)

Her mother had deserted her, gone over to join a group of women gathered around the fire. Carrie stood alone by the door. In each hand she carried a plastic shopping bag full of Christmas presents. At least they gave her something to do. Looking with simulated pleasure at the green plastic Christmas tree in the far corner of the room as though she had never seen it before, she crossed over to it and knelt down, head lowered, distributing her parcels among the pile already arranged around the tree's base.

She rose, looked around, and went over to a tall lanky boy with whom she used to play Indians in the laurel bushes at the end of her old garden, less than a quarter of a mile away. In those days they'd been in and out of each other's houses and gardens (he lived in the same street) as though they were brother and sister. Parting from Richard had been one of the hardest parts of the move. Remembering the earthy smell under the laurel bushes where they used to leave buried messages in code for each other, another pang of longing struck her.

She sat cross-legged on the floor beside him. "Hi!" she said, happy to see him again. "How goes it, my long-lost coz?"

He seemed to have trouble replying. His face flamed round the pallid

9

pyramids and craters of the acne pustules that he could never resist picking at, and a hoarse choking sound emerged from his mouth. He coughed to clear his throat and tried again, but a falsetto squeak followed by a dive into profundo bass betrayed his agitation.

For a moment Carrie misunderstood the cause of his embarrassment. He had been eating a sausage roll when Carrie spoke to him, and she assumed he had swallowed the wrong way. Unthinking, she leaned over and thumped him vigorously on his back. He spluttered, and unmistakably pulled himself away from her. Then she understood. She looked up and saw the whole tribe of Loweses openly staring at her with the expression on their faces she remembered so well from before, a kind of fear combined with unwilling fascination. Instantly she understood she had broken a taboo: she, the contaminated one, had laid her soiled hand on a virgin Lowes body.

Shamed, but obscurely angry too, she drew herself away from Richard, clutching her hands together in her lap. Perhaps he had been told it was catching.

The incident was quickly smoothed over, glasses being refilled and more sausage rolls passed around; but when finally they all sat down to supper, crushed tightly behind conjoined tables shrouded in white cotton bedsheets, she was acutely aware that instead of sitting together with her young cousins as she had always done in the past she was imprisoned between Nancy Pringle's husband, the headmaster, and her rigid-backed grandmother. She knew her grandmother's opinion of her—the day after it had happened she'd overheard her say to one of the aunts, "It's in her blood. I don't suppose she could help it. She's got bad blood, she got it from *him*," and had thought her grandmother was making an excuse for her, though it hurt. The image stuck in her mind for days. Now she realized the old woman never had liked her anyway—why hadn't she realized that earlier when she was still a child?

Worse was still to come. Carrie had a cousin who was also named Caroline, and to distinguish between their presents it had been the family custom to write the girl's surnames as well as their forenames on their gift labels. This year everyone had remembered her new identity except her grandmother (or was it done out of malice?). As Carrie was handed her grandmother's present she looked at the label and there, printed large so that everyone could see it, was the forbidden, dead name—CARRIE WARREN.

Carrie Warren. For the first few seconds it seemed absolutely natural to Carrie. Then suddenly the name became a blow, a deliberate insult; a moment later it was warm and lovely and she wanted to hold the label against her cheek. *Carrie Warren.*

There was another embarrassed silence. Then at the same moment all the grown-ups began to talk rapidly in a variety of false voices so that it was worse than if they had not spoken at all. She knew her mother had seen the label too because later on during the bus journey home when Carrie, almost weeping, said she'd never go to another family party ever again, Agatha Lowes looked thoughtful, then said, "We'll see." Which under the circumstances was almost as good as an agreement.

It was quite true that at her new school Carrie had made many friends. After a year or two she became one of the most popular girls in her class. No one knew about her past, not even her teachers—her mother had seen to that—and they all took on trust that pretty, fair-haired Carrie was exactly what she seemed: a normal, untroubled girl who never caused anyone any problems. A few of the more perceptive teachers felt that something—perhaps the unfortunate death of her father—was holding her back and that probably her intelligence was greater than most people suspected, but this was common enough among the older girls. By Carrie's age most of them were more interested in clothes, pop music, and boys than in their studies, and there weren't many teachers who retained enough enthusiasm for their jobs to view someone like Carrie as an interesting vocational challenge.

Perhaps it was inevitable that the more secure Carrie appeared, the more bitter Agatha Lowes felt toward her. She did her best to conceal it—she was not a vicious woman—but Carrie soon learned that for a few days after the term reports her mother would treat her especially sharply, and the better the reports the sharper she would be. At these times Mrs. Lowes would go on about the stringent economies they had to make (she had been forced to take a job, but she earned so little she often complained she'd be better off on Social Security though living on public money was something no Lowes did lightly).

At this stage in her life Carrie was perpetually hungry—the starchy food she ate never seemed to make any flesh on her—and she would finish her meals in a flash. Bread was the only food that was not rationed out, and she would fill up her cavernous emptiness with endless slices of the

11

substance sold as bread at the supermarket where Agatha worked. But during the post-report days even bread was short. Agatha Lowes would plunk down the remains of a wrapped loaf in front of Carrie and say coldly, "Go on then, eat it up. There'll be nothing left for my supper, but never mind—I don't matter." Then Carrie would remove one thin slice only and push the rest away.

Occasionally after school she would go back to one of her friends' houses for tea, but she took care not to do this very often. She felt instinctively that if you ate with someone you grew closer to them, and that she was frightened of—she had too much to conceal. Mostly she made friends with lightweight girls only, girls whose minds flitted like butterflies from subject to subject—boys, other girls, the latest disc, that lousy teacher who'd kept them in late twice in one week for nothing at all.

There was one girl, though, a quiet rather strange girl, that none of the others liked much, to whom Carrie felt drawn. Janice was always sitting around reading in a corner of a room when everyone else was wandering around the playground arm in arm giggling. She was often in trouble because in lessons that bored her she would conceal a book on her lap and read instead of listening to the teacher. She made the others feel uneasy because she was so obviously "different," a mistake Carrie had been careful never to make.

She and Carrie had spoken together a few times, and Carrie had felt the exhilaration that comes from discovering someone with whom you know you can truly communicate. At first—she was still only fifteen then—Carrie submitted to the tug of friendship, at night dreamed long involved dreams about the two of them, the details of which she could never remember in the morning except that they were full of adventure and weird happenings. But soon she began to realize the special dangers for her in such a relationship. Carrie knew that giggling about sixth form boys or the younger male teachers, which passed for intimacy with most of the other girls, was not for Janice. She was as fascinated by romance as they were, but found it in books—Mallory's *Morte d'Arthur,* the Brontës, Wordsworth—not people. Except for Carrie, whose quality she recognized.

Carrie longed for the sort of closeness Janice offered, but knew that sooner or later she would tell about herself. Already there were times when she could hardly bear not to talk openly to her new friend. But tell such horrors! Tell things that could never have happened to anyone else in the world? In any event she no longer knew what the truth was, so obscured was it by her mother's half truths and outright lies.

In the end, out of pure funk, Carrie deserted Janice and returned to her other friends. But it was no longer quite the same, and more often than not her laughter sounded artificial. Although she was still liked, the other girls no longer sought her out as they used to, and she missed her old eminence.

At seventeen Carrie fell in love. Paul had hardly noticed her at school, but seeing her in a party dress at a friend's house he had instantly moved to her side and stayed there for the rest of the evening. She was, of course, flattered—she was still not aware how pretty she had become. Paul had already taken four "A" levels and done so well no one had any doubt he would sail through the Cambridge entrance examination at Christmas. Tall, good-looking, witty, he was a catch for any party, especially for Carrie's friend Shona, who, like herself, was still only a lower sixth former. All the girls in the room had glowed when he arrived—there wasn't one who hadn't at some time daydreamed about him—and Carrie couldn't help noticing the envious looks.

But when, taking her home, he tried to kiss her, she refused him. When he persisted she slapped his face and ran indoors. He couldn't believe it. It had never happened to him before. Girls ran after him; everyone ran after him. Unaccustomed to having to work for success, he found the experience novel. He couldn't get her out of his mind. After a couple of letters and an abortive visit to her home he decided he was in love with her. Finally she relented and went out with him one evening to the cinema. As they roared back home on his motorbike Carrie, clutching him around the waist, was terrified but joyful. By the end of the evening she, too, decided she was in love.

At first it was a delicious experience, no doubt of it, one of the most delicious sensations she had ever known. The sun shone out of everything. It was the same for him. He'd been attracted, even temporarily obsessed, by other girls, but it had been straightforwardly their bodies he'd wanted; individually the girls hadn't meant much to him. He had plenty besides sex on his mind—he studied hard, played squash and tennis, ran three or four miles every day, made and flew his own radio-controlled model

13

planes, spent hours stripping down his motorbike and zooming around the place with like-minded friends. Girls were fun and easy and easy to forget.

Carrie was different. Every time he thought he'd got somewhere with her she'd retreat into some inner space, and he lost touch with her. It infuriated him because he wanted to know her beyond her body; he sensed something about her that was special and that he might not meet again. He had never been denied like this before, and he tried to grab what he wanted. The more clumsily he reached out, the more Carrie fluttered away from him. And yet sometimes she would sit on his lap with her arms around him letting him kiss her and kissing him back with more open passion than any girl he'd ever known. But always, unexpectedly, perhaps when he merely tried to touch her breasts or when she had let him strip her almost naked and he really thought that this time she would—she wouldn't. She'd suddenly freeze, push him off, and dress quickly.

Carrie herself couldn't have told him what the matter was, because she didn't understand either. It was as though she inhabited two separate bodies at the same time. One body yearned for sex, desired with an intensity that amazed her. She had not imagined it was possible to have such a powerful need for another's hand to touch her. But the second body was a chaste little thing that in a previous existence had known sex, and yet had not known it. This body, with its emotions, its loyalties, still belonged to another man. A dumb homunculus, unknown and unrecognized after years of deliberate forgetting, it haunted the flesh and bone she thought to be her only body. Betrayal of its first lover was out of the question.

So she and Paul drove each other nearly mad. Paul, because he was frustrated on every count—he was in love, he wanted total possession, physical and emotional, and he could not make out what was wrong. Carrie, because the warfare between her two bodies had awakened old pains. At times she lay almost prostrate under the pressure of the past. She was a dozen people at once. She was ashamed, angry, humiliated, brazen, distraught, happy. She didn't know what was happening to her. She wouldn't remember the past, couldn't remember it if she tried, but she knew it was there behind the wall she herself had constructed. When she wasn't with Paul she yearned to see him, when he telephoned she lit up, face shining; but when she saw him she wanted to run away. Paul, clever and successful though he was, had no way of reaching through to her.

14

Gradually she began to push him out of her life. The sunshine of the first few weeks was replaced by clouds so inpenetrable it was as much as she could do to get up in the morning and drag herself to school. In the evenings she could not concentrate on her homework, and she wasted the free periods during the day, when they were supposed to do private study, drinking cup after cup of coffee in the sixth-form common room or gossiping with other disaffected students.

Everyone at school noticed the change in her. She could no longer be bothered with the niceties of friendship that had once made her popular. When she felt bored, she showed it and was often downright rude. Soon she hadn't a single friend left who cared enough about her to brave her moods and try to find out what was wrong.

At the beginning, she and Paul had met every lunchtime in the school canteen, but now she avoided him and went outside to local cafés or simply wandered about the streets without eating. Then she ceased bothering to return to school after lunch. Soon she hardly turned up at all. She would get up reluctantly in the morning when Agatha called her and eat as much breakfast as her mother insisted on. Then, the moment the front door closed behind her mother, she would undress and climb back into bed again. Or, if the weather was good, she wandered out to the local park where she would lie curled up on the grass or sit huddled over on a bench looking endlessly at her shoes while the hours passed unnoticed. Vaguely she noticed the flowers in the park opening up or shedding their petals, passed hours watching sparrows searching beneath benches for missed crumbs, but she couldn't even be bothered to throw them her own scraps. Sometimes she would make herself stand up, even take a few brisk steps as though she had every intention of going somewhere, but the impulse that had got her to her feet would soon fade and at the next bench she would sit down again. She was appalled at her own weakness. She felt she was disintegrating, but there was nothing she could do about it. At night she would creep out of bed and walk around and around the flat, her face anguished as she tried to take hold of herself, but the most she achieved was not to cry out aloud. Soon she gave up trying and sank into passivity, pretending to herself she was no longer there. She became quite good at that, arriving at a blankness of mind that at least was preferable to the earlier pain.

After a few weeks of this the school contacted her mother, who had not realized what was happening. She looked closely at her daughter and saw

15

signs of strain. Agatha immediately assumed Paul was the cause of Carrie's misery, since he had not been to the house lately.

"It's not surprising he's dropped you," she said tersely, taking her annoyance out on the egg she was beating up for Carrie's breakfast. "Look at you! Your hair's a mess, you're getting thinner and scraggier every day, and the expression on your face is enough to put anyone off. For goodness sake cheer up. You won't get another chance like him in a hurry!" Critically she looked her daughter over. "I don't know what he saw in you in the first place," she said finally. "You don't take after my side of the family at all. There's nothing of you!" She turned her back and poured the egg into the sizzling pan. Impatiently she shoved the sticky mixture around, banging the sides of the pan with her wooden spoon.

Carrie replied listlessly. "He hasn't dropped me. It's just I don't feel like going out with anyone at the moment."

Agatha Lowes snorted. "That's likely! A good-looking boy like that— going to Cambridge and all. You're a fool. He'll end up someone important, with his brains. You ought to have hung on to him when you had the chance."

Carrie didn't bother to answer. It was true. Paul hadn't called her for a week. Well, she couldn't blame him. As her mother said, someone like Paul wasn't going to wait forever. Tears filled her eyes, and she put her head down onto the table and cried.

Agatha came over, plate in hand, and looked down at her. Conflicting expressions crossed her face. Awkwardly she put out her hand and patted Carrie gently on the head. "There, there," she said, "it'll be all right. It's not the end of the world. I expect you're a bit run down. You don't eat enough to keep a bird alive. I'll make a nice bit of stew for you tonight, and you can have a hot glass of milk before you go to bed to make you sleep." She put the plate down in front of Carrie and pushed a fork into her hand.

As she watched Carrie poking without appetite at the scrambled mess in front of her she added, "That's one of your troubles, you don't sleep enough." The old tone entered her voice again—she tried, but couldn't prevent it. "You wake me up every night, lately, getting up and walking around. You might at least try to be quieter. I need my sleep even if you don't. *I* can't take time off during the day." For once she heard her voice from outside her anger, as a stranger might. She forced herself to stop and patted Carrie again, but it was too late. Carrie merely cried harder.

A few more days passed. Twice she went to school but she couldn't take in anything anyone said. Then one afternoon she went home and, without planning to, she went into the bathroom and swallowed a dozen or more of the pills the doctor had given her to help her sleep better. At least it was action of a sort. She couldn't go on doing nothing any longer.

Fortunately for her she had eaten quite a good lunch, and, though she was thin, she was not unhealthy. So that although, when her mother found her two hours later, she was already in a coma, the hospital to which she was rushed was able to save her without much trouble.

Everyone combined to cover up the incident. It was clear, they all said, that it was only a gesture. For a start, she'd swallowed less than half the bottle, and if she had really meant to die wouldn't she have taken the *entire* bottle early in the day instead of an hour or two before her mother was due back? No, it was obviously a gesture—a call for attention—wasn't that so? Wouldn't she agree with that, they asked—her mother, her doctor, and the psychiatrist. "I suppose so," Carrie would say to each of them, "I don't know. I can't remember. I was very muddled."

After a couple of days, they brought Paul to see her in hospital, but she turned her head away and wouldn't look at him. Then, when they all thought she was asleep, she overheard her mother telling the nurse that Paul had treated her very badly and it had broken her heart. Carrie realized that probably that was how everyone else saw it, too, and that Paul must be going through hell. So, though the thought of even looking at him made her sick inside, she asked to see him.

When he came she forced herself to look straight at him, and once she'd done that it wasn't so bad. He looked so strained and worried, clutching a bunch of red and purple de Caen anenomes, that there was no resemblance between him and the urgent boy whose infectious passion had shattered her three-year-long sleep. She made herself smile at him, the first time she had smiled, and reached out a weak hand.

"It was nothing to do with you," she said, patting the bed so that he would sit down on it. He looked so tall and embarrassed standing towering over her, the flowers crushed against his stomach. "You didn't do anything wrong."

Relief breaking through the concern on his face, he sat down on the edge of the bed and dropped the flowers on top of a heap of grapes, magazines, and Kleenex piled around the cabinet separating her bed from her neighbor's.

"Why then? What made you do it?" he asked uncertainly, not daring to look her full in the face again after that first frightened glance.

She shook her head wearily. "It wasn't your fault," she repeated, then shut her eyes. She turned her face away. She couldn't do anything more for him.

After a minute or two he tiptoed away. When he had gone she opened her eyes again and beckoned to the nurse. She pointed to the flowers. "I can't stand anenomes," she said. "Will you give them to someone who doesn't have any visitors?"

"Oh, now," said the nurse briskly, beaming at her. She knew who Paul was. "You mustn't feel so badly about him. Young men at his age—they're all the same—here today, gone tomorrow. You mustn't be bitter. You've got to reconcile yourself, so you can get well again. You must learn to face up to facts." And she hurried out to a side room, returning a few moments later with a hideous vase of cheap orange glass that someone had once won at a fair. She thrust the gaudy flowers into it. "The colors clash a bit," she admitted, "but it's the only vase left. I'll ask Sister if she's got a nicer one tucked away somewhere. There!"—she pulled the blooms out a bit and stood back in admiration—"don't they look pretty?"

Carrie sighed and muttered some reply.

It was no use fighting other people's good will.

Soon she was allowed home. Because her mother had seen to it that neither the psychiatrist at the hospital nor her own doctor knew the truth about her father, the suicide attempt was dismissed as the act of an adolescent temporarily unable to cope with school examinations and her first experience of sexual tension. "A father's death," explained the psychiatrist to Agatha Lowes in front of Carrie, "is a crushing experience for a young girl, and there are often problems when they come to have boy friends. It's common enough, but she won't be so silly again, will you, Caroline?" and he gave her the earnest smile that later she was to associate with many memories of the hospital. She tried to please him, though she could not manage a smile of quite the same broadness as his. Encouraged, he leaned forward and patted her knee. "There," he said, looking sideways at her mother, "isn't she a good girl? She'll be right as rain in a few weeks, you'll see." And he closed his file with a firm slap.

Going home on the bus Agatha was as nice as she knew how. She determined to be warmer, to show more affection. It had, after all, been a terrible shock to come in and find her own child breathing in that terrifying way, her mouth open and her face so white. She would never forget the anguish she had felt then—and the shame.

Only Agatha Lowes was not given much time to change because not very long afterward she was killed in an accident at a crossing where three roads met. Characteristically, Carrie took the blame upon herself. It was true that, if she had not called out to her mother at the crossing, Agatha would never have stepped into the street so that in a sense her guilt was justified. But equally she was innocent of any real blame, for how could she possibly have known that a motor bike would suddenly come roaring around the corner, or that her normally cautious mother, instead of just waving to her—they'd been together half an hour earlier—would take it into her head to attempt to cross over without even looking to check if the road were clear? She knew all this but also knew that if it had not been for her, her mother would still be alive. How could she not, then, feel guilt? It is impossible to be entirely logical about such things, least of all for someone like Carrie who was already worn down by the burden she had been carrying for so long.

Before her mother's accident, she had apparently recovered some of her old spirits. It might have been Agatha's attempts at maternal fondness that helped, or the pills they gave her, or that without a boy friend her savage homunculus sank back deep into its cave and went to sleep again. Whatever the reason, quite soon she was able to go back to school, to laugh, and join in whatever amusement was going on. Although her work varied wildly, most of the staff considered that if she really got down to work she would still have a chance of scraping through her "A" level examinations.

But her mother's death shattered her. Alone now in the flat, the telephone disconnected, with no one to force her out of bed in the mornings, she rarely bothered even to get up. She had recently had her eighteenth birthday, and although the school authorities sent a social worker, school visitors, and even old friends to hound her she refused to listen to any of them. She slept, got up, went to bed, starved or ate as she chose, living on social security. Officially an adult, no one had the right to make her do anything she didn't want to do, and soon the interference stopped.

Eventually she became ill enough for her doctor—whom she had to see in order to collect her sleeping pills—to insist she go into the psychiatric wing of a hospital for a few weeks.

19

Something happened to her in the hospital. It wasn't the individual treatment she received—she didn't see the psychiatrist alone for more than a couple of hours altogether. She herself could not have explained the exact cause of the change. Perhaps it was a combination of a variety of things: being forced back into company; living among others far worse off than herself; being made to eat regular meals; having to attend twice-weekly therapy groups that excited her with the possibility of communication, though she herself never managed in the brief time she was there to open her mouth. She began to feel a lifting of her spirits, but feared it was only the pills. Gradually she stopped taking them, pretending to swallow them but in fact throwing them down the lavatory. She felt better after that instead of worse, less confused, more in charge of herself. This encouraged her, and there began to grow in her a sense of impatience. This impatience had a physically exhilarating effect so that soon she found it impossible to sit around all day as most of the other patients did, and within a few days she was spending hours walking around the hospital grounds.

There was another patient, a middle-aged man who was manic-depressive, and he was in one of his manic phases. Together they strode through the gardens, Carrie pushing herself to keep up with him, and, though he rarely stopped talking long enough for her to answer him, sometimes she was able to talk back. Not about her father, of course, that was still a taboo area in her mind, but about her mother's accident, and school, or just pointless chatter. It didn't matter what they talked about—his enthusiastic gabble was so much better than the silent depression of the other patients. He loved gardening and often would kneel down and begin fussing with a plant that seemed to him to need attention. She would kneel beside him and take up handfuls of leaf mold or earth in her hand and sniff it, recalling earlier days. She hadn't realized before how much she had missed the old garden, living these last four years in the flat. She was grateful to the man for reminding her, and, when he leaped to his feet and strode on, she would run and catch up to him, patiently listening or pretending to listen to his endless flow of words.

But this time lasted only a week or so, until the worst of his manic phase was over, when he was sent home. By then his pills had damped him down so much she hardly knew him any more, and it frightened her. She imagined it happening to herself and wondered what would become of her.

Then she had a row with one of the nurses who caught her throwing

20

her pills away. The nurse refused to believe she hadn't taken any for a fortnight and shouted at her as though she were a stupid child. What am I doing here, Carrie asked herself that night in bed, why am I putting up with this? So she discharged herself and went back to her flat.

Back at home the sense of being newly alive left her, and she began to feel depressed once more. But she made herself think about her situation, brooded about the man with whom she had walked and the effect the pills had had on him, and she determined she would not let it happen to her. She regretted now that she hadn't been able to make herself join in the therapy groups she had attended. Suddenly, talking openly to other people seemed to be the most desirable thing in the world. For years she had kept silent about everything that mattered to her, even with Paul. Now the need to talk grew so strong in her she would even stop people on the stairs and breathlessly say something she knew was inane, but it didn't matter—words were rising in her and had to spill out or she would drown in them.

When she visited her doctor, he saw this change and was delighted with it, though he also saw how unstable she still was. He tried suggesting that she visit the hospital as an outpatient but she refused. Later that day he asked around, and someone mentioned a probation officer called David Parry who ran a group for disturbed adolescents. At first Carrie objected, said she wasn't going to sit in with a lot of thugs and addicts, but in the end her need overcame her. One evening in early October she put on her coat and left the flat, the first time she had been out at night for several months.

Carrie noticed Aidan the first day she joined the group. It was not that he said anything remarkable: he hardly ever spoke. But everything about him set him apart from the other boys. Even his clothes seemed different though he wore the same sort of jeans and sweater as everyone else. When he spoke, he mumbled as badly as the other boys so that you had to crane forward to hear what he was saying, but when, just occasionally, he opened up, his voice would suddenly clear and it was obvious he was unusually articulate, for that group at least. Then—always unexpectedly—he'd shut up, sometimes in mid-sentence, and close his mouth tight, refusing to say anything else for the rest of the meeting.

There were about nine of them in all, including David, the probation officer. Everyone liked David—he had a knack of making them feel good about themselves. For most of them, he was the only adult they had ever met who didn't make them feel defensive. With him, words like "criminal" and "delinquent" and "disgusting behavior" and all the other labels each had carried at various times were freed of emotional overtones: if he used them at all, it was to describe certain acts—as white describes snow or blue the sky. A delinquent act was a delinquent act—you couldn't fudge that. But people were individuals. He didn't go in for tagging people with names it was difficult to shake off.

Today for some reason everyone was in a good mood. The weather was brisk and cold, and spirits were high. It was Carrie's third session, and already she knew all their forenames and a surprising amount about their problems and their thoughts. She hadn't expected this. Usually you learn quickly enough the basic facts about acquaintances, where they live, what school they are at or what job they do, but you know very little about what goes on inside them. Here revelations about inner feelings would pour out as though the talker were confessing to a lover, or mad jokes would be made that set the whole group choking.

The three blacks in particular had taken it upon themselves to be the entertainers of the group. They would beat their hands on their knees and fling back their heads full of such infectious laughter that even Aidan, the most withdrawn of them all, would have to smile. But the laughter would die as quickly as it came, often followed by gloom.

Carrie had been one of the last to arrive that night. Winter had come early: although it was not yet November there had been a heavy fall of snow several hours earlier, and everyone had been fooling around outside the offices where they met, scooping up handfuls of snow and bombarding each other. Carrie was thinking about something else as she turned the corner. Coming across the group unexpectedly she felt momentarily alarmed. In the lamplight dark figures danced and leaped, waving their arms threateningly. Then she heard laughter, saw snow whitening their hair and jackets. She hesitated shyly a moment, then she too crouched and gathered up a large handful of snow, but at that moment David came out and called them in.

She didn't mind: the more she saw of David, the more she admired him. At first she had expected an authoritarian figure, a kind of policeman, but he behaved more like an elder brother. He had an especially attractive smile: there was an almost female tenderness about it that had instantly relaxed her. Within minutes she found herself talking freely to him. She had even told him about her father being in jail, though she gave

22

no details and he did not ask.

Now she followed him into the main office and watched him as he moved around the room arranging the chairs into a circle. Suddenly she felt a tug on her sleeve. It was Aidan, the quiet one. "I've brought you some coffee."

She looked at him in surprise. She had never seen him approach anyone before. "Thanks," she said, smiling at him. She wrapped her hands around the hot mug, then held one of them to her cheek as though to warm it too.

He smiled at her gesture, and, when she moved over to the circle of chairs, he followed and sat next to her. Pleased, she took a surreptitious look at him. Though he was very good-looking, there was something slightly sulky about his mouth that disturbed her. But she liked his eyes—clear blue, fringed with black lashes. She had noticed them before on one of the rare occasions that he had looked up, and had found their clarity somehow awesome. His hair was only slightly darker than her own, but it was thick and curling with the crisp spring of animal hair. He did not look back at her, but stared gloomily at his shoes. Already he seemed to have forgotten her.

Carrie found herself unable to concentrate properly on the meeting with Aidan sitting at her side. She was fascinated by him—she couldn't make him out, he was the oddest mixture she had ever met. It was his voice that always surprised her most: it had soon become clear to her he was ashamed of his accent, and he would do his best—when he spoke at all—to disguise it into an amorphous late adolescent mumble, but sometimes he would forget and the upper-class voice cutting through that smoky and somewhat odorous room (grubby parkas and wet boots were drying by the radiators) startled everybody, Aidan included. Sometimes other members of the group would tease him about his voice, imitating him, and he would redden and look furious. Tonight they did it again, and, though the bantering started out amiably enough, it soon became unpleasant enough for David to have to interfere.

Carrie felt embarrassed for Aidan. She wanted to protect him and was about to protest when several of the other members began to make angry comments about Aidan that she didn't understand. She did not know what had brought him to the group, only that, except for herself, he like the rest of them was on probation, and that fact in itself seemed absurd. She couldn't connect crime with people of Aidan's sort. Nor could she under-

23

stand why whatever it was he had done should upset the rest of the group so. Most of them had spoken openly about what they were there for—petty crime of various sorts—but Aidan had volunteered nothing about himself. Now, under attack, he muttered that it hadn't been as they supposed, and Carrie wanted to ask him *what* hadn't been as they supposed, but did not dare. Already she liked him too much. She did not want to find out anything about him that would change that. But she became a little frightened of him and spent the rest of the evening snatching quick glances at him, trying to see signs of violence in his face. She consoled herself that David had stood up for him, had told the group that Aidan had done his best to defend the woman, but since she didn't know what woman they were talking about or what it was Aidan had tried to defend her from, it didn't help her much. She only knew that the more she saw of him the more she was drawn to him, regardless of who he was or what he had done.

It was several weeks before she finally agreed to go out with him.

As much as anything she was frightened of herself, remembering Paul. Aidan took her hesitation to be fear of him, as it was also, although this fear gradually lessened during the group meetings as she watched his face, his eyes. Whatever he had done, she could not see him as a vicious man.

When eventually they did go out together they were already in love, though neither would have admitted it, even to themselves. In group they had avoided sitting next to each other after that first time because each wanted to look at the other without it being too obvious. Both imagined their interest was their own secret, but they fooled no one except each other. Each developed a sensitivity to the other's reactions; they knew to the hundreth of a second when the other was going to look up and would look away just in time so as not to be caught out. Carrie thought Aidan had lost interest in her and was surprised every time he approached her. Aidan so rarely caught Carrie's eyes on him that he was not at all surprised when she refused him. Sometimes at the end of the meeting Aidan would leave without talking to Carrie at all; other evenings—the group met twice a week—he would drift up to her and after chatting aimlessly for a few minutes suggest a late cinema or a drink, but always she said no, she had to hurry home.

Soon the growing need to be physically close overcame the desire to

24

look, and they began to sit side by side again during the group sessions. All evening they would be aware of little else other than the proximity of their not-quite touching shoulders and thighs. At last, after several nights of this absorbing torture, Aidan risked pushing his chair up close to hers. The moment their bodies finally touched they both felt a shock of fusion. Shoulder to shoulder, thigh to thigh, they sat like a pair of Siamese twins—but still they didn't look at each other, or speak.

At the end of the meeting Aidan followed Carrie out of the door. David, who had contacted the jail where Carrie's father was, saw them go. He was pleased. It seemed to him to be a helpful development for both of them, and he made a mental note to have a quiet chat with Aidan about her vulnerability.

A cold November wind ripped at their clothes and blew Carrie's headscarf off. Aidan ran after it and made a great fuss about tying it on again for her. He stroked her blond curls and told her she was beautiful, but lightly, as in joke, for he was still not sure of her. Then, when he had finished knotting the scarf he put a hand on each cheek and tilting her face up, kissed her. Carrie hesitated, then with a sigh slid her arms up around his neck. They stood embracing in the middle of the pavement until an elderly couple walked sedately past them, heads carefully averted. They laughed and kissed again, but suddenly Carrie felt a return of her old fear. She pulled away and said she had to go. But at least she agreed to meet him the following night.

What followed was in some ways a repetition of the affair with Paul, with Carrie playing hot and cold. But the essential difference this time was that Carrie was really in love. For the totally admirable Paul—with his brains, his academic success, his promising future—she had felt little real respect; for Aidan, a dropout with a criminal record and an enigmatic future, she sensed such heady possibilities that in comparison Paul was nothing.

Carrie was no fool. She knew that part of this perception of Aidan was because she was in love (even with Paul for a week or two the whole world had glittered in the light of a metaphysical sun). She loved everything about Aidan—his looks, his intelligence, his voice, which was warm and deep. With her he had begun to talk again; sometimes she found herself just listening to the sounds he made as though it were music. He was never out of her mind for an instant; she saw him everywhere. He brought delight, and he brought pain.

Pain, because although he could be more tender than anyone she had ever known, sometimes she would remember that time in the group when they had attacked him and she would be frightened. Yet, even then, when fear of him dimmed his brightness, she still knew he was someone special. That beyond her silly daydreaming he had a quality that made him different from anyone else she had ever met, except perhaps Janice. There had been the same kind of silence about her too, a kind of knowing.

Then Carrie would feel frightened once more that she would expose too much, and she would withdraw into herself. She was learning to talk, drew strength from the group, but there were still areas in her mind she could not reach. She openly accepted that her father was alive, even told the group that, but could not tell them what he had done to her because that last dreadful day when the police came, and everything that went before— all that had gone from her consciousness, blocked out beyond her power of recall. She knew one day she would have to face it, but not now, she would tell herself, not now.

There were days when Aidan, too, was racked by his own problems. When their bad phases coincided they behaved like a pair of sulky school kids and parted, hating the sight of each other. But they always came back together again. They couldn't help themselves.

After the party Aidan thought that at least the problem of sex had been solved. To Aidan sex was very important. He was strong, healthy, and twenty. There had always been about him the kind of sexual magnetism that attracts girls, and he had never been short of willing partners. Carrie was the first to refuse him.

His attempts to seduce her weren't made any easier by the dreariness of his room at the top of a decaying house not far from the probation offices. Every morning now when he rose he looked with disgust around him, at the sagging divan on which he slept, the spluttering gas fire, the threadbare strip of carpet ringed with cigarette burns, and held his breath against last night's stench of cooking seeping up from the warren of bed-sitters below. Coming back alone to his room, by the time he had climbed the five flights of badly lighted stairs, stepping over the occasional pile of cat shit (the house was plagued with unneutered cats and their hordes of whining kittens), he felt sickened enough to think about moving. It was impossible to ask any girl he cared about up there. But, he'd remind himself, it was cheap, and convenient for the probation and social security offices—he saved pounds not having to take buses. And in a way he liked the sordidness of it all, got from it the kind of enjoyable shudder you get from taking medicine so unpleasant you know it must be good for you.

Once had liked. The necessity didn't seem to be there anymore. He had a vision of a large sunny room with whitewashed walls, and determined soon to move.

Carrie had still not told him she lived alone. She didn't lie but brushed off any questions he asked, while he enjoyed his own privacy too much to willingly break into another's. So they kissed at the back of cinemas, in doorways—anywhere there was shelter. Winter had settled in, and the parks were cold and wet. In that area, tarts managed their business against walls, but lovers had a hard time of it until the better weather came.

Sometimes Carrie herself was so frustrated by their public embraces she almost took him back home. But the prospect of making love awoke in her terrors she couldn't bring herself to face. So they fumbled and groped and began to quarrel until one evening, just before Christmas, Nicholas, a friend of Aidan's, invited him to a party.

Carrie tried not to look too impressed. It was a large house in an expensive part of Hampstead, with the Heath close by and a wide, tree-lined road in front. All the lights were on in the house, and the front drive was crammed with cars and motorbikes. The music was so loud she guessed a live group was playing there. She hung on Aidan's arm, suddenly very shy.

"They must be very rich," she whispered. It was the grounds in which the house stood that most affected her. Professionally landscaped, several neat little hillocks had been raised and topped with clumps of rhododendrons. The crest of the highest bump bore a doll's house forest of half a dozen young birches, from the center of which broke a minute stream. Running straight for a few yards, the stream then tumbled over the rocky edge of a lower hillock and poured down a fall of artistically-arranged Westmoreland rock, finally splashing into a fish-filled pool. Carrie thought the river was natural: the hum of pumps did not reach her ears.

Aidan looked curiously at her, saw how little they knew about each other. Vaguely he supposed that Carrie lived in a small house somewhere with a little back garden where her father had once grown beans and standard roses, but more than that he couldn't guess. He knew nothing about suburban lives. In his crash downward, he had plunged straight to the bottom.

"To afford a live group!" she persisted, clutching nervously at Aidan.

Aidan smiled and gave her a hug. "It comes free. Nicholas plays the drums—hear him? Not bad for an amateur!"

"But the group?"

"Just friends. They've played together since school."

"Don't Nicholas' parents mind the noise?"

"They go away a lot. As long as the house isn't messed up, it's OK with them."

She looked at him dubiously. "Are they away tonight?"

He hesitated. He didn't want to lie, but he'd rather she wasn't fore-warned. He compromised by shrugging his shoulders and was saved from having to answer more directly by the arrival of a low-slung white sports car that spattered gravel all over them as it screeched to a stop outside the front door.

A couple climbed out, and the girl—diaphanous yellow muslin flowing from her expensive limbs—ran up and threw her arms around Aidan's neck. "Darling! You wicked, wicked boy! I've been hearing dreadful things about you! Is it all true! What exactly did you do? Oh, it's so exciting, tell me all!"

She glanced dismissively at Carrie, running her eyes over her worn coat, her chain store flowery skirt and cotton top, then turned back to Aidan. But before Aidan could reply her partner came up. He avoided Aidan's eyes and took the girl's hand. "Come on, Jackie, we're late already. Hello, Aidan," he added coldly, "nice to see you," but walked off without once looking straight at him.

Aidan flushed. If it had not been for Carrie, he might have left. He looked at her excited face, then firmly taking her arm marched her inside.

Wandering up the stairs, leaning against Aidan whose arm was around her waist, Carrie quietly hummed to herself. She was happy.

At first she had been stunned by the noise, the exuberant laughter. She had never been in a private house before with so many rooms, such expensive furniture: deep leather armchairs, Persian rugs, polished floors. And paintings everywhere—originals framed in narrow strips of shining metal, paintings and prints that made no kind of sense to her, though she thought them bright and cheerful enough. Bottles of beer and wine crowded every surface not already filled with empty plates. Downstairs in the kitchen under swags of holly and mistletoe, platters of rice and chicken were emptying fast. Like all the other guests, Aidan and Carrie ate and drank as though they had done neither for some days. They spoke to few people. Aidan did not want a repetition of the earlier incident.

Carrie knew she was drinking too much, but tonight she didn't care. They wandered from room to room, dancing, talking. The more they danced the more trance-like her state became. She was in a daze of happiness, high on music, alcohol, and love. When Aidan took her by the waist and led her upstairs, she leaned against him humming, quietly. He tried the doors of several rooms before he found an empty one. Even when he led her in and locked the door behind them, Carrie didn't rebel.

There was a moment, as Aidan pulled the cotton top over her head and took hold of her breasts, when the old fear rose. She grasped at both his hands with the intention of pushing them away, but instead she found herself pulling him even closer. Through a haze of surprise she watched as this uninhibited creature—not her—unbuttoned and stepped out of her skirt, shamelessly ripped off her pants, swung them around her head like a trophy, then flung them to the other side of the room where they slithered down the wall and fell on top of a bowl of snowdrops. This watching self gasped in shock, then—it couldn't help itself—began to shake with silent laughter. And joined her sisterself.

Carrie, united now, perched naked on the edge of the bed and with a concealing hand over her mouth sat watching Aidan as he undressed.

Aidan had a difficulty. The advanced state of his arousal was making it almost impossible for him to unzip his skin-tight jeans without injury. Conscious of her attention he turned his back to her to wrestle more privately with his problem. He, too, had drunk a lot, and his coordination was not what it usually was. At last, after a few muttered curses, he succeeded in freeing himself, and bending down pulled off his jeans.

Carrie, faced with the unexpected revelation of a heart-shaped bottom with its hanging baggage demurely pressed between muscular thighs, let out her laughter. The sight was at once tender and ludicrous, and it flashed through her mind that all over the world there were these millions of men—severe dignified men, all-powerful men capable of handing out life or death—all hiding beneath their pin-stripe trousers, khaki pants, burnooses, or whatever, this innocent squashy bit of flesh pocked with strands of straggling hair. And she had been so frightened of it and its attachment! Her laughter peeled out, rang without restraint around the room.

Aidan, hearing the laughter, was nearly demolished. Straightening, his straightest member freshly released from its prison reared up, then fell under the onslaught. He turned, angry at her amusement and fearing disappointment. She was now lying collapsed backward on the bed, her legs carelessly open, still laughing. Only her eyes were closed. He flew at her, rising again in flight.

Carrie caught her breath, but he gave her no chance to resist. She struggled for a moment or two, then, like an unpracticed swimmer who one lovely day finds himself at home in the water, let go, wholly present in each vibrant toenail, nipple, and curling hair.

Aidan, grateful, loved her back with all the knowledge he had, which was not—bearing in mind his age—inconsiderable.

And yet, good as it was at the time, an event stemming directly from that night was to be the cause of Jess Bennett's grief three months later.

But was it grief that Jess felt? The police were less than sure, that first evening when they left her house after interviewing her. They had reassured her, of course—it was their duty to reassure relatives, it was more like being a social worker, this part of their job—but all the same they had expected a tear or two. Crasswell, the young sergeant, wasn't far off the mark when he commented, "It's enviable, in a way. If she couldn't keep her cool, she wouldn't have got where she has. She's no ordinary woman." The Inspector, who liked womanly women and had taken a dislike to Jess, made the theme of coolness the basis of an unprintable conjecture about Jess's sexual parts. Crasswell did not laugh. He had found Jess's restraint rather heroic. The Inspector noticed. His dislike of Jess spread to Crasswell—they were two of a kind, he thought; too much education dried up your natural feelings. His comfortable wife rose before his mind, and he thought how she would have put her head in his lap and wept if little Sammy or Rita had been snatched from their pram when they were that age, and tears came into his own eyes.

His eyes had moistened when Mrs. Bennett first opened the door and he saw her face. She had learned the terrible news only five minutes earlier

when she'd arrived home from the interview with the geriatric playwright in Surrey. His immediate instinct was to comfort her. He reached
out and patted her arm. Most people liked that, an Inspector showing
human warmth. It made them feel secure—*there was nothing like the
British police force.* His heart swelled, and, as he followed her inside, he
wanted to take her into his arms so that she could break down and have a
good cry, but it wasn't possible, of course, not in uniform and in front of
Crasswell.

Jess did indeed feel comforted. She shrank from the soppy emotion
expressed in his dog-eyes, but her inbred response was exactly what he'd
intended—the British police were marvelous, and she could rely on them.
Order began to return to her life.

"Mrs. Bennett," he said, "I'm very sorry to disturb you at a time like this,
but there are certain questions we must ask. I hope you understand?"

She nodded, unable just yet to speak. She led the two men into the living
room, gestured toward the deep armchairs, and opened an antique corner
cupboard. Taking out three sherry glasses, she paused. "You will have a
drink, won't you?" she asked.

The Inspector was longing for a drink; had he been on his own, he
probably would have accepted one. Instead he shook his head. "Never on
duty, Mrs. Bennett. It wouldn't do," and he looked firmly at Crasswell.

Jess replaced two of the glasses and filled the third to the brim with
whisky. The Inspector expected her to make some comment such as that
she didn't usually but under the circumstances—but it never crossed Jess's
mind to apologize in her own house. She sat down in the middle of the
sofa, her slim legs neatly crossed, and sipped the whisky without any
redeeming show of distaste. How different from his own wife! Behind
her, a spray of imported white lilies rose from a small checkered rosewood
and ivory table. The lilies rayed out behind her long dark hair, and the
Inspector was reminded of a painting in his school bible that he had loved
as a child, a painting showing some saint or other—or was it Mary?
He couldn't remember—dressed in a white robe and looking sadly
thoughtful.

Jess spoke directly to the Inspector. "I suppose you've no news yet?"

He shook his head. "Nothing yet, I'm afraid. But you mustn't worry,
Mrs. Bennett, we're doing everything we can. I expect we'll find little
Matthew within a few hours. That's the usual pattern."

"So soon? You're telling me the truth? I don't know anything about . . .
baby snatching, what the chances are he'll be safe, that he won't be hurt."

31

She surprised both men by how exactly like her television self she was—the same steady, controlled voice, interested and intelligent, the enunciation flawless, the accent impeccable. Her face looked slightly older off screen, but if anything more beautiful. There was a delicacy about the pallor of her skin, and the hair shone blacker. Crasswell, with plenty of opportunity to observe her, decided she was marginally more human than he had thought, and wasn't sure whether he was disappointed or pleased. He noticed that the hand not holding the glass of whisky lay tightly clenched in her lap, the knuckles showing white.

The Inspector saw only the smoothness and the rapidly emptying glass, and the first stirrings of distrust woke within him. "You can rest assured," he said, "he'll be safe. It's not like other crimes, baby snatching. It's not done by the criminal classes, you see. It's usually committed by young girls or women who've never done anything wrong before, and they take the child because they want to love it. Like a pet, you might say. And they look after it as though it was their own because their intentions are the best. In fact, they usually claim they truly thought it *was* their own child. Personally I find that difficult to believe, but that's what they claim. A sort of amnesia, you might say. I suppose it could be genuine."

Jess was not convinced. "Don't I remember some dreadful case where a baby was found in a . . ." she couldn't say it—a child dead in a ditch, the parents distraught. She rose and poured herself out another whisky.

The Inspector flashed Crasswell a look. "That was unusual, that case. The woman was a madwoman, completely out of her mind. It hardly ever happens like that," he said reassuringly, but there was less warmth in his voice now. "You mustn't think about it. It's nearly always the same pattern. They take the baby from the pram, walk around with it for a few hours, then they come to their senses and leave it somewhere, in a hospital corridor, say, or outside a church. Or a neighbor is suspicious, knows perfectly well they don't have a baby of their own, and rings us. Oh, don't take it hard, Mrs. Bennett, it'll all be over in a few hours, and you'll have little Matthew back in your arms." He watched her in concern as she emptied her glass. "When will your husband come in? You shouldn't be alone at a time like this."

Jess thought of David rather than Adam. He was with his group again tonight. The first time she'd ever really needed him, and he wasn't there. "My husband is abroad," she replied to the Inspector's question, "in Denmark. I haven't had time yet to send him a cable." She saw the

Inspector looking at her glass. "Don't worry, I shan't take to drink. Are you sure you won't have one?" polite, cool to the point of frostiness.

He shook his head in embarrassment, feeling reproved for his familiarity. He became a little pompous. "Removing a child under the age of 14 years with intent to deprive the parent or guardian having lawful care of the child is an offense under Section 56 of the Offenses against the Person Act 1871 . . ."

"Sixty-one. 1861," interrupted Crasswell.

"1861," the Inspector corrected himself, not looking at his sergeant, "and is punishable by a maximum of seven years' imprisonment. But they hardly ever get it. Not more than a couple of years, usually. They plead insanity or mitigating circumstances, or someone gets up a petition, and then they're let off, like as not."

Jess, relieved at the turn of conversation—she could cope with facts, graspable data—commented, "You don't sound as though you approve?"

The Inspector considered. "It all depends. I've never dealt with a case personally before, mind, but I've read about it. I'm a sympathetic sort of person, not one of your hard type, and I feel sorry for them. But I feel even sorrier for the mothers, for the terrible distress they suffer."

Jess looked down at her lap. She was aware that the Inspector expected more obvious signs of grief from her, and her mouth hardened. "Inspector," she said after a pause, "as you can appreciate this has been a dreadful shock. You've been very reassuring, and I'm very grateful to you. But now there are many things I must do. I must send a cable to my husband, there are some phone calls . . ."

"Of course, of course, I understand." He gave her another of his dog looks, and Jess felt she couldn't stand much more of him. He had fulfilled his function—shown the law was in action, made her feel there was some solidity left in the world. If only he'd go now and let her get on! It was unbearable sitting here doing nothing—as soon as she'd started some sort of action, it hardly mattered what, she'd be herself again.

"We'll be as brief as possible," he said, leaning forward in his chair. "Your . . . nanny"—he enjoyed using the word, it made him feel temporarily part of the upper classes—"your nanny told us all she could at the station, but I'd like more details from you, if you don't mind."

Jess shook her head, trying to hide her impatience. "You know as much about it as I do. I'd only just got home when you came."

"But if you could tell us in your own words . . ."

"I don't see the point. But if you think it will help . . ." she sighed and sat back. Only she knew how close to tears she was. "Iris had been shopping, taking Matthew with her in his pram. When she got back home, she realized she'd forgotten to post a letter, so she ran inside to get it, leaving Matthew outside in the street."

The Inspector clucked disapprovingly. "Surely you'd told her never to do that, leave a baby unattended in the street?"

Jess frowned. She was not accustomed to slurs on her efficiency. "Of course I had. She's a very good nanny, I've absolute trust in her. It's impossible to blame her. The letter was on a table in the hall—she shouldn't have been away more than a couple of seconds, just the time it takes to go a few yards up the path, open the door and straight out again." She could hear Iris's sobbing voice going over and over just that point, how she'd looked around twice, as she went up the path and before going into the house, to make quite sure Matthew was all right. "You must have noticed there are three steps down into the street—it's very difficult getting up and down them with a pram. She only thought she'd be a moment. But when she opened the door the phone was ringing. She answered the call meaning to ask whoever it was to hold on, but it was her mother in the country—her father had had a serious stroke. You can understand the news put everything else out of her mind. She forgot Matthew, she forgot everything. When she did remember, five minutes or more must have gone by. She told her mother to wait and rushed outside. But he'd gone."

Jess stopped. The whisky had dulled the nausea that had gripped her when Iris first told her the news, and now what she mainly felt was disbelief. She couldn't shed the feeling that if she shook herself hard she'd wake up, that she only had to run upstairs to the nursery and she would find Matthew fast asleep in his cot as always at this time of the evening.

"Imagine her feelings," she heard herself continue just as though she were on her own program, giving a synopsis of a new play before launching into the criticism, "her father possibly mortally sick, the baby stolen." She stopped again. Feelings. Feelings were best ignored. They were treacherous; at best they only muddied your decisions, distracted you from what really mattered. She looked straight at the Inspector. In a different voice she said, "You seem so certain he'll be all right?"

He nodded, reassurance beaming out of his pale round face. He, too, could act quite well if he needed to. He'd had plenty of experience over the years. "As certain as anyone can be." He put his hands on his knees and said quietly as though frightened of being overheard, "Tell me, Mrs. Bennett, do you entirely trust your nanny? There's no question. . . ?" He paused. He didn't want to introduce too openly the possibility of kidnapping for money; it was better no one brought that up for the time being. But the family was obviously very well off. Always had been, by the look of it. Nothing flash about the Bennetts.

"I told you, I trust Iris absolutely. We're good friends. She's a nice girl—not all that bright, but very trustworthy and kind. She loves Matthew as though he were her own."

The Inspector and Crasswell exchanged glances. It fitted. "Where is Iris now?" Crasswell asked hopefully. "Have you seen her since you got back?"

"I've already explained. It was she who told me what had happened. She's upstairs putting my daughter Emma to bed at this very moment. I've tried to persuade her to go home to her father, but she refuses to leave me until Matthew's found."

The two men looked disappointed. It would have been too good to be true, if it had been as easy as that.

They questioned Jess for another minute or two, then the Inspector asked if she had any photographs of Matthew. "The press are very helpful in matters like this," he said.

"The press!" exclaimed Jess. "I won't have the press in on this!"

The Inspector shook his head. "Impossible to keep them out, I'm afraid. I'm surprised they're not on to it already, you being famous and all that. No, I'd like a photograph, if you don't mind—they'll be able to show it on the nine o'clock news tonight. But you'll know about that sort of thing better than me."

Jess carefully put down her glass, then sat still with her hands clenched in her lap. "The best picture of him is in there," she said at last, pointing to a Sunday color supplement lying on a low coffee table. "It's last week's issue, but they took the photograph over a couple of months ago—he's changed quite a lot since then. He's seven months old now. I took a few myself recently, but they were . . . destroyed by accident." Pictures of Adam and Matthew—Matthew in Adam's lap. Matthew being tossed in the air by Adam, Matthew crawling toward Adam's encouraging hands. She'd been sitting in front of the fire last Friday looking at them when Adam came in and told her his decision about Frances. She'd said nothing at first, just looked at the photographs lying loose in her lap, then she'd gathered them up, ripped them in half, and flung the lot in the fire, shouting at him in such a rage Adam could only stare. It was the first time in their entire life together he had ever seen her lose control.

"I have the negatives still, though." Cool again.

The Inspector picked up the magazine and flicked through it. "Ah," he said, spreading it open at the center pages, "Here we are . . . *Ideal Marriages*. That must have made you very proud."

Crasswell stood up and looked over his chief's shoulder. The center spread showed a close-up of Jess, sitting on the sofa just as she was now, but with a spray of white roses in the place of the lilies that now haloed her. Also on the table behind her head was a large leather-framed portrait of a dark-haired man, full-faced and handsome, a man obviously in charge of his life. On Jess's lap lay a baby of a few months old, looking straight at the camera and smiling. To Crasswell it looked exactly like any baby he had ever seen—two eyes, a turned-up nose and a pale fuzz of hair—he failed to see how it could be of any use as an identification picture.

" 'The brilliantly successful Mr. and Mrs. Adam Bennett,' " the Inspector read out with pride as though they were his own children, " 'the first couple in our new series . . .' Ah, *that's* your husband, is it?" he asked. "Yes, yes, it says, 'Adam Bennett, barrister . . .' Barrister? I didn't realize . . ." a note of special respect came into his voice.

"Yes," said Jess with some impatience. Then, feeling she had been too short with him, she added, "He wouldn't let them photograph him in the flesh. Barristers are touchy about personal publicity. Like doctors. But he didn't mind appearing at second hand, as it were." She tried to keep bitterness out of her voice.

The Inspector put down the magazine. "Of course, of course," he said importantly, as one in the know. "Very nice indeed. Well, now, if you would be kind enough to look out those negatives I'll send someone along to pick them up. We probably won't need them at all, Mrs. Bennett," he added hastily. "I'm sure he'll turn up in an hour or two."

Jess stood up. She could not bear inaction any longer. As the men rose with her, the telephone rang. Jess went to answer it, and came back in, her face white. "You were right," she said, "It's the press."

"Let them come," said the Inspector gently. "It's unpleasant for you, but they'll be very sympathetic. And it can only help. Tomorrow the whole country will be looking out for Matthew."

Jess looked at him. "That's unlikely to be necessary, you told me. If you meant what you said, he'll be back before tomorrow morning's papers are out."

"Of course, of course, but we shouldn't leave any stone unturned, should we? Sometimes it can take two or three days, if the person who's taken the baby tries to hide, as it were. That's where photographs come in useful—and publicity. People notice things—they're very helpful, the public are. But Matthew will be all right, you can rest assured of that. Whoever took him is probably bouncing him up and down on her knees right now or mixing him up a nice warm bottle. That's what you've got to keep your mind fixed on, Mrs. Bennett, that whoever she is, she'll love him just like her own. That's what you've got to remember."

But once outside the house the sympathy left the Inspector's voice. As they got into the waiting police car, he replied to Crasswell "You're right about her being no ordinary woman. The question is, just how extraordinary is she? There's something odd about it all. I don't know what, but something's going on."

Crasswell looked at him in surprise. "What do you mean? You're not suggesting she's stolen her own baby, are you?"

The Inspector gave his instructions to the driver and waited until they had moved off before he answered. "I suppose not. It would hardly make sense, would it? But something's up, I'm sure of it. Most women would be in floods of tears in her situation. It may be she's just a cold bitch, of course, who doesn't give a damn about anything except her work. I've got a feeling she's keeping something to herself. I can't make it out. She doesn't seem to have any maternal feelings at all."

Crasswell refused the cigarette the Inspector offered him and opened a window. "That's hardly fair. She was obviously very upset when we first arrived. After all, you kept telling her the baby would be all right, so why be so surprised when she seemed to believe you?"

The Inspector stubbornly shook his head. "It's not natural under these circumstances to be as cool as that. But I suppose it's true that if the kiddies were brought up by a nanny she wouldn't get to grow much in the way of maternal feelings. My wife always says it's the everyday things—changing their nappies, wiping their noses, all that—that makes you into a mother. *She'd* have gone off her nut if any of our kids had been taken. That poor little bastard, being brought up like that, without any love. Perhaps he's better off right now than he's ever been."

Crasswell protested. "Oh, come on, that's absurd. You don't know anything about the family. Jess Bennett's a professional—she knows how to keep her feelings under control. You wouldn't expect a type like her to go into a screaming fit. And her husband looked a pleasant enough sort of chap. Even a barrister can have feelings."

The Inspector looked sour. There was an air of invincibility about the woman, and the same was true of her husband. People like that always made him uneasy.

"The thought occurs to me," Crasswell said, as they waited in a queue of cars at a red traffic light, "that the portrait of her husband wasn't on the table behind her today though it was there in the magazine."

The Inspector looked at Crasswell with new interest. "That's true. Very observant. Perhaps you've got something there. *Where is the husband?* Yes, indeed, you might have something there," he repeated thoughtfully. His eyes were following the swinging bottoms of two teenagers running down the hill past the waiting cars. "Cherchez les femmes," he said aloud to Crasswell. "Toujours cherchez les femmes." He sucked in his lips with satisfaction.

Jess, left alone at last, went to the coffee table and picked up the magazine. She opened it at the center spread, looked closely at it, then threw it down. Then she went up stairs to the nursery. She had not yet kissed Emma good night.

DAY 2

The second day the press played it straight. Jess Bennett was a national heroine in distress, and the same sympathy was extended to her as would have been accorded a factory worker's wife from the Midlands. There was no hinting at that stage that had she been at home where she belonged instead of passing her responsibilities to a paid childminder the snatching might never have occurred.

In any case there were still very few facts to record. The principal "heavy," accustomed to walking with the great, kept its dignity:

Last night the police were searching for the 7-month-old son of Jess Bennett, the well-known television critic, snatched from his pram outside his home in Village Row, NW3, late yesterday afternoon.

They described correctly what had happened and finished by issuing police descriptions of two possible suspects:

The police are anxious to trace a man in his late forties seen peering into a pram in Camden Town earlier in the afternoon. He was wearing a shabby gray raincoat over frayed workman's dungarees, worn brown shoes with one blue sock and one yellow sock. He had long greasy brown hair and wore a soiled gray felt hat. They would also like to interview a woman in her early thirties with long mousy hair, wearing jeans and a knitted cardigan. She was seen carrying a crying baby in her arms in Hampstead High Street shortly after Matthew was taken.

The populars were much more excited. One wrote:

Distraught TV star Jess Bennett, whose 7-month-old baby Matthew was snatched from his pram yesterday afternoon, pleaded last night with tears in her eyes for the return of her baby. "My fame and success mean nothing to me," she said, "without my children." Emma, Jess's three-year-old daughter, lay upstairs asleep in her nursery, as yet unaware of the calamity that had overtaken her family. When at bedtime little Emma asked why her brother's cot was empty, she was told he was spending the night at his grandmother's. "I will protect her from the truth as long as I can," said her mother bravely. "I cannot believe that whoever has stolen my baby will make us suffer much longer."

A head and shoulders photograph of Jess did not reveal the described tears—in fact she looked remarkably composed—but newspaper reproductions lose much detail. As to the two suspects, the paper contented itself with a brief comment that the police wished to interview a shabbily-dressed man and a woman in her early thirties.

Inside, the middle pages were full of various pictures of Jess taken during her career: Jess in cap and gown at Oxford; Jess at her desk as a young reporter; Jess interviewing the stars at a film premiere; her first television appearance in a quiz program (by then she was theater critic for one "serious" paper and film critic of another, with a growing name for her original and witty occasional pieces, but this aspect was not expected to be of much appeal to the paper's readers); and finally—Jess in triumph, her first appearance on her own television program, BBC's answer to women's demand that a woman head an intellectual series in her own right.

Adam was hardly mentioned; thanks to professional etiquette no one knew much about him at this stage.

AFTER the party—at three or four in the morning—some friends gave Aidan and Carrie a lift most of the way home to her flat, and they walked the rest. Then, still full of love, she had seen no point in keeping her address secret from him any longer, though even before she was fully awake again she regretted what she had done. Everything. Fucking; letting him come home; the breaking of the shell she had so cautiously grown around herself. A shaft of noonday sunlight fell on her face; dazzled, she kept her eyes closed, but every pore of her was aware of the male body next to hers. He was still sleeping. Lying on his back with open mouth his breath came heavily—not exactly in a snore, but each breath laboring in and out, fuel for an alien mechanism that lay there ticking over in her bed, a large autonomous engine over which she could have no control.

She was frightened. The breathing went on and on, so regular it half hypnotized her. She considered putting a pillow over his mouth, not thinking of stifling him, only of stopping the noise, which bore no relation to the imaginings that had filled her mind all those other mornings when she lay, just like this, dreaming pretty dreams about him. This solidity, this invincible masculinity that lay next to her in her own bed, unmovable as an outcrop of primal rock, menaced her with its independence. She could do nothing to affect it. It would move only of its own free will. For so long, a lifetime it already seemed, her flat had been an inviolable nest, a hiding place of feathers and softness for the thin-shelled egg she had become. Now of her own accord she had betrayed her solitude, had taken this monstrous otherness into her own bed. How could she have!

She forced herself to turn onto her side facing toward him. Now that her eyes were no longer sealed by the sun she risked opening them. The alien, swollen in her imagination to an immovable grossness, was revealed as a sleeping boy, lips turned in a slight smile, chin smudged with a day's growth. The horror shrank, and its passing left behind an emptiness in her stomach that would only be pacified by stretching herself

41

alongside him, pressing her belly and breasts against his side. Her right arm slid over his body curving around him in an embrace. In his sleep he turned toward her, wrapped his free arm about her, and buried his head in her hair. His breathing quieted, and as soon as she was sure he was still asleep she let out the breath she had been carefully holding and breathed normally again.

She lay quite still, watching him, absorbed in the joy of contemplating someone she loved. She thought about this love for some time. She no longer had any doubt that what she felt for him was love, love of a kind that was quite new to her. There was a part of her that was ecstatic, a part that rang with wedding bells and happiness. She wanted to smother him with caresses, tell him how much she loved him, hear him respond. But that other side, that darker side of her, kept her silent, watching, waiting for his first move.

It came sooner than she expected. Abruptly, as though he had been awake all along—had he?—he opened his eyes, instantly smiled at her, and sliding his other arm under her waist pulled her flat against him so that their bodies touched everywhere.

The gentle dreaming was shattered. She felt him grow large and press against her, and all the peace, the joy, instantly evaporated. She was flooded with shame at what she had already allowed herself to do with him. Pushing him away, she began to fight against the arms that gripped her. But he was too strong for her. Thinking she was fooling, he hung onto her and laughed. She reached out and drew her nails down the back of his hand, drawing blood.

Aidan swore in amazement and put his scratched hand to his mouth. Freed, Carrie flung back the blankets and leaped out of bed. From the panic in her face she might have just awakened from a virgin sleep to find a rapist clawing at her.

"Look!" Aidan shouted, holding out his hand. "You've bloody scratched me! What the hell did you do that for?"

She ignored him. Snatching up her old blue wool dressing gown she wrapped it around herself, not waiting to put it on properly, and sank down into the wicker chair in the corner of the room, burying her face in her hands. Some of the split canes that bound the wickerwork together had broken under the strain of time and use, making sharp-pointed little spirals that stuck into her. She was so accustomed to it she didn't even notice. The chair was home. It had always been hers. It was part of her life.

Aidan got out of bed and slowly came over to her. He watched her carefully for a minute, then, crouching down in front of her, put his hands on her knees.

"Carrie," he said as gently as he could, his anger subsiding, "what's the matter? I thought after last night . . . ?"

Dumbly she shook her head, not looking up at him. He tried stroking her arm, but the more he persisted the more she sobbed. At last he got up, and still naked went out to the kitchen to make coffee.

The state of the kitchen shocked him. The sink was full of dirty dishes, and dozens of milk bottles lay around, sour curds coagulating at various levels inside them. Distastefully swabbing the antique crust out of a couple of stale cups his feelings about her changed. He'd make coffee then go. If she wanted to play that game . . . He had too many problems of his own without taking on anyone else's. But spooning the coffee powder into the cups his thoughts began to soften. He remembered her suicide attempt. If she cared so little about life that she hadn't minded dicing with it, why should something so basically trivial as domesticity matter to her?

By the time he took the coffee to her, he felt gentle again. The childlike way she huddled herself into the chair made him want to stroke her as he would have stroked a distressed animal. He held out the cup. "Come on, drink up. It'll make you feel better. You've got a hangover, that's all."

He didn't realize it was only an accident when she knocked the cup out of his hand. She had reached out to take it, but her eyes were so bleary with crying she misjudged and sent the cup flying. Some of the hot liquid splashed over Aidan, scalding his bare flesh; the rest ran down the floral wallpaper behind him.

The self-restraint Aidan had been painfully learning to develop these last months under David's care disappeared. He swore at Carrie. He called her names he was afterward ashamed of, said things she didn't even understand. The look of fear on her face infuriated him, stung him more than her shrewish fingernails had.

Grabbing hold of her he pulled her out of her chair, wanting to shake the life out of her. Her passivity and fear drove him wilder than any response would have done. But as his fingers sank into her limp arms, his anger merged with a rush of desire so strong all conscious thought was obliterated: there remained only an overpowering necessity to subdue once and for all this impossible female who was driving him crazy with her moods. All tenderness vanished.

43

Carrie was terrified. Then she found herself fighting like a trapped cat to free herself—scratching, biting, kicking. In the struggle her dressing gown fell off, and wrestling with this naked creature Aidan's mood changed again. He felt a spring of pleasure in his power as a man to take what he wanted. Triumphant, his hands firmly grasping her by the shoulders, he held her away from him, looking at her body with open desire. Then picking her up he threw her on the bed.

But he saw her face. Her expression of terror and despair were no counterfeit. Whatever she had done last night, however she had behaved, today she was virginal again. He hesitated. The anger, and with it the desire, melted away. In their place came a drained depression, growing into a black emptiness of body and spirit as though he had been deeply sick.

Bending down he picked up her dressing gown and threw it over her. His face dark, he turned his back and began to dress.

A couple of minutes later—they had not spoken a word—he slammed the door of the flat behind him. Going down the stairs he kicked out sullenly at the wooden bannisters. When one shattered he felt so relieved he smashed the next one too. In the street he deliberately pushed a middle-aged man off the pavement as he passed by him, shoving out with his shoulder. The man's shouts after his retreating back made no immediate impression on him, but after a while he calmed down and tried to think rationally about what had happened.

However he looked at it, it made no kind of sense. She had made love once, she'd obviously enjoyed it—so why not again? He went over every minute of the previous night, but he could think of nothing he'd done, nothing he'd said, that might have upset her. He thought defensively of other girls. They'd all liked it well enough! More than liked it!

His face was flushed with hurt pride. She needed a thrashing, he told himself angrily—bloody little pricktease. But remembering her face he could have cried.

It was a fucking awful world.

He came back, of course. It wasn't in him to stay away. He loved her too much. Not that he'd admit it. Not even to himself.

That was the cause of the next row, his refusing to tell her he loved her. He had been to see her at her flat a couple of times, and he didn't try once

44

to touch her. He had sworn to himself he would try to play it her way. He had not even kissed her when they first met—the most he did was to hold her hand very gently, the way you'd hold a child's hand. Then, the third meeting, they went out to the cinema and at first she snuggled up to him, perhaps reassured by the presence of other people. After a while he risked putting his arm around her shoulders, and when she leaned her blond head on him he sighed with relief. Each thought more about the other than the film they were supposed to be watching.

Even so, Carrie was not won over. The familiar struggle, the struggle she had fought with Paul, was never absent. She could not help it. In the dark intimacy of the cinema her body warmed to Aidan. Her breasts were autonomous creatures yearning to be touched, all of her longed to press itself into him—but her mind lashed her melting limbs with worse than Puritan scorn. It was also the pain of Judas she suffered. She saw her father's face looking at her, and part of her cried.

Around them other couples were sitting necking without embarrassment. It was a dull film, and few people were much absorbed in it. Next to Carrie a man sat alone, a formally-dressed man in collar and tie and pressed trousers. She became aware that for some time he had been looking at her intensely. He seemed to be leaning his entire weight on the elbow propped on their shared armrest, so that having pulled herself away from Aidan she now found the man's shoulder pressing more and more heavily against hers.

She considered telling Aidan about the man but decided against it. She was still frightened of the violence in him, although sometimes she found herself almost thrilling to it, felt protected and safe when she was with him. After a while the man shifted his knee so that it rested against hers, and when she still didn't look back at him he began to move it up and down in a way that disgusted her. Surreptitiously she moved as far away from him as she could though this meant her pressing into Aidan's side, but now the man's foot sought after hers. Why didn't Aidan notice! She endured the repellent pressure against her ankle for a minute or two—partly out of fear at what Aidan might do, partly out of embarrassment—but when the man suddenly slid his gloved hand over her thigh she reacted instantly. Giving his ankle a vicious kick, she openly turned and glared at him. Then she looked around the half-full house as though searching for an usherette or the manager. Immediately the man got up and moved to a seat on the other side of the aisle, where he sat staring at the screen in apparent absorption as though he had moved merely to get a better view.

Aidan, lost in dreams of Carrie's sweet thighs, had noticed nothing. In the steamy depths of his imagination the hand that cupped her wool-clad shoulder was elsewhere. The auditorium could have been crawling with perverts; he was absent, sweating in heaven with a torrid Carrie.

Carrie, the real Carrie—cold—shuddered in the rising temperature of the back row and thought of snowfields.

But later, in the relief of leaving the cinema, her spirits soared. Aidan bought them both hot dogs in the foyer, and arms linked they strolled together back to her flat, not hurrying in spite of the chill in the air.

Carrie lived at the end of a small street in a north London suburb. Nearly all the houses in her area had been built in the pebble-dash and bow-windowed style of the mid-thirties. The front gardens of the street in which Carrie lived were tiny, but that did not deter their owners from cultivating them with an intensity of passion peculiar to English town dwellers. Roses, hydrangeas, tulips, and crocuses all bloomed in their season behind neat privet hedges. Only a few patches here and there of rough seeded grass and untrimmed hedge betrayed where immigrants, mostly Pakistanis or Indian refugees from East Africa, had settled. None of these had yet caught the gardening bug, though recently the longest-settled family had borrowed a pair of shears to trim back their knee-high grass and had even accepted a bundle of mixed cuttings from the next-door neighbor. Most of these plants were destined to die through lack of knowledge, but a start had been made, which was as well. An influx of brown faces was one thing—tatty front gardens that meant parachute invasions of immigrant dandelion seedheads were another.

Now, in the light of a moon so full even the street lamps were eclipsed by it, the gardens showed empty and dry. As yet few early bulbs had broken through the ground, and only an occasional winter jasmine, its yellow flowers whitened by the moon, and the faded heads of last year's hydrangeas betrayed the local obsession.

Carrie shivered and pulled her coat tight about her.

"Cold?" asked Aidan.

"Mmmm. It was so hot in the cinema."

Aidan hugged her to him, then suddenly laughed and gave her a quick kiss. She kissed him back, then pulled herself away.

She shivered again as they walked on. "Aren't they beautiful?" she said after a while, looking up at the stars. It was such a clear night the Milky Way stretched like a dusty ribbon across the sky. He talked about the galaxy and taught her how to find the North Star. She was impressed by his knowledge and thought of all the things she didn't know.

They reached the entrance to the building where Carrie lived. It had been built on the site of three houses that had been flattened by a landmine during the war. Square, of raw red brick and with pseudo-Georgian sash windows, the building bore no relation to the prewar style of the rest of the street. An attempt had been made to soften the building's harsh outline by planting half a dozen flowering cherries along its narrow front, but somehow they made it look more stark than ever. It was this very frigidity that had attracted Agatha Lowes when she first came searching for a home for the two of them five years previously. It was a place in which you could be anonymous—unspoken to and unspeaking. It suited her exactly.

Carrie didn't really see the building any more. She lived there, that was all. She had wished it were more impressive the first time she took Aidan home after that smart party, but it was inconceivable that she should move. The apartment was the only solid thing in her life. It contained all she owned—her books, the wicker chair, bits of furniture brought from the old life—all her permissible memories. She felt safe there. She couldn't imagine living anywhere else.

Now she let Aidan follow her up the stairs. At her door she hesitated. "Just come in for a coffee, then," she said finally. "But I don't want to stay up late. I'm really sleepy."

He knew what she meant to imply but hoped for better. While she moved around the kitchen, he said nothing about the mess, and it never even crossed her mind he noticed or cared about it.

Carrie was in a peculiar state. The last few days she had tried to make herself think clearly about Aidan and what she wanted from him, but she found coherent thought about him almost impossible. If she sat down to think she immediately wanted to jump up. If she got up she felt restless and found herself thumbing through her books or nervously plumping up the cushions. No matter how hard she tried to concentrate her mind, it refused to settle on her problem. It wasn't that she needed to waste any time wondering whether or not she loved him. That at least she was clear about. Since Paul she had come to believe that, after what had happened to her, she could never live a normal life like other girls. Yet here she was loving a boy just as though she were any normal girl and, she hoped, being loved back.

It was at that point that her thoughts came unstuck. *Did* he love her? Aidan would cuddle her, gently or roughly according to his mood, but always attentive to her; she knew he thought continuously about her—he'd told her so—and that apart from wanting her physically he wanted to be in her presence anyway, just as she wanted to be in his. And he was always saying how much he really liked her. So what was that, if it wasn't love? But nothing would make him admit it. He wouldn't say the words. Several times she had tried to bring him to the point of saying them, but always he evaded her, changed the subject or just grinned at her.

The evening after the cinema it came to a head. They had taken their coffee into the little living room and were sitting side by side on her old red moquette sofa, its ancient pile flattened and faded from years of wear. Carrie glanced up at Aidan and was struck—as she often was—by his good looks. He had been staring absent-mindedly at the carpet, but as he suddenly looked up the sheer blueness of his eyes made her put out a hand and stroke his face. He smiled back at her but said nothing.

"Do you know . . . ?" she began without thinking, meaning only to say something vague about his eyes, but to her dismay she heard herself saying "Do you know, I really do love you!"

Now she'd said it, she blushed and buried her head in his chest. He had been gently stroking her arm, and he went on stroking it, but his arm had gone rigid. Cold with misery she waited: at that moment nothing in the world was more important to her than that he should tell her he loved her. She could feel his hesitation in the stiffness of his body. But after a minute or two it had become obvious he wasn't going to say it. He had swallowed several times as though clearing his throat prior to speaking, but that was all.

She sat up, angry at what she interpreted as stupid pride. "Don't you care about what I said?" she cried.

He looked embarrassed, wouldn't meet her eyes. "Love's a big word."

Now she was really mad at him. "You mean I don't understand what I'm saying?"

"Not necessarily. But it's not a word I ever use."

"*That's* true enough. I've noticed that already."

Aidan turned to her and tried to pull her back into his arms, but she shrugged him off. He took a deep breath. "Look," he said in a tight voice, "I know what you want me to say. And I know it hurts you that I don't say it. I would if I could—you know what you mean to me! Isn't it obvious enough without my saying anything?"

She shook her head. She was holding her back straight, and she kept her voice firm, but she couldn't keep tears out of her eyes. "How can I know what you really feel if you don't tell me?"

"I've told you a hundred times how much I like you."

"Like! Like! Anyone can *like* me!"

"If liking was all I felt for you, then we wouldn't be sitting here arguing like this, would we. Of course I feel more than that."

"Then *say* it!"

He hesitated. "I can't. I can't use a word I don't understand. Not a word like that. I don't know what it means—'love.'"

She laughed bitterly. "That's ridiculous. Everyone knows what 'love' means. The stupidest child knows what love means. It's just pride, that's all. You feel you'll be giving part of yourself away if you say it."

He put a hand tenderly on her knee, but now it was her turn to look away. "You can have all of me if you want it," he said.

She still wouldn't look at him though her heart had begun to beat heavily at his words. "Then say it."

He looked stern. He took his hand away. "I can't. I just can't. Not yet, anyway, not when I'm told to say it. Because it's all a fraud, perhaps. When it comes down to it I don't know that anyone genuinely loves anyone else. They want someone to *fuck*. Or they want something the other person's got and they haven't. Or they want to be able to say to the world, 'Look, I'm so clever I've managed to win this desirable object for myself.' Or they want a walking wallet to keep them for the rest of their lives. And they go all dewy eyed and pretend it's love . . ."

Outraged, she glared at him. "Is that what you think! You think I see *you*, you of all people, as a bread ticket?"

"Don't be crazy, I wasn't talking about you and me. Why do you have to make everything so personal?"

A look of scorn came over her face. She drew back from him. "Are you crazy! I was saying I love you! How am I supposed to say that without being personal?"

He pushed himself against the back of the sofa and stretched out his

49

legs. His face was completely closed now—she could see no signs even of friendliness in it. She felt she didn't know what was happening to her: she had a desperate desire to fling herself on him and drag the words out of him with her bare hands.

"I was trying to discuss it impersonally," he said stiffly. "To make you understand. It's a con, the whole thing. I don't think there's any such thing as love, except maybe self-love."

She was silenced. She looked away from him. "That's a terrible thing to say," she said at last. "How can you sit there and say that? I'd rather be dead than think like that."

For the first time he looked at her. She noticed the strain in his eyes. He looked older; a sad man. "If it really matters to you that much, then I'll say it." He paused. "I . . ."

Quickly she leaned toward him and slapped a hand over his mouth. "Don't you dare! If you say it like that I'll never speak to you again. I mean that, do you understand? I really mean it. I think I'll kill you if you say it to me like that."

Aidan could not suppress the sudden desire to be cruel, to hurt back. A sarcastic smile widened his lips. "*To love and to hold,* is that what you want? *Until death us do part, for ever and ever amen* . . . all that?"—he droned the marriage vows in a nasal hum—"Is that what you really want? Can you honestly believe in all that?" He laughed, then said quietly, "Why can't you let us enjoy what we've got without bringing all that super-annuated romanticism into it?"

Carrie jumped up from the sofa. She was trembling. "I'm sorry for you," she said in a low voice. "I'm really sorry for you. I wish I hadn't said what I said. I'd take it back if I could. And I wish I could pretend I didn't mean it when I said it. But I can't. That would be a lie." The expression on her face made him lower his eyes. "But it's different now. I made a mistake. I thought you were another kind of person. If this is what you are, then I don't want to know you. If that's all you think there is—self-love—then you're not worth knowing." Her control broke. To hide her emotion she went to the hall and picked up his coat. An old air force great coat bought from the army surplus stores, its familiar smell and the starchy roughness of its coarse wool brought back vividly the times she had rested her cheek against it. She hesitated a moment, then flung it at him. All kinds of bitter comments rose in her mind, but she kept silent.

Slowly he put it on and buttoned it up. He looked at her. "I'll see you at the group."

"All right. But I shan't speak to you. I mean it, do you understand? I don't want ever to have anything to do with you again."

At the door he turned. "It's only words," he said. "Words don't mean anything. Do you absolutely have to have it said?"

"Yes. But only if you mean it."

He paused, then opened the door and left.

Carrie couldn't believe he'd gone. She ran to the door, almost opened it, but stopped herself. She listened to his disappearing footsteps, felt her heart contract when they stopped, despaired when they started up again. She called to him, but too quietly for him to hear. When at last he was gone she went slowly back into the living room and threw herself down on the sofa, burying her face in the cushion on which he had been sitting. She wrapped her arms around it and kissed it fervently. "The stubborn bastard!" she cried aloud, "the stubborn bastard. I *hate* him!"

That night she cried herself sick.

For several days Carrie stayed in bed. The world was a black place. Beyond the walls of her apartment no one cared about her. It was only here she had any life.

She didn't bother to cook for herself—lived on nothing but warm milk and stale bread. She didn't even wash. Her unhappiness was complete. There seemed to be no light anywhere.

But the fourth day she suddenly felt a revulsion against what she was becoming. Late that morning she had hauled herself out of bed, heavy as though each movement involved severe effort. Bending to put on her slippers she became aware of the smell of stale body odor. Straightening, she looked at herself in the full-length mirror on the door of the mahogany wardrobe that half-filled her bedroom—once her mother's, now hers. She stared at her stained nightdress, her hair darkened with grease. It was the Agatha in her who said aloud in tones of distaste, "You're a *slut*! A dirty little slut! You're disgusting."

The sound of her voice surprised her. It was the first voice she'd heard since the row. Tentatively she repeated what she had just said but less severely. She said it again and again, rearranging the words to make a rhythm to which she began to rock, watching herself in the mirror—

"You're a slut, a slut, a dirty little slut." The gloom that had kept her in bed these past four days lifted, and she made a face at herself, sticking her tongue out.

In the bathroom she ripped off her crumpled nightdress and dropped it on the floor. Then she picked it up and put it inside the dirty-clothes bin. As she waited for the bath to run, she took up a cloth and squirting Ajax around the sink began to rub it clean. Then she wiped the mirror, the lavatory seat, the window sill. For the first time she noticed fist-sized balls of fluff, collected in the corners and behind the water pipes, which had been invisible to her before. Full of eagerness she ran to the kitchen, returned with a broom and dustpan, and swept the floor clean. It was lovely, she thought, looking around her when she'd done, really lovely.

As she was sinking into the hot water of her bath it crossed her mind that in two days she'd be seeing Aidan at the group. Against all her cautioning to herself, her heart sang. As though she didn't know he loved her! He was right, why should she need words? What were words!

After the bath she put on old jeans and settled down to clean up the rest of the flat. She wondered if Aidan had ever noticed how dirty it was and decided not. Men didn't notice that kind of thing. In the kitchen she was shaken to find she had a total of thirty-three milk bottles. As she emptied the coagulated dregs into the sink, the whole room became filled with a nauseatingly sweet stink. Even with all the windows in the flat opened she couldn't get rid of it. It was horrible. It smelled like death.

That thought jarred her into stillness. Cleaning rag in hand, she saw the whole flat—herself, all of it—with an extraordinary clarity as though she were looking down from above at a model stage set. As well as the still dirty kitchen, she saw the sad little living room with its dull wallpaper of pink and beige flowers, the worn sofa and sagging armchairs bought for a larger room, the Van Gogh sunflowers and Chinese girls with green faces that her mother had once bought in a sale, the mottled green and cream tiles surrounding the empty fireplace.

She'd called it home! Home! What was it? Just a collection of bits and pieces, stuff you could find any place you chose to look. There was nothing unique about it, nothing that had *her* mark on it, that said this is me, could only belong to me. It was just a piece of wrapping paper, that was all, a piece of wrapping paper to protect her from other people.

Not only her. Them too. Those other people as well. For a moment she had a vision of everyone sheltering from the world and its threats within their own personal scraps of wrapping and saw how flimsy the coverings were, how easily blown away. How courageous people were, she thought, tears in her eyes. They persisted, survived, even enjoyed. More than enjoyed! Laughed. Loved.

She stood still, overcome. How beautiful people were! In the face of everything, how beautiful!

She didn't have to wait for the meeting before she saw Aidan again. He turned up the next afternoon carrying a bunch of early daffodils. For the first few minutes they said nothing, but just clung together. Then Aidan, still holding her close, said gently, "We mustn't quarrel again, love. It hurts too much."

They held each other a little longer, then she pulled herself away and took the flowers out to the kitchen. He followed her.

"Hey, you've been busy!" he said, surprised.

She looked up sharply. He had noticed, then? She unwrapped the damp white paper from around the flowers and threw it into the wastebin. She left her foot on the pedal longer than was necessary, hoping he would see how clean the bin was. It had taken hours of soaking and scrubbing before she had been able to scrape off the dried collage of egg and tea leaves glued to its sides.

If he noticed he said nothing. He brought her a blue and white milk jug that had been standing on a shelf. "They'll look good in this," he said and filled it with water for her. When it was done, she buried her nose in the daffodils, breathing in their earthy woodland scent.

"I love them," she said. "I love them best of all flowers. I think if I were dying they'd bring me back to life. Do you feel like that? Nothing stops them, not the cold, not snow—not anything. They'd come out even if the bomb fell—everything could be blasted to hell, but in the new year somewhere the daffodils would come out just the same, smelling like spring."

He looked sober. "You think of death too easily. It's a sad way of thinking about a flower."

Her eyes glowed. "Sad! Why sad? It's just the opposite. Everything dies—everything has to die—but however we mess the world up flowers go on blooming, grass goes on growing. Don't you find that makes things seem better, rather than sad?"

53

He touched her face. "You're smiling like an evangelist. Is that your gospel, then—nature?"

"It's the only thing I've really got faith in." She pointed out of the window. "Look at those cherry trees down there. In another two or three months they'll be covered in horrible bright pink blossom like some artificial pudding out of a packet, but when the blossom falls it's suddenly beautiful—millions of tiny petals lying around all over the pavement as lovely as any petals from a *real* tree. However much you distort nature you can't completely muck it up. It's so relentless, so unchangeably *itself*, not like us never being sure who we are or where we're going."

"It's a very primitive sort of faith. Haven't you any time for mankind at all?"

She carried the daffodils into the living room and carefully put them down on a small coffee table in front of the sofa. "About as much time as it's got for me," she replied in a low voice.

He followed her and, putting his arm around her shoulders, pulled her down on to the sofa next to him. "That's crazy. A lot of people think a great deal of you. There's David, and there's me, for a start."

Aidan stopped. He didn't know how to go on.

Earlier that day he had been talking about her to David when David let slip a remark that Aidan had pounced upon. Eventually he had dragged from him as much of the story as David knew.

David, conscience-stricken at his betrayal of professional secrets, had warned Aidan to go easy how he told Carrie that he knew. "She's never talked to me about it again," he said, "not after that first time when she told me her father was in jail. I tried once or twice to talk to her about him, but she clammed up so tight I decided to wait until she knew me better. I'm still waiting."

"She's told me nothing about him," Aidan had said.

"It won't be long before he comes out. Two or three months, if he gets parole."

"Do you think he will?"

"Probably. They tell me he's been a model prisoner. He was put in a special security wing to stop other prisoners getting at him—they don't like child molesters in jail—and he's kept himself to himself. I'll be surprised if he doesn't get parole."

"Shouldn't Carrie know that?"

David had shaken his head. "I don't want to tell her until she's ready to talk about him openly. Maybe it's as well I've told you. No one else is as close to her as you are."

At that Aidan had looked away. It struck him that he had been unbelievably selfish the other night.

Now he sat with his arm around Carrie's shoulders, thinking of her father. He wanted to tell her he loved her but still felt shy of it. Finally he blurted out what David had told him, hugging her tight as he did so. She became rigid, even stopped breathing. Then she said in a cold voice, "You hadn't any right to ask David. It's nothing to do with you or anyone else."

"Carrie! It's everything to do with me. I love you. I had to find out what the matter was."

At his words she looked up. Her limbs relaxed, and she let out a deep sigh. He'd said it now. It gave her strength.

Tentatively, resting against Aidan, she tried to think about her father in jail. But she couldn't. Not even when she tried, she couldn't. As though there were nothing there to think about.

"Carrie," he said, his arm supportive around her shoulders. "Try. Try and face it."

Could he read her thoughts then? All of a sudden she began to cry.

When she had quietened he said gently, "It wasn't *your* fault, Carrie. *You're* not guilty of anything."

Her eyes were red. "*He* wasn't either. They were all lying about him. My mother said he raped me. It wasn't true! It wasn't like that at all."

"Tell me about it."

She shook her head. "Not now. Let's go out for a walk. Later, perhaps. But not now. Let's talk about something else."

Later in the afternoon as she sat on the kitchen table swinging her legs while Aidan made a cup of tea for them both, she suddenly started talking about a dog that her mother had had put to sleep when they moved. "She said it wasn't right to keep a dog in a small flat like this. She said it was too old to change its ways, it was used to a garden and it wouldn't be happy here. But that wasn't it." She looked fiercely at Aidan. "It was because my father had loved it that she killed it."

She paused. She became aware of what she was doing. Once she let herself go—where. . . ?

Aidan put a cup of tea into her hand, thinking of the Labradors he had been brought up with. Working dogs, they were never allowed in the house. He'd begged for a dog of his own, but his mother had an aversion to house dogs. "Muddy brutes," she used to say, "covered in ticks and fleas. Certainly not." And that was that.

"What was it called, your dog?" he asked to prompt her.

"Flopper."

He laughed. "Why on earth?"

Carrie smiled back, warm with memory of the dog. "Because she had this crazy way of flopping down with a sort of groan. Other dogs sit or lie down in a fairly tidy way, but Flopper used to collapse on the floor like one of those pajama-bag dogs after you've taken your pajamas out, with legs all outspread in the most ungainly sort of pose. She was a funny sort of mixed-up spaniel—very cuddly. I really loved her, she always looked so daft and sweet."

Aidan saw it exactly. He'd dreamed of such a dog. Fond, and stupid, and devoted to him alone. "Your mother can't really have had it put to sleep out of spite?"

Carrie considered, then said slowly, "Not out of spite exactly. It was more that after my father . . . went away . . . she couldn't stand having anything he'd loved around her. It wasn't just Flopper. She got rid of everything—his favorite chair, his special books, even a picture he'd bought, a great big painting by Turner of a ship caught in a storm at sea—it was marvelous, wild and violent, everything going berserk—but so beautiful; I can't tell you how beautiful it was. I loved it. So did he. She gave it away—it was a very good reproduction, he'd paid a lot for it—but she gave it away for nothing because she didn't want to have anything in exchange for it, she hated it so."

Aidan was surprised at the intensity of his dislike for Carrie's mother at that moment. He sat next to Carrie on the edge of the table and took her hand. "Was Flopper your dog or your father's?"

Carrie's mouth drooped. "Oh, neither. She was my mother's dog. *We* loved her, but it was my mother she obeyed. She doted on my mother."

There was a day—she was about ten or eleven at the time—when Carrie came to realize her father was a very lonely man. It had never crossed her mind before that it was possible to be lonely if you were married. Her parents talked to each other companionably enough although, when she thought about it, she realized that her father never said much himself—it was mostly her mother who talked; and if she thought of them when she was in bed, the picture that came into her mind was of her father sitting at one side of the fireplace in his armchair—the red moquette looked fresher in those days—and her mother sitting in its twin on the other side, talking while she knitted. She was a passionate knitter of socks, Agatha; she enjoyed shaping the toes, but it was turning the heel that gave her the greatest pleasure. When the dangerous corner was safely negotiated she would sit back for a moment, look at the half-completed sock lying in her broad lap and, after a satisfied sigh, remark, "It won't take long now. I *can* knit a good sock, though I say it myself." Then she'd pat her tightly-permed graying hair with a smile, pick up her knitting, and return to whatever she had been talking about as though she had never interrupted herself. In this tableau her father was always holding a pen poised over a slip of paper (he went in for competitions of the kind that asked you to say why this brand of X was so much better than any other brand of X: though he never won anything the daydream that one day he might buttressed him against the nightly tedium). Occasionally, sensing the need to pretend he was listening, he lifted his eyes and appeared to be looking at Agatha, but his face was blank with concentration as he continued to search for the *mot juste*. She never noticed, or if she did it didn't bother her. She had long ago given up expecting much interest on his part in her daily doings; when she found the need for reciprocal gossip too powerful to ignore she would waddle to the telephone and phone a sister or a cousin.

Carrie had Flopper to talk to. Flopper was an amiable dog who never minded lying quietly, one ear cocked attentively, while Carrie—flat on the floor in front of the fire or lying outside on the grass, her arm resting over the dog's barrel-like body—confided whatever was on her mind at the moment.

But she had no doubt in her mind at all that what was right for her wasn't at all right for her father. The shock she'd felt when she caught her father talking to Flopper reverberated in her mind for weeks afterward.

One Saturday morning she had been out shopping with her mother, and they had returned earlier than usual. Just as Carrie was about to close the front door behind her—ever since her father had weather-proofed it the door could only be closed by giving it a hefty slam that shook the whole house—Agatha told her to leave it open, she was going out to pick a few flowers from the front garden while she still had her coat on. Which was how Carrie caught her father off his guard.

She quite deliberately tiptoed into the livingroom where she expected to find him working at his competitions, hoping to make him jump. But

57

this Saturday morning he was not sitting at the table. Instead he was crouching on the floor in front of Flopper, the dog's muzzle supported between his hands so that they were face to face, no more than a few inches apart. His fair hair had fallen forward, completely obscuring his expression, but Carrie could hear his voice. It was that which was so shocking. It was the quiet voice of a lover when the last barrier of shyness is down and the most intimate thoughts can be uttered. With a look of infinite patience the dog sat listening while its master talked.

At first Carrie watched in bewilderment. Then recognized herself in him. But for *him*. To be adult—married!—and to have no one, only a dog, to bare your soul to! Her heart broke for her father.

She lowered her eyes and crept backward away from the room. Soon the front door slammed, and her mother's voice called her.

"Run and put these in water for me," she told Carrie, thrusting a bunch of pompon dahlias into her hand. "Put them in a jug, any old one, it doesn't matter. I'll arrange them properly later." Then, taking off her coat, she said loudly, "Where's Flopper then? Flopp-er! Flopp-er!" Instantly the dog tore out of the living room and hurled itself at her, tongue hanging out, wet brown eyes soppy with adoration. Mrs. Lowes bent down and patted the dog briskly. "What were you up to then, you silly old thing? Getting round your master, eh? I bet he was spoiling you—giving you a biscuit if I know him, or a sweetie. Gerald!" she called, "you shouldn't spoil that dog so, she's getting fat. You're always feeding her titbits, it's no kindness. She'll have a heart attack if she gets any fatter." She turned back to the dog and patted her again. Flopper jumped up and down in joy, her tail thwacking the wallpaper. "There," she said in satisfaction, "*he* may spoil you, but I'm the one you love, aren't I? Sit!" Flopper instantly sat, eyes fixed on her mistress, full of love. "Good dog. Lie!" Flopper lay, her irrepressible tail thumping the carpet in an ecstacy of happiness. Agatha bent and patted her. She turned to Carrie. "He's got no idea how to train a dog, your father. None at all. He'd ruin her with his softness if I didn't keep a close eye on him."

Carrie had watched in horror, knowing her father was hearing every word. There was nothing new about the scene, her mother was always going on like that, yet he'd never said a word, never once retaliated!

She turned away. It was none of her business. Grownups were very odd, they probably felt quite differently. They must, or her father would have shut her mother up, wouldn't he?

Pushing the plastic-like blooms her mother was so proud of into a jug,

58

she longed to rip the nasty things apart and fling them into Agatha's face. She was chilled with shame; it was days before she could look her father in the eye again.

The rest of the afternoon Carrie fought with this memory. She had not wanted to recall it, it brought back too much pain, but now that it had arrived it was with her for the rest of her life. She almost told Aidan about it, but loyalty kept her back. She wondered to whom she was being loyal and couldn't decide. Though in her heart she knew.

She felt very frightened. But also eager. All amnesiacs are desperate to recover their identities but even more desperately fear what discovery might reveal. She wanted to remember—there was no other way forward, she knew that—but she did not know if she had the strength. There was growing in her an extraordinary sense that she was not quite of her body, as though she were on a kind of high as when one drinks too much coffee. She wanted to take charge of herself because if she didn't, who else could? At times she felt almost powerful enough to throw aside the past. Look at me, she'd say to herself—I'm intelligent, pretty, healthy. I've got a lot going for me. All I have to do is to stand up and be free. But when she stood it was only to find that her feet were still stuck firmly in the mud. It wasn't even mud that she could see, but a thick heavy blackness that lay somewhere at the back of her mind, intangible but solid.

Today, though—memories were beginning to break through—she felt a shaky sense of movement. And of adventure. Terrified and brave at the same time. Things have to change, she told herself, nothing can be static forever. I am capable of change. She kept looking at Aidan and wanting so many things at once that she was totally immobilized. He thought her frozen, didn't know of the whirling inside.

They had been sitting next to each other on the sofa for over an hour by the time the light had faded from the sky, and Aidan's self-restraint was wearing thin. So was Carrie's. Gradually she allowed more and more.

Aidan, though no angel, had so far behaved impeccably. Carrie, not wearing a bra, did not stop him when his hands exploring under her sweater reached their target. She meant to, but she couldn't bring herself to. Encouraged, he explored further but met resistance. He reverted to what he had been allowed. She let him pull her sweater up but not off. She also permitted him to loosen her skirt and draw it down onto her hips, but no further. There, she finally drew the line. Venus de Milo didn't offer more, he comforted himself but wasn't convinced.

Dusk, even a cool Northern dusk, is no time for puritans. There is something about those last minutes before daylight finally vanishes that stirs atavistic memories and pricks even the staid into an awareness of longing. Fires are lit, women's voices soften, and men turn away from work. Owl and urban fox call, and desire wakes for the shelter of the cave.

In Carrie's darkening flat, the worn furnishings were transmuted into rock and pelt as the lovers throbbed with the eternal pulse. Aidan, a man true to his heritage, tugged with hope at the final veils. But Carrie, still unfree, had no choice but to scream and leap up, pulling at her clothing.

Swearing aloud, Aidan thrust himself into the corner of the sofa and buried his head in his hands while Carrie, having some idea of what he was feeling, ran out of the room and locked herself in her bedroom.

Later, after a cup of coffee and a lengthy silence, he took her to a Chinese take-away. Their mood changed to one of hilarity though on Aidan's part it was somewhat forced. Carrie was entranced by the fringes on the painted lanterns. She had never eaten Chinese before. "Nor Indian, either," she confided. Loving her again—because there was so much she'd missed out on? he wondered—he read out the menu in comic-strip accent. They bought a cheap bottle of wine and back home attempted to eat with knitting needles. Agatha would have been horrified at the rape of her craft.

After supper, they cleared up and lay down together on the sofa. Carrie's earlier scream lay like a sword between them, and Aidan merely held out his arm so that Carrie could snuggle more comfortably onto his shoulder. They talked gently for a while and—a little drunk—laughed at pointless jokes, then they fell silent.

Carrie was lying with her eyes shut, conscious of nothing but Aidan's closeness, when without warning a scene began to run in her mind. It was as vivid as though she were actually present. Her father was standing rigid, pale, a policeman behind him, and in front of them both her mother, ice-cold, saying again and again, "He raped her. He raped his own daughter." She saw herself; she, Carrie, was sitting huddled on a chair in the corner of the room, staring at her father's face, not saying a word in his defense. Not a word! He wasn't looking at her, he was sparing her that. She was longing to rush to him, to defend him, but she couldn't move— how could she, a child faced with a policeman, her icy mother, the horror on everyone's face? How could she even open her mouth, when she was dead with shame?

The scene faded, but the shame remained. And guilt. She murmured something, but shook her head when Aidan asked what she had said. She searched again for her father's face, unable to leave the raw nerve alone.

Suddenly she said, "Last night I dreamed I was quarreling with my mother. I'm always dreaming that. She's been dead for over a year, but whenever I dream of her we're quarreling. I hate it. I feel so guilty that I should do that when she's dead."

"Guilty!" Aidan said angrily. "You! What have *you* ever done wrong?"

"I can't help it. I feel guilty about everything."

He wanted to shake her. "You ought to feel fucking mad at the world—not guilty!"

"What's the good of being angry?"

"It's much healthier, for a start. It's better than rotting away from the inside."

She was silent. Then, "I let my father down. I should have tried to defend him."

Aidan looked disgusted. "Defend him! What from? He's a grown man. Whatever his marriage was like there's no excuse for him doing what he did to you. He deserved everything he got."

She shook her head. "Please let's stop talking about it. I don't want to talk about it any more. Please."

He was so angry it was painful for him to lie quiet. He longed to hit out, but not at her. For her, he was filled with tenderness. His suppressed violence only revealed itself in the trembling of his mouth as he kissed her. Carrie was surprised at this and misinterpreted it, thought it due to a near feminine sensitivity on his part. She lay against him as trustingly as on a mother's breast. Aidan sensed this and suffered accordingly. His endurance amazed him. He wondered how much longer he could stand it. Lying silently beside her he thought about the complications of love and how little he had understood it. He listened to her heavy breathing but was hardly able to breathe himself, he felt so choked with love for her.

It grew late. Aidan's caresses—at first too delicate to be noticeable—became more insistent. Carrie was in that state between sleeping and waking when the mind is sufficiently awake to imagine that only a slight effort of will is needed to make one fully conscious, yet the body is virtually asleep and incapable of responding to any but the strongest of commands.

61

Such an effort was in fact beyond Carrie. Her mind half-veiled in sleep, she was aware that Aidan had drawn off her sweater and was now quietly undoing her zip and sliding her skirt down over her hips. As he lifted and gently replaced her limbs on the cushions she made no resistance. It seemed to her she had the choice of fully waking, but was unable in fact to do anything except to drown gladly in the warm pleasure of his hands.

It was the most exquisite of dreams: now and then her limbs moved languidly; sometimes she sighed deeply, and once even whimpered like a sleeping child. Whenever she stirred Aidan kissed her mouth and whispered tender things to her she heard like music, taking in their sound only.

At some barely conscious level she was aware that once before this had happened—the gentle hands, the tender whisperings, her sleep-filled submission. There had been no moment then, and there was none now, when she could have borne to push aside the loving body wrapped tight around her. Then, as now, she submitted to the urgency of the other's need, which was her own also, each gone beyond the restraints of conscience or prudence. And when it was finished, then as now, she fell immediately into a sleep of such profundity it seemed impossible that any but the most blameless act could have preceeded it.

The first night her father gave her an awkward kiss: no more. She had expected nothing more and was content.

Carrie and Gerald Warren were strangers. As like as father and daughter could be, they were divided from each other by the implacable jealousy of Agatha, who was quite unconscious of the extent to which she was terrified that one day these two would meet and communicate at a level incomprehensible to her. Her husband, her daughter—she alone knew what was good for them. They were weak; their gaze wavered toward the world outside the family, and no good could ever come of that.

At a cave entrance, attacked by savage warrior or starving bear, big-breasted Agatha would have been magnificent: as a twentieth-century housewife she was a disaster.

When, then, it was found that her womb was in need of repair and she was packed off with toothbrush and nightie to the local hospital, what she left behind was not a family but a kindergarten for two whose headmistress had flown.

Like children, they felt both pleasure and fear at their sudden freedom.

Carrie was twelve, her father thirty-eight, but they were as unpracticed in emotional relationships as babes in arms. All they knew was dependency: Gerald Warren had married Agatha for her strength and had never stood on his own emotional feet, while Carrie had been brainwashed since her first gulp of milk from Agatha's flowing bosom. In most families some outside influence usually loosens the mother's stranglehold, but until Carrie went to school her mother's was the sole voice she heard. It was an organ of firm control whose message was reinforced by their only visitors, other Lowes. Gerald never spoke much, cuddled Carrie warmly until at four her mother decided the child was too old for male embraces— from then on he was allowed only a good-night peck.

That first night alone together, Carrie and her father were both subdued. Efficient as always, before she departed Agatha had put on a pot of stew to cook in the oven, and as they ate it seemed impossible not to believe she was out there in the kitchen and would come bustling in at any moment. They didn't say much, but each began to feel a tentative excitement and stole occasional looks at the other. Gerald helped Carrie wash up, which normally he never did. Agatha—at home all day—believed in family roles. Afterward he put the kettle on and made them both a cup of tea. At nine o'clock as always he looked at his watch and said it was her bedtime. She went upstairs without a murmur, and when he came in to kiss her good night she lay with the sheet pulled up to her chin and her eyes shut, pretending to be half asleep already. He stood by her bedside looking at her for a moment or two, then whispered that he was sure her mother was thinking of her. She shouldn't feel upset, he added, her mother would be quite all right and in no time at all she'd be back home again to look after them. Carrie opened her eyes and gave him a proud smile. "I'm not worried about that," she said. "I can manage on my own. I *am* twelve, after all, not a child anymore. I'm going to go shopping tomorrow." He nodded approvingly. "That's a good girl. Quite the regular little housewife."

All the next day at school she thought about what to buy and how to cook it, frequently touching the five pound note he had given her, which she had stowed away safely in her breast pocket. She shopped on the way home from school and spent ages in the kitchen preparing a fancy pudding. Even so, the time until he returned home dragged interminably. He had warned her he would be late as he was to visit Agatha in the hospital first, and Carrie tried to settle with her homework, but she wrote a poor essay and knew it.

63

When he came in, he seemed unusually excited. He had not been able to speak to her mother, he told her, as she was still asleep from the operation. It had been slightly more complicated than expected, and it would probably be a couple of weeks before she'd be well enough to come home. But there was nothing to worry about, he assured her, they'd found nothing . . . nasty. And Carrie knew he meant that her mother hadn't got cancer, which she had already learned was something that never seemed to be very far from grownups' minds.

"I saw her, though, just for a few minutes," he said in a strange tone. "She looked . . . very peaceful. Very quiet." They stared at each other in disbelief. Carrie tried to imagine her mother lying asleep, off guard, while others were awake, and could not. "I'm very relieved she's OK," he added, and she was too, so relieved she immediately burst into tears. He patted her, then awkwardly pulled her head against his chest (she was still sitting at the table with her homework spread out in front of her) and stroked her hair. "There, there," he said gently, "it's all right, really it is. She'll be home soon." And as certainly as she knew how happy she was her mother was safe, she knew also she wanted her not to come home for months and months. She stopped crying and smiled up at her father through her tears. She had the extraordinary sensation that he knew exactly what she was thinking and that when he smiled back at her he was telling her he understood.

That night after supper they couldn't stop talking—not about anything in particular but rather the way strangers who meet on a train and take a liking to each other begin to find all manner of subjects in common. They got on so well it was ten o'clock before Gerald thought to look at his watch, and as he packed her off to bed there was an atmosphere of fun quite alien to the normal atmosphere in the house. As soon as he heard her leave the bathroom, he came upstairs and chatted to her while she brushed her hair, carefully not looking at her as she was wearing a rather skimpy blue nylon nightdress without a dressing gown. But when she climbed into bed, he came over to tuck her in and sat chatting on the bed for a few minutes. Then reluctantly he said she mustn't be tired for school tomorrow, and he kissed her, but a proper kiss on the lips this time, not the usual quick peck on her cheek. She stayed awake for hours afterward, hearing him come upstairs, clean his teeth, use the lavatory, and finally climb into bed. It was all she could do not to make some excuse, pretend she'd woken up out of a nightmare, and run into his bedroom and get in beside him. The snugness of her babyhood, when she had done just that and crept in next to her

64

mother, came back to her, and she fell asleep at last, imagining she was cuddled up against him.

The following evening he came in late again after his hospital visit, looking serious. Agatha had been awake this time and so much her usual self that afterward in entering the house he had been unpleasantly surprised to realize what a relief her absence was. Carrie saw his expression. Immediately she was worried that there might be something wrong with her mother. But when he assured her that Agatha was getting on well and might come home earlier than they had expected, she found she was not as pleased as she thought she ought to be.

Over supper they were both very quiet. Gerald praised the meal she had cooked, and when they had washed up they sat down together on the red moquette sofa, drinking their tea, talking soberly. When they had finished, he put his arm around her shoulder, and she curled up against him, resting her blond head against his chest. They sat like that for some time, rarely speaking. When his hand dropped to her breast she did not move. She could not decide whether or not it was deliberate (she felt so shy and uncertain about her breasts anyway—they had only recently begun to burgeon and were hardly any larger than a pair of saucers glued onto her rib cage), for his hand stayed quite still, merely resting there as casually as earlier it had rested on her shoulder. But the feelings his touch aroused in her! She didn't know what to make of them. "Down there," as her mother called it, throbbed and grew moist, and the pit of her stomach contracted. But after a few minutes of them both sitting rigid in this position, he took his arm away and picking up a magazine from the table said quietly, "It's nearly nine o'clock. You were so late last night you'd better have an early night tonight to make up."

Without a word she jumped up and went upstairs, quickly cleaning her teeth and undressing. When she was in bed, he came up and looked down at her gravely. "You forgot to kiss me good night," he said. His voice was strange to her, tight and a bit shaky.

"You always come up," she replied, not looking at him.

He didn't reply but sat on the bed next to her stroking her hair. She looked at him at last and thought his eyes were wet. She pushed back the blankets and buried her head in his lap. They sat like that for some time, him stroking her hair while she lay with her eyes closed, surrounded by the unfamiliar smell of wool trousers and maleness. When he finally kissed her good night, it was a brief kiss on the cheek, and he hurried out of the room.

65

The next night they avoided each other. She said she had a lot of homework, and he said he had his competition forms to fill in. At nine o'clock she went straight up to bed and had her back turned to him when he came in to kiss her good night. He sat on the bed a minute or two, then pecked at the back of her neck and left.

Carrie could not sleep. She turned from one side of the bed to the other trying to find a comfortable position, but thoughts of her parents ran endlessly through her mind. Every time she thought of her father she felt those strange disturbing feelings she had had two nights previously when she sat curled up in his arms, until in the end—some time after her father had gone to bed—she got up and went downstairs to make herself a cup of hot chocolate.

She was drinking from the large brown mug decorated with yellow bunny rabbits, given her last Easter, when he came into the kitchen. He was dressed only in his pajamas, and he was yawning as he opened the door.

"I heard you," he said sleepily. "What's the matter?"

She wrapped her hands round her cup. "I just couldn't sleep, that's all. I thought I'd make myself a drink."

He patted her affectionately on the shoulder. "That's a good idea. What are you drinking? Chocolate?"

She nodded.

"I'll have one too," he said and took some milk out of the refrigerator. They did not speak while he warmed up the milk but glanced at each other occasionally. Smiling, when he'd made his drink he came and sat down companionably next to her.

They chatted gently for half an hour or so, then Carrie gave a great yawn and said she thought maybe she could sleep now. He picked up the two mugs, took them to the sink, and ran hot water into them. She got the dish towel and polished them as though they were best china.

As they left the kitchen they looked at each other like conspirators. Their voices were low—it was difficult to remember that Agatha was not in the house. He followed her up to her room, and after he had tucked her in he sat uncertainly on her bed. He shivered.

"It's cold," he said. "I should have put on my dressing gown."

Carrie hesitated. She wanted to say get into bed and warm up, but something stopped her. Though why not, she argued with herself? Why shouldn't he? What could be wrong? She pushed back the blankets. "Get in a minute and warm up if you like," she said, "I'm not all that sleepy yet."

He did not reply for a moment. She guessed he was struggling with all sorts of prohibitions. Feeling very grown-up she reached out and touched his hand, smiling at him gently. "It's all right," she said. "Just to warm up. Like I used to get into your bed when I was small."

With embarrassment he pulled back the blankets further and lay down beside her. She snuggled up into his arms and shut her eyes in contentment. For half an hour or more he lay stiffly beside her, hardly moving at all except once or twice to stretch his legs. Sometimes they spoke, but gradually she felt too sleepy even to talk. They lay silent, their two fair heads close together, her arm loosely around his waist.

When his hand began to stroke her back, she didn't move, pretended to be asleep. As the hand slowly crept around to her front and began to caress her breasts, she thought she would die of pleasure. His hand moved down to her hips, gently crossed over her stomach, then crept up to her chest again where it hovered uncertainly, then slipped inside her nightgown. Now he was stroking her bare breasts, touching her so delicately she wasn't quite sure she wasn't dreaming—she almost persuaded herself she was. She forced her breath to come quietly, regularly, feigning sleep. She was certain that if she so much as stirred the spell would be broken, he would be off like a disturbed bird, and he'd never come to her again. She lay as though paralyzed, not moving even when his hand pulled up her nightdress and slipped along her thigh and up to the forbidden place, where even her own hands had never been permitted to go. She felt herself wet there and was alarmed at this, knowing nothing, but the pleasure she felt was so intense she wouldn't have cared if the house collapsed, if the world collapsed, so long as he didn't stop. When finally, he lay on top of her, breathing hard and making urgent little grunts, she didn't know what he was actually doing, only that in spite of his weight and a momentary pain her feelings were so extraordinary she couldn't stop a gasp from leaving her, nor her hands from tightening around him. When he had finished he rolled over to one side, pulling her around with him, and though she didn't want him to stop, wished he would go on for ever, she still kept her eyes closed, pretending to be asleep.

Which soon she was. Gerald himself lay awake for some time, then he too slept, though his dreams left him heavy-eyed and weary when he woke next morning.

The following morning was hardly endurable, although Carrie was not yet

67

fully aware of the true seriousness of what had happened. She only knew he had broken an injunction forced on her from the day her pudgy hand first began to explore her infantile body.

By the time she was a year old "down there" was already associated with "ugh-ugh!" noises of disgust, although the message was not yet entirely clear because sometimes her mother made lovely noises of approval, sounds Carrie quickly came to associate with the flowing out of her water or of delectable warm turds from her bottom into the potty seat upon which she was perched after every meal. But even this approval ceased by the time she was two and a half and fully house-trained, from when on bodily functions became unmentionable—apart from an occasional embarrassed inquiry from her mother if she had not spent the requisite amount of time in the lavatory after breakfast. Whenever, later, her pajama trousers pinched her "down there" she learned to wriggle herself free rather than let her hands enter the forbidden zone to pull the material away, though so early had her training begun she had no idea why she was doing it that way or even that her hands were so restricted.

So that when she was twelve and her father made love to her, all Carrie was sure of was that he had offended against her mother's teaching that "down there" was dirty and mustn't be touched. That she had allowed him to left her full of guilt. That she had loved every moment of it filled her with confusion. If they had been somehow magically transferred to an island, just the two of them, they might have lived happily ever after. They were gentle and full of good will toward each other—it is unlikely much harm would have come of it once they had grown accustomed to their defiance. But there was to be no island, no forgetting of rules.

Inevitably when Gerald woke he was tortured at what he had done. He tried to creep out of bed without disturbing Carrie, but she was awake instantly, and, throwing back the blankets, she was out of bed almost as quickly as he was. They turned to look at each other from opposite sides of the bed, then their eyes fell onto the stained sheet. Both faces whitened. Carrie felt faint. Until that day she had never spilled any blood except from cuts or extracted teeth: the sight of her own blood now, with its associations of pain and loss, sickened her. Turning to her father she wanted to blame him, accuse him of hurting her—until she saw his face. There was pain enough there already. Instead she ran to him and put her arms around him, burying her face against his chest.

During breakfast they scarcely spoke to each other, though several times they looked at each other shyly. That evening he rang her from a call box immediately after leaving his office to ask her if she was all right. All day she had moved around in a daze, but now she suddenly felt very alive though full of tears. He asked her about school, what lessons she had had, and she found herself chatting to him as though nothing had happened. Then he reminded her he would be visiting Agatha as usual before coming home, and that put a stop to the conversation. To both their relief the operator released them; claiming—though it was untrue—he had no more change, he put down the phone.

When that night she met him at the front door he was clutching a bunch of de Caen anemones in his hand. Always she had disliked the blood-red and purple flowers, although they were her mother's favorites, but today she especially hated them. There was something about them— was it their gaudiness? their lack of grace?—that she found repellent.

"I bought two bunches," he said as he gave them to her, "one for Mum, one for you."

She tried to smile, but she was upset. How could he have bought them both the same! He didn't even like them himself: she'd overheard him say once to her mother that, for himself, he'd rather have daffodils any day. Couldn't he have guessed she'd like the same as he?

She took them and stuffed them into a cut-glass vase, not even bothering to remove the rubber band that held them together. He was watching her, and she could see he was hurt, but she didn't care: if she hadn't loved him so much, she'd have thrown them away into the dustbin.

"You didn't like the flowers I gave you," he said tentatively later in the evening as they stood side by side washing up.

She shook her head. He stacked their supper plates away in the cupboard, saying nothing for a while, then said:

"I'm sorry about that. Mum likes them best of all flowers."

"Mum's not me," she said, and suddenly they were in each other's arms—Carrie crying and Gerald holding her tight and begging her to forgive him. He said it many more times that night—"forgive me, forgive me"—and said it again when he climbed into bed beside her, but she stopped him by putting her arms around him and kissing him.

That night she didn't pretend to be asleep. When he took off her nightdress, she held out her arms to make it easier, but he left his own pajamas on. They were flannelette and rather furry, and it was as though the teddy bear she'd held tight every night of her life had come to life, grown big and warm and embracing her back as she'd often daydreamed. She knew so little about passion she had no inhibitions, and Gerald took care not to startle her. He allowed himself some dreamy fantasies as he did on the rare occasions he made love to Agatha, but he explored no further with his daughter than he did with her mother—apart from Carrie being naked, which seemed almost natural to him, having seen her unclothed often enough as a small child. Somehow it would have been quite indecent, both for him and for his wife, if ever Agatha had stripped off and allowed him to see her as she was. He had wanted it once but had never liked to ask. Now he preferred not to think too closely about what she might look like under the Vyella nightdress she wore in winter, or the voluminous cotton nightie she wore in summer. Enough was enough. Naked flesh can be too raw an experience to face without valor.

Agatha was away for a fortnight. By the time she returned Carrie and her father were real lovers. Carrie thought of nothing during the day but him, and the happiness that during the first few days had been tempered by anxiety now swamped every other feeling. The teacher standing in front of her class didn't exist for her; her friends spoke and she spoke back, but her mind was elsewhere. She longed to talk about her father to them, but knew she must not. Sometimes, casually, she mentioned him, engineered the subject of their conversations so that it was legitimate to bring his name in. But she never let her passion override her caution. Sex as a subject was not yet openly discussed among her schoolfellows. There were smiles and one or two half-comprehended jokes, but to none of the other girls was it a real experience. Suddenly Carrie had found herself isolated, set aside by what was happening to her. As this stage—before Agatha returned—she was too happy to care. It was only later, when the euphoria had gone and she would have liked to talk it over with someone, that she realized how separate the experience had made her.

Gerald always rang her as soon as he left the office and before going to visit Agatha. At the weekend Carrie went with him to the hospital and sat silent at her mother's bedside, unable to open her mouth. Agatha looked from one to the other of them and later told her husband she was sorry he and Carrie were getting along so badly. Home was not home without a mother, she added, smiling so smugly Gerald had an almost irresistible urge to hit her across the face and was appalled at himself.

At home Carrie ignored her homework, instead spending hours preparing supper. Every dish was elaborately decorated with carefully selected pieces of parsley, strips of cucumber, or scarlet tomatoes cut into zigzags. Posies of small flowers from the garden adorned the dining table, and when it was time to wash Gerald's clothes even that she did with adoration, ironing and re-ironing his white shirts until they shone like glass. She made mistakes, not being used to the work: some supper dishes were failures; a shirt tail got burned; woolen socks were shrunk, but he pretended not to notice and called her his darling, and "little mother." They embraced when he arrived home as though they had been separated for days rather than hours, and often touched each other during the evening. They went to bed early and did not sleep until midnight. Too often Carrie was late for school and her house tutor called her out, asking what was wrong—was she not sleeping well?—she looked so baggy-eyed. Already she had had three late detentions. When Gerald heard this he panicked and made sure after that she slept earlier and rose in time.

The day before Agatha was due out was terrible. It was a Sunday, and although they didn't once mention her homecoming, her ghostly presence was already creeping between them. Together they cleaned the house from top to bottom in preparation, polished furniture, and filled flower vases. Once Carrie found a rubber bone in a cupboard that had belonged to the dog before Flopper, and though she scarcely remembered the animal she burst into tears over it, holding it to her breast as though it were a memento of a dead child. She said nothing to her father, though, and put it back where she had found it. In the afternoon she refused to visit her mother, saying she felt tired. Close as she and Gerald had become, she was still too shy to be entirely open with him.

That last night they slept together but did not make love. It was as though they feared Agatha might burst in on them at any moment. Next morning they woke early and lay unmoving in each other's arms, saying nothing. It seemed to Carrie there had never been any time when she and her father were not lovers, and the future threatened such desolation she could not bear to think about it. At school that day she looked so white her teachers wanted her to leave early and were surprised at the tone in her voice when she refused. When in the end the final bell rang and there was

71

no avoiding it any longer, she put on her navy coat and dragged herself homeward. Gerald had taken the afternoon off to fetch his wife, and when Carrie got home he had changed their previous roles and had prepared tea for her. Agatha, large and white, sat propped up among satin cushions in the middle of the living-room sofa.

She took one look at Carrie, whom she had not seen since the previous Sunday. "What's the matter with you, then?" she cried triumphantly. "I knew you wouldn't look after yourselves properly! Look at you both—thin as rakes, the pair of you. I'm really disappointed, especially in *you*, Carrie. You might at least have taken better care of Daddy than that. What a hopeless pair you are ..." She nagged on, while Carrie, frozen, sipped her tea and forced herself to eat the chocolate cupcake Gerald put in front of her, purely because he had bought it for her. Once, and once only, they dared to look at each other, a look of absolute understanding, and love, and despair. It was Gerald who looked away first.

Had Agatha seen? Did something of what had happened make itself felt? Carrie never knew. There were times when it seemed to her that Agatha was hinting at something, times when odd comments were made, little digs that seemed to have no point unless she had guessed.

And yet, thought Carrie—filled as she was in those early days with a turbulent unhappiness—if she had known, wouldn't her mother have come right out with it and condemned them both roundly? Then she began to wonder if it was not her after all that her mother was getting at. Since her operation Agatha had refused her husband "his rights," as she called it. It was Gerald who told Carrie this, not Agatha, who would never have mentioned such a thing to her daughter. Gerald said he thought the hints were fear on his wife's part that he might be looking at other women. It was inconceivable, he said, that she should have guessed at the truth and said nothing. And yet Carrie wondered, unsure. She could not rid herself of the feeling that, even if she had not admitted it to herself, her mother knew. There were periods when she hated her mother intensely, felt she was being betrayed by her every bit as much as she herself was betraying her mother. Felt she should have been protected from what was happening to her.

For she and Gerald remained lovers. Sometimes, in the middle of the night, she would be woken by a hand stroking her hair or the awareness of a warm body curling up beside her. They almost never spoke; mostly Carrie, genuinely half asleep, pretended not to wake and in the morning was often not quite sure whether or not she had dreamed it. He was always very careful: he carried a handkerchief with him and made sure he left no signs behind him. Later, when she was a little older, he stopped coming inside her and finished in the handkerchief—fearful, as he explained, that she might become pregnant. This really horrified her. In her absurd innocence she had never connected what he was doing with pregnancy, and from then on she worried, until he went out and bought a packet of condoms, which they both detested. The horrid things loomed large in their lives as objects whose discovery by Agatha would bring a retribution so terrible it could not even be thought about.

Gradually her feelings toward her father changed. Agatha saw to that. She was never one to build up anyone's confidence, but now she began to denigrate her husband, made unpleasant little comments about his character that usually had just enough truth in them to strike home to Carrie. It *was* true he was not an ambitious man and had not risen very far; it *was* true he was sometimes weak (if only he'd tell her mother off, even hit her, Carrie thought angrily after one of these sessions) and allowed others to dominate him. It *was* true he was not physically strong, and this now seemed particularly irritating to his wife. "Handsome is as handsome does," she said one day in the garden picking up in her own massive arms a slab of paving stone Gerald had been unable to shift. She even suggested that physical slightness implied cowardice. Since her father took all these hardly-veiled insults without once retaliating, Carrie reluctantly found herself thinking that of him too.

Gradually these insinuations eroded something inside Carrie, began to destroy the pride she had always had in her father, until she found herself avoiding him. She no longer caught his eye, and she tried not to be alone in a room with him and spent a great deal of time trying not to think about him.

But Agatha could not destroy everything. Sometimes when he came to her at night, Carrie clung to him, tears running from her closed eyes, even though she still tried to pretend she was sleeping. He wept too, overcome with guilt, but he could not stop himself. At school Carrie's work improved, and on the surface she seemed to regain the ease and pleasure in her friends that she had lost for a while, but those who knew her best drifted away from her in the way that girls do, sensing a lack of openness that made them, ever so slightly, distrust her.

Carrie was fourteen when Agatha was at last brought face to face with the facts, and there was no longer any way she could ignore them.

Agatha had been out shopping, leaving the two of them alone. Usually she was insistent that Carrie accompany her, but recently Carrie had started her periods, and today she was due for one. She pleaded a headache and a stomach ache, and after grumbling a little about having to carry everything herself without help, Agatha allowed her to stay at home. But she returned much earlier than normal, came into the house very quietly, not closing the front door behind her, and found them in each other's arms.

She went mad. She screamed—hollered and yelled until the next-door neighbor ran in. White-faced, fainting, Agatha sank to the sofa, moaning as though knifed in a vital artery. The neighbor, a large brusque man with no children of his own, could not at first make out what the matter was. When he did, he advanced on Gerald and struck him violently across the face, then hurried to the phone and called the police.

For the next few days, before Carrie froze the whole horrible scene out of her mind, she tortured herself with questions. Had her mother not suspected, after all? Had she imagined that, just to give herself an excuse so that she needn't feel guilty about taking her mother's place? Or—a new idea occurred to her—perhaps her mother *had* known all along and it was her conscience that had at last forced her to catch them out and put a stop to it? To protect her.

Or was it hate, vengeance, that had driven her to come home early that afternoon? Or love? It had not looked like love. No, it had not looked like love at all.

They had been in each other's arms, she and her father—not talking, just holding, standing up in the middle of the living room with arms wrapped tightly around each other, bodies pressed together. When Agatha walked in there could be no mistake about their intimacy, no possibility that Agatha could any longer ignore it—for whatever motive.

Gerald never attempted to defend himself, not from the outraged neighbor, nor from the police. Not once did he suggest that Carrie might have wanted what he gave her. They had only been caught kissing, but when Agatha accused him of everything, including rape, he said nothing, only looked down, so that they all knew—the neighbor, Agatha, the grim-faced policemen—that the worst, the very worst, had taken place.

All the Loweses were to accept among themselves that he had raped her: for all her difference, Carrie was half a Lowes, and it was not possible that a Lowes could have accepted such a thing happening to her

74

without force. In the police station, however, it was different. When it was explained to Carrie and her father (separately—they were not allowed to see each other), that if Carrie claimed she had been raped she would be medically examined and possibly have to give evidence in court, her father decided it was best to admit he had not forced her physically. Still trying to protect her, though, he said he had used emotional persuasion. After this Carrie was not made to speak and tell the truth of it; it was enough for her to shake her head firmly when she was asked if he had forced her. They did not press her any further. The policewoman put her arms around her, saying with a hardly-subdued sob that people like Carrie's father ought to be shot—done away with like vermin—and hugged the girl even tighter when Carrie at last burst into convulsive crying.

The worst pain had begun the first time they accused him of rape in front of her, and she had said nothing—there in their own living room, where less than half an hour previously they had been holding each other in love. Wordlessly she had betrayed him. He did not ask her to help him: on the contrary, he had deliberately lowered his eyes and not looked at her at all. He had allowed her to deny her own desire, and she had accepted his protection. But no amount of willingness on his part could later assuage her own grief that she had not stood up and proudly told them she had loved him of her own free will. Perhaps, had there been more time, she might have. Had she had time to think and to see that her mother had lied, that he was *not* a coward, that he had taken on his own shoulders her sin as well as his own and never once asked for mercy, then perhaps before they took him away she, too, would have found the courage. But there wasn't time, and she did not.

Before they took him, the police searched his bedroom, his clothes, his wallet, looking for evidence of his depraved mind. She heard them in his bedroom, their voices stiff with outrage as they searched for what one of them kept calling "feelthy pictures," which they did not find. All they discovered were photographs of *her*. Clothed photographs. Photographs of her in her christening robe; in her first short dress, still plump with baby fat; wet and laughing at the seaside; sprawled across her mother's lap half asleep; running across a field (she remembered that time, although she was only six—she was chasing after Flopper who'd run off with her sock); and later photographs showing her losing her plumpness and grown gawky, plain; then a later one still, the last one, taken only the previous holiday when she was suddenly pretty again, a colored photograph exaggerating the blondness of her hair, the blueness of her eyes, the tan of her face. They had all known he loved that picture—he had had it enlarged and bought for it an expensive metal frame, which he stood on top of the upright piano. What neither Carrie nor his wife knew was that he also had a small print of it in his wallet, carefully wrapped in plastic to protect it, and another in his cigarette case. There was nothing he owned that didn't have a photograph of her stowed away somewhere. In the breast pocket of the suit he wore to the office, in the anorak he wore on walks, inside his driving license, in the drawers where he kept his competition forms, his underclothes, his shirts—even tucked away inside his current library book.

The police were clearly disappointed. They straightforwardly despised him for what he had done; he had offended against everything they believed in, and they could only see him as a monster. It disgusted them, this exaggerated front of being a normal father, and before they left they threw down the entire collection of photographs on the table in front of Agatha, making clear from their expression what they would do with the pictures if they were she.

Agatha needed no prompting. When the door had shut behind them, she rose slowly from the chair where she had been sitting. She totally ignored Carrie, who was huddled whitefaced in the corner, too shocked even to cry. Silently the woman went to a shelf where her sewing box was stored and took out her sharp-pointed dressmakers scissors. Holding them in front of her like a bayonet, she turned toward the center of the room and advanced toward the table. Arrived, her thoughts betrayed only by a tight viciousness about the mouth, she slowly raised the scissors high in the air then in a quick flashing arc brought them point down and stabbed the pile of photographs, stabbed at it again and again, regardless of the damage to the polished table. After a while the passion lessened, then one by one she picked up the mutilated photographs, cutting each one into many pieces. When that was done she picked up those pieces and sliced at them again, cutting them smaller and smaller until in the end there was nothing left but tiny segments small as confetti, which littered the table or fluttered to the floor.

Carrie watched in horror. Only once—when her mother took up the photograph of herself running after Flopper—had she made a pleading gesture, but the mechanical hands continued to slice, to chop until that memory too was demolished.

Finally, when nothing was left of her father's treasure, the grim figure

76

scooped up the remains and, walking like a stone ghost, carried them to the fireplace where they flared up and were gone forever within a few seconds.

Carrie, thus broken, fainted. It was the only mercy shown her that entire day.

David, his mind still mostly on his work—in particular Carrie whose present state of emotional upheaval was causing him considerable worry—was surprised when Jess's front door was unexpectedly opened by a red-eyed girl whom he had never seen before. She stood there silently in front of him, attempting to suppress her sobs. David stared at her, trying to make out who she was before giving his name. He had hoped to find Jess alone. Short and squarely built, the girl had a pleasant but unremarkable face not improved by a swollen nose and rubbed eyes that leaked continuously in spite of her constantly dabbing them with a sodden, screwed-up handkerchief.

David spoke cautiously. "Would Mrs. Bennett be at home?" he asked, uneasiness bringing out a slight Welsh lilt.

The girl nodded, but said doubtfully, "She said not to let anyone in from the press."

He felt a little indignant at the mistake. "I'm not the press. Will you tell her it's David Parry. There may be something I can do to help."

The girl stared up at him with the unseeing gaze of someone under deep shock, then without another word disappeared inside the house. To David's surprise he could hear loud talking, almost as though a party were in progress.

Iris pushed through the group in the living room and took Jess to one side, tears spilling freely once more. "There's a man outside," she said in her wet voice. "I told him you didn't want to see any more press."

Jess did not hide her impatience. "Send him away, Iris," she said shortly. "And do stop crying, for heaven's sake, it doesn't help anyone. No one's blaming you."

Iris dabbed uselessly at her eyes. "But he's not press. He said his name was David Parry. I've never seen him before."

Jess's expression did not change. She gave Iris a slight push toward the table where the drinks stood. "Iris, pour yourself out a large whisky, then go to bed and get some sleep. Go on, off you go. I'll fetch David myself."

Iris shook her head doggedly. In three years of devoted admiration for her employer she had absorbed some of Jess's qualities. She could not remain as apparently cool as Jess, but give in she would not. "I'll get him," she said determinedly and went back to the hall.

David, looking over Iris's head, hesitated uncomfortably at the living-room door. With Adam in Denmark he had imagined Jess alone, grieving, needing comfort. Of course he was appalled at the cause, but all the same he had to admit to himself he was glad of an opportunity to show Jess the professional side of himself. He'd planned how he would assure her it was very unlikely anything harmful would happen to Matthew, how it was nearly always some deeply disturbed girl who did a thing like that, but they doted on the kids, cared for them as though they were their own. He knew the statistics. While he talked, he'd have his arms around her, comforting her, giving her the warmth she needed. It gave him deep satisfaction, thinking that. Usually she was so bloody independent.

Far from seeming distraught, Jess, caught up in a group of a dozen or so people, appeared to be her normal self. She was looking very beautiful. Her figure, in spite of two children, was that of a young girl, with slender hips, small waist, and high, though small, breasts. In contrast to the more formal dress of some of the others, she wore jeans and sweat shirt, which made her look even younger. David, who even now was still somewhat awed by her fame—he had first met her as a guest on her own program three months previously when she was discussing the worth of a documentary on delinquent adolescents—for the first time realized he was falling in love with her.

David had deliberately not looked too closely at his motives for sleeping with her, but love, he had always known, was not one of them. Now, seeing her toss back her long black hair with that slightly impatient jerk so familiar to viewers, not bothering to smooth it with her fingers as another less confident woman might have done, he felt for the first time a pang of delight in her as a lover. Raising the glass that Iris had brought him to his lips he caught Jess's eye; she smiled, but made no attempt to come over to him.

He stood watching her, surprised by his feelings. Each time they'd met he'd thought it might be the last—a woman like her could have any lover she wanted. She'd be bored, would chuck him. So why let himself get really involved? It was extraordinary that it had ever happened at all—he still couldn't believe his luck. But at nights his conscience troubled him. His Welsh puritanism told him he was wrong, *wick-ed,* and he resolved to give her up. But in the morning it seemed pointless: she'd end it herself, for sure, in a week or two.

Surprisingly, the affair had gone on. They had never, either of them, talked about their reasons. There was not much time for talk. Mostly they met at her house, chatted for a few minutes over coffee or a drink, went to bed and made love, dozed in each other's arms for quarter of an hour or so, then hurriedly dressed and went on with their respective jobs. They seldom saw each other more than once a week, but that was enough, given lack of passion on both sides. It was this last that worried David's conscience most. Love excused a lot of things—but how could he justify a sophisticated affair of this kind? It didn't fit in with his idea of a moral life at all. But give her up? Jess Bennett? It was too much to ask of himself, wasn't it?

Watching her, it occurred to him that he might be falling in love with her so he would feel better about the affair. He was not so far in he could not stand aside and evaluate the situation. He tried to look at her critically, to find fault, but found her flawless. Even her apparent lack of emotion he knew was due to her will power, her professionalism. She wasn't the sort to break down—it had been unperceptive of him to expect it.

Finding her flawless did not please him. He was like a craftsman whose main delight was not in creating but in restoring broken ware. His pleasure lay in searching out the potential in people damaged by life, consoling them in their worst times and working at bringing out the best in them. There were times when he suspected he needed them as much as they needed him, but usually he pushed this reflection aside, rejecting it as pointless, destructive. He thought of them as seabirds clogged with oil—once he'd cleansed them, he opened his hands wide and sent them off back into the world. Often this last was surprisingly painful—he did not expect gratitude, rarely got it—but did at times feel his investment in the emotionally wounded brought very little return. Then he would sharply remind himself of his own good fortune, and tell himself he had no need for reward except the work itself. Mostly he believed himself.

Had he ever been alone he might have searched deeper. But there was always someone needing help. He worked late at nights, seeing clients in their homes or running groups, went back worn out to his flat, slept deeply, and got up early to face another busy day. Sometimes he was awakened by the phone at night to deal with a client in a crisis. Much as he groaned to himself at being disturbed—quite often he wouldn't get any

79

more sleep that night—the reviving breakfast cup of tea would have an especial sweetness it lacked other mornings.

David looked away from Jess at the people separating him from her, wondering who they all were. Most were rather elderly, apart from a tall, heavily built man of about thirty-eight with a thick mane of black hair already showing a touch of gray here and there. With a shock David recognized him as Jess's husband from the portrait she had until recently kept on the little chess table behind the sofa. It seemed that Adam had felt David's eyes on him; looking up from the old woman at his side to whom he had been talking, he briefly returned David's stare.

David's first impulse on recognizing Adam was to walk out. He felt embarrassed, guilty—absurdly so since he knew Adam couldn't possibly have known who he was. He disliked the man on sight. He had met his type in court, always felt steamrolled by the weight of their confident self-sufficiency before they'd even opened their mouths. It had never occurred to David Adam could have returned home so quickly. If it had, he would never have come.

He looked swiftly at Jess. She was absorbed in conversation with someone. She receded from him; his growing love shrank. Not that he'd ever been under any illusions she'd go so far as to marry him even if he'd wanted it: he knew he was being allowed to borrow her the way he borrowed an expensive book from the public library—she was tagged and date-stamped and would have to be returned at the end of the permitted time. You didn't keep classy ladies like her on a probation officer's pay. It would never have occurred to him that he might be the one to be kept. Adam's presence merely rubbed in what he already knew but today had nearly forgotten.

He decided it would be unwise to walk out without first talking to Jess—it would look odd, distinctly suspicious. Then, once he'd done that, he'd go.

Not wanting to push through to her too obviously he stood at the edge of the group for a minute or two, sipping his drink. It was an odd collection: a circle of well-heeled older people who appeared to know each other stood in the middle of the room talking animatedly almost as though they were at a party. Two or three more casually-dressed younger people stood by Jess. They too surprised him by the brightness of their manner. He wondered about it, thought them callous under the circumstances, until suddenly he recognized the apparently out-of-place vivacity of these guests for what it was: the wake syndrome. They were neighbors, local friends—dropped in to sympathize. At that he wanted to laugh, in spite of his anxiety for Jess. There was something ludicrous about the thought of this obviously well-off lot behaving like any group of mourning peasants anywhere in the world. What was their main objective—a genuine desire to support Jess, or a morbid wish to join in, to be part of the excitement? He chided himself for his cynicism but traced signs of inner glee on these smooth faces, and he recalled old aunts back in his Welsh valley who, knocking back the port, would whisper in joyous hisses about the dreadful last agonies of the coffined body lying in the bedroom upstairs. Death brought unification. Even enemies joined hands in the face of it.

Was it ever different? There flashed into his mind the image of a white-robed Greek chorus, hands flailing, voices keening, and for a moment he was irradiated with a sense of the rhythm of the world turning on its axis, eternally, and eternally people grieving, loving, weeping, Himself and all these others in this room, a part of the everlasting cycle. Looking about him he warmed to them, was irritated less by their prosperity.

Until he looked again at Adam. The dislike he had felt for this grave, good-looking face with its slightly heavy jowl and dominant nose grew stronger. It was a face of power. He saw him in wig and gown, convincing judge and jury of the inevitable rightness of his case. David looked away. He had an uneasy suspicion that if Adam Bennett ever looked straight at him he would instantly discover all.

Had not Jess at that moment moved forward and taken David by the arm, he might after all have slipped out of the room, driven by adulterer's panic, but he was caught, pulled forward and forced by the woman he loved—he loved?—to endure introductions. She hardly listened to his words of sympathy but pushed him forward toward the others. Fortunately for him, struggling to find the correct social inanity for such a bizarre occasion, half a dozen people simultaneously began to cry they really must be going. Instantly, the atmosphere altered. With the putting down of glasses, the party spirit was abandoned. Faces lengthened under the weight of renewed commiserations and hopeful assurances. Suddenly everyone was expert on the subject of baby snatching, and they all assured Jess the prognosis was excellent: Matthew would be back in her arms tomorrow at the latest. Arms reached out to pat her, and thin, veined hands flinched at Adam's returned handshake. Jess bore these unwanted physical intrusions stoically. Adam stood at her side. Like a pair of

81

automated twins the couple, with sad smiles, indiscriminately muttered, "Thank you, thank you, so kind of you to drop around," and with no sign of reluctance ushered the callers out of the room.

David, too, tried to leave, but Jess wouldn't hear of it. "You've only just come!" she cried too brightly. "You really mustn't go without meeting Adam! I've been longing to get you two together for ages." David felt alarmed. Behind the cool exterior there was a hint of flushed recklessness that made him wonder if she had been drinking. Ignoring his urgent whisper, she took his right arm and led him up to her husband. David felt his nerve shrinking even further. Adam topped him by at least four inches. Adam was, besides, a good deal broader in the shoulders and chest; his was the heavy build of a natural rugger player, while David had the slim wiriness of the long-distance runner.

Gently David tried to remove his arm from Jess's grasp, but her fingers dug into him. It was a relief when Adam held out his hand; Jess had no choice then but to free him. Taking his mistress's husband's hand in his, David shook it, but could not bring himself to look the man straight in the eye.

Jess was chattering to Adam about how she and David had met. "I knew instantly," she said, smiling from one to the other, "you two would have a lot to talk about. You both spend so much time with lawbreakers. David is a probation officer," she explained to her husband.

The men nodded politely to each other. David hesitated: he had intended to talk about Matthew but for the moment the subject seemed taboo. "I should imagine our approach to *lawbreakers* is somewhat different," Adam said after a moment's pause, and there was no disguising the arrogance of his tone. "Though as a species probation officers are not as anarchic as social workers," he added coolly, "most of whom seem to consider lawyers, judges and policemen to be the only true criminals alive. They appear to have no concept at all of the inviolability of the law."

As Adam had turned to Jess as he said this, David was uncertain whether or not he was included in the last comment. Jess looked angry. "Darling, I know you're tired after your journey, but you are being rude," she said in a hard-edged voice, and taking David's arm again she led him over to two elderly couples who were sitting talking to each other in a half circle around a lit fire.

David's nervousness left him. He would have liked to have stayed with Adam and argued. The patronizing bastard! Felt he owned the world because in court he could play around with men's lives like God. The rage

82

that always filled him when certain magistrates emptied themselves yet again of their venom against what they insisted in calling the "criminal classes" boiled in him now. He nodded briefly to the four elderly people sitting by the fire whom Jess introduced as her parents and parents-in-law. Unwillingly he sat down in the chair Jess had indicated but perched on its edge to show he meant not to stay. When Adam pulled up a chair and joined the group by the fire David did not look at him. Iris came back into the room, hesitated, then said good night and went out. Only the family and David were left.

David looked curiously at the two grandmothers who were engaged in a long converstion about education. It was not every day he had a chance to observe the role of grandmother in families like this one. He had been thinking only recently that grandmothers were a neglected study.

Both women seemed impeccably ladylike, from their curled gray hair down to their narrow suede shoes, but virulently anti-snob that he was, he had already sniffed out a difference between them. Just as Adam Bennett had made no attempt to disguise his social superiority over David, so Mrs. Ingram was projecting a similar aura toward her daughter's mother-in-law. It was clear that Mrs. Bennett, plumper but well-corseted, was conscious of the social perfume wafting her way. A constriction of her throat, showing itself in a tightened voice, betrayed her. Here and there a vowel slipped, elongated into uneasy refinement. Suddenly David became aware that beneath the careful middle-class voice lay a discarded Welsh accent. How was it he hadn't noticed the inflection earlier—he had all along been aware of an odd sense of familiarity with Adam and his mother. Mrs. Ingram's voice, on the other hand, flowed with the silky ease of a woman who had never had to give her accent a second thought. She was unshakeable, and he did not take easily to unshakeable people.

He turned to examine Mr. Bennett. While there was a distinct physical resemblance between Adam and his mother, there was none at all between him and his father. Slightly shorter and less bulky than his wife Mr. Bennett sat silently smoking his pipe, ill at ease away from his own familiar armchair. From the walking stick propped against his chair and the way he occasionally shifted his leg or rubbed it automatically as though unaware of what he was doing, David guessed at an old war wound.

Mr. Bennett saw David looking at him and, after giving him a friendly nod, asked him his opinion as a probation officer as to what type of woman would do such a "cruel, wicked thing" as to snatch somebody else's baby.

It was the first time David had heard Mr. Bennett speak, and he was not prepared for the sound of his own native valley. The old Welshman had made no attempt to change his accent to impress his son's in-laws. Rich and smooth the deep voice flowed through the southern living room: "wo-măn"; "cru-ĕl"; "wick-ĕd," the old man sang in a bass voice trained from adolescence in the sad laments of the annual Messiah. Straightaway David was back in the slate-floored kitchen of his childhood with his mother singing in her shaky alto as she rolled the pastry while he sat playing on the floor—"He was des-pi-sĕd . . . des-pi-sĕd and re-ject-ĕd . . ."—the disbelief in her voice as she swooped down to the tragic "re-ject-ĕd"! he'd always stopped playing then, wanting to comfort her but knowing obscurely her sadness was nothing that he could touch—"re-ject-ĕd of men . . . A man of sor-rows . . . a man of sor-rows, and ac-quaint-ĕd with grief . . ."

While his voice politely replied to Mr. Bennett's question, his inner ear listened still to the sounds of the Oratorio. He glanced at Jess. She was staring at him with a far from sympathetic look. He wondered if his emotion had shown on his face and, embarrassed, blew his nose.

Adam—whose deep voice was his father's, David saw now, Oxford replacing Welsh but the essential music unemasculated—was speaking about the cases of baby snatching he remembered. The mood of the family group was changing; for the first time they allowed a sense of fear, of uncertainty, to surface. It was Mrs. Ingram who rescued them from an unthinkable breakdown: bringing around the conversation to Emma, she asked if they had settled the question of her granddaughter's future school yet.

Mrs. Ingram wanted Emma to follow the family tradition and go to Jess's old school. She brought up the subject every time they met. "It's so good for them to be away from home, though of course it is terrible to part with them . . ." she paused, realizing her gaffe, then continued in her determined clear voice, "I loved it, and so did you, Jess. You were very happy there. And it gave you a splendid education, the very best."

Adam, who had conquered the emotion he had begun to feel a few minutes before, settled back in his chair and crossed his legs, tugging at his pin-striped trousers as he did so. With an irony his mother-in-law missed, he said, "Oh, the very best, Mama, absolutely splendid. It turned Jess out the equal of any man. Indistinguishable from one, in fact. You'd hardly

84

know she was a woman apart from certain obvious . . . attributes." Jess's father, a tall spare man with the air of one unaccustomed to having his opinions contradicted, nodded his head in agreement.

"Oh, I don't know," Mrs. Ingram said vaguely, "they'd given up cricket and that sort of thing, more's the pity. Jess didn't even have to wear a tie! But the ethos of the public school, *that* they retained, thank heavens. There are certain qualities in which this country has always excelled, and I'm not ashamed to admit I would rather pack up and go abroad than live in the kind of England those Labor people want."

The elders nodded, except for Mr. Bennett who raised an eyebrow and looked as though he would have liked to qualify her statement.

Adam could not leave Jess alone. "Are you a real gentleman, Jess?" he asked, his cool smile covering his intentions. "That's what your mother seems to be saying. I think perhaps you are. Yes, of course you are. Isn't that why the BBC gave you your own program—they knew you could be relied on to play the game."

"Game? What game?" She looked at him suspiciously, not yet seeing where he was heading. She was finding it difficult to concentrate on the conversation.

"Being a front. Window dressing. So that they can say to all the other struggling females who don't stand a chance of getting out of the typing pool in spite of their degree in anthropology or whatever—Look! We have integrated: Women's Liberation is achieved! Jess Bennett rules supreme, not in a despised woman's program but in your genuine male-type intellectual slot. So be good girls. Put down your guns, pick up your notebooks and take a message: *Jess Bennett is a true gentleman and can be relied on not to rock the boat.*"

"That's a lot of balls! There are plenty of marvelous women producers, women with real power."

"Agreed. But could the public name one of them? Yours is the only female name, Jess, that anyone knows apart from news broadcasters, talking reporters, chat queens, and so on. You're unique. The only brain in her own right. You're even *better* than a man—you've got tits!"

"I'm no hermaphrodite!" she spat at him.

"I never said that. A *true gentleman* was what I called you. I presume hermaphrodites are unstable creatures, and that's your main weapon against the world, Jess—you're so bloody stable."

85

"Adam!" his mother cried, "I don't know what's got into you tonight! And you too, Jess. You're both using language I've never heard decent people talk!"

"Then you've led a sheltered life, mother," Adam said, not taking his eyes off his wife.

Jess ignored her mother-in-law. She stared at Adam. How could he, at a time like this! "You're talking nonsense," she said coldly. "My program's a breakthrough, not a dead end. It proves a woman can run a serious program as well as any man and get as good ratings. Others will follow."

"Oh, yes? A philosophy series with Iris Murdoch in the chair? Maggy Drabble's Saturday Night Arts Parade? A twenty-part History of the World's Greatest Art by some female Kenneth Clark? Maybe. Maybe one of them, even two. But the public wouldn't stand for more, and you know it. It's still a man's world, Jess, and you've only succeeded in it because you've played the man's game and won. If winning is what you call it."

The older couples, startled at the bitterness in Adam's voice, looked from Adam to Jess and back again in alarm. What was happening to their children?

It was David who broke the silence that followed. Watching Adam talking he had suddenly recognized him. The same stance, that assured voice, that challenging glare—as an eleven-year-old hadn't he watched Adam in admiration, though even then with dislike—Adam Bennett, the star of the sixth form dominating the school Debating Society's annual open meeting? Adam Bennett, Captain of Cricket, Captain of Football, the leading light of the Drama Society; the tall, the handsome, the brilliant One-and-Only (as the juniors snickeringly called him) Adam Bennett. It was extraordinary how little he had changed. He was broader in the shoulders, heavier in the face, but still the same self-assured bastard he had always been—how was it he hadn't recognized him straight off?

It was an unpleasant surprise. From the moment he had set eyes on Adam he'd thought, yes, he's exactly the sort Jess would marry. Top public school, everything made for him from the word go. No possible rival. How could it have occurred to him Adam might have been, like himself, a grammar school boy from the Rhondda? Had started out with the same chances.

Without thought, he said to Adam, his amazement showing in his voice, "You're Adam Bennett!"

They all stared at him. Adam held out his empty glass to Jess who was pouring herself another drink. "Who the hell did you think I was?" he said irritably.

Feeling like a fool, David explained. It was immediately clear that his old school was not a favorite subject of Adam's, and enough of the ancient nugget of first-year awe remained within David for him to have no desire to annoy the resurrected sixth former. Adam muttered something but obviously had no desire to indulge in nostalgia.

There was a moment's pause while everybody's thoughts reverted to Matthew. Except those of Adam's mother. She was a woman whose passions—apart from her feelings for her son—had never run very deep. She looked delighted at the coincidence. With a gracious smile and a tilt of the head like the Queen Mother's, she asked David his name again. "It's such a small world," she added. "You never know."

"Parry. David Parry."

She beamed. "Oh, dear—Parry. There are such a lot of Parrys."

David told her where he had lived. "Why, yes! Indeed I knew your mother!" she exclaimed with pleasure. Then suddenly her hand flew to her mouth and she stared at David. He stared back, puzzled by her expression. Then it came to him. Mrs. Bennett. Mrs. *Bennett,* for God's sake!

He began to smile, he couldn't help himself. He wanted to laugh aloud. He looked around the impeccable room with its bowls of roses, the Meissen china and the display of rare Icelandic carvings; at the linen-covered walls studded with original drawings; at the antique cupboards full of glass and leather-bound books—and looked back at Mrs. Bennett, earnestly middle-class Mrs. Bennett, hardly able to believe the truth: that at one time she had scrubbed his mother's front steps. She had gone down on her hands and knees to clean up the dirt of the Parry household and had been glad to do it. Mrs. Bennett from the council houses on the other side of town, the scraggy char with the chronically sick husband.

There was a brief moment when David knew temptation. He felt the exhilaration of cruelty and looked at Adam with wicked joy. Then Mrs. Bennett, pale, leaned toward him, holding out a pudgy, ringed hand. "It's so many years since I saw your mother, Mr. Parry, not since Adam was a boy. We got completely out of touch. I don't suppose you even remember me."

Looking into her eyes David read her message. He recalled his mother's admiration for Mrs. Bennett who was working, he was told, in order to buy books, encyclopedias, games gear for her clever son. His mother, always particular that her swarming family treated her cleaning woman with proper respect, had been especially thoughtful to Mrs. Bennett whose husband, she had often reminded them, had had a bad accident and it could happen to any one, such a disaster—even to them! But she had never told David what school Adam was at, and it had never occurred to him to wonder.

So it was for Adam for whom those knees had ached, those hands had blistered. That was how he had got the expensive cricket bat and the fancy tennis raquet that all the juniors had envied. Adam Bennett! It had never even crossed his mind! He'd assumed a quite different background. A thought occurred to him—if his mother had told him who Mrs. Bennett's son was, would he have been able to resist the temptation to take the One-and-Only down a peg or two? Had his mother been right not to trust him, knowing for a whole year they would be in the same school?

David looked at Adam—from the man's face he could see the penny had dropped with him too—and colored as though it were his own secret in danger of revelation. Hastily he said, not looking at anyone at all, "I don't, I'm afraid—my mother knew so many people."

Neither Adam nor his mother were fooled. His knowledge lay between them, linking all three. Jess, who had brought Adam's drink, was watching them curiously. She passed Adam his glass, looked down at him for a moment with a raised eyebrow, then turned to David. "David," she said casually, "you asked to see the transcript of that program you did with me. I've got it upstairs in my study—would you like to come up and have a look at it?" Without waiting for his reply, she said to her father, "Daddy, do help yourself if you want another drink. I'll be down again in a few minutes," and went to the door.

Jess and David were standing looking down at Emma. A few minutes earlier, faced with the sight of Matthew's empty cot, Jess had for the first time talked about him to David. Now she laid a gentle hand on the mass of black curls that hid Emma's sleeping face and whispered, "If anyone took her, I'd go mad."

"You love her so much more?"

Jess shrugged. "It's not so much a question of loving. She's me. I know everything about her. Her reactions are my reactions. She's part of me. With Matthew it's different. Of course I love him as much. But he's Adam's child. I feel a stranger to him sometimes in a way I never do to

Emma." She bent over her daughter and kissed her gently. "Let's go out now, I don't want to wake her."

They tiptoed out and went into Jess's study, where they embraced. David, meaning to return to Matthew, said instead, "I think I'm falling in love with you. Did it show downstairs?"

"I thought you looked different, somehow."

"It happened tonight, when I first came in and saw you. I hadn't felt like that about you before." He looked anxiously at her and took her hand. "You don't mind my saying that?"

She shook her head. "No. I wasn't in love with you, either. I'm not in love with you now. At least, I don't think I am. How do you tell?"

"You're joking. You've been in love? With Adam?"

She looked abstracted, but answered him.

"Yes, of course. But that was different. I was overwhelmed by him as much as anything. He always stood out, even at Oxford. Lots of girls were in love with him, though they managed to be in love with other *real* people at the same time."

"*You* said it."

"Mmmm."

"Jess, I really do love you." He was surprised at his need to tell her that, even though he wasn't entirely sure he fully meant it. He began to kiss her again.

She freed herself. "We haven't long. We'll have to go down in a few minutes. I don't want anyone to suspect."

"I don't give a damn about them. I love you."

"I heard you the first time. But the world doesn't come to an end because you're in love. Don't look like that," she added more gently. "I meant we can't do anything much more than we've been doing already, can we?" Her expression changed. "And that's dangerous enough! Even if we never hear anything more from Yvette, I'll never . . . Anyway," she looked at him dryly, "you've only fallen in love with me now because I've suddenly become someone with a problem. Admit it. You like me better because of Matthew. You didn't think about anything except my cunt before."

"Jess!"

"Oh, don't be so prudish, you with your stuffy Welsh background." She gave him a quick look and said casually, "What was all that going on between you and my ma-in-law, by the way?"

David showed his confusion. "Nothing was going on."

89

"Yes it was. Something was up."

David let go of Jess's hand and flipped through the pages of the transcript she had left out for him. Then reluctantly he said, "If you must know, Mrs. Bennett used to help my mother out sometimes. For money. That's all."

Jess stared in disbelief. "Helped your mother out! How? Do you mean she babysat?" She drew in her breath. "No! She cleaned for you! Mrs. Gracious Bennett!" She put her hands to her face and began to shake with laughter.

David could not help laughing too. After the tension of the evening the absurdity of it was too much for both of them. Then Jess's voice changed. David took her by the shoulders. "Jess! Stop it! You're getting hysterical."

She stopped instantly. "Well, who wouldn't be under the circumstances. But is that honestly true? About Ma Bennett?

"Yes, it is. I truly don't remember it very well—my mother had a number of temporary helps—I know that Mrs. Bennett's husband was knocked over or something and couldn't work for a long time. She had to earn money to buy Adam all the extra bits and pieces he needed. Or which she thought he needed."

"Oh, he would have needed them all right. He has a great need for all sorts of bits and pieces. Especially *pieces*." Jess pushed David's hands away and, hoisting herself up, perched on the edge of her desk. She seemed to be making a decision. She swung a leg freely as though to show her lack of concern, but there was no disguising the bitterness in her voice. "In fact he's gone off with one," she said finally, looking down at David. "It's pure Victorian melodrama, he's left me for a *fancy piece,* a shop girl called . . . Fanny!"

"Left you? But he's here right now."

"Only because of Matthew. We had a terrible row last week, and he packed his bags and went off. We've kept it quiet because of the QC business. Tonight he's going to sleep on the sofa in my bedroom. He can't sleep in the guest room because his parents are staying there tonight, and anyway we don't want them to find out, not until we've got Matthew back. I couldn't take any more . . . sympathy."

David reached up and wrapped his arms around her. He wished he were taller. When Jess wore her highest heels she even rose above him—sitting on the desk put her almost out of reach. She let her head rest against his, but her body stayed stiff.

"What QC business?" he asked, gently trying to pull her off the desk.

He couldn't tell if it would help her most to talk about Matthew or Adam. He had never known her so tense. Resisting him, she sat up straight again. "Didn't I tell you? Well, it's not something to gossip about. He's hoping to be given silk this Easter. He stands a first rate chance, he's been told, but it's a couple of weeks before the announcements are made. It wouldn't do to have any scandal before then. That would muck things up completely. You can't imagine how sensitive barristers are about their reputations—you'd think they were bloody royalty."

"You sound very bitter."

"Are you surprised? When he's so crazy about a woman he can't even wait a couple of weeks for her."

"He's left you for good?"

"I told you, last week."

"Why didn't you tell me about it then?"

He saw her freeze. "I don't *have* to tell you anything, darling."

It was true. But now it hurt. He let go of her and walked over to examine a portrait of Jess as a young girl. It completely missed her toughness: done in pastel it made her look insipid, a chocolate-box beauty. With his back still to her he said in a conversational voice, hiding what he felt, "I suppose it's tremendously important to him that he becomes a Queen's Counsel."

"Of course. It's essential to him. If he's not successful this year then he almost certainly will be next year, or the year after that—*provided* he doesn't do something stupid to offend the mores of the pious gentlemen at the top. He has to pass this hurdle with flying colors—there are plenty more. Oh, he'll get there in the end—can't you just see him, a Law Lord, white-haired and fat, pontificating along with his peers in the House."

He turned around and faced her again. "God, you are bitter!"

"We were so close! We were like twins. Someone once said just that—that it was indecent for us to marry, we were so alike it was almost incest. And he leaves me for some sock-darning, dim-brained tart who makes him cups of Horlicks when he's tired and strokes his brow. Yes, strokes his brow! He told me! That's his exact phrase. 'I love her because she strokes my brow when I'm tired, and she darns my socks.' Can you imagine! Adam!" She took David's arm. "I think I'm going to be sick."

"You've drunk too much. You're overwrought. Do you want me to make you a cup of coffee?"

She shook her head. "I don't want to go down just yet. Let's sit on the sofa for a minute or two and chat." She slid off her desk. "Do you honestly think Matthew's going to be all right?" she said, not looking at him.

Putting his arm around her shoulders, David pulled her down next to him on the small sofa. "Yes, I told you. It's a hundred to one it'll all be over in a day or two. It's a terrible time for you, but, honestly, the odds are completely in his favor."

She sank against him, but looked toward the door to check that it was ajar so they would be able to hear anyone coming up the stairs. "When the press came they wanted me to cry, but I was damned if I would. It wasn't just keeping a stiff upper lip and all that—I've got this feeling that as long as I *believe* it will be all right, it will be. That if I once started thinking that anything could . . . go wrong, then it would be bad luck, it would actually make something bad happen. As though I can keep him safe by will power. How's that for a first class honors graduate? Got a bit of wood handy? I haven't touched any yet!"

"Don't make yourself feel guilty because you think he'll be OK."

She looked at him in surprise. "Why should I? I'm *not* guilty. Not in the sense that I'm culpable for what happened." In David's arms she felt her guard slipping. She pulled herself up straight. "Of course, you could say that I am guilty in one way—if, as Adam so sweetly put it when he first got home this morning, if I'd been a proper mother this would never have happened."

"The bastard." He hugged her tight. Thoughts of future possibilities entered his mind.

"No-o. It makes a rational argument. If I had not employed Iris, then that particular phone call from her mother would not have been made and Matthew would still be asleep next door."

"That's a pointless line of argument. Something else even worse might have happened on another occasion. No, if anyone's guilty, it's Iris."

"I don't see why. It was very understandable, what happened. It's impossible to blame her. She's being very sensible about it, fortunately."

"It didn't look that way to me. She was howling her head off."

"Oh, that's because of shame, not guilt. She's ashamed she's been made to look a rotten nanny. She's failed in the eyes of the world. But she doesn't feel guilt about what's happened to Matthew. She might think she does, but that's only because she doesn't understand the difference."

"How can you split philosophic hairs at a time like this?"

She was able to smile at him. "I've always told you, we're very different, you and I. *Your* problem is that you're just a walking sense of guilt. Anything can make you feel guilty. You jump at the chance. But not me. I

92

don't feel guilty, not *your* sort of undefined guilt. Guilt isn't lying there around the corner waiting to get me the way it is for you. Can't you understand that?"

He shook his head. "No. Not really. I can't even imagine what it must be like. I can't see how anyone can grow up in this world and not have a strong sense of guilt about . . . so much. How can you have any moral sensitivity if you don't have a sense of guilt?"

"Now who's talking philosophy? Listen, darling, we've got to go down or they'll get suspicious. Besides, I daren't leave them alone much longer. Adam's always particularly frightful when the four parents-in-law are all together. He's such an awful snob. But give me a last kiss first." She wrapped her arms around him and pulled him close, but not before he had caught a glimpse of her face. It betrayed what she had been so carefully hiding all evening. Now he knew he loved her.

When he came downstairs, Jess had already settled herself next to her husband. David felt uncomfortably out of place. For some reason Aidan came into his mind. The thought that this was the sort of house Aidan might well have grown up in startled him—he tended to forget that once Aidan must have taken this kind of luxury for granted.

It surprised him how easily he could imagine Aidan sitting there, a part of that group—a grandson of Mr. and Mrs. Ingram. He saw, too, the arguments, the quarrels, the problems that would inevitably arise between someone as intensely individual as Aidan and these solid guardians of the status quo. But he would fit in in a way he, David, never could. He himself, Aidan, Carrie, the other kids in the group, they lived in a different world to this set. You'd hardly think they belonged to the same race.

And yet, wasn't there a kind of similarity between Aidan and Jess—a sort of arrogance?—no, not exactly arrogance, he told himself, but something not far from it, a hands-off-me-don't-get-too-close-without-permission attitude that was superficially very like the attitude of some of his more recalcitrant lads, but was in fact miles away from it. It was more than the confidence born of good parenting. He cringed from the word "class"—he preferred when he could to pretend it didn't exist—but he recognized the same thing in all the Ingrams, and to some extent in Adam, though there was a subtle difference there. He tried to pin it down, feeling more at ease with himself once he was able to see it as a social symptom, almost a kind of sickness. In the Ingrams he thought it arose

93

from an unshakeable conviction of their own personal superiority born, perhaps, of growing up with such a large share of life's goods. But no, he thought after a moment's reflection, it wasn't simply possessions alone that produced that assurance. Not all the rich had it. Was it then a matter of being impeccably socially acceptable? Today? *Still?*

Jess, suddenly breaking into loud laughter, interrupted his thoughts— apparently some remark of Adam's had set her off. Her laugh was so close to hysteria that her mother rose and went over to her. Before Adam could reply the doorbell rang. David jumped to his feet. "I'll go," he said, "I was just about to leave anyway."

At the door were two men, one fat, one thin. The fat one introduced himself as the Inspector, to whom David had spoken to earlier that day on the phone. The two men talked together about the case for a minute or two, then David took the Inspector and Crasswell into the living room. As they entered he heard Jess giggle, "Oh god, it's Laurel and Hardy again." He looked rapidly at the Inspector, but he gave no sign of having heard. David decided not to leave after all, not with Jess in that state.

Jess, taking hold of herself, rose and introduced the Inspector to the group around the fire. He was clearly relieved to see that Adam had arrived home and shook his hand warmly, speaking to him as one colleague to another. Adam, in spite of his fatigue—it had been a long, emotional day—was full of questions as to what the police were doing. He drew the Inspector aside to speak to him privately.

Crasswell, the young sergeant, was left talking to Jess and David in the middle of the room. Crasswell looked pointedly at Jess. "We mainly came to ask you a few questions about Yvette Grüber. I understand she doesn't live here anymore," he said.

Jess looked distinctly annoyed. "That's right. She left last week."

Crasswell glanced down at a paper in his hand. "Yes, we gathered that. She was your *au pair*, right?"

Jess nodded but said nothing.

"She didn't have to register with us, so we don't have any details, but we'd like to have a chat with her. Could you let us have her new address, by any chance?"

"I've absolutely no idea where she's gone. What on earth do you want to see her about?"

Beneath the coldness of Jess's voice Crasswell sensed some agitation. He looked at her curiously. He had already noted that her speech was slightly slurred, though he didn't think any the worse of her for that under the circumstances, but he did find the presence of so many unexplained undercurrents puzzling. "Well, I'd have thought it was obvious." He hesitated. He was aware he had spoken with a kind of social intimacy that his presence there as a police sergeant did not warrant. "I'm sorry, but from the way you spoke I gathered you didn't exactly part friends."

David answered for her in a tone that puzzled Crasswell even more until he thought about it later, going home. "Mrs. Bennett is very tired and upset. Can't you leave routine questions like that until the morning?"

Jess interrupted him, her voice restored to its usual crispness. "Thank you, David, but I'm perfectly capable of answering for myself. The truth is, Sergeant, Yvette was a rather difficult young lady—to be honest, she was quite impossible—and last week I told her to go. I gave her a couple of weeks' wages, and she walked out. It's as simple as that. I've no idea where she went, and if you're thinking she had anything to do with Matthew I'm certain you're wrong. The last thing that wretched little . . . girl would do would be to saddle herself with someone else's child, I promise you."

Crasswell made a note in his book. Then, holding his pencil up in the air as though hoping for more, he asked, "And you have no idea at all where she's gone?"

Jess shook her head firmly. "None."

"Did she have any friends?"

"I've no idea. She'd only been in the country two weeks, and she wasn't the type to make friends easily. Quite frankly, I was glad to see the back of her. She was not at all a pleasant girl. So I'm sorry, but I can't help you." She nodded at the sergeant, then turned and walked over to the Inspector. Crasswell wrote a few more words down, then thoughtfully closed his notebook and put it away in his pocket.

Later, driving back to the station, the two policemen agreed that it would be worth asking the press to run a description of Yvette along with a request for her to contact them. Adam had been more forthcoming about Yvette than Jess, and though he, too, had disliked the girl's character he had described her physically with obvious appreciation, which led the Inspector—whose mind was never a subtle one—to hazard a guess as to the reason for Jess's objection to her.

Crasswell made no comment. It might possibly be true, he thought to himself, but he suspected something else was involved though he had no

95

idea what. He had noted with interest David's protective manner to Jess—he had been standing close by her side—and the way he looked at her; though she hadn't once returned the look she had swayed slightly toward him several times. Crasswell assumed she had had rather too much to drink and the sway was unintended, but in his experience the instinctive barrier people put up between their own and other people's bodies was so strong that a considerable amount of alcohol—certainly more than Jess had taken—had to be consumed before physical touching between those who were not intimate ceased to be taboo. He had expected her to jerk herself back at the last moment; instead she had briefly leaned against the probation officer's shoulder twice—for less than a second, it was true, and each time she had quickly recovered herself—but those two separate moments told him as clearly as though the pair had openly admitted it that they were probably lovers, were certainly no strangers to each other's bodies.

It never occurred to him to tell the Inspector of his discovery; since it seemed to him to have no bearing on the case—at least for the moment—he let class loyalty sway his judgment. In certain ways he was a fastidious man; he would not have cared to listen to the Inspector's inevitable comments about a woman whom he, Crasswell, found more intriguing each time he met her. Adam, on the other hand, he hadn't cared for. There was some lack there, something he couldn't pin down. The unlikelihood of ever being surprised by him—was that it? he asked himself. Adam Bennett looked solid all the way through—it was difficult to imagine any vulnerability there. And it was their vulnerability that made people interesting.

Many men, as they face the onset of middle age at thirty-nine or forty, know despair and throw up their jobs and/or their wives and begin life anew. But barristers—successful barristers, that is—have a midway change of life built into their profession. When as young men they first enter their chambers they sit around waiting, praying for work. Gradually, if they are any good, the clerk fixes them up with more and more work until soon, like the sorcerer's apprentice, they long to fling up their arms and beg the taskmaster to stop. But stop they cannot, for the gilt carrot that is dangled before the eyes of all junior barristers has now filled their hearts with desire. If only they can keep up the pace! Holidays, free weekends, gentle leisure—all become a thing of the past. Toward the end of his thirties, when other men are beginning to grow bored, the junior barrister is so snowed under with work he hardly has time to kiss his wife good morning or his children goodbye as he disappears into his study to bury himself once more in the monstrous volumes of Chitty on Contracts or Lloyd's Reports (if he is a commercial lawyer, as Adam was), or to sit writing advices, opinions, pleadings for presentation in court. Copies, drafts, reworkings, telephone calls, searches among the hefty tomes in his home library or through the nobler collection in his chambers; papers; files; work; work—there is no end to it. Twenty, thirty cases a week pass through his hands until nothing exists except work—and the Goal.

At last comes the time he has been waiting for. He decides he has earned his spurs and, just before the winter solstice, makes his application for silk to the Lord Chancellor. Until Maundy Thursday the nerve-wracked applicant must sweat it out; four months of pretending he doesn't really mind, of listening to gossip as he eats in Hall or chats in the chilly corridors and cramped changing rooms of the courts, exhausted by work and worry, but excited by hope. If his luck is in, the miracle happens—his application is successful. Invited to "join the front row" at the bar, he relaxes with the deep joy of a mother after a protracted childbirth. Posing for a commemorative photograph of his new self, in white wig, bulky gown, and black silk stockings, looking for all the world like some character out of Gilbert and Sullivan, he already dreams of future photographs, splendid in the full panoply of High Court Judge, even finally—dare he think it?—in the regal robes of a Law Lord, a peer among peers.

As a Queen's Counsel, life is pleasant indeed. Holidays, money—even fame—now become possible. Instead of thirty cases a week he can tackle the real meat, tastings that can last three or four months a sitting, even longer. He is treated with awe by the lesser inhabitants of the courts. Life (though since abolition no longer the death), the prosperity, or the ruin of his fellow man, is his province. Freedom or incarceration, the dice he plays with. Is it any wonder that some tend to develop an air of stately invincibility—even, dare one say it, of pomposity?

For the most part honorable men, they live and die content in the knowledge that as long as good and evil, truth and mendacity exist, there must also exist a body of men and women whose job it is to argue for one man against another in the courts of law. Such people must be upright and clearheaded, proof against inappropriate emotion. If you are trying to send a man down for twenty years, it is better not to reflect that if you'd had *his* early life you, too, might have ended up in dock, and it is essential not to envisage what those twenty years will in truth be like. Imagination and empathy are no assets in a job like this: it is easier if black remains firmly black, untinged by unsettling shades of gray.

Adam was born to the job. Every quality a good barrister needs, Adam had. If he had a flaw, it was only that he was not quite as self-sufficient as he thought he was. Fanny had found this out, and while the flaw need by no means prove fatal, it would certainly hold up his ambitions for a year or two if made public. Lawyers, like Caesar's wife, are supposed to live lives of moral rectitude. As young daughters used to be advised—be good, and if you can't be good, be careful.

Adam had meant to be careful. He *had* been careful. Then, for some reason that he still didn't fully understand, one night he had felt he would crack if he didn't go to Fanny. He'd packed his bags and left—to his own amazement as much as to Jess's. He couldn't help himself any more than a cube of ice can help melting under the warmth of a lamp.

When he had first met Fanny he was not even aware how dissatisfied he was with his marriage. He and Jess had always been a perfect pair, everyone had said so. In many ways they were extraordinarily alike. They were both tall and dark-haired, though Jess was slender, small-boned, while he had the broad shoulders of an athlete, a man of bulk and presence. Both moved lightly on their feet, he like a boxer, she like a dancer; both radiated a kind of intensity and enthusiasm for whatever they were occupied with that set them apart from more mundane couples; above all, their minds worked in similar ways. The last was less obvious to Adam because their interests were different, and besides it had always seemed to him he was the more intelligent of the two, though it was she who had attracted the most notice at Oxford (he'd never quite got over his chagrin at her talent for attracting publicity for whatever she did, nor that even now she still earned more money than he; there was also the slightly humiliating fact that she had brought with her a good deal of inherited money as well). But whatever the truth about their respective intelligences, their viewpoints were remarkably similar. The world was their oyster, to be prized open and devoured with little sympathy for the feelings of the living matter inside. It was not that they were callous, it was just that they had no idea how to put themselves in another's place. They saw no reason why most other people should not be as confident as they were and assumed any failings in that direction could easily be put right if only the person concerned would pull up his or her socks. The delight they felt in their own successes spurred them on and satisfied them. Life had always smiled at them: they felt it was no more than their due.

That other people's needs could be different from their own was a matter of absolute unimportance. They knew it was so, of course—they were not entirely unobservant—but it had no direct relevance. This attitude made life very simple. Especially parenthood. Not for them the anguish of the post-Freudian, post-Bowlby majority. They were both very satisfied with the way they had been brought up, and, making a few allowances for the inevitable changes between the mores of one generation and the next, that was the way they intended to bring up their own children. When, for example, they viewed the neat pile of freshly-laundered clothes set out every night in the children's bathroom by the nanny, their feeling was one of pure gratification—Jess because it showed her competence as a mother and organizer and Adam because it not only showed his cleverness in picking a competent wife, but also because it reminded him of his increasing affluence; he too had had clean clothes every day as a child, but they had been patched and washed by his own mother and were set out on a second-hand chest of drawers in his little bedroom, not in a private bathroom as were Emma's and Matthew's. It had never occurred to either of them that Emma might have been happier wearing muddy jeans and a ripped sweater rather than the nicely-ironed dresses that Iris did not at all like seeing torn or muddied after all her careful work. Perhaps, being truly Jess's child, Emma would have hated messing herself in the winter mire of Hampstead Heath along with the other local kids. No one would ever know because who would ever think of asking?

This, then, had been the pattern of their life together. They did what they wanted to do, with flair always and usually achieving excellence. Their house was exquisitely furnished, thanks to money, taste, and knowledge. They had a large number of amusing, intelligent friends, though no really intimate ones—they were too busy for that. They went to theaters, concerts, films when they had the time, though lately there had been none. Were they happy? They never had time to think about it, which may well in fact—had they ever stopped to ask themselves—have been their definition of happiness.

So their lives were full. They had two children, one of each sex. They each still had a complete set of parents. Neither Jess nor Adam had ever suffered a close death. If either of them had had a failure, such as losing a best friend in childhood, or doing less brilliantly in an examination than was expected, they had wasted no time in regrets. They never brooded over the past or feared what was to come. Present action was the thing, not awareness. So that, working toward future goals, they devoted all their energy to living in the present. Adam, sitting at his desk reading a brief, would give his entire concentration to that brief. He was not at all aware of himself, buttocks pressed into the leather chair, chest rising and falling with slow quiet breath, stomach comfortably full but not overfull; nor was he conscious of the ticking of the pretty carriage clock on the marble mantelpiece, nor of the bowl of flowers placed summer and winter on a small Sheraton table between the two windows of his study; nor of the other rooms of the house, one containing his children, another a cleaner busy polishing the furniture or sweeping the carpets, others empty unless Jess was in one of them.

And that was the point at which it had all broken down—that Jess might be, but probably was not, in one of the other rooms.

Until he met Fanny, Adam had had no idea that he minded this. On the contrary, he would have told anyone how proud he was of his wife, what a success she was, how he could never have stood being married to a woman without a mind, a woman whose greatest ambition was to have a comfortable home and a husband to cherish. They suited each other perfectly, he would have said, he and Jess. It was a relationship of genuine equality.

Then Adam met Fanny. That was not too disturbing to the marriage at first. Each had always agreed that if ever such a thing should happen the other would be sensible and take it in their stride. In fact both had been too busy for affairs. When Jess realized what was happening, she decided quite rationally that the best way for her not to mind was to take a lover herself. The following week she met David, and by the time the program was completed and shown they had become lovers. She had no need to persuade herself she was in love—she liked David, they talked easily together, she found him physically attractive. There was no danger she would get hooked—even if he were the type she could fall in love with, which he wasn't, she had no time to waste in mooning. There were too many other more interesting things to do. No, he had a function to fulfill, and he fulfilled it admirably. He didn't ask much, made love well but not so well it might become obsessive, knew none of her friends, and so was absolutely safe.

100

She did not tell Adam about David, and he did not guess. She felt no guilt, no more than if she'd gone to a dentist to have a troublesome tooth seen to. Adam thought her serenity was merely further proof of her mental superiority over other women.

Including Fanny. Fanny wouldn't have stood for such a betrayal by a husband for a minute, he knew that—she'd have gone wild. Amazingly, against everything he thought he believed in, he loved her even for that. And for much else. In a few brief months he learned to love her for a lot of things it had never crossed his mind before to want.

As he had sweated harder and harder those last years to keep up with the flood of work, he had occasionally thought how good it would be to have a feminine bosom on which to rest and an attentive ear. For Jess had never given him that. If, exhausted and stiff with long hours of sitting, he left his study to search for her, she was either out or in her own room with her glasses on, deep in a reference work or someone's manuscript or making notes. She would look up, say briefly, "If you're making a cup of coffee, darling, do make me one too," and down her head would go again, back to her work. He'd bring her the coffee, sit hopefully next to her and tell her how tired he was, and she'd pat him sympathetically on the knee, saying "Poor old chap, you *do* look beat." Then she'd shift her papers about and pick up her pen. If he didn't take the hint, after a minute she would straightforwardly apologize and say she was pretty beat too and wanted to get this lot out of the way so she could go to bed.

He met Fanny in a shop—in Liberty's, to be precise—when he was buying a kimono for Jess's birthday present. Fanny served him. She had tried the robe on at his request so that he could have a better idea of what it looked like. He had taken one look at her in it, and her body was so full of rounded, strokable things it was impossible for him not to imagine her naked under the painted silk. Straightaway his imagination soared; he saw her kneeling at his feet, eyes humble with dutiful love. It had ended with him buying *her* the kimono and something quite different for Jess. It would have been wasted on Jess: Japanese wifely humility was not exactly her line.

When Jess learned where he had first met Fanny, she couldn't resist a bitchy dig about him picking up a shopgirl. Adam protested that an assistant at Liberty's wasn't exactly what was usually meant by a shopgirl. Jess sneered that was just like his bloody snobbery—even when he picked up a shopgirl she had to be from one of the very best shops. "I don't care if she's a deb," she'd added, "if she's working in a shop she's a shopgirl."

They'd quarreled about that, and he forgot to call the girl Frances but used instead his own pet name for her, Fanny. Jess had really hooted then and cried he'd been reading too much Cleland. Surely he didn't expect her to take him seriously!

He'd agreed it wasn't serious, and up to that instant it was true—it was nothing serious, merely a gesture to himself. He and Jess kissed, and they didn't talk about it again. But from then on it changed.

Fanny was everything Jess wasn't. She was short, plump, quite pretty but not especially so, fair-haired, gentle, clinging, and lower middle-class, the same as he had once been.

How he relaxed in her company. In her flat, it was as comfortable as being back home in Wales. There was nothing expensive or antique to damage. If he flung his coat down on the sofa, she didn't mind at all: if he kicked off his shoes and left them in the middle of the carpet, maybe she'd pick them up and put them down somewhere else, maybe she wouldn't. Either way it didn't matter. He would yawn and put his stockinged feet up on the sofa, and instead of raising her eyebrows she'd sit down beside him, pick up his feet and, resting them on her lap, would gently tickle them, which hadn't happened to him since he was a child. If he said he had a headache, she'd rush off and fetch him a couple of aspirin. Then she'd make him lie down and, kneeling beside him, would stroke his forehead, his eyes, his brows until the only reason he didn't fall asleep was because he couldn't bear to miss a moment of such joy. She cooked his favorite dishes, made him bowls of tripe and onions even though the smell of it turned her white; would have fed it to him, too, if he'd asked. She insisted on darning a hole he had not noticed in one of his socks, and when it was finished showed him her work with pride. She was indeed a fine darner, he said, and for no reason that he knew tears came into his eyes. Jess had never done that for him. There was no point, she'd said in the early days of their marriage—once socks had gone through it was a waste of time to repair them. Best throw them away and buy new ones.

Suddenly it seemed to him that Jess could never have loved him because she wouldn't darn his socks.

In bed Fanny was less original than Jess had been in her younger days, but less expectant too, and he wallowed in the generous pillowing of her breasts, not experienced since the days of suckling at his mother's fount— for Jess's breasts, though neat and well-formed, were distinctly on the sparse side.

102

He wallowed. He wallowed in it all. And never once did he mind that Fanny said nothing bright or witty. Who needs wittiness when being told how adored they are? Never once did he care that she had no ambitions except to have a wedding ring on her finger and a man to care for. Her lack of education didn't worry him at all; her manners were smooth and her voice polished by her experience at Liberty's, so she never grated on him—altogether he was totally delighted that he need never be daunted by her, that there was no way in which she was his superior.

It never occurred to him he was a fly being caught in a subtle web spun with a knowledge inherited from generations of homemaking women. If he was a victim at all, he was a willing victim who walked into the trap with his eyes voluntarily and firmly closed. For he knew that in her heart Fanny was as simple as her exterior. The web was not made of deceit— what she promised she would give. And what she promised was what most men want. Who can blame them? Wouldn't most of today's women, slogging away at the burden of their dual lives, also jump at the chance of such a dream companion? Jess had no little wife though she could have done with one. Adam hadn't had one either until he met Fanny.

After a while he began to leave his house on the nights Jess was out late, propping up a message on the hall table asking her not to disturb him (they had had separate rooms for years because of their working habits, though they mostly slept together in one or other of their rooms) and take a taxi to Fanny's flat, coming back in time for breakfast. Later, even when Jess was there but working, he'd knock at her door, say he was slipping out for a while and wouldn't disturb her when he got back, and guiltily, but full of joy, go off to Fanny.

Jess did not let herself mind. It gave her a momentary pang each time it happened, but she'd already sorted out the situation and didn't intend to waste any more time worrying over it. He wouldn't leave her, she knew—he wasn't the type to fall deeply for the sort of clinging brainless twit that that girl Fanny—Fanny, for God's sake!—so obviously was. So there was absolutely no point in dwelling on it when very soon it would all be over.

But she hadn't reckoned on love. The falling-in-love type of love. As a girl she had known its delights, as had Adam, but the affairs had been transient and comparatively innocent. She was nineteen and Adam was twenty-one when they met. They themselves had not so much fallen in love as known right away they were a pair.

If love is instantly satisfied—as it was with them, they were in bed within a week—and the beloved is always around, it is impossible to indulge in dreamy yearnings: and where is the in-love emotion without a reasonable amount of thwarted desire and, preferably, distance? Where would Romeo's passion have been if Mr. Capulet had opened his arms and said: welcome, son. Or Jane Eyre's if Mr. Rochester had proposed the first week and there had been no mad wife in the attic? Or Abélard's if he had been able to marry his favorite pupil and settle down to happy domesticity? Gone in no time, transmuted into married love no doubt in the last two cases (Romeo would have been unfaithful within the year), but passion would have been doomed from the first moment of felicity.

So it was with Adam. Because he was so certain that permanence with Fanny was out of the question, he allowed himself to fall passionately in love with her. Then, when he began to wonder if after all he might not throw everything up (well, not his job, of course) and marry Fanny, the almost impossible idea became so overwhelmingly seductive he could think of nothing else. Working at his desk; pleading at the bar; at lunch, supper, tea; brushing his teeth, scrubbing his back, even kissing his children goodnight—which was about all he ever saw of them—there was nothing he could do without Fanny floating in front of him. He couldn't think; he couldn't concentrate; he couldn't do any damn thing at all. He lived in a perpetual state of delight and misery so hopelessly combined he sometimes wondered if he were not out of his mind.

The climax came one night when, after working straight through from seven in the morning to eleven-thirty at night he staggered, half blind with a headache, to the bathroom cupboard for aspirin. There weren't any. He went to Jess's bedroom hoping she might have some there, but Jess was in the throes of polishing her critique for the following night's program and she snarled at him, exasperated because she hadn't been able to get the flow of the words quite right. Irritated beyond reason at the interruption, she even added shrewishly, just as though she weren't the world's most competent and impeccable wife, "Why don't you buy your own bloody aspirin, anyway!"

That was all there was to the row. A twelve-year-old marriage sunk and two children abandoned for the lack of a couple of aspirin. But that is how it goes. Marriages, children, can be replaced. Or so it seems at the time. He swore, she swore; they said things to each other they had never said before and even now only partly meant: and that was it. He went back to his room, packed a suitcase, and moved out that night. He knew it was potentially disastrous, that if his rashness became public he'd ruin his chances of silk for that year at the very least, but by then he could no more keep away from Fanny than an addict can keep away from his next fix. He did not choose to go—choice never came into it—he was as impelled toward Fanny's little nest as a baby to the nipple, and Jess was left behind, hurt and betrayed for the first time in her life.

As for Fanny, she wasn't at all surprised. She had known he would come sooner or later. She didn't even get out of bed (he had his own key, of course) but merely pushed back the coverlet so that he could see she lay naked. Patiently she held out her arms to him and waited with a steady smile on her vacuous little face while he ripped off his pinstripes and Zimmerli underpants and leaped into bed on top of her. It was funny, she thought, as she sank out of sight beneath his hot bulk, how everything always turned out all right in the end if you waited long enough.

DAY 3

Unfortunately for Jess's peace of mind the international news remained depressingly unexciting. Yet another Italian millionaire had been kidnapped and his ear posted. In Ireland two patriots on opposite sides of the religious fence had blown each other up. The dollar, which had been sinking, rose slightly. At home the union trouble at British Leyland had blown over, but a Ford workshop had come out on strike because an over-enthusiastic plant engineer unwisely fetched a screw from the storeroom instead of waiting for the man whose job it was to fetch screws to fetch one. And a minor Royal personage was expecting another baby. None of it was enough to oust Matthew from the front pages.

The papers did their best with what little they had on the case. Two of the heavies printed the same photograph of Jess and Adam, taken on their wedding day. It was a moving picture of two people in love looking into each other's eyes with confidence, both in the other and in their combined futures. It brought tears to many eyes. Alongside, each showed snaps of Matthew beaming happily at the world.

The populars had chosen a different emphasis: they ran press pictures of Adam coming out of his house half-shielding his face, and sad portraits of a tear-stained Iris. Two also showed old photographs from the files of Jess laughing happily. Was the incongruence deliberate? It is true that in these last two cases the captions made it clear the photographs were old *ones, yet seen adjacent to weeping Iris the first impact was one of shock. Doesn't she care? people thought. He means no more to her than that? And even after—if—they read the captions, that first impression lingered.*

All the papers reported that the police were organizing a reconstruction of the baby snatching in Hampstead that afternoon and that ten women in jeans and baggy woollies answering to the previous day's description had been interviewed but that in every case the crying child had been the woman's own. Equally disappointing, the tramp in the dirty raincoat turned out to have been sleeping off a hangover in the local police cell at the time of the snatching. Perhaps because of these letdowns, none of the papers made much of Yvette Grüber, the ex-au pair. They obligingly reported that the police would like to interview her, but lacking photographs or titillating details there was nothing else to write about.

All the interest fell, therefore, on the little-girl-and-her-banana story. The fullest version of this was obtained by the first reporter to arrive— pockets amply lined—at Sarah Binney's house (later reporters were unable to find the mother at home). Under the banner headline "BABY SNATCHER SEEN?" a photograph of a smirking child almost filled the lucky paper's entire front page. The story, continued inside, began:

Mrs. Binney, mother of nine-year-old Sarah, proudly told me how her observant daughter had spotted a woman trying to feed a whole banana to a young baby yesterday afternoon outside a bookshop only a mile away from Jess Bennett's home. "I shall be so happy," said Mrs. Binney, hugging Sarah to her, "if Matthew is found because of this clever daughter of mine. Jess Bennett may be famous, but at heart she must feel grief the same as any other mother." She told me that Sarah, "always a bright little thing," was coming home from school when she spotted the woman, aged about thirty, with fair curly hair and of middle height, unsuccessfully trying to make a small baby hold a half-peeled banana in its hands and eat it. "Sarah thought this was very suspicious—she's helped me bring up my two youngest, so she knows about babies, you see—and when she heard about Jess Bennett's baby on television last night she turned to me and said, "Mum, I think I saw the woman who did it!"

Clever little Sarah was apparently too tongue-tied to speak to the reporter herself, but the facts she had given the police the night before had been so clearly presented the duty officer had sent a junior out to buy her a bar of chocolate. The description was indeed admirable. There was only one error, but that was fatal: to the nine-year-old's eyes Carrie, under stress, looked at least thirty. If the possibility of this childish error had occurred to the police, someone—David for example—might have put two and two together. But it did not.

IT was early February. Carrie, driven by anguished uncertainty as to whether she was at once one, or two, people, and if she were two whether she was happy or appalled, had been walking all day. Inaction was impossible, it was as though her feet possessed springs that thrust her upright every time she tried to rest.

She hadn't worried at first when her period was late: she was often slightly irregular, sometimes by as much as three days. But never four days. Or five. Or six.

At six days she knew. She'd really known at four. Some inner knowledge—maybe no more than an expectation of doom, maybe a genuine percipience—had lodged in her belly, growing in weight and size like the fetus she feared.

Or longed for? How could she know what she felt when no part of her body or mind would keep still for a single second? Thoughts whirled chaotically while the springs in her legs forced her out of the house, up unknown streets, on into central London, through the parks, the shopping streets, into the dingy areas and out again into unexpected pretty squares—the crisp February weather encouraging her day after day until after two weeks of it she found herself ringing the doorbell of a doctor's office close to Piccadilly, drawn by the worn plate and the absolute anonymity of a doctor who practiced over a chemist's shop and within sight of Eros.

An elderly man, he sighed when he saw her. Girls with drawn faces coming in off the street without any appointment—how many had he seen in the course of his life? Half an hour later, as she stood up to leave, he put a hand on her shoulder.

"Listen. If the test is positive, don't do anything you'll regret later." She looked so young. She'd never speak to her family about it. Or her own doctor. That sort never did. Someone had to play the parent. But he was tired of it all the same—too many years of the sheer messiness of people and their inability to live neat orderly lives. It had worn him out. Wearily he added, "It's a pretty desperate thing to take a life. If you *are* pregnant," he hesitated again, for what right had he to tell this girl to go through with it? "it's better to have the child, even if you have it adopted afterward. It's better for you in the long run."

Carrie was flabbergasted. To carry a child inside yourself for nine months, then to give it away like a Christmas present to someone else? He couldn't know what he was saying.

She walked along dazed for some time, the address of the clinic he had given her clutched unthinkingly in her hand. When she remembered it, she told herself she would get the test done, but it would only prove what she already knew. What he had known.

She was at the entrance to Green Park when she began to smile. It was a smile of absolute happiness. She had misunderstood him. He'd been saying it was OK. He'd been speaking to her like a father, telling her it was all right, she should go ahead to have the child. He'd given her his blessing, told her she wasn't disgusting.

Weight fell from her. She felt so light she thought she would certainly float upward if she let herself go. The week before she had lain awake unable to sleep all one night, crying with shame, in spite of her love for Aidan. Ever since she had started her periods she had often thought of them as dirty, as filth being expelled from her—no amount of rationalizing helped her then. When she suspected she was pregnant she couldn't help fantasizing the fetus as being a huge clot of menstrual blood—she could not allow herself to see it as a baby, the result of hers and Aidan's love. Then she had wanted to tear her belly open, to rip it out. But now it was all right. Suddenly the baby was a real baby.

Slowly she walked through the gates of the park, then stood looking at the still wintry trees and the people strolling along the paths, children running, dogs hurtling after balls. It was all incredibly beautiful. She wanted to shout aloud in triumph, it's all right! I'm pregnant, and it's all right!

A woman pushing a pram passed her. Their eyes met, and they smiled at each other. Did it show? Coming toward her was another woman, hugely swollen. On each side of her a small child gamboled, laughing at some family joke. Again the woman's eyes met hers, and again they smiled. Everywhere—everywhere there were children. Every woman seemed pregnant. She'd never been aware so many women were pregnant at any one time. Walking briskly now, she strode out along the path by the lake and watched with laughter amorous pigeons chasing their hens all over the grass. She looked with curiosity at passing old people, divining whether or not they were grandparents, and had tears come to her eyes for those who seemed to her wasted with virginal atrophy, isolated forever from the fertility that was everywhere that sharp morning.

How happy she was! A thin sunshine, only marginally diluted by cloud, sent a glitter of catspaws rippling across the surface, gilt sparks flashing as though the water were phosphorescent. The grass, the lichen on the trees, the shining feathers of the birds, everything everywhere seemed to glow with interior light—*which was within her too,* so bright and warm she laid her hands on the source, already curving her fingers in anticipation.

She was no longer alone. This was what her hands told her. Inside her was an Other, an Other that was at the same time herself. The two of them were one, divisible but a unity. A wholeness. A oneness. She need never be alone again.

Glowing she walked along, slowly now, sipping at the delight she had discovered. After a while she thought of Aidan, and although she was frightened of the violence she knew was part of him she was glad he was the father of her child. He was a good man, she was sure of that. She imagined him walking next to her, then played through a scene in which she told him she was pregnant. He put his arms around her and held her gently, kissing her with tenderness as though she were very fragile. She particularly liked this part of the scene and played it through several times.

As she walked along, wondering if she'd pretend to Aidan the doctor had warned her against having sex, she thought about her fear of it and tried to pin it down. She dreaded it and yet—she reddened even at the thought—she loved Aidan's hands on her. No ice maiden, she. Yet how could it be that an act she found so shameful that she could only bring herself to do it when she was either a bit drunk or nearly asleep, how could such an impure act result in something so innocently beautiful as a baby—her baby? *Could* something truly shameful result in something truly good? How was that even a possibility?

The mothers into whose eyes she had looked did not appear to be crushed by a sense of guilt. She herself was not crushed by guilt, not today. *What,* then?

She paused, stood with hand resting on an iron rail, watching a pair of slowly drifting swans. She did not feel guilt! On the contrary, she felt uplifted, truly happy.

Had conceiving a baby purged her of the guilt of sex?

How could it, since the one was impossible without the other?

113

Her mind whirled with these thoughts. She had a vision of her head as a room full of hopelessly complicated equipment of which she was in charge but about the workings of which she was almost completely ignorant. If only she had the knowledge to sort out these questions about guilt and absolution and shame. How she had neglected her brain, these last years!

She walked on again, gnawing at the questions her thoughts had led her to. But even trying to think made little quivers of panic rise in her. A rush of thoughts obliterated the present. Uppermost among them was the memory of that moment when the person she had most truly loved was being taken away, carried off in a car by bitter-mouthed policemen acting as though he were something subhuman crawled out of a drain.

She had never really talked to anyone since. Not properly. Not even to Aidan. It could end in too much hurt.

Crossing the bridge over the lake, a sudden chill on her face made her aware she was crying. She stopped to lean over the bridge, resting her arms on the rail. Unnoticed by the quick-stepping passers-by, her tears fell into the water. But soon they ceased. Idly she began to watch the hopeful ducks below, circling as they waited for offerings of bread. The rushes at the side of the lake parted, and a mallard appeared, leading a dangerously early brood of five chicks. Straight onward the hen paddled, her newborn chicks following so fast, so light, they skimmed over the surface as weightless as blown leaves.

Carrie smiled again. Her hand crept back to her belly and nestled over her child. One day, she promised herself with love, one day they would bring bread here, just the two of them, and as they fed the ducks together she would tell her daughter how that very day, the first true day of her existence, she had seen five tiny chicks perform a miracle and run on water.

It was probably inevitable that the dreams she had had ever since she was a child—that she was quarreling with her mother—should now intensify both in frequency and in bitterness. Many of these dreams centered around Flopper being put to sleep. In real life her mother had simply gone ahead and done it, not warning Carrie in advance. At the time Carrie had not even dared to dream about it. But now she raged half the night away; violent, shrieking. She! who had never shouted at her mother, never once in her whole life!

It was Aidan who, trained by personal experience in dream interpretation, told her that she was substituting Flopper for the baby inside her,

114

and that what she was actually doing was fighting her mother's wish to have the baby aborted. If her mother were still alive, he said, wouldn't she have done anything rather than face what she would have seen as the public shame of having an illegitimate grandchild? At first Carrie denied this, said that the dream Flopper was the real Flopper, that at last she was openly grieving for her beloved dog. OK, said Aidan, that too: dreams are very economical.

One day, sitting next to him on the sofa after they had been out shopping, she saw he was right. She was flooded by such feelings of hatred for her mother she became speechless, could only bury her head in his lap and clutch tightly at his leg. He bent forward and hugged her to him, but part of him was angry, too. Part of him wanted to hurt her as she had hurt him. For she had filled him with happiness at the news of her pregnancy—he hadn't had a second's doubt about his feelings, his face had broadened and broken into an instant smile of pleasure, and he had held her close—but the moment his caresses turned sexual she broke away, told him the doctor had warned her she might have trouble and they shouldn't have sex for several months.

It was not that he hadn't believed her. He trusted her fully. It was that she couldn't hide her relief as she told him this. She tried to, but her real feelings were so evident it was as painful to him as though she had hit him physically in the belly.

Now unexpectedly, before he could stop himself, his anger burst out. Pushing her away, he said bitterly, "It's time you grew up. You and your bloody mother! You're like a fucking casebook." He knew she hated him to swear, and that in itself gave him some relief. "Your fucking mother! Your father! Your guilt! You're in love with the whole bloody thing. What you really want is a permanent analytic session flat out on a couch with some nice father figure stroking your mind but keeping his filthy physical hands strictly to himself. *Wake up!* Or haven't you got the guts to face real life?"

Carrie pulled herself upright and looked at him in disbelief. He had never spoken like that to her before. "Guts!" she answered angrily, "you know about guts all right! It really takes guts to beat up pregnant women. Oh, you're a big man! You really know the right way to work your problems out."

"That's a rotten lie. You know I didn't touch that woman."

"That's *your* story. How do I know it's true? You've nearly hit *me* more than once."

"That's another lie! I've never hit you."

"I didn't say you had. I said you *nearly* hit me."

"For God's sake what's that got to do with it? Do you think all men are as soft as your father? It's natural for men to want to hit out sometimes. It doesn't mean they'll do it."

"Leave my father out of it. He was a really gentle man. He never wanted to hit anyone."

"He didn't have to, did he? He got what he wanted without it!"

They stared at each other. Aidan already regretted what he had said. Sickeningly he saw the danger. At any moment they'd say things that would never be forgotten no matter how many years they lived together, or things so bad he'd have to walk out and never return. As he fought to hold back a rush of comments, Carrie put her hand to her belly. It was an unconscious act of protection, one she would never have allowed herself to make deliberately.

Instantly Aidan softened. The child was as miraculous to him as to her. He placed his hand alongside hers. They did not look at each other, but the danger had passed. They sat in silence for some minutes.

Then Aidan said, "We'd better clear up what happened when that woman got beaten up. Then we'll drop the subject. Right? I don't see any sense in dragging up the past all the time. I think it's better to put what's happened behind you, whether it's good or bad. Especially if it's bad." He put his arm around her shoulders and with a show of reluctance both knew was unreal she cuddled up to him, letting her head rest against his shoulder.

Outside, rain beat against the window so that although it was not quite four o'clock it seemed the evening had already come. Carrie stretched out a hand and turned on a table lamp, then snuggled back into his arms again. In the darkening room the lamplight spotlit the two of them huddled perilously together like survivors on a raft.

Aidan thought for a while, then said, "It's defeatist to hark back all the time to the past, don't you see that? You'll never get it off your back if you don't learn to say . . ." he made the gesture of "fuck off" with his fingers.

"I can't, don't you understand? I just can't."

"You could if you tried. All this self-analysis stuff, you're driving yourself mad with it. Forget it! It's all finished, that. Especially now. You're on the brink of a new life, there's you and me, there's the baby. It's time you put it all behind you."

"You make it sound so easy. But I . . ." she hesitated, "I don't know what it *is* I'm putting behind me. I did what you say, for years I didn't think about the past. I did more than not think—I blanked out on it so successfully I couldn't have made myself remember what actually happened even if I'd tried."

He took her hand and squeezed it. "You can't have totally forgotten, not everything."

"Almost. I think I even really believed my father was dead. At least, that was how I always thought about him—as dead, someone I'd never see again. But these last few weeks all sorts of things have started coming back, and I have to allow them to, don't you see that? If I've got to live with a past like that, it had better be the true past, not a fairy story. Anyway, it was you who made me think about my father again. To everyone except you and David, he's dead. I don't have a father."

"Well, all right. Maybe you really do need to wallow in it for a while. But when you've remembered, Carrie, when you've got it all clear in your mind, climb out of the pit and leave it behind you. We've got other things to think about. Like what to do about the baby."

"*What* about the baby?"

"Well, do we get married? That's not a proposal," he added hastily. "I'm just saying we've got to think about that sort of thing."

"Marry!" she looked shocked. "Marry? You and me!"

"Who else?" He laughed, but he found the prospect as breathtaking as she apparently did. They stared at each other with unexpected shyness. Then he looked away. "Let's get what happened with that woman out of the way first. But when I've told you—that's it, OK? No post mortems."

She nodded, but she would rather have stopped him. It had become very important that she should be able to go on loving him. "Tell me about your parents first," she said, putting it off. "What happened to them? So that I understand."

He shrugged. He truly had little interest in his past. Reluctantly he began.

Aidan was one of those unfortunates who seem born with an unquenchable knowledge of the Grail. Their occasional moments of ecstacy are too rare a reward; anguish is the more frequent visitor. Sometimes they enviously imagine what it must be like to be content with regular Saturday afternoons at a football match or neighborly coffee mornings without even a suggestion of consciousness-raising. But such easy contentment is not for them.

Aidan's parents were both quite normal. His father, wealthy and intelligent, had—apart from a hot temper—only one flaw as a family man: an inability to be interested in anything other than the stockbroking firm of which he was managing director and dry fly fishing. Aidan's mother, bored, discreetly took to drink.

Away at boarding school from the age of seven Aidan knew less about his parents than he did his headmaster, and that was little enough. Up to fourteen, his life centered around school and reading. He was good at games, gifted at history and English, mediocre in math, but more than adequate in all his other subjects, so that a straightforward path through his "O's" and "A's" and on to Oxbridge was confidently predicted for him.

The remoteness between his nearest and dearest and himself had never appeared to trouble him; many of his friends had a similar relationship with their own parents. Not for them the forced intimacy of a two-roomed council flat or even the day-in day-out habituation of the middle-class day-school child. Certainly the spartan conditions under which he had spent his school life were later to help Aidan put up with his horrid little attic, while the meals he learned to cook for himself were preferable to anything school had had to offer.

So then, no one expected much of a problem when his father turned up at school on his fourteenth birthday, took him out to lunch, and explained after drinking his health that he was divorcing Aidan's mother and marrying a charming lady he had met at a house party in Scotland who shared his passion for trout fishing. At the time Aidan said nothing. He just nodded, refused a second helping of pudding—a sign of distress his father thought only right and proper—and changed the subject.

Not even Aidan had realized to what extent he had idolized his father and mother. Even his mother's proneness to drink he had ignored, which was easily done since she always retired, pleading a headache, whenever she felt her exterior control in danger of slipping. She had always appeared calm and beautiful—and still did. As a boy he had cherished an image of her as an immaculate being whom he was privileged to look up to. His father similarly. In some shrouded niche of his inner self they had stood, the pair of them, side by side, stone idols in an occasionally visited cathedral from whom he imagined he asked nothing other than that they should be unchanged by time.

Now, abruptly, he was faced by reality. It was not so much a question of fallen idols or the discovery of clay feet that broke him up as the sudden revelation that he had never in any true sense had any parents at all. Of

118

course he grieved that they were divorcing, of course he suffered the usual irrational suspicion that it was he who was really to blame for the separation, but he could have endured all that. No, what turned him from a pleasant, easy-going responsive pupil into a sullen malcontent who couldn't even be bothered to clean his teeth or brush his hair was the realization that he had missed out on what he now believed to be a human right unthinkingly accepted by most people, the right to be reared by concerned loving parents. He had been deprived, institutionalized like any orphan, denied what suddenly seemed to him the most precious thing in the world, and never ever could this deprivation be put right. His chance was gone for all eternity.

Aidan staggered along for a while, then fell. Into the school sanatorium.

They didn't know what else to do with him. He was eating so little he grew thinner and paler every day, and caught every cold germ floating around that damp spring. He spoke to no one voluntarily, seemed to suffer from bouts of amnesia, wouldn't (he claimed he couldn't) study, was boorish to the masters and rude to his peers. A week of lying in bed being fussed over by the matron, who had decided he needed a bit of loving, poor boy, improved his condition. Color came back to his cheeks, he put on weight, and, though he remained silent, at least he stopped being rude. But he was not as improved as they thought, or maybe the matron's temporary tenderness had been a mistake, because, dressed in full gear once more and about to be thrown out of the nest, he suddenly turned to the matron in whose sitting room he was and told her she was a fucking old cow. Then he flung the suitcase in which he'd packed his books and other odds and ends through a closed window, kicked in her glass-fronted cupboard in which was exhibited her prized set of Spode dinner plates, tore out of the room, bowled over a couple of small kids hanging around in the corridor outside, barged right into his math master and would have knocked him out cold—so crazy was he by then—if another couple of teachers hadn't come running up to see what the disturbance was. He was out of his mind for more than an hour. He fought, screamed, hit out, shouted abuse, and it took four of the toughest teachers to restrain him. Then a doctor arrived and injected him with a tranquilizer that was so effective he stayed asleep for twelve hours.

The matron refused to have him back in the sanatorium—Aidan was right, her tenderness had been purely professional—and he was transferred to the psychiatric wing of a nearby hospital where he stayed for a couple of weeks until he seemed cured. The school took him back, but cautiously. He managed to behave himself reasonably well—there were a few further outbursts, but no overt violence, and though his grades dropped badly they decided to allow him to stay on. He wasn't the first boy to break out like that, and he wouldn't be the last, they said.

Aidan could not understand himself. He wanted to study, to do well, but it seemed he wanted *not* to even more. He saw less and less of his friends who now were studying hard for their "O" levels. A few of his closer friends tried to persuade him to work, but after half an hour's concentration he always gave up, sick with tension.

Inevitably, when the time for the examinations came, he did badly in everything except the English language and literature papers. On the strength of the last they decided to let him enter the sixth form, where they hoped he'd settle down at last, but the increased concentration now required of him was too much, and gradually he stopped trying altogether. At the end of that year his father was asked to withdraw him from the school. They could do nothing more for him, the headmaster said; it was up to his parents now.

He hung around his mother's house, moody, silent most of the time, sleeping a great deal, until she packed him off to his father's Scottish country house (it being summer) where he mooched over the moors all day until nightfall. He never spoke to his father's new wife, but she was a kindly woman and bore with him, and when they couldn't stand it anymore, he was packed off back to his mother's again.

Periodic attempts were made to get him to work with private tutors, but they all gave him up in despair. Eventually Aidan stopped his parents pestering him by walking out. He left home one day carrying a few belongings in a paper bag, joined a squat in Hammersmith, learned how to claim social security, and eventually found his little attic where he had lived ever since.

He had not meant to get involved in lawbreaking, and it happened in such an unexpected way he was hooked into it before he'd had time to think it over.

He had gone along with a couple of friends from the squat to the Roundhouse near Camden Town to hear a new group play. He was disturbed by the beat of the music; the subtlety of the rhythm penetrated his bones and made him restless. He needed to move, to work out the beat with his body, but people were listening, not dancing, so when a piece had finished he pushed his way through the crowd and stood for a while on the

120

balcony of the outside staircase, breathing in the evening air. It was late autumn, and a full moon hung heavy in the sky. The traffic was light, the theaters and pubs not having emptied yet, and the air, with Hampstead Heath so close, smelled fresher than the polluted gasses he breathed most of the time. He thought briefly of the damp moors of childhood holidays, and the contrast between that abandoned life and this was so immense he found himself looking at that boy as though at a stranger.

He was thinking about these differences when suddenly he found himself jostled aside by a group of lads in black leather motorcycle jackets. Instantly he reacted. "Watch it!" he growled, automatically clenching his fists.

The group stopped, surprised. There were four of them, only one actually taller than Aidan, but because of the black leather and their huddled closeness all seemed bulky and vicious. The tall one pressed close to Aidan. "You startin', then?" he asked threateningly.

Aidan wished he'd kept his mouth shut. "Sorry, mate," he said placatingly, "I wasn't thinking." The others still stared at him. "Been to the concert, then?" Aidan added, but glancing quickly around to see if there was anyone about to whom he could yell for yelp.

"Yeah," the tall one said slowly, still glaring at Aidan, who obviously puzzled him. "We walked out, like you. A load of fuckin' crap, were'n' it!" Suddenly he raised his arm. Aidan started back, expecting a blow, but the other, grinning at his alarm, merely turned his grubby fist toward himself and stuck a broken, black fingernail into his earhole. He dug around for a while, saying nothing. The other three had not moved. They stood watching him, chewing silently, with the blank faces of cows backing up a more investigative sister.

Aidan suppressed a desire to praise the music: there was no point in getting his teeth knocked out over a question of musical appreciation. Finally he mumbled "Yeah," in a voice equally laconic.

The leader of the group visibly relaxed. He, too, started chewing, though he appeared to have nothing in his mouth. They all continued to stare at each other for another twenty seconds or so when unexpectedly the leader said, "Wanna come on a joy ride then, mate?"

It was not a popular move with his friends. They shifted about, and one even muttered " 'ere, Nick!" but Nick spun around, and the protest immediately died out.

Aidan breathed more easily. "Yeah, why not?" he said. It was not until they were clattering down the steps that the penny dropped. Joyride. That meant a stolen car. For a moment, because of their leather jackets, he had assumed they meant a pillion ride on the back of one of their bikes. Hastily, he stuck out his wrist and looked at his watch.

Nick grinned. "Time don't mean nothing!" he said before Aidan could make his excuse. He nodded at his mates. As one, the other boys closed in around Aidan making escape impossible. Wandering through the rows of parked cars jammed into the tiny courtyard, they fooled around amiably among each other, with Aidan caught miserably in their middle. Nick surreptitiously tried the handle of every car they passed. After half a dozen failures he gave a grunt. "OK," he said, and the door of a roomy cream-colored Rover swung open.

Aidan swung his head around hoping for help, but in a moment he found himself bundled roughly into the back seat.

"Relax, mate," drawled Nick, grinning at him through the driving mirror. "We're just 'aving a larf, that's all. Ain't you never done this before, then?"

Aidan felt sure Nick meant him no personal harm. And whatever the others felt about him, it was obvious they wouldn't go against Nick. The panic passed, and a mild excitement took its place. "Wow!" he thought to himself, and an image of his father's appalled face came before him. Instantly he laughed, a laugh so exuberant that after a moment's surprise all the others joined in.

It took Nick only a few seconds fiddling with the wires under the dashboard before the engine roared into life. Then they were away, tearing up Haverstock Hill toward the Heath.

Aidan sat back and prepared to enjoy himself. He liked this set of new friends.

It was all right up to the day of the Post Office raid. It was a new world he was living in, but they accepted him, and that was good. They had almost nothing in common—they weren't even bright, Nick's mob—but for a while at least they suited each other. Among themselves they didn't speak much. They drank in pubs, smoked dope occasionally but not often, it cost too much, talked about girls and sometimes got some, but none of it was serious. Aidan found himself shocked at their attitude to women—"cunt" they always called them—but the girls didn't seem to mind. They giggled back and obliged happily enough. It was all very casual and easy, and no one seemed to take anything very seriously. Including the right of other people to keep their own possessions.

That also shocked Aidan at first, but, their friend, he tried to look at it from their point of view. *Why* should other people have so much when they had so little? What did it matter, nicking a few things when everyone else was doing it, either directly by shoplifting or robbery, or by cheating through expense accounts and tax fiddling? Or plain corruption. That was yet another shock, coming to accept that there really were bent policemen, that money left behind the lavatory cistern in a certain pub bought off detectives or softened a forthcoming charge. Everyone knew about it in his new circle; it wasn't just gossip, it was fact.

During the early weeks of this new life Aidan found himself unable to think straight. Anger was gradually building up in him, anger directed against so many targets he sometimes found himself snarling—not at anything in particular, but against the whole of it, the so-called civilized life. Strangely enough, his rage against his parents softened. They, too, were diminished by the system like everyone else. It was the *system* he detested, he came to see, it was the system that needed breaking up and kicking out.

He never quite knew why he went along with Nick and his mob on their shoplifting jaunts. The others straightforwardly did it partly for kicks, partly for money. Aidan was surprised how easy it was. They stole small things like transistors, cameras, calculators—the cheaper kind because the expensive ones were usually locked away out of reach—working in pairs or threes. The day they finally kidded Aidan into actually picking up something himself instead of merely acting as a shield he was rigid with fear. But once he'd done his snatch and was safely outside the shop he felt nothing but exhilaration.

That night they all got drunk in the pub, and when he woke up in the morning he found a girl crushed up against him in his narrow bed. He stared at her in amazement, sure he'd never seen her before. She looked terrible. She had blond hair badly dyed, crooked teeth already yellow with nicotine, and streaked mascara like bruises all over her eyes and spotty cheeks. He was shattered to be in bed with such a sordid little clown and worried for his health. Then he saw she couldn't be more than sixteen, and his disgust mixed with sorrow for her and what her life would be. Gently he moved onto his back trying not to wake her and, looking at the ceiling, came to the decision the time had come to make a break. All this wasn't for him. And what if he got caught?

That evening when he went to meet Nick in the pub he had decided to tell him he was dropping out, but Nick didn't give him a chance to speak. He was full of a new plan. Aidan listened, appalled.

"Look, mate," Nick said, seeing his panic, "it'll be a fuckin' pushover. She's on 'er own in the shop every night. 'Er ole man don't get in 'til gone six, and she locks up regular at 'alf past five. We wait outside 'til she's got shot of the last customer and just as she bends down to lock up—I've watcher 'er three nights now, she always bolts the door from the bo'om up, stupid Pakki cunt—we shove against the door, send her sprawlin', and there we are! Like I said, there's nuffin' to it!"

And he was right, about that part of it. It went exactly as Nick had said. It was a cold dark evening, and no one was hanging about the streets. Sharp at half past five the elderly assistant who helped out behind the sweet counter put on her woolly coat and trotted off to catch her train. Through the gaps between advertisements on the windows the boys watched the plump little postmistress in her bright blue sari writing something in a ledger behind the grill at the far end of the shop where the post office work was done. A larger black man in a heavy overcoat stood tapping his fingers impatiently on the counter, partly obscuring her from their view.

"Bleedin' wog," said Nick, zipping up his black leather jacket against the cold and stamping his feet. "Wot the soddin' 'ell are they doin'?" At that moment the woman pushed something across the counter for the man to sign. Nick grunted in disgust. "Fuckin' monkey. Wot makes 'er think 'e can write? Don't suppose 'e even knows 'ow to make a bleedin' cross!" His friends sniggered. Aidan said nothing.

Suddenly Nick gave a low whistle. The boys gathered around him. The last customer came out of the shop, tucking his wallet away in his breast pocket. Seeing the group of boys he hesitated a moment, then swiftly turned and made off in the opposite direction. A minute later the woman in the sari opened the wooden gate separating the post office from the shop and walked slowly toward the door. She reached out to a piece of cardboard hanging from a loop of string on which was printed in large uneven letters: "OPEN." Smiling serenely at some interior thought she turned the notice to its opposite face. Aidan caught a glimpse of large eyes set in a plump brown face. A thick black braid wrapped around her head intensified the impression of calm placidity. It was only as she bent down to lock the door he saw she was pregnant.

Before Aidan could shout out to stop him, Nick had lunged at the door, shoving it open with his shoulders and—just as he had predicted—the woman was sent sprawling across the floor. She gave one loud scream,

124

then began to moan. Aidan found himself running with the others inside the shop. Nick, the last to enter, bolted the door behind them and drew the blind. The woman lay on her back, staring up at them, her belly rising large and vulnerable. The rucked-up tinsel border of her sari revealed her legs, the calves thin and unmuscled like a child's. One of her sandals had come off and lay upside down on the marbled lino floor against the sweet counter. Aidan wanted to cover her legs, but stood ineffective just inside the door. After a moment he moved forward and picked up the sandal, holding it out.

"Shut that fuckin' row or I'll smash you!" Nick shouted at the woman, swiftly crossing over to her. He swung his foot back as though to kick her. There was a look of malice on his face that Aidan had never seen there before. Hesitating no longer, he ran forward and grabbed Nick's arm. The other boys were poking around among the goods on the counter seeing what they could pick up; they seemed uninterested in the woman on the floor.

"Pack it in!" Aidan shouted. "Can't you see she's pregnant!"

Nick looked at him in surprise, then laughed in his face. Shaking off Aidan's arm, he said loudly so she should hear, "The less Pakki bastards the better!" But he lowered his foot and said to the woman contemptuously, "C'mon, get up. We ain't got all fuckin' night."

She did not move except to roll over on her side with her arms protectively over her belly. Her braid had come undone and snaked over her shoulder. She was muttering something now that no one could catch. Nick stood over staring down at her. "C'mon, get up, I said!" He lifted his foot again and swung it back. She screamed.

Aidan shouted out and flung himself at Nick, who staggered back a couple of paces before recovering his balance. His face, white with anger, seemed that of another man. He looked much older. Moving slowly, never taking his eyes off Aidan, he pulled out a flick knife. Opening it up he pointed it at Aidan. "You fuckin' keep out of this," he said coldly, "unless you want to be done! Right?" He turned back to the woman and pulled her roughly to her feet. She stood trembling, looking pleadingly at Aidan.

But Aidan was motionless now. When Nick had drawn his knife, the other three had done the same. Standing there in the bright neon lighting of the shop, surrounded by racks of gaudy birthday cards and bins of cheap toys, he looked with disbelief at the open knives and the shivering woman and felt his guts melt. He went to follow as Nick pushed the woman through the gate into the post office section where in open view stood an

125

old-fashioned safe, but the others shook their heads at him, indicating he should stay where he was. They seemed to think it all a huge joke and shouted encouragements at Nick.

"Open it," growled Nick, giving the woman a shove toward the safe, "go on, open it!" Mutely she shook her head.

Nick gave her a vicious swipe on the cheek. She winced but kept her hands on her belly. Beneath her fear there was a clear look of determination on her face.

At the blow, Aidan had once again started forward, but instantly the others surrounded him, grinning and flashing their knives.

"Whacha worrying about a Pakki cunt for, then?" one of them asked. "Doing the country a service, Nick is, showing fuckin' scum like that what it's all about!"

Once more the little postmistress turned to Aidan, holding out her bare arm to him, the gesture of a beckoning girl. On her wrist she wore half a dozen glittering bangles that tinkled prettily. Perhaps even Nick was moved because it was then that he struck her down. He went berserk. He kicked at her belly, ignoring her screams, shouting a stream of racial and sexual obscenities. The grins on the faces of the others broadened in their excitement. They pushed through the gate to see more clearly, taking Aidan with them.

Aidan had been frozen by the knives. Watching—because looking away would have been easier—he knew that for months he would not shut his eyes without her face rising before him, that he'd never lose the sound of her voice. Yet even through the horror one part of his mind was ticking over rationally, saying to him: well, what did you expect then? That she'd say, yes sir, certainly sir, and hand over the keys? Nick had reckoned on that, but why had he?

As in his mind he himself took the blows now landing on her, an appalled understanding came to him—that he'd known all along that sooner or later there'd be violence. He'd known perfectly well that the mob's gestures had not been empty—hadn't he himself been affected by them?—and that someone somewhere would reap that anger. Wasn't this what he had been waiting for? *Hoping for?* A catharsis of violence that would finally free him from himself?

There she was then, the unwitting agent of that catharsis lying huddled on the floor—a brave, stupid little woman whose loyalty or whose cupidity gave her even now the useless courage to endure.

It was in his head to throw himself on the knives if necessary, he was on the point of risking all to save her (or so it seemed to him afterward) when the choice was taken from him. There was a hammering on the door, and at the same moment the three friends leaped at Nick, pulled him away from the woman, and dragged him out through a back entrance just as a couple of men came crashing through the glass door at the front, drawn by the noise.

Aidan, left behind, began to shudder. He felt, but could not see, an authoritative hand grasp his arm. Quaking, he pushed it aside, then leaned over a basket of plastic windmills, and was violently sick.

"What happened then?" Carrie said after a while, her face white. "After those men broke in?"

Aidan shrugged, relieved to have finished. "I told the police everything they wanted to know. The woman had nearly died. She lost her baby, of course. So I told them. They picked up Nick and the others, and they went to jail. I got off with probation. It was different for me—it was my first time, but they'd been through the courts dozens of times already, done Borstal, the lot. And the court knew I'd tried to stop them. She told them that, she made a great point of it, how I'd tried to stop them but couldn't. I think that was very decent of her, don't you?" He laughed, but there wasn't much humor in it.

"They wouldn't talk to me when we came up for trial. Can you blame them? I felt they thought I was getting off because of my ... background. That wasn't true. They'd had plenty of chances themselves before, but I felt lousy about it, all the same." He didn't look at her, but his voice changed. "I felt it wasn't so much what I'd told the fuzz—it wouldn't have taken them five minutes to find out who my mates were, we'd been hanging around together for a couple of months. It was that I felt certain that my getting off while they went inside was just one more thing for them, one more bit of proof. A final nail in the coffin, d'you see?"

Carrie shook her head. "I don't understand. It doesn't make sense, any of it. Why did they hate that woman so?"

"People need scapegoats," Aidan said.

For over a month Carrie went about hazy with joy. The only flaw in those nearly perfect days was Aidan's frustration. He was very tender with her, taking her arm in the street, never allowing her to carry anything heavy,

127

but through it she sensed a withdrawal on his part. They were never separated; they went everywhere together, sat hand in hand in David's office, occasionally joining in the talk of the group but more often silent. It was obvious even to a stranger merely glancing at them they were in love. But there were moments when Carrie saw Aidan watching her, judging her, and for a second or two she was frightened. Then she'd recover, blinkered from fear by her maternity.

David also sensed something was troubling Aidan. Ostensibly to discuss his getting a job, he took him into his private office for a few minutes one day, but Aidan was too loyal to Carrie to talk openly. He and David discussed the subject of marriage vaguely—David was anxious that they not marry purely for propriety's sake—and Aidan told him Carrie herself seemed unhappy with the idea. He admitted after some delicate probing on David's part that she had been told to be careful by her doctor, but David—always slightly shy about sex—respected Aidan's reticence, which was unfortunate but probably inevitable.

Aidan and Carrie had made love two or three times since Carrie had seen the doctor, but as usual it happened only when she was nearly asleep and her natural randiness had led her to press herself up against Aidan in such a way that he was unable to restrain himself. Then he took her so gently she hardly appeared to be aware it was happening.

He feared for the future. What if she stayed frightened of sex, permitting it only when she was half knocked out by sleep or drink and never ever letting him do anything to her? It distressed him, it made the whole act sordid, as though it were something so dirty she needed anesthetizing to make it bearable. Sometimes he tried to discuss it with her, but always she changed the subject, smiling at him with that new interior glow of hers that left him quite defenseless.

For to Carrie life had suddenly become very simple. She had found the strength to take her life in her own hands and had made a pact with herself to forget her father, her mother, her guilt and everything else that had made her previous days a misery. Aidan was right, you should put the past behind you and get on with the present. It was all quite simple, really. How simple she had never suspected before she became pregnant. And once the baby was born she would be much too busy to even remember that past, let alone wallow in it. She'd even be able to tackle the sex thing, then.

The morning she began to bleed, Carrie was alone for the first time in weeks. If Aidan had been there to comfort her things would almost certainly have turned out differently. As it was, his mother had written and asked him to come home for a couple of days because his grandmother had died and she wanted him there for the funeral. Aidan had been fond of the old lady, and he went. He had asked Carrie if she wanted to come but was clearly relieved when she said she thought it better if she didn't. They didn't want to have his family interfering at this stage.

The miscarriage was a time of pure misery for Carrie. She had been so happy before, as if after years of being locked in some dingy room the door had swung open showing beyond it a world of loveliness and sanity she had never suspected could be hers. Mercifully, after some hours when it became obvious she was losing the baby, her mind partly blanked out as though she had been given some analgesic, and the earlier tears gave way to dumb resignation.

It took so long! All afternoon and evening and through most of the night the birth pangs came, growing more and more frequent. It seemed so unfair to suffer like that, merely to achieve bereavement. Mostly she lay in bed, occasionally staggering to her feet to fetch a new towel to lie on or to make herself a cup of tea. At the beginning she had cursed, thumping the bed in anger, unable to really accept what was happening. Then she began to cry and yearned for Aidan to be there to give her comfort. But after a while she made herself stop thinking of him. Now she dreaded his homecoming; he had so wanted the baby. She had failed him. Failed herself.

The door closed again in her mind, and the old terrible thoughts returned. She couldn't stop them. The baby, Aidan's baby, had been the source of her strength, and this strength was too delicate to entirely survive such a blow. Enough remained to stop her breaking completely, but that was all. It seemed to her all her old shamefulness had gathered up in her and pushed out their lovely baby. It was no more than someone like her deserved. She had done such bad things. Hers was not a body that should give birth to a new human being.

She recalled that first day walking in the park, wondering how something so beautiful could come out of sin. Now she had the answer. It couldn't. Not ever. She turned her face to the wall.

Early in the morning the fetus came away in a sudden flush of blood and water. She felt its warm passing, a small wet fish slithering over her thigh. Later, dry-eyed now, she bundled up the towel on which she had been lying, eyes averted, and thrust it into a plastic bag. She felt very weak but

129

managed to sponge most of the mess off herself. Then, sitting in her familiar old wicker chair, she washed down four aspirin with a mug of water and finally returned to bed. Worn out, she soon fell asleep.

Late next morning after lying awake for some time thinking heavily of the alternatives, she climbed out of bed, took some firelighters, made a fire in the small living-room grate, and burned the plastic bag and its unseen contents. Anything else would have been even worse. Unthinkable. She didn't watch but sat slumped in the corner of the sofa with closed eyes, waiting until she was sure everything was consumed. Then she ran a bath and lay soaking in it. Only then, when it was too late, did she allow herself to think about what the fetus might have looked like. She invented a clear picture of a perfect girl baby, five or six months old, with blond curls like her own and bright blue eyes, but minute—so minute she could have held her in the palm of one hand. It was holding out its arms to her, this tiny image, and smiling.

At that moment, although her grief was intense, she knew she had done right: had she made herself look, the reality would have haunted her for the rest of her life.

The loneliness afterward was atrocious. She had been two; the whole, and a part, of a perfect unity: now she was one again, and destined to be only one for the rest of her life. She had been orphaned at both ends of her existence; for her there was no physical past and no future, other than the bones and the flesh of her own body. Aidan, returned, would put his arms around her, but he could not comfort her weeping center where there was nothing but a snowy waste.

She did not tell him of the miscarriage. She dare not. He had come back from his visit surprisingly altered.

It had been the sight of his aged grandfather—whom everyone had expected to die long before his considerably younger wife—standing grief-stricken at the grave that had brought home to Aidan the finality of his grandmother's death. She had been a great lover of celebrations and had always infected everyone with a sense of her own childlike joy at birthday gatherings and Christmases. No one else in the entire family was half as alive as she had been. It was impossible to him that such a lively spirit could be extinguished. It seemed to him it was because she was not there to cheer them up that the gloom lay so heavily on all their faces, not because it was she who was being buried.

With bowed head he stood among his black-clothed relatives, his father and mother on either side of him. As he thought of his merry grandmother and of past celebrations he found himself smiling. He looked across to where his grandfather stood, half expecting to see her standing there beside him, wanting to exchange a grin with her as they so often had in the past. He saw instead a shrunken elderly man, straining forward toward the grave, supported not by *her* but by one of his daughters, grim-faced and clutching his arm like a wardress restraining a prisoner. Brought up sharp by the shock of the wrong woman on his grandfather's arm, he faced at last the immutable fact of his grandmother's death, and wept.

Yet, later, in spite of his genuine grief, he also felt buoyant for the first time in years. Perhaps it was the discovery that he had in fact, after all, been part of a real family. His father, who had ignored him since the court case, had even taken his hand, as the coffin was lowered into the grave, and squeezed it. The sensation of that hand grasp had stayed with him right through the train journey home to Carrie.

He expected joy when he returned, but he found Carrie subdued. She said she'd had flu and felt terrible. In spite of his improved spirits, he could not bring back the glow to her face, and they spent dismal evenings side by side on the sofa watching the small fire burning in the grate, an extravagance Carrie suddenly insisted upon.

Carrie would not let him make love, certain he would realize she had lost his baby. Discovering how hopelessly inadequate she was, what could he do but leave her? When one afternoon he touched her breasts tenderly and remarked how full they were, she burst into tears and shut herself in the bedroom.

Aidan, confused almost beyond bearing, came to the conclusion she was worried about the future, and one night he proposed properly to her, love in his face and voice. He was not prepared for the storm of tears that followed, but still he persisted. He talked to her about hormonal imbalances, psychological changes, and other things he only partly understood, not being experienced in paternity, and she quietened but would not give him an answer.

It was early the next morning that David called on them, carrying a letter in his hand. It was obvious from his expression he had disturbing news. Carrie made him a cup of coffee, and while he drank he asked Aidan about his grandmother's funeral. He seemed pleased with what Aidan had to tell him. Then he stood up, went over to Carrie who was standing at the sink peeling potatoes, and put his arm around her shoulders. Carrie

131

looked up at him alarmed. David often patted people in a friendly sort of way, but this kind of embrace meant trouble.

"Carrie," he said after some hesitation, "I don't know how you're going to take this, but try to look on it as good news. Your father's coming out in a couple of week's time." Seeing her face he tightened his grip and hurried on. "They write that he's been a model prisoner and has earned maximum parole." He looked anxiously across at Aidan and signaled with his head for him to come over. Quickly he continued, "Look, Carrie, I know it's happening earlier than we all thought—you aren't prepared, it must be a shock—but there's no need for you to see him yet if you don't want to. Though I hope you will," he added finally in an unconvinced voice.

Carrie, shattered, could say nothing. With a sharp toss of her shoulders she shrugged David's hand off and went on peeling potatoes as though she had not heard. Aidan took the knife away and wrapped his arms around her. "Carrie," he said after a minute, "You don't have to see him. It's up to you. Tell David what you want."

Still she said nothing. David put the kettle on for more coffee. Spooning powder into three mugs he began to talk about the process of parole, telling her (though he doubted she was listening) that her father would first stay in a hostel for ex-prisoners not too far away where she could visit him if she wanted. "Or he can come here to visit you, if that's what you prefer. I'll come along with him if you want." He did not look at her as he spoke. He went on talking, chatting about hostels and the various problems prisoners faced, not caring much what he said, his intention being to give her breathing space. He was worried about her, but not too worried—she had Aidan and the baby, she was not alone.

It did not occur to Carrie to reply. Not that she was short of words. Just like that! she was thinking bitterly. Casual, just like that—"your father's coming out." *The bastards!* First they kill him off, then they resurrect him, just like that.

She tore herself from Aidan's grasp and ran and locked herself in her bedroom.

Alarmed, David and Aidan banged on the door. When she did not reply Aidan shouted out he'd break it down if she didn't come out. They waited half a minute then together the two men hurled themselves forward, smashing their shoulders into the cream-painted panels. The door creaked loudly, and Carrie let out a small scream. Before they could launch themselves at it again she turned the lock and let them in. She had a bottle of aspirin in one hand, but the lid was still on and in any case the bottle was

132

almost empty. She said she had a headache. She said nothing else, so they had no means of knowing.

She came into the living room and started to drink her coffee, but halfway through suddenly put her cup down and started to laugh. It was a weird, high-pitched sound, unlike her usual throaty giggle. As she laughed she rocked backward and forward, her hands on her knees with head well back, as though she were some fairground dummy. Then, as suddenly as she had begun, she stopped, reached out and picked up her cup, drank down the coffee, and finally lay back against the sofa with shut eyes, pale but apparently calm.

David stayed with them for an hour or so, then decided he could safely leave. He had already spent longer than he had meant; Jess was expecting him, and he had to be in court soon after noon, so there was little enough time. He picked up his briefcase, patted Carrie's knee, whispered to Aidan to keep an eye on her and not leave her alone, then left, believing the worst was over.

For the next two weeks, until the day before Carrie's father was due out, Aidan obeyed these instructions faithfully, never letting her out of his sight. That he was no longer able to obey them after that was not his fault, but Carrie's.

Or David's, for not keeping a closer eye on her.

Or her father's, for what he had done to her.

Or her mother's, for what she had not done to her.

Or Jess's, for enjoying a career and leaving her child in the care of another.

Or Iris's, for forgetting her charge.

Or Jess's father, for teaching Jess the joys of independence and power.

Or Iris's father, for having a stroke.

Or . . .

Or

The chain of events is infinite. So how can any act ever be self-contained or wholly someone's "fault"?

The excitement among the mobile members of the nearby old people's home was intense. For one thing they had taken the trouble to read the chalked messages on the blackboards set up by the police as they prepared for the reconstruction. Many of the shoppers—mostly busy housewives accustomed to film crews using Hampstead village and the Heath as picturesque background for television advertisements or feature films—did not pause long enough to realize this was no ordinary piece of stagecraft but the re-enactment of reality. Of those who did stop to read the boards, most had heard by now of Matthew Bennett, but many of the younger ones—kids, layabouts enjoying the spring sunshine, *au pairs* with a free afternoon—hadn't bothered to follow sobstuff like that and, imagining a film was being made, searched hopefully among the huddled groups for the famous.

As the afternoon wore on, the mob around the junction of Heath Street and Village Row grew so thick the police had repeatedly to shout through their megaphones that the re-enactment could not take place unless the crowd dispersed. Would they please keep out of the road and let the traffic through! The underground station around the corner disgorged batches of seemingly endless newcomers, eyes hopeful of vicarious excitement. Now even the local shoppers became aware something was up and stayed to gawp. In the end, the area was so congested the police had no choice but to set up barriers at each end of Heath Street and redirect the traffic through to the High Street.

The Inspector was thoroughly flustered. He had not anticipated such crowds and realized now what a fool he'd been. But it was not the prospect of coping with such numbers that was flustering him—he was a very able policeman—it was the fact of his sudden stardom. All afternoon press photographers had been snapping him, catching him in various angles, hand on brow, frowning, bending over to consult with a shorter colleague, holding up an admonishing arm. And now, to crown it all, the television cameras had arrived, and microphones were being thrust under his nose. Already he was wondering if he could persuade someone to let him have a videotape of his interview and was dazedly anticipating his wife's embrace on his return home that evening. He was in luck, he knew. With the Chief Superintendent away sick and everyone else still working overtime on the unsolved Vale of Heath murder he had been left in charge of the case—but soon, perhaps tomorrow, or even by this evening, he would be ousted. Such luck would probably never come his way again.

It occurred to him, as he obligingly posed for the cameras, that he'd particularly like a picture of himself talking to Jess. He looked around but could not see her. Wasn't she going to bother to turn up? His suspicion of her grew. Every day he became more and more certain there was something, something odd there, even though he couldn't put his finger on it.

134

That woman was not as innocent of knowledge about the snatching as she pretended. She was hiding *something,* he was too old a dog not to know that. But what? he asked himself. And what on earth could have been the motivation?

He looked at his watch. The time had come. Holding the megaphone to his lips, he called out instructions for everyone to leave the area except for anyone who had been present in the street on the afternoon of the twenty-first. No one moved. "It's impossible," muttered one of his colleagues, "it's a complete waste of time." The Inspector shook his head. Now three mounted policemen on huge gray and white stallions appeared from Prince Arthur's Road, tall awesome beings. With godlike grace the centaurs moved carefully through the crowds, calling down to them, urging them to cooperate. Gradually most of the people were persuaded to retreat, slowly moving backward so as not to miss anything. Arriving at the barricades, they blocked the view of those who had behaved themselves and stayed behind the barrier. Outraged, the noisier among these muttered aloud, then began to shout. The horses were undisturbed by the noise, moving sedately, delicately through the crowd, occasionally tossing their heads but totally under control—except for one that paused a moment to drop a steaming heap of glossy turds on the road at the foot of the BBC cameras, delighting the watchers, who giggled among themselves.

Jess, standing incognito on the edge of the crowd at the top of her own street, heard them and thought: For some of them it's just a picnic, a day out.

She had covered her hair with a paisley headscarf, an old one from Marks and Spencers, and wore lightly-tinted glasses and no make-up. No one had recognized her. When she had woken in the morning she had decided she would watch everything from her windows, but it had suddenly occurred to her that after all the publicity there'd probably be people waiting outside just to see *her.* If it had been winter time, or a wet day, few would have bothered to turn out, but on a lovely spring morning like this, with the Heath only five minutes away, there would be enough people with nothing to do and a curiosity about the famous to spoil everything. The least she could do was to make herself invisible.

She was pleased to see how rational she was still able to be, even though it was now three days. Dressing, eating breakfast, working at her desk, she had remained—at least on the surface—her usual self. From time to time

135

she paused, pen in hand, wondering at the extent of her self-control. It surprised even her. When people rang she would swiftly cut off any sympathetic comment and return to the business in hand with a curtness that was never allowed to appear on the screen but which, in the past, had sometimes offended those who worked with her. Today of all days, she thought, finally turning her phone over to the answerphone service (it was ridiculous how many people were finding excuses to call), she needed to stay calm. Work was work. If she'd been a man, they wouldn't have gone on like that. Hadn't they learned yet she wasn't going to play the weepy little woman just because they felt it was appropriate? It was bad enough having one hysteric in the house already.

For Iris—who was supposed to be the star of the re-enactment, pushing the pram along the road, doing the shopping, repeating everything she had done two days ago— had finally broken down and been put to bed by the doctor, too sedated to be of use to anyone.

Jess had been immensely irritated by that. If *she* had kept control, surely Iris could have managed it? She had not quite been able to keep the contempt out of her voice as she talked to the doctor, and for Iris that had been the last straw. She had burst into a fresh fit of moaning and tried to bury herself inside the bedclothes.

Now, alone in the crowd, Jess stood thinking about Iris and wondering whether she ought to sack her when all this was over. She could never again have the same old easy relationship with her. On the other hand, what was the alternative? She thought of Yvette and shuddered. She wondered again why the police should want to interview the girl. She couldn't have had anything to do with it. But if she turned up and the press got hold of her! If she'd kept those photographs! She was capable of anything.

Jess's face burned. Nothing so horrible had ever happened to her as what that girl did.

It was at this moment, when Jess's thoughts were furthest from Matthew, that she was brought back to the present by a sudden murmur from the crowd, a soft shocked sound—not quite a wail but containing within it a hint of pity and fear, the noise a Greek chorus might make at the occurrence of yet another stroke of inevitable misfortune. She looked down the street and saw Iris carefully bumping Matthew in his pram down the steps of their house. Arrived safely on the pavement Matthew looked around him crowing with delight as he always did. Safe in his leather harness he burbled and flung out his arms to all the world in full trust, just as he always did. Iris bent over him, adjusted the pillow behind him to make him quite comfortable, then slowly began to push the pram up the street toward Jess.

It was now, for the first time in her life, that Jess knew real grief. Had she truly thought, only a few seconds ago, that that shameful morning had been her most terrible ordeal? How shallow, how unimportant it was, beside this sorrow. She had a sense of disintegration. Was it possible to suffer such anguish and remain whole?

Oh, it was cruel, such simulation! That first moment at the top of the steps, with Iris leaning back as she took the weight of the pram and Matthew gleefully waving his arms, it had been all so normal. She hadn't even been surprised to see them—the sight was so ordinary it had seemed almost banal.

It was diabolical! Had they no feelings? With shame she remembered herself despising Iris for breaking down at the thought of it. *Had she no imagination, then, that she hadn't understood how it would be?*

The pram approached. The not-Iris was a policewoman with Iris's short square build and a not dissimilar round plain face, the likeness increased by the fact that she was wearing Iris's navy blue headscarf and the same sloppy green sweater and maroon slacks she had worn that afternoon three days ago. The not-Matthew was dressed in borrowed clothes, a replica of the blue and white jumpsuit Jess had bought Matthew only a week before. The familiar stranger sat there in Matthew's pram, glowing and batting his hands up and down on the pram cover, full of joy at all the unexpected fuss.

As they passed by the baby looked straight at Jess, and she could have sworn he gave her a special look—a look of happy complicity aimed especially at her. It took all of her strength not to rush forward and snatch away this child, gather him up in her arms and rush off with him before anyone could stop her. Was this how the baby snatcher had felt, she thought as the pram passed by, the policewoman pushing it along with exactly Iris's heavy country gait—that Matthew was really hers? Fierce anger and a need for revenge had already been mixed with her grief. Now there came an unexpected pity, a sense almost of understanding and comradeship with that desperate woman, whoever she was. Had the woman been there, Jess thought with passion, she would first have killed her, then wept over her.

She was standing quite still, tears running down her face (she was not alone, other women were crying also, reliving imagined terrors) when suddenly she felt a hand on her arm. She looked up. It was Adam. He gripped her tight, looking at her with a depth of love and compassion bred of long—even if rejected—years of marriage. Jess could not speak but leaned back gratefully against his broad shoulder.

Once before, when Emma was being born and it was feared the child might not survive, Adam had sat by her holding her hand and encouraging her through all the birth trauma with just that same look of love and concern for her on his face, totally forgetting his own fears for his firstborn.

Now she looked up at him and wondered why she had not remembered that brief time of married communion more often. Something precious had been revealed to her then, and she had ignored it. They both had: neither of them had ever referred to the incident again—Emma, in fact, was born perfectly healthy, and it was not their style to linger over the past.

Now she thought, why didn't we? We opened up to each other then— why did we take it so for granted and not build on what might have been the first step of another kind of relationship?

Even at this moment, with most of her mind grieving for Matthew, her independent spirit instinctively rebelled at the thought of such a building up. She saw it literally as a bridge between herself and Adam welding them together, two pillars united by an arched span. But when a bridge collapses it is a useless edifice, no good to anyone! They had chosen to remain separate beings, independent of each other, and that had seemed the wise, the right thing to do. But had she, in spite of her intentions, become tethered to Adam after all? Was that what marriage was, a creeping union of body and soul that conjoined two people, regardless of their happiness or unhappiness, so that even if they had learned to hate each other separating was as painful as tearing bare flesh away from the tentacles of an engulfing sea monster?

Not-Iris, dimly seen behind a shop window, was choosing invisible items from an unseen shelf, not-Matthew balanced on one arm. The whole thing's a farce, Jess thought hopelessly, searching every face for signs of dawning recognition, a relevant memory. But saw no such thing.

Adam, sensing her growing distress, tightened his grip on her. Holding Jess like this it seemed impossible he had walked out on her, yet the other reality of Fanny waiting back home for him in her little flat was just as clear in his mind and just as important. He was married to both of them, he saw with astonishment; he had known Fanny such a short time, but already she had wormed her way into his consciousness so thoroughly there seemed hardly any difference between his attachment to either of them.

As he watched the charade his thoughts turned to Matthew and Emma, whom he had so easily abandoned only the week before. He fought the feeling that he was being deliberately punished for his betrayal, that some judicious god was sitting up there throwing measured thunderbolts at him. Standing behind Jess, his arm around her waist, he stared as the policewoman came out of the shop, buckled not-Matthew back into his pram and walked slowly up the street to the cleaners. He pressed an unthinking kiss onto the back of Jess's head and felt her fingers tighten in his hand.

But Jess was lost in new thoughts. Watching the policewoman buckle up the baby she had suddenly recalled herself at about three years old, trying to pull off the straps of newly-imposed walking reins. She had screeched her head off, but her mother had been adamant—Jess was so reckless she'd be out in the road and under a bus before anyone could stop her.

It came back fresh as ever—the despair at being tied down like that, reduced to creeping slowly along the London pavements instead of rushing from shop to curb, snatching at the experiences offered so freely everywhere. It was bad enough with Nanny, but worse with her dull, correct mother, who kept stopping to chat with some equally boring friend, while she, Jess, stamped and pulled and tugged impatiently at her straps. With her father it had been different. She had had no objection when he took her out, though that was a very rare treat. With him she had played horses, run along in front dropping her head and rearing up, pretending she was pulling him along in a grand carriage, proud to be of service to this regal, handsome man. But the service was between equals: as often she pretended it was she who was leading him, it was she who was in control. Did he ever guess that? He had smiled and enjoyed the game but noticed how she detested it when it was her mother who held the reins, and soon the harness was abandoned. But for some years afterward she had tied her skipping rope around herself and, giving the handles to her father, had played the game with him again, romping around the lawn with her colt's legs, tossing her black head proudly.

He had always made her feel so good, her father, taught her she could be whatever she wanted. It's up to you, he'd say, you're free to make your own choices. No good blaming anyone else if things go wrong—your life is in your own hands, no one else's. Her mother had quietly, tactfully, fought him, tried to turn Jess into a woman in her own mold. "Men like feminine women," she used to say privately to her daughter, and at first Jess kept quiet, but later when she was older she'd laugh and say, "Not the sort of men I like."

Now she was close to weeping. She had believed her father. He was right, she knew he was right. She still knew he was right. And she'd always played straight and worked for what she wanted. So what have I done wrong that everything should suddenly turn upside down? Why me? Why now?

The day before she had overheard Emma playing with her doll in the garden. At first Emma had been rocking the doll in her arms, saying in a gentle crooning voice, "I'm never going to leave you alone in your pram, never ever." But a minute later the child's mood had changed. Scowling she had turned the doll over onto its stomach, whacked it firmly on its bottom, and said in hard tones, "If you ever do that again I'll put you in a pram and leave you outside the house. And see if I care what happens to you then."

It burst on Jess that there could never be real freedom. You couldn't cut yourself free of the ropes linking you to the world around you. Whatever action you took had its reaction elsewhere. Freedom was an illusion. Right now she was in theory as free as she had ever been, but in reality she was tethered to Emma, tethered to the policewoman pushing that pram, tethered to Adam's arm, tethered to the real Matthew wherever he was, tethered to a thousand lesser things she was scarcely even aware of.

She was not free. She never had been.

It was now that someone in the crowd recognized her, or maybe they had recognized Adam from his photographs. There was a murmur that rapidly led to an excited chatter (everyone's emotions had been worked up by the sight of the baby, everyone wanted to reach out and touch) which ended in a crowd of faces suddenly milling toward Jess. She cringed back against Adam, who, himself again, led her effortlessly through the faces back to their house.

140

On the steps Jess turned and faced them. She tried to smile, but for the first time in her adult life her body refused to obey her will. Instead she gave a kind of grimace that was caught by a waiting photographer, the image of which—appearing in the press the next day—changed the minds of many people who had previously thought of her only as an ambitious bitch.

DAY 4

Considering that apparently there were still no facts to go on, the press managed to fill a surprising number of columns on the Matthew Bennett case. There was a general feeling it would stand one more day before public interest waned. Other news remained unexciting: readers were so surfeited with industrial strikes that editors hesitated to blow up the Ford workshop affair. The evening before there had been an unsuccessful assassination attempt in the Middle East, but the Middle East had also been rather overplayed recently. All three heavies decided to lead with a statement by the Prime Minister on the EEC, but the populars, knowing what caught the mass heart, filled their front pages with pictures of the reconstruction scene. The lucky staff photographer who had caught Jess grimacing at her front door saw his scoop filling his paper's front page, topped by a banner headline—THE FACE OF GRIEF. By that evening his photograph had been syndicated all over the world. He was very pleased with himself: only the previous week there'd been a hint that his work had grown boring.

The paper with the pictorial scoop treated Jess in its inside columns with the awe and gentleness due to a Madonna. The other populars stepped up their already barbed comments in their later editions (having seen The Face of Grief), reporting that Jess had been too busy to attend the reconstruction. Their correspondence columns reflected this growing bias—one letter commented sarcastically on the shortcomings of career mothers, another straightforwardly said that if Jess had been half a mother she would have been at home where she belonged, in which case the abduction would never have happened.

Adam was left alone.

The paper that considered itself the most socially conscious of the three heavies not only ran a couple of reconstruction pictures but also printed an article on baby snatching on the Woman's Page, which, considering how quickly it had been thrown together, was reasonably accurate. Dr. d'Orbán, the only known expert, had parted up with his wisdom over the telephone. The interviewing journalist compressed the material, duly reporting there were three types of baby stealers, the "comforting," the "manipulative," and the impulsive psychotic, all unstable. Her inadequate description of this typology was to lead to a furious correspondence from a variety of interested people, including Dr. d'Orbán himself, but her other comments such as that publicity was often followed by outbreaks of baby stealing caused less controversy. She cited the 1973 Bristol case where, after a young mother had reported her baby was stolen, there followed over a period of seventeen days an epidemic of reports of baby snatching. Parents of young children began to panic, there were calls for vigilante groups, and information poured into police headquarters following the publication of identikit pictures. That it was eventually discovered no child had actually been stolen at all, including the original "stolen" child (whose mother, together with her own father with whom she had been living, was six months later convicted of incest), the journalist chose not to comment on since it spoiled the story. She had also managed to contact a sociologist who considered baby snatching an ancient custom connected with women's need for "primary identification," in which mother and baby are one, and who cited the old legends of fairies stealing away nursing infants as proof of the antiquity of the habit.

The most Tory of the three heavies printed a long letter demanding a drastic tightening up by the police as it was evident law and order was rapidly becoming a thing of the past and complaining that it was truly appalling that such a model family as the Bennetts, ideal citizens of a clearly unworthy state, should be defenseless against the increasing nihilistic elements in our society. It's them or us, was its ancient cry; woe, woe, the civilized world is cracking up.

Speculation about who had done it was widespread. Some nut had rung the police demanding a ransom of £5,000,000 and the release of twenty unrelated leading terrorists imprisoned in jails throughout the world. The police had dismissed the caller as an obvious fraud, especially since he had not mentioned a certain item of "secret knowledge" (a lemon-shaped birthmark on Matthew's bottom). Several editors, however, pounced on the phone call; one liked best the idea of straightforward kidnapping for money and wondered whether the habit was at last spreading from the continent to Britain; a couple of others preferred the terrorism angle, reporting the crank phone call as though it were genuine (they could have been right and the police wrong, after all), and suggested that all celebrities should guard their offspring carefully since there was now bound to be a spate of similar crimes. The theory of a connection with terrorism had some justification since two weeks previously Jess had taken a documentary on that subject for her weekly piece. Since just about every terrorist organization had been covered in it, from the defunct Bader-Meinhopf sect, the Palestinians, the Irish brethren, right through to the Basques, it was only too possible that at least one of the groups had been outraged by her acid comments to the point of action.

Such speculation was encouraged by the fact that the only other lead had been demolished. The "banana" woman had apparently been found and cleared. She was a progressive mother who believed in "stretching" babies, and the child was her own. It is true that Sarah Binney, the little girl who had first reported having seen the "banana woman," failed to recognize the suspect in a police line-up. But since the woman had been more or less in the right place at the right time, the police decided Sarah's suspect had been she. The fact that she was nearer forty than thirty, that her hair was gray not blond, and that it wasn't a banana but a sausage roll she had been feeding her baby was of little importance to the police. Such reporting error was typical of uninvolved witnesses. Poor little Sarah's self-image was demolished. Severely scolded on the way home from the identification parade by her mother, who hated to look a fool, Sarah tried to explain that the woman had looked so ancient and ugly, not at all like the one she had originally spotted, that she didn't know how to tell the truth without sounding terribly rude. But her mother was too absorbed by her own shame to listen. At least Sarah learned from the experience a useful lesson for adult life—that to mind your own business is the safest policy in an unjust world.

Jess and Adam, who had spent the night together as a married couple, *sat drinking coffee at their breakfast table as they worked through the pile of morning papers. Outside the window the spring sun shone on a huge rhododendron bush smothered with its annual load of white blossom already noisy with the droning of early-rising bees, but the two people at the table had no eyes for nature. Each had first flicked through the papers to insure the press had not found out their private secrets (Jess knew what Adam was frightened of, but Adam had no idea of Jess's terror), then with increasing apprehension they read their way through the possibilities offered—that Matthew had been abducted by, among others, a power-mad maniac, a terrorist gang, a money-seeking kidnapper, a sadistic psychotic or an unstable, unhappy girl with a strong "comforting" urge.*

That morning for both of them, suddenly anything seemed possible.

WHEN Carrie woke she knew her periods had started again. Jumping out of bed she watched the blood trickling down the inside of her left leg. At first she eyed it almost dispassionately. She had known it would happen and had prepared herself for it. But when she touched the red with her finger she began to cry.

The act of washing restored her to a state of comparative calm. Clean and dressed she stood dithering in the little living room. She wanted badly to get out of the flat, but to leave would be an act of treachery: she had promised Aidan she would not go out without him and for a fortnight she had kept her word. At the beginning she had agreed willingly—she knew it was only sensible that she should do as David had suggested.

But she had promised before the blood. Now she needed to be alone, to make decisions. Soon Aidan must see she was growing thinner, not fatter: would see the blood. Her lie would expose itself.

The thought let loose chaos in her head. Thoughts flew everywhere— to Aidan; to her dead baby; to her father sitting in his prison cell waiting for tomorrow's dawn and a return to life; to her mother lying on the road, the motor cyclist sprawled beside her.

She sat down on the sofa, spread her fingers protectively over her head. The doctor would help. He would give her something to see her through.

But what if he sent her away to that place again? He knew her too well now. This time he wouldn't take chances.

She had to get out of the flat quickly. Aidan would be back. He'd take one look at her and know something was up. Oh Aidan! Oh love!

David. Why hadn't she thought of David? He'd help. Even if she didn't tell him, just being with him would calm her.

She snatched up a coat, her bag, checked that she had money and keys and ran out of the flat, down the stairs and all the way to the bus stop, desperate not to be caught.

When Carrie arrived half an hour later at the probation offices she met David bounding down the steps two at a time, car keys in his hand. He had

147

an eager look on his face. He was obviously very surprised and apparently not too pleased to see her.

"Carrie! What's up?"

She forced calmness to her face.

"Nothing. I just felt like getting out on my own for a bit, that's all."

He relaxed. She seemed her usual self. He gave her his special smile. "Where's Aidan?"

Carrie absorbed the smile. She'd been right. Just seeing him was settling her.

"He's gone shopping. I'm OK on my own. Really. Don't worry about me. Where are you going?"

"I'm driving over to Hampstead. One of my clients appeared in Court there this morning and got sent down for a couple of months. I want to go and commiserate with him, poor bastard, before they take him off. He asked for it, I suppose; if there has to be such a thing as prison he's a natural. But I hate seeing one of mine go back in, all the same."

"You're in the wrong job."

"I hope you don't really think so."

She smiled back at him. "I was thinking of you, not me. Can I come with you?"

He looked doubtful. "To Hampstead? Well." He glanced at his watch. "I'd say come in and have a quick cup of coffee, but I'm already a bit late. The traffic can be terrible sometimes."

She moved closer to him and looked up at him appealingly. "That's all right, I don't mind about coffee. But I'd like the trip, honestly. It would make a real change. And we can chat on the way."

He still looked doubtful. His face hadn't lost its usual friendliness, but something was obviously bothering him. "Was there anything special you wanted to talk about?"

She let her head drop so he could only see the top of her blond curls. Then she looked up and the pure blueness of her eyes—the sun had deepened their color—made him catch his breath. "Let me come, please. Please," she begged, almost childishly.

He gave in and led her to his car. Inside he leaned across her to tighten her safety belt. Suddenly he was glad he had let her come—she was really a nice kid. Before moving back to his own seat he looked down at her appreciatively. "Hi," he said, grinning.

She sank back against the seat smiling. Now everything seemed much easier. It was not yet three o'clock, and sunlight made the dingy streets they were passing through look cheerful. Held up at a set of traffic lights she was aware David was watching her, and she looked back at him with such an open, frank smile he was completely reassured. He reached over and patted her knee, a pleasant casual gesture that warmed her with gratitude, almost love for him. If only everyone could be as nice as David, she thought.

The journey was disappointingly quick. There were no traffic jams, and most of the lights had been in their favor. Looking at his watch David said casually that since they were so early he had time to return a book he had borrowed from a friend, and instead of stopping at the Magistrates Court he continued straight on up the hill and through a side road to Village Row. There was no free space outside Jess's house, so he drove down to the end of the road where it swerves around the old church, leaving a broad patch of unused road useful for parking. Self-consciously he drove into an empty space, slamming on the brakes, and unbuckled himself. "I won't be very long," he said. He reached into the back of the car and put a magazine into her hands. "There are some more in the back if you get bored." He opened his door and got out quickly, then as an afterthought stuck his head back inside. "I don't know if my friend's in or not. I won't be long, anyway."

Carrie sensed something unusual about him. She looked up sharply, intuition telling her it was a woman he was seeing. She felt a momentary stab of jealousy, which she dismissed immediately. She did not want to be left alone. No, that would not be comfortable. "I'll go for a walk, I think—I won't wait." She tried not to sound hurt.

David looked at her anxiously, picking up her reactions. He tried to persuade her to stay. "I won't be long, really. It's quite possible my friend is out, and I'll be back straightaway. Then you can come to the cells with me. Give Harry a last glimpse of the delights of freedom."

"Thanks! No, honestly, it's such a lovely afternoon I'd really like a walk. It's so beautiful here. It's like a film set, these lovely old houses and that yew tree and all. I'll wander around the churchyard a bit and explore." Getting out of the car she put a hand on his arm and looked him straight in the eyes. "Don't worry about me, I'll be all right, honestly."

Reluctantly, he shut the door behind her and locked it. He felt uneasy about abandoning her, but it was true—she seemed OK. And he'd been thinking about Jess all morning, hoping he'd have time to slip in to see her. He'd never had a chance to surprise her like that before. "All right, then." He put his arm around Carrie's shoulder and gave her a quick hug. "Have a good walk." He pointed back up the road toward Heath Street. "If you turn left at the top of the road you'll see the underground station on the corner. You can easily get back home from there."

She smiled at him, waving her hand as she walked off. "Don't worry about me; I feel really great, honestly."

And it was true. Suddenly she did. She felt terrific. The sun was flashing back at her from the windows of the church and everywhere there were yellow daffodils—daffodils sprouting out of window boxes decorating the nearby houses, daffodils planted among the flagstones outside the church and on the jostling graves of the famous and the obscure—yellow trumpets proclaiming spring and renewal. In the churchyard she knelt down to sniff a clump so old and degenerated in size they might have been wild flowers—perhaps, she thought, they *were* wild ones, native daffodils left over from the days when Hampstead itself was still wild, a distant place of green hills and dangerous highwaymen.

Oh, how dull, how dull her life had been these last years! Terrible things happening inside her, but outside—nothing! She climbed a gravestone and looked over the churchyard wall down into London. It quivered below her in the warmth of the afternoon sun; a foreign city, gilded by sunlight, unknown. And here, beauty and age: old graves, the last homes of people dead so long it was impossible to be sad for them, only glad they rested in so quiet and lovely a place.

A black bird sang in a yew tree that spread its flat branches over her. She crouched beneath and looked up through the ancient growth, searching until she saw the belly of the singing bird. Pleasure filled her, and she thought how good it was to be alive, after all, and looked back with astonishment and sorrow for that sad girl standing, no more than an hour ago, in her bedroom touching her damp thigh.

She was young! It was not too late. Anything was possible, still. She ran her fingers through the mat of dried needles dropped during many lifetimes from the yew. Then she dug down among the roots and sniffed the still damp leaf mould. Its tang excited her even more. She imagined herself a field mouse burrowing through this redolent earth, whiskers atremble, nose twitching, and she laughed, laughed aloud. In front of her a half-collapsed slab of limestone leaned right over, its wording worn away a hundred years ago or more by wind and rain. Green ivy—planted in the still visible hump of earth in front of it—clambered over the gravestones, tentacle and root binding together sea-pressed remains of fossilized mollusc and oak-encased bones, the bones of the long-dead worthy who had once walked, curled wig bouncing on his shoulders, elegant cane striking the same slabs on which she had just walked, looking vaguely— so long ago—at the church front and thinking, just as she had, of life, and adventure, and fate.

She rose and laid a hand on the weathered stone. Then briskly she walked out of the churchyard and up past the houses of Village Row toward the shops, suddenly feeling like company. As she passed the spot where David had parked his car she saw it was gone. Poor David, his friend had been out then. What a pity for him.

Not far from the end of the road she was stopped abruptly by the sound of a wail.

The wail hit Carrie's consciousness with the ripping violence of a super-sonic jet zooming unexpectedly over a summer field, when the mind is full of the flutter of butterflies and the quiver of grasses. It tore through her calm joy, indicating pain of such magnitude there was no enduring it.

There, in front of her, not three doors along, was a pram; and in the pram a propped-up baby, its hands flailing the air in urgent grief. Carrie hastened to it, and—inexperienced, but instinct informing her—took hold of the handles of the pram, a large old-fashioned one with big wheels and carriage springs, and rocked it.

Later, recovering, she tried to explain to her therapist what had happened then, but she never could. Even she, at that later date, could not quite recapture the feel of that instant recognition, her absolute certainty that here, neglected and unhappy, was her own baby. With its face screwed up she had not recognized it, but no sooner had the rocking commenced than the wailing stopped, the mouth unclenched and the eyes opened. Large blue eyes, *her* eyes, her father's eyes, the eyes that all the paternal side of her family bore. The blue eyes looked straight at her and in miraculous transformation melted in a conspiratorial smile as mouth tilted and cheeks spread with new-found happiness. Gurgling, splutter-ing, the baby held out its arms toward Carrie.

She didn't stand a chance. These were the eyes, the flaxen curls, the embracing arms of the child she had played with so often in her mind this last month, the laughing girl baby for whose sake she had given the bundle

151

to the flames unexamined. Phoenixes are not ten a penny—there had been no other child looking just like that, at just that age, who had chuckled at her with instant familiarity. Perhaps even if there had been, last week or the week before, she would not have known who it was. But today her vision was not as on other days. Today her understanding was inspired.

Yet she hesitated. Something told her she must not take up her child. She drew back. Straight away the baby screwed up its face again and, opening its mouth, drew in a deep breath. Hastily, before it could utter that desolating wail once more, Carrie fumbled with the buckles of its safety harness and lifted it out of the pram to comfort it.

There again, later, she was never able to describe properly the intensity of her emotions then. As she took the baby into her arm she became acutely aware of the emptiness in her belly that had racked her this last month, but even as the emptiness reproclaimed itself it was at the same moment filled, as though the child in her arms had flowed through the pores of her body and returned into her womb, recharging the void its absence had created. There was no separation between her and the child—they were one—and her arms closed around it as naturally as the womb encloses the seed, the two of them perfect and indivisible.

How could she afterward explain these feelings, except as bliss and joy and a completeness she had never known before? No words were adequate for the sensations of that moment.

Even so, after a minute during which she stood unmoving, totally unaware of the outside world, of the traffic passing up the street and the wrangling of two middle-aged passers-by locked in marital disagreement, she still doubted her right to take the child. She hesitated, then made herself put it down. It giggled and waved its arms in pleasure as she refastened the buckles and tucked the blanket around its legs, but the moment she stood back it sensed her withdrawal; the child's face began to pucker, and the first pathetic sob burst from its lips.

Anger filled Carrie. How dared anyone treat her baby like this! To leave her unattended; crying; unloved! The child's pain was her own pain. Inside herself she felt a return of anguish, and there flashed through her mind her mother's face, stern-mouthed, telling her to be quiet. "Shh, shhh, my love," she hushed and, bending over, kissed the baby on her cheek. She smelled her milky warm scent and felt a pudgy fist pushing into her breast. She straightened, and without a moment's further doubt pushed the pram away, after scowling at the closed door at the top of the steps before which the pram had stood.

The door remained shut, and was to remain shut for another three minutes, by which time Carrie was invisible among the crowd of shoppers.

The walk home was long. With that pram there was no question of going by bus or tube. It was not easy, finding her way. There was no problem getting to Camden Town—it was all one long straight road downhill into London, which she recalled from the drive out with David, but finding her way after that eastward to Islington and beyond was difficult. She hesitated to ask openly for help. For although she knew the baby was hers, at another level she knew equally well there were those who would not understand, would not realize the truth of it. She solved this problem by popping into shops to ask for directions, leaving the pram outside where it could not be seen. In this way, she reasoned, no one would associate her with the baby should there be any inquiries.

In the first shop she went into she bought a pound of bananas before asking for help. Afterward, as she walked along proudly pushing the pram, it occurred to her the baby might be hungry. This thought made her realize how little she knew about babies, what to feed them on, how much sleep they needed—all that sort of thing. But this slight anxiety did not disturb her euphoria: she looked so bonny and healthy, this lovely baby of hers. All the same, when a little later she found herself passing a bookshop she stopped. Books held many answers. She placed the pram just beyond the windows of the shop where it would not be noticed, just in case some nosy assistant peered out. Her daughter smiled up at her, so delighted with the unexpected long walk that she made no attempt to cry when Carrie prepared to leave her.

Bending over to implant a quick kiss on her forehead, Carrie whispered a few loving words, then took a banana out of the brown paper bag dropped among the blankets at the foot of the pram and half peeled it, leaving the flaps dangling. Gently she pressed the unpeeled base of the fruit into the baby's hands. It gurgled, and let go. "Come on!" said Carrie tenderly and tried again, closing the plump little fingers around the banana once more. They clutched it tight this time and jogged the fruit up and down. Carrie pushed the white flesh gently toward the baby's mouth. Taking her point and liking this game immensely, the giggling infant attempted to get the fruit into its mouth but underestimated its length and instead jammed it firmly into its own eye. It let out a yell of outrage and pain and dropped the treacherous toy in disgust.

Carrie, fearing for its intelligence, tried several more times before it came to her how complicated an act she was demanding of the child.

My goodness, she thought to herself, I've got a lot to learn! And throwing away the mangled banana in the gutter, she entered the bookshop where, telling the assistant she wanted a helpful book on childcare as a present for her pregnant sister, she was soon initiated into the worldwide sisterhood of Spock disciples.

When at last she arrived home she was very tired but triumphant. She had thought a lot about Aidan during the walk, thought of him with love and pleasure. Pregnant, she had been selfish. No, she corrected herself, not selfish—uncomprehending, rather. In the last month they had grown close together; he had become a part of her, and she could no longer imagine him entirely absent from her life. Was that what marriage was? A growing together through living side by side and sharing everyday things? Yet she had not been happy then; there had been something grossly missing. She smiled down at her daughter—Aidan's child as well as hers. How happy Aidan would be, how clever he would think her. She searched for signs of Aidan in the baby and thought the line of her chin, her lofty forehead bore a strong resemblance. Her heart overflowed again, and she could only just stop herself from grabbing the child to her and hugging it tight.

During the walk she had bought tins of baby food: strained prunes, carrots, beef, custard, rice—a bagful of different flavors recommended by the plump elderly woman whose advice she had asked (for her sister again, this time laid up with flu and her baby hungry and in need of nourishment). "Is she weaned?" the concerned woman had asked, and pressed on Carrie tins of evaporated milk when Carrie admitted she wasn't quite sure. Carrie went to another shop to buy a feeding bottle and diapers—and was pleased with herself for her caution.

There was a lot to think about. For a start, it was not possible to tell Aidan straight away. A certain period of time would have to pass, as though she had been in the hospital to have the child. She couldn't present their daughter to him just like that—he would think it very peculiar. The same applied to the other people in her building. No, she'd have to conceal the baby for a few days, maybe a week or so, until she had learned how to look after her and until she could reasonably be expected to arrive home from the hospital with her baby. Oh, it wouldn't be difficult, but it would be wise to be careful—she couldn't rely on other people understanding the situation. Not even Aidan.

Back at the building she was lucky: there was no one in sight. The pram was too large to fit into the tiny elevator, so she had to bump it step by step up the stairs to the fourth floor. The baby, thumb in mouth and eyes sleepily half-closed, hardly stirred.

Once behind her own door all she wanted was to draw up a chair and worship in silence. But there was too much to be done. Her worst fear that Aidan would be waiting for her outside (for he did not have a key) had not been realized. Though he had been there. Pushed through the letter box she found a note saying he was out searching for her, and where on earth had she been. It ended, "I love you—Adian," and had a postscript begging her to stay where she was and not to go out again.

She held the note to her cheek, then hurried into the bedroom and began to pack his things. He had brought over some of his gear in a rucksack, which she now fetched out from under the bed and stuffed full with the clothes and books she thought he might need. Lastly she packed his toothbrush. She hadn't time to fold up his clothes properly and hoped he would not be hurt, for she didn't want to imply she was careless of his affection. Before she put them away she held his belongings to her mouth, kissing them tenderly. There was one thing she could not part with, the old blue sweater she particularly loved him in. The very first time she had ever seen him he had been wearing it. She had started to pack it, but it was far too familiar. It bore the smell of his body, had several of his hairs caught in the ribbed neck; pressing her face against it she half expected his arms to come up and enclose her. She hesitated, then laid it on her lap. That, she would keep for herself.

She was only just in time. She had hardly put the rucksack outside the door and come back in again when she heard his footsteps. She heard him before he'd even reached the second floor. He was running, taking two steps at a time. On his own he always did that, never took the elevator. She pressed her hand to her heart, dreading the moment when he saw the rucksack. The footsteps were loud now as he rounded the last bend in the staircase, half a dozen rapid footfalls clattering on the uncarpeted composition-marble floor. They slowed, then stopped. There was a muttered exclamation, followed by a brief shuffling noise—had he picked up the rucksack?—then a thud on the floor as he dropped it. A moment's silence was followed by a loud hammering on the door.

"Carrie! What the hell! Let me in!" His voice showed anger, shock.

Carrie, her body pressed against the door that separated them, sank trembling to the ground. She held his blue sweater in her hand. "I can't," she called out weakly, "I can't let you in."

"You're there! Christ, I was frantic..." Then anger returned. "Are you crazy! Let me come in."

She shook her head. "I can't."

She spoke too quietly for him to hear. "Carrie! I know you're there." His voice, though loud, was frightened. "Open the door, and let me in."

She lifted her head up and spoke more strongly now. "Aidan, trust me. Just for a few days. You can't come in now, not right now."

"Why not, for God's sake? What's happened? What's the matter? Has something happened?

"It won't be long, I promise. Just for a few days."

The baby, awakened by the noise, began to whimper gently in the room next door. "Hush," Carrie whispered as loudly as she dared, "be quiet, my love."

Aidan heard her. He began to attack the door, first hammering, then kicking at it. His voice when it came again was thick with fury. "You've got someone there! Who is it? Let me in!"

Terrified the baby would break into a cry Carrie ran into the little living room, picked her up in her arms, jigging her tenderly as she hurried back to the front door. "There's no one," she cried, staring at the blank wood as though she could see through it. "I was talking to you. Please, Aidan, *please*. Take your rucksack, and leave me alone. Just for a few days."

He attacked the door again. She was frightened he'd break it down or that neighbors would come. "Stop it!" she cried, mouth pressed to the door, "Stop it! I love you! But I can't let you in. Please!"

Now there was silence. She could hear him breathing. She could hardly bear not to open the door and show him what she held.

"I've such a surprise for you, Aidan," she said pleadingly. He didn't reply. "Can you hear me?"

"Yes."

156

"You'll be so happy. But I can't show you now. You've got to wait for a few days. I can't bear making you stay out there—but I can't let you in now. Please understand, Aidan. Trust me."

When at last he answered, his voice was still angry. "I know you've got someone else there. I know it. If you . . ." he couldn't say it, but jealousy overtook him, and he began to pound at the door again.

It had never occurred to Carrie he might misunderstand in this way. As though she could ever look at anyone else! She didn't know how to reassure him. "I love you," she cried out, "but I can't let you in. Why won't you understand?"

Now she heard other footsteps running up the stairs, then Aidan, very angry and a woman's voice arguing with him. Aidan must have made some violent gesture as he shouted, "Fuck off! It's none of your business!", for the woman gave a gasp, then saying something Carrie couldn't quite catch retreated back down the stairs.

Frightened the woman might call the police, Carrie called out urgently, "Aidan! Don't make trouble. You've got to trust me. I'm all right, I'm not going to do anything silly. I'll be quite safe, honestly I will."

She waited. Was he still there? She heard nothing for a minute or two. In her mind's eye she could see his face as he struggled to keep his temper, to do the right thing. He tried so hard!

At length he spoke. "Carrie? You're there? OK. I believe you. But you know what David said. It's a difficult time for you. You shouldn't be alone." His voice was wheedling now. "Let me come in just for a few minutes, just to make sure you're OK. Then I'll go away if you want, I promise. Just let me in for a minute or two so we can talk." His voice changed. "I love you, goddammit!"

She weakened, but the baby, clutched against her breast, puckered up its face, and she knew that at any moment it would begin to howl. It was probably hungry. A rush of tenderness went through her. She wanted to whisper its name to calm it, and she realized she hadn't given her one yet. She almost forgot Aidan in this discovery. As she half-listened to him talking to her, there ran through her mind a list of names—all useless: how could any name be good enough for this marvel in her arms?

"Carrie? Darling? Are you there?"

She nodded, forgetting he couldn't see her. Then said, "Yes. Yes, I'm here. But I've got to go now. I've a lot of things to do." Her voice sharpened. "Promise me you won't fetch David. I'm all right, I really am. I promise I'm not going to do anything silly. So don't fetch anyone. Please, Aidan?"

He hesitated. "I'm not making any promises. I'll go away now if you really want me to. I'll come back later tonight."

"No! I told you! Not for several days. A week maybe. I'll tell you when I'm ready."

"I'm not letting you alone that long."

"You'll have to. Goodbye. I'm going now." She started to walk away, then turned back to the door again. "Oh Aidan, I do love you. I've got such a lovely gift for you. Be patient."

Then she went through into the kitchen and shut the door firmly. For a moment she considered turning on the radio to drown any noise, but dismissed this thought immediately. She wanted to be alone with her daughter—this was no time for strangers. As she took up one of the tiny tins of food her eyes were wet, whether for joy at her baby's presence or regret at turning Aidan away, even she couldn't have told.

At no time in her life had Carrie suffered such a violent, totally unexpected shock—even her mother's discovery that dreadful day had been half-anticipated. She was paralyzed with the pain of it.

She was standing in front of the kitchen table on which lay the baby stretched out on a towel, naked except for a brief vest and corner of a heavily-soiled nappy that curled over its plump thigh. From the cleft between the child's legs—her daughter!—rose a miniature steeple. A pointed finger. A minute but outrageously stiff, indubitably male, phallus.

She had jumped backward, her flesh crawling. Her first instinct was to get rid of the creature. It didn't matter by what means so long as she was no longer forced to see it, touch it. Touch it! She could as soon have touched a tarantula! The monster's blue eyes looked at her penetratingly. It knew! It knew her shock and was amused.

She turned and ran to the sink. Heaving, fighting down nausea, she tried to regain control, but her head swam with hallucinatory visions. She saw her father's face—distorted, demonic. She saw her mother, frigid with false smile. Hate flowed from them into her, corroded her veins with fire.

For some minutes she dared not look at the child. She feared what she

158

might do. Then she forced herself to turn toward it. She had not imagined it—it bore her father's face. Its eyes, *his* eyes, which tomorrow would look at the forgotten world (but not at her!)—his eyes stared at her, returning her pain.

She advanced to the table. She no longer saw a child lying there, but an amalgam of all that had injured her, not least her own weary burden of hate and guilt. It was evil, what lay there. It was her duty to do away with it.

She stood over the table, her hands stiff at her side. Forced herself to wait. She shut her eyes against what she saw. More time passed. The fight within her was barely conscious. Then the sense of the presence of evil began to pass, leaving her heavy, and cold. She had never felt so tired. But she had won. Whatever dreadful force she had been fighting, she had won.

When at last she dared to open her eyes again the thing was moving— breaking into a variety of shapes. She watched, astonished. Stalks grew from it, undulating like seaweed in water.

Then it began to make noises, noises that at first grated on her nerves but which slowly took on a lighter note. Gradually the sounds grew to resemble the trilling of birds. At the same time the stalks began to turn to flowers, to pink roses, to waving legs and arms and curling fingers, and suddenly there was her child again, all malignancy gone. Resting on the uppermost point of its thigh lay a small worm, collapsed and harmless. The trilling was laughter, a lovely delicate noise that obliterated the trembling inside her and made her, in spite of the aversion not yet faded, smile a little in return.

She stood there for some time, while the blue eyes gradually closed and the chest rose and fell in sleep. Deep sighs broke from her, and once she cried, not for long but long enough to expel some of the regret. Then, arming herself with sheets of tissue, her face tight, she set about cleaning up the mess that filled the child's nappies.

The lack of hard news about Matthew's disappearance meant that by the afternoon of the fourth day the newspapers were scraping the bottom of the barrel for the following morning's editions. The case was about to be relegated to a small paragraph as a filler on the home news page. Only one paper, the most scatological of the populars, had a potential scoop; all that afternoon the editor had been deep in consultation with his lawyers as to whether or not he dared publish a nasty little story offered him by a vengeful *au pair*—a story, complete with photographs, about an incident that had occurred ten days previously.

That morning, ten days ago, Jess had taken a taxi to the British Academy of Film and Television Arts in Piccadilly to see an advance screening of part one of a new television series. Walking up the lush marble staircase (for the sake of her figure) she noticed as always the accumulated dirt at the foot of the bannisters, though it was nothing like Lima Grove—or backstage at most theaters—at least the marble was real, not paper. She noticed such details: she liked her surroundings, people included, to be based on solid foundations. Had she made the wrong choice, she asked herself, not for the first time, in turning down the academic life? But the memory of various dons of her acquaintance made her mouth twitch. Who supposed the stone walls of Academe were any more real than the mock-up sets of the TV studios with their two sides missing and no roof?

Lately it had come to her quite frequently, this shock of surprise at finding herself in the midst of all this stagecraft, *as part of it*. Before, she'd only dipped in and out, a swallow snatching at hovering flies—now she was a full-blown resident, part of the whole peculiar setup.

But her own programs, she defended herself, were different. They were real, not illusion. Or were they? Illusion discussing illusion? Like that philosophy program she'd done? Hoping to pass unnoticed she walked through the bar into the club room to help herself to coffee. There was a fresh jugful steaming on the hotplate. She sat down, thinking about illusion and reality, and whether talk about talk as it came over to viewers—who were seeing only a picture, after all—could be construed as reality under those circumstances. It interested her, promised her several minutes of absorbed argument, when to her annoyance an epicene voice behind her said, "Queen Jess not holding court today?"

Before she could move away a self-indulgently fat man had drawn up a chair beside her and lowered himself into it. "Not exactly your cup of tea—today's offering—is it, ma'am?" he continued, looking partly at her, partly around the room, his pale eyes almost lost in the surrounding layers of bulging skin.

"I won't know until I've seen it," Jess countered. She quickly finished her coffee. "It might turn out to be fascinating."

He looked her up and down critically. "You shouldn't wear black," he

160

said after a pause, "it makes you look like a young widow. Ah! Bill!" he turned to a slender newcomer who had been hovering nearby, "I was saying to Queen Jess here that I didn't think today's offering of tits and bums and slave chains was exactly up her street." He turned back to her, his eyes narrowing. "Or do you go for that stuff? Yes, perhaps you do." He giggled. "What a superb subject, though. What opportunities for lightening the dreary evenings of the weary commuter. The mind boggles! Now if they include those delicious little boys they say can still be had for . . ."

Jess rose, turning her back on him contemptuously. "It's time to go in," she said coldly, and walked away.

As always she was greeted enthusiastically; everyone wanted her good will, even those whom she knew hated her guts. Once, she had lapped it all up. Would it corrupt her too in the end?

In the tiny cinema she chose a seat next to a critic who was notoriously incommunicative. Sinking deep into it she rested her head on the high back. She shut her eyes and thought about David, whom she was meeting as soon as she could get away. She smiled to herself at the contrast between his rigorous goodness and the indulgent luxury of this place, where everything was new and rich and expensive. And comfortable; above all comfortable. David wasn't comfortable. If it weren't for the fact that she never felt guilt, she might almost have said at times he made her feel slightly guilty.

The program began. She opened her eyes to watch the credits— afterward in the bar she didn't want to slip up—though she wouldn't choose to base a program on it if she could avoid it. Or maybe she ought? If only to show she wasn't an intellectual snob? There had been hints her programs were getting heavy—it *was* TV, they'd said, not radio, after all. But it went against the grain—a *documentary* on slavery was OK, but fiction? Wasn't it fundamentally wrong, to make light entertainment out of something so loathsome?

She watched more than she'd intended. To her surprise she found herself caught up by it. It was as slushy as she had expected, but it was gripping slush. In spite of herself its sexual undertones reached through to her and by the end, with its expected cliffhanger of a luscious young thing—half clad and bound—face to face with her new owner, Jess was so aroused she was fearful that when the lights went up her excitement would show on her face.

She need not have worried. She was not alone in her reaction as was

161

obvious from the banter that took place in the bar afterward. The producer of the program came up to her just as she had filled her plate with quiche and salad and asked her what she thought of it. She hesitated and finally compromised. "Gripping, but immoral," she said and refused to be drawn out on whether she was going to use it.

A circle gathered around her. The two stars of the piece joined it, courting her briefly but too full of their own glamour to stay long. Soon they were seduced away by press photographers: gracefully they leaned together over a balcony and smiled rich loving smiles at each other. Free of embarrassment, they turned love on and off as easily as a child flicks a light switch.

Jess watched with amusement—actors always fascinated her—as she half-listened to the heavy jokes about ropes and chains being woman's proper dress. Knowing they were partly aimed at her and her success, she countered them automatically but without much interest. All that feminism stuff was old hat as far as she was concerned; it was difficult to get riled about it anymore unless some obvious case of discrimination was thrust under her nose.

She thought of David; looking at her watch she found it was later than she had realized. Hurriedly she finished her quiche, and, distributing kisses and unmeant congratulations all around, she departed down the stairs, aware of an unusual desire to return home as quickly as possible.

David had been waiting on the doorstep. It had been an unexpectedly cold day for mid March, and as the taxi drew up he was rubbing his hands together to warm them. She waited for his special smile—sometimes she thought it was the most attractive thing about him—then she hurried up to him, house key in her hand, and let him in. Inside the hall they embraced.

"I'm sorry," she apologized. "I've been to a showing at BAFTA. I'm later than I expected."

He rumpled her black hair and smiled again at her to show he didn't mind. "I rang but no one answered. It didn't matter—I was a bit early."

"Yvette must be out. It's her day off. And Iris has taken Emma to lunch with a school friend."

"*School* friend? At three?"

Jess laughed. "Nursery school. They're great buddies. You'd laugh to see

162

them together. Two black heads bent earnestly over their drawings or whatever—they're a very serious-minded pair. They're always working at something. Matthew won't be like that, he never stops giggling. Everyone takes to Matthew."

David smiled at her. "When can I see him? Now?"

She put her arms around him again. "He's with Iris and Emma, silly. There's just the two of us. Isn't that nice?"

He held her tight. Kissing, he was aware of a new kind of passion between them. She pulled herself away. He followed her.

"You're a great organizer, Jess, but you never let me see you with your kids. I can't really imagine you as a mother. It's odd—it doesn't show at all, your motherhood."

"Do you mind that?" She'd hung up her coat and was brushing her hair out, looking at herself critically in the mirror as she spoke. She picked up a loose lash off her cheekbone. "Do you prefer fat motherly women?"

He laughed and ran a fond hand over her waist and bottom. "No, idiot. Let's go to bed." It still shocked him, being so frank. He suppressed a sense of—what, me? With *Jess Bennett*?

She turned and took his hand. "I've been thinking about nothing else this last hour. They were showing the first part of a new series; it was dreadful—nubile slaves, masterful owners, bits of liberalism thrown in—and the language hopelessly anachronistic, of course, but it turned me on, all the same."

"A film in the morning! God, that's decadent." He half meant it and grinned at his own reaction.

"I thought you'd think *me* decadent, to be turned on by trash like that. I'm not sure I'm not rather disgusted with myself."

He looked closely at her. Was she joking? "I don't think you're decadent," he said uncertainly. "*Are* you?"

She took his head between her hands and kissed him deeply, her tongue exploring his mouth. Then she broke away with a laugh. "Let's have a drink. I left halfway through the launching party, so I've hardly started."

Following her into the living room he drifted around while she poured out drinks, picking up various expensive knickknacks and putting them down again.

"I wish you wouldn't do that," she said, trying to keep irritation out of her voice. "I feel you're pricing everything."

"Like an auctioneer, you mean?"

"In a way. I feel you're summing me up, thinking rich bitch, or something like that."

He put down the Icelandic carving he had been examining. "I've just come from one of my cases, right? and I can't help being aware of the difference."

"If I'm rich, I've earned it."

"All of it?"

"No. Not all. I've inherited some. But I've added to it, and that's what matters."

"You're lucky to have something to add to. Most of the people I work with start with zero and end with minus zero."

She put a whisky in his hand. She was thinking about the last scene in the film she had just seen and was not really listening. "There's always sex," she said.

"What's that supposed to mean?"

She shrugged. "It's free, that's what I meant."

They settled close together on the sofa. She leaned against him, letting her arm lie across his legs. She began to stroke his knee, but David was not to be deflected. "At the lower end of the scale sex tends to cost a lot. One way or another."

"And what's *that* supposed to mean?" She stopped stroking him.

"I was thinking about Carrie, a girl I saw this morning. Sex in her case meant sex with her father, and she's still getting over it. The price of that particular bit of sex was very high."

Jess gave in. She drew slightly away from him. "What happened to the father?"

He looked at her rather sternly, wanting to impress her with reality. "He's done five years in prison, his family's broken up, and he lost his job, of course. All the usual trauma. He'll be coming out soon, and God knows what'll happen then."

"And the girl? What was her name—Carrie?"

"She tried to kill herself."

"How terrible!" She meant it. It was awful. But honestly! Hadn't he any idea?

"In a way. But hopeful, too." He looked boyishly pleased: it wasn't often Jess gave him a chance to talk about his work. "Unless it's obvious someone meant to make a thorough job of it, I always see attempted suicide as a form of communication. A rather extreme form, but communication all the same. And in some cases that's a real breakthrough."

"A bit extreme, yes."

He missed her irony and nodded.

"Was it that in Carrie's case?" Jess asked politely. She could feel the sex draining out of her.

"Oh yes. She was making a very definite statement. And a request."

Jess put her drink down and stood up. "How complicated people make life! Is it really necessary to pretend to kill yourself in order to communicate with someone?"

David looked at her sharply. "I didn't say that. There's no pretense about it, not in the kind of case I'm talking about. They have to mean the suicide, or the gesture's meaningless. At least they have to believe they mean it. If they make it a hundred percent safe then it's nothing more than a bit of hysteria. That's another sort of case altogether." He settled back comfortably against the cushions and crossed his legs. "It's interesting, isn't it, how you don't respect someone who pretends to kill himself purely for effect, but you do if someone is desperate enough to take a genuine risk. I suppose it shows they've got courage, and you can't not respect courage."

She looked down at him firmly. "David. We haven't got all that long. If we're going to go to bed together I'd rather not start by talking about incest and suicide and speculations on courage." She smiled at him to take the edge off her words, but she could not remove the irritation from her voice. "I'm going to check the answerphone to see if there's anything important, then let's go upstairs. Help yourself to another drink. A *strong* one."

He saw his incompetence. Her husband Adam would never have made such a mistake. He often wondered about Adam, looking surreptitiously at the photograph on the little chess table behind the sofa, and thought he was exactly the sort of sod women fell for: strong-minded, selfish, irresistible. He jumped up and grabbed Jess's hand. "Leave the phone alone—you can check it later," he said.

She pulled her hand away. "It makes me uneasy not to have the phone working when I'm in the house."

He found himself standing alone with his hand out, empty. He felt

165

unexpectedly angry. "You talk about me! You never relax. You're always doing something. Pouring out drinks, organizing something or someone, never just sitting down doing nothing."

She picked up the phone, then put it down again without listening to it. "Doing nothing's a fine way to get on." She, too, was angry.

"Who has to 'get on' all the time?"

"Well, don't you want to? Make something of your life?"

He looked puzzled. "Haven't I? Do you think my job's so negligible?"

"Being a probation officer's not exactly high flying, is it?"

His fair skin flamed. He'd always thought of himself as having done rather well. "You bloody snob!" he said, stung. "Is that how you've thought of me all this time? What did you think you were doing? Slumming?"

Her own anger burst out. "Don't you talk to me like that! I'm not one of your cases."

He was enraged at this. Did she honestly think that he'd ever dream of speaking like that to one of his clients? Didn't she know him better than that? It came to him she didn't know the first thing about him. Or about other people. And yet there she was, on the box, every week... He spoke out loud what he was thinking, his voice rougher, more Welsh than usual. "You don't know what you're talking about," he said, knowing instinctively she'd hate that. "You haven't the faintest idea how real people live, with your Icelandic carvings, your Turkey carpets, your barrister husband. There you sit every week in your grand leather chair like a high court judge spouting off as though you know it all—but what do you know about real life? Any of my kids know more than you do."

She looked at him flabbergasted. How had she ever let this . . . this moron into her house! "Reality!" She was so shocked at his attack her voice came out almost in a thin scream. "Incest and murder and theft . . . and suicide! You call that reality? Normality? You think that's the kind of life most people live?"

They were standing close together, not more than a foot apart. There was such scorn in her voice he longed to hit her. This upset him even more. "It's closer to reality than the kind of life you live," he said furiously. "You've been sheltered all your life! Everything's been given to you on a plate."

"I've worked for every bloody thing I've got," she shouted, not caring what she sounded like. "Real work. Planning. Organizing. Creating. What

166

do *you* do? You just sit there listening to people nattering on, holding their hands while they kid you they're special. You call that work! It's self-indulgence, that's all it is. Most people do that for nothing."

"Careful," he said. "Watch what you're saying."

She ignored him. "You let them trample all over you! You're just a sponge, soaking it all up. You'd be nothing without them and their problems."

"Then why did you pick me up if I'm such a nobody?"

"Pick *you* up! Christ! You couldn't take your eyes off me!"

"It was you who suggested going to the pub. Not me."

She threw her head back and sneered at him.

"That's exactly like you. Gallant! Full of old-world charm! 'It was you, not me'" she mimicked, taking off his accent. "I'll tell you why I picked you up, if you want to call it that. I wanted somebody to go to bed with, and though you're a bit short in the legs and not all that brilliant, I thought you'd do for a night or two." She was shocked at herself. She hadn't known she could be such a bitch.

He reacted without thought. He lifted his hand and struck her across the face. The raw outline of his hand stayed imprinted in scarlet on her cheek. Jess drew back.

They stared at each other, unable to speak. David, his hand still tingling, looked inward with shame at the pleasure he had felt in giving that blow. He too could behave like that? With violence? He wasn't just a bystander?

Jess herself was less angry than she would have expected. She had asked for it, she knew that. She had spoken outrageously to him. She suddenly thought of the film she had seen earlier and understood she had learned something more about pornography. Thoughtfully she put her hand to her cheek. She looked at him, her anger subsiding.

"I'm sorry," she said in a low voice. "I shouldn't have spoken to you like that. I didn't really mean it. But if you ever do that again . . . !"

He was flushed. He didn't know what to do. He held both his arms out. "Jess, I don't know what to say. I've never hit anyone in my life. I can't understand what . . ." He put his arms around her and she didn't resist. He went on apologizing—she remained silent but let him hold her. Then she put a hand over his lips and said, "It was my fault too. I was in an odd mood. Let's drop it. It was out of character for both of us." She gave him a kiss on the cheek, then took his hand and led him out to the hall. They

167

were silent, each occupied with their own thoughts. David, the apparent aggressor, could not understand why he also felt himself a victim. The only thing he was certain of as he climbed the stairs with Jess was that his feelings at that moment had little to do with romantic love.

Jess's bedroom was as tastefully comfortable as the rest of the house. The extra-large bed was covered with a moss-colored bedspread hand-crocheted in Ireland. Formed of hundreds of medallions shaped like daisies all stitched together, it lay like a vast negative over a white linen sheet, green daisies on a pristine white background. The carpet on the floor was white; thick cream-white wool covered the chairs and dressing stool. White curtains hung at the window, deep hems of green linen meeting the fleece of the carpet. Had it not been for all this white the moss-green walls might have been oppressive: as it was the room was as cool and light as an opening in a pinewood, lit only by the shining brass rails of the bed.

Into this room Jess led David. Jess loved her bedroom. Curled on the bed in her gold bathrobe she felt like a cat, a tiger, a creature of the forest. She felt strong, alone, capable of taking on the world. But today she wished it were different. She would have liked scarlet, and lace, and Tiffany lamps. She sent David into her bathroom and searched among the clothes in her wardrobe until she found what she was looking for, a red lacy peignoir that Adam had once bought her for a Christmas present.

"Don't come out until I call you," she shouted to David. She was aware that if she weren't slightly drunk—downstairs she'd given herself a really large whisky on top of the wine—she'd never have the nerve to do what she was going to do. Rapidly she searched through her chest of drawers for some gilt chains bought a decade ago when chain belts were fashionable. It took only a few seconds more to unwrap a couple of luggage straps from a suitcase stored on top of the cupboard. But once the straps were in her hand she was frightened. She! What the hell was she doing? In a moment of revulsion she flung them down on the floor. She laid her hand against her face where he'd hit it. That was the sort of thing you got when you behaved like that. She recalled her anger and her pleasure. Yes, pleasure. Had she been leading up to that all along?

She'd made him do it. She'd gone on until he'd hit her.

It was incredible. Her!

She went to the bed and looked at it thoughtfully. Then with a quick decisive movement she pulled off the green daisy-spread.

David, washed and waiting naked in the bathroom, was trying not to think. Later, he knew, there would be a time of self-castigation. Right now he could not be himself. What had happened still left him reeling. He forgot her words, remembered her eyes. In this rich bathroom, scented and full of opalescent glass, he imagined himself an aristocrat, a voluptuary with no conscience—only desire. He felt guilt, of course, but for once relished it. The bathroom, which normally he disliked, today seemed exactly right: he imagined what she might be doing that was taking her so long. When at last she called him he flung open the door and strode forward fully armed, lance blatantly upstanding.

Until he saw her. Then he stopped, momentarily winded. On the bed in front of him Jess the unconquerable lay outstretched, her wrists tethered by golden chains to the rails at the head of the bed, her legs stretched apart and tied by leather straps to the foot. Rumpled around her and half pushed aside as though someone had already attacked it lay a transparent red lacy thing. On the plumped-up white pillow her long black hair lay spread out, though when she saw him staring she turned her face away and shook her hair over it. In embarrassment? Stagecraft?

David looked; hesitated; called on his Welsh forebears to protect him from the dreadful perversion of it. But before they could answer he had jumped at her with a shout that echoed through the house, reaching up to the upper floor where the *au pair* Yvette lay brooding on the dreariness of her present life.

They'd known nothing like it before, either of them. They were out of themselves, mind completely absent. Imagining themselves alone in the house they moaned, bit, cried out and struggled. They did things inconceivable to their normal selves. "Tie me!" Jess cried, as the straps at her feet came loose, and waited feverishly while (overcoming a vision of weeping walls and manacled prisoners) David bound her fast to the rails. As he plunged into her the hairs on his body prickled with aggression. He had thoughts of rape and conquest and joined in spirit the looting armies of history. She struggled and fought him, closed her teeth on whatever she could reach, kneed him (but with caution), and scratched, raising weals colored here and there with slowly seeping spots of blood. He tore at her nipples and bit her belly, though not so deep as to break the flesh. On the floor lay the remnants of the peignoir, ripped across its lacy seams (an accident but it had thrilled them both—no habitual slut or Don Juan could have felt their shocked pleasure at the ritual shredding of that nominal garment).

They fought a genuine battle, for all it was make-believe (it was her own handgrip that tethered her to the gilt chains wrapped round the bedhead). She could never have permitted it with Adam—it would have been too dangerous: one slip on her part and he would have assumed dominance for life. The indulgence was only possible with a stranger, a stranger weaker than herself, but one in whom the enemy was strong.

"Ah!" she cried as she succumbed to the pain of his violence, arching her back against his thrust, and for a moment accepted this pain—her mind temporarily awakened—as the price demanded of women for existence. Then,"*I accept only on my terms!*" she swore in grief, and thought she heard a mocking laugh.

For a moment she nearly dried. Almost pushed him off. He sensed it and became gentle. Knelt and kissed her, licked her gently, parting her hair with delicate fingers. She had felt angry, but now she remembered herself as a girl, leaping and laughing in the garden, skipping rope tied around her waist, long black hair tethered in a pony tail flying behind her. A sense of ineffable happiness flowed through her, and with it came a long shuddering of joy. She pulled David down in gratitude, and it was like that—David oblivious in his own moment of release and Jess, head raised, with hands still wrapped in chains and feet strapped in buckled leather—that Yvette caught them within the frame of her camera, preserved them in their moment of stasis like a pair of rare butterflies pinned out for display.

Yvette was an unpleasant girl. Even she knew it, which didn't make her any more pleasant.

Jess had known the moment she set eyes on her it wouldn't work out. The doorbell had rung, and there on the steps was a tall, broad man, fair-skinned like a Swede, prosperous in expensive cream Burberry and fine shoes, blond hair cut short, smelling faintly of some expensive cologne. From the taxi outside emerged two equally tall women, one young, one middle-aged. The man briefly announced his name, picked up the trunk at his feet as though it were a paper bag and advanced on Jess obviously expecting her to get out of his way. It was only then that Jess realized who they were. She looked quickly at the girl, and saw down-turned lips, narrow unsmiling eyes, and a broad jaw. Her mother walking up the steps behind her bore the same features, and, though the mouth moved in a luke-warm social smile, the set of the face clearly foretold her daughter's future appearance. Jess pressed herself against the wall to let the man pass, then amused herself letting him wait before she told him in her coolest, most superior voice to take the trunk up to the attic.

The battle continued later in the living-room where Jess felt obliged to offer the Swiss family drinks. It was an unusual occasion—no other *au pair* had ever turned up with parental escort—and she was enjoying it. It was a nuisance the girl was so obviously hopeless, but it intrigued her, this sudden intimacy into which these three prosperous strangers and herself were thrust. The mother, having examined the furniture and status of the family, relaxed a little while the father settled down to interview Jess and satisfy himself that the house was a moral, properly run one and that his daughter would be carefully chaperoned. During all this Yvette said not a word, just sat there mouth turned down looking vaguely out of the window as though it all had nothing to do with her.

As far as she was concerned it hadn't. She had as little intention of remaining in the house as Jess had of letting her stay. She was about to escape the parental prison. The rest had nothing to do with her. Within a month, at most, she'd be off.

Jess had made a better guess at the timing, for the situation exploded within a fortnight. Though even Jess had not anticipated the nature of the explosion.

During those two weeks it was as if the house were filled with gray dust. The air was infected with Yvette's discontent. The Bennetts had always felt obliged to eat breakfast and lunch with their *au pairs* whenever they were at home, and even Adam, usually too absorbed in his work to take much notice but not adverse to young female company with his bacon and coffee, said she ruined his appetite. Thank God, he had said more than once, they ate dinner alone, or he'd become a shadow.

Not eating dinner with the family was one of Yvette's interior complaints. She knew it was impossible—their hours were too irregular—but she persisted in seeing it as a personal insult. A worse insult was doing the housework although that was what she had come for. She, product of an expensive school, with the promise of her own car if she returned home with fluent English, having to stack the washing machine and vacuum the stairs while that silly *dummkopf*, Iris, half-witted peasant, walked out like

171

a *grosse Dame* with the children, refusing even to touch a duster! Her only relief was being unpleasant to the twice-weekly char, an old woman who came in to scrub the floors and clean the lavatories.

By the end of a fortnight Yvette was heavy-eyed with hatred. She had no friends and ignored Jess's offers of introductions to other *au pairs*. Jess had made it clear she did not consider it part of her duty to chaperone a girl of twenty, but apart from mooching around the coffee bars of Hampstead there was nothing to do anyway. London itself Yvette thought a dirty, disgusting city, full of derelict buildings and impertinent foreigners. Everywhere she went men of every color tried to pick her up, so on her days off she mostly stayed in bed. Sometimes if the weather was fine she took her camera, an expensive one equipped with all the refinements Swiss francs could buy, and photographed odd things that caught her eye. She had a talent for catching bizarre moments, mostly unpleasant—a dog peeing against a placard saying Salvation is Due; an old man spitting phlegm; a child surreptitiously pinching her baby sister. She had hopes one day of turning professional: nothing else would have made her bother with learning English. She despised her father for making her work her way—convinced herself his real reason was to make her suffer—though *he* claimed it was because close contact with a family was the best way to learn. The *bastard,* the *rotten selfish bastard* she used to say to herself, and she consoled herself by imagining photographing him in humiliating poses.

Photographing Jess and David was no problem to her, technical or ethical. She was about to leave the house that afternoon with her camera when, hearing them—who could not? it was a wonder the whole street wasn't peering through the windows, the racket they were making—she stopped to watch through the half-open door for a while. At the right moment she merely held up her camera and flash! click! click!

And out of the house to safety. Out before David had time even to fully realize what had happened and Jess to go white. Out into the decaying street of eighteenth-century houses that in any decent country would have been pulled down years ago and replaced with good new buildings. Ah! she thought to herself in hate, I detest the English with their past and their hypocrisy and their dirt. I detest every one of them. And stormed into the cemetery at the bottom of the road where she photographed fallen gravestones and littered corners filled with candy wrappings and condoms until she ran out of film.

DAY 5

It is a strange seeking that makes even the mildest among us scan the morning's paper as it drops through the letter box or hurry to switch on the TV so as not to miss the day's headlines. What news are we all waiting for? Annihilation? Christ reborn? Martians landed at last? All those editors all over the globe scratching their heads struggling in hundreds of different languages to assuage our yearning, and mostly coming up, out of necessity, with nothing but dross!

On Day 5 of the Bennett drama, the world was comparatively quiet apart from the usual trouble spots, and even there nothing new was happening. Variations on the bomb circled peacefully over our heads, piloted by men doubtless thinking of their income tax bills or that evening's date. The men owning the sacred fingers that alone are permitted access to the button were mostly absorbed in modest thoughts about their votes, their rivals, their family problems, their peptic ulcers.

All, even the most eminent, need a dash of the trivial, the personal, in their daily news. But the Bennett case was proving a wash-out. In most papers, it had been moved to the inside pages, stuck among the minor reports of pools wins, rapes, and court cases. The language used was no longer dramatic: even the populars had dropped emotive words like "distraught," "agonized," "tormented," "heartbreak," and now stuck to straight reportage. A couple of papers contented themselves with print-

ing identikit pictures (different), one showing a desperado with black staring eyes, stubble and crooked mouth, the other a pretty, anonymous-looking girl of twelve, both pictures compiled from information resulting from the reconstruction scene. The girl was the most promising, it seemed, and police were visiting suitable schools in nearby areas. "Was there an empty place in your class that afternoon?" they asked the excited schoolgirls. "Have you noticed anyone acting strangely lately?" In one school a girl (absent that fatal afternoon and known to be a bit odd) fainted, to the pleasure of everyone present, not least the hopeful policeman.

Two papers, the most venerable and the most junior, printed personal appeals to the baby snatcher to return the child, the former an appeal from a woman who had stolen an infant several years earlier and had served two years in prison for her offense.

("Telephone a friend," she begged, bravely giving her phone number); the second paper printed a request from the Inspector's wife for the snatcher to consider Jess Bennett's feelings and to leave the child in a church ("God will forgive you," she predicted confidently).

The most socially-concerned tabloid was the only paper to restore Matthew to the front page, on which it offered £1,000 reward for information leading to his recovery. This resulted in a great deal of fruitless work for the police, but it was well meant.

Only one newspaper had something positive to say, and that was not about Matthew but about his parents. For the titillation of thousands, Adam's chances of taking silk that year and for several years to come were destroyed. For there, right across the middle pages, was a photograph of Fanny, face half-covered with one hand, looking unattractive and dumpy, hurrying into her flat. The story was carefully circumspect, reporting that the Bennett marriage had broken up and before Matthew's disappearance Adam had been living with Fanny.

Husband and wife read and reread the report, Adam searching in vain for a careless word, a phrase that would allow him to get them for libel. Never had he felt so intensely angry. Little was said about Jess, but it seemed to her that what they did say was peculiarly ambiguous.

Did they know? They must know. Someone knew. Suddenly she was as convinced of that as surely as though she had been there when Yvette arrived at the editor's office with the photographs. She almost wished *they had come right out with it and said it! For they would. If not today, then tomorrow.*

She drew in her breath. Tomorrow was Sunday. There was less restraint on the Lord's Day, for should not sinners be held up for all to see? The most notorious of the Sunday papers would find a way to print it: were not their lawyers well-practiced in what could and what could not be safely revealed?

Sitting next to her was one of the finest barristers in the country: how bitter it was that he was the sole lawyer whose opinion it was impossible for her to seek.

CARRIE sat contemplating Matthew's phallus. It was Thursday, two full days since she had brought him home. Already she had grown accustomed to his sex. Her face was peaceful, bore the contented look to be seen on the face of any animal mother—cat, ape, sow—after full tits are emptied and the infant temporarily satiated.

A bright sun shone through the pseudo-Georgian windowpanes of her little flat, spotlighted both the baby on the rug at her feet and her right hand, which rested lightly on her knee. It lay unclenched and open, fingers only slightly curved inward, the hand of a totally relaxed person. In the same beam of light, motes of dust slowly floated upward, disappearing again as the gilt fire left them. A tree outside, stirred once in a while by a barely perceptible breeze, caused occasional shadows to flicker across Matthew's face. Sleepily he reached out to the shadows and tried to catch them with his open hands. A robin perched on a branch close to the window endlessly sang its complicated song, breaking now and again into Carrie's drifting consciousness, beauty added to beauty.

An outsider, unaware of Carrie's circumstances, could hardly fail to have been touched by the archetypal scene of maternal bliss. The shared blond curls, the clear blue eyes, the obvious contentment between the two, spoke clearly of their relationship. Carrie, hot in Aidan's blue sweater, which she had worn continuously day and night since the day she had turned him out, had slipped off her socks and shoes and rolled up her jeans. Sometimes she gently stretched out a bare toe and poked the baby, who giggled back at her and waved its arms in pleasure. He lay on his back. When he tried to roll over, she did not help him, for on his right buttock there was a small birthmark, not more than an inch across, shaped like a plump lemon.

She couldn't help feeling slightly superstitious about it, as though some foreboding hand had touched him at birth. But the mild distaste she felt for the flaw was forgotten in the quiet happiness that had been her rarely interrupted emotion for most of this day. Soon, she had thought earlier, she would be able to kiss the mark: this was what love was, loving the

177

imperfections along with the rest. Lucky baby, she had thought sadly, to be so loved. Or had her mother loved her like that once, when she was small, and had not yet become offensive?

She was surprised at how easily she could push that reflection away and wondered if it was permanent, this new feeling of detachment from her past. Had it been necessary to make a new attachment—this insoluble bond with her own child—before she could break the tie with her mother? Was it always like that, for everyone?

She bent and gathered Matthew up into her arms, and again there was an answering contraction in her womb linking the two of them as in the days when she used to spread her hands over her belly, delicately seeking as a water diviner seeks.

Now, watching the afternoon sun flickering over his body, she wondered what his thoughts were. She had no philosophical doubts as to whether, without language, he was capable of thinking, for it was clear to her from the changing expressions on his face—as he puzzled about the refusal of the shadows to submit to his grasp, or turned to search for the source of noise as a clock chimed, or suddenly looked up at her with a strangely curious gaze—that some kind of thought processes were taking place in his brain. Sometimes he frowned, not with bellyache but with the frown a thinking man has when cogitating some problem. Sometimes some interior perception caused delight to flash over his face, or his eyes would go blank in a momentary concentration on physical matters.

For hours she sat watching this gradual entry of a new human brain into the world. She saw in him a trailing of immortality and quoted Wordsworth to herself.

While he drank from his bottle she caressed the fine silk that covered his scalp and amused herself by gently stretching out the tight curls and letting them go again. Feeding him, she would hold the child with his head resting on her left arm—it seemed impossible for her to hold him any other way—and always he pressed the back of his head firmly down into the crook of her arm while staring thoughtfully up at her as he sucked. From birth an amenable baby, at seven months he was still prepared to take life as it came. He had inherited all the Bennett assurance and, as his father had before him, smiled so confidently at the world it could rarely bring itself to disillusion him. It never occurred to Carrie to be surprised at Matthew's constant sunniness. This is how she imagined all babies were, the dream children of advertisements. That a child of hers and Aidan's

178

would be born reaching out with searching arms, anxiety never far away, was a probability she did not consider.

Her present peace had not been easily won. But gradually she had grown accustomed to washing his dubious parts, patting them dry, powdering them, and the necessary tenderness of these acts sponged away the remaining repugnance and fear. Sometimes his tiny phallus would stiffen and rise. Then she would search his face, but his expression did not alter: he seemed quite unaware, unbothered. Was this it then, the unpredictability of this sleepless little organ, this untamed remnant of a wilder state that had appalled her mother so, given as she was to order, and control, a neat and tidy life? What could ever be neat and tidy about this little animal that leaped around even while its owner dozed?

And her own desires? Had they been any less wild before her mother had trained her so effectively that now she could no more touch her own parts with her bare fingers than she could go dancing naked down the street? Could not even face her periods without disgust. Could not fuck without getting drunk.

But could love. That at least had survived. She loved the baby. She loved Aidan. At the thought of Aidan her heart jumped inside her, and she wrapped her arms around herself with longing for him. She hadn't known it was possible to want to be with someone so intensely, to feel such violent need to hold and be held. Yesterday, the day after she had brought home the baby, she had seen Aidan. She had crept out of the flat late in the afternoon to do some shopping, leaving the baby asleep in his pram. She had gone out the back way, hoping not to be observed by anyone, and she was glad she had been cautious when she returned because, as she came up the road, she saw Aidan squatting on the steps outside the building, huddled in his army surplus greatcoat, head sunk between his hands. It had been drizzling on and off all afternoon, a fine gentle rain not much heavier than mist, and Aidan's gray-blue coat looked as though wet spider's webs had been draped all over it. Drops of rain quivered on his hair and ran down his cheeks making him look as though he had been crying. He had obviously been there a long time, seemed pressed permanently against the door. His eyes were closed, knuckles pressed white against his cheeks, and he appeared to be asleep. It was terrible for her to leave him there like that, wet and desolate. She stopped not more than a dozen yards from him, her shopping clutched in her hands, and had he opened his eyes at that moment she would have run to him regardless of

179

the consequences, but he did not. He shifted his position slightly, as though aware at some level of her presence, but fatigue had temporarily obliterated the world for him. Carrie looked with longing, then somehow found the strength to leave, ran around to the service entrance at the back of the flats and up the stairs, just as though part of her was not desperate for him to catch up with her.

It was true. Aidan was totally exhausted. Since he had left Carrie after she refused to let him in to the flat on Tuesday afternoon, he had not been to bed. At first he had not known what to do with himself. His immediate reaction was to go around to David's and fetch him. He was half way to the probation office when he changed his mind and went instead into a café where he sat drinking coffee for hours. He even bought a packet of cigarettes, something he hadn't done for a couple of years, and smoked the lot, one after the other. When the café closed he went home to his attic but couldn't stand being there alone and went out again, walking the streets until dawn came. Then he returned to Carrie's flat. He crept up the stairs, but the door was locked; so he propped himself against it and slept fitfully for an hour or two until a neighbor from the apartment above passed and woke him. He knocked on Carrie's door, but she only told him to go away, that she was fine, he was to be good and leave her alone for a few days. He was too tired to argue, but he couldn't bring himself to leave her completely, so he went downstairs and waited outside on the steps for her, assuming that at some time during the day she would come out to do some shopping.

He didn't mind that people stared at him. By the afternoon one of the old women inhabitants of the flats had gone so far as to complain to the police about him, and they sent a young constable of Aidan's age to investigate. At first he had been brusque, seeing Aidan's old greatcoat and the stubble on his chin. But hearing his voice and observing his courteous manner (Aidan was too tired to be aggravating) his attitude changed. Back at the station he reported the man seemed to be some hippy type meditating or something—harmless, in his opinion. When he'd asked him to move on, he'd said he was waiting for someone.

"Who—God?" joked one of the policemen, and they all laughed.

All Wednesday Aidan went over and over in his mind what had happened. He could make no sense of it. He told himself he should have gone to see David immediately, as he had started out to do yesterday. But

180

the argument that had prevented him was as powerful today as then. It was a straightforward question of trust. "Trust me," she had said. He hadn't promised anything, he had carefully chosen not to promise her anything, even when she had asked him to. But then she had said, "Trust me. I promise I'm not going to do anything silly." And how could he go and get David after that when she'd asked him not to? It would be a clear statement on his part that he didn't trust her, that he didn't believe her own promise that she wouldn't do anything stupid.

They had to trust each other, or it was nothing, their love, he told himself. He'd never felt like that about anyone before, never felt this extraordinary amalgamation with another person. Didn't the bond between them mean that there was no choice but to trust?

But what if the strain on her had been too much? What if she were cracking up? Then for her sake shouldn't he do something, and do it quickly? Before it was too late?

At that thought he had run up the stairs again, but instead of hammering on the door as he had first intended he put his ear against it and listened. He could just hear her. She seemed to be talking to herself, making cooing gentle noises, and suddenly he realized that when, yesterday, he had thought she was talking to someone she had in fact only been talking to their baby. Crazy kid, he said to himself, talking to a fetus! but somehow it seemed such a normal act, a happy act, that he smiled, remembering how he himself had often laid his mouth on her belly and whispered to the child inside. He had not wanted to interrupt and crept back down again and resumed his place on the steps outside. He thought fondly about their child for a while, then suddenly panicked, fearing for it, and rushing up the stairs hammered on the door—Jesus Christ, she had no right . . . ! But she ignored him, though he heard her moving about in the kitchen, singing a little song to herself that sounded to him brave, defiant, as though she were telling him she was all right and he shouldn't worry.

By now it was late afternoon, and the light was fading from the sky. He returned again to his post at the top of the steps, and propped his head on his clenched hands. There was a fine drizzle but he ignored it. He was now losing hope that she would come out, and it was becoming clear to him he had to do something, take some action. Trust or no trust, what she was doing wasn't normal. He had to face it. Normal people didn't lock themselves up like that and refuse to come out. But when he thought for a while about normality he came to the conclusion that probably it didn't exist at all except as a useful sociological concept.

Sometimes he dozed and then would wake with a start. Carrie was on his mind all the time. Once, waking, he saw with absolute clarity that his love for her had passed beyond any option on his part. That he could no more stop loving her than he could stop breathing. Whatever she did. He remembered how they had quarreled that day because he wouldn't say he loved her, had insisted that love was a con and only self-love existed. Now he looked with amazement at the self he had been then and wondered what it was about Carrie that had made such a change in him.

For a while he sat lost in contemplation of love. When darkness fell he made a last attempt to persuade her to open the door, but she ignored him, though he thought he heard footsteps creeping to the door. Was she there, listening? Quietly, so the neighbors shouldn't hear, he begged her to open up, but there was no answer, and he was not certain he hadn't imagined the footsteps. Then he left and went home to his attic. He was too distressed to eat and sat huddled up in his damp greatcoat, only stirring to make himself coffee.

The next morning, Thursday, he went straight to David's office. David's head was still full of meeting Adam the previous night and worry for Jess. His first action on arriving at the office had been to ring the Inspector, but there was still no news of Matthew. Faced with such an immediate anxiety he found it difficult to take very seriously Aidan's concern for Carrie.

"I saw her only the day before yesterday," David said, picking up his mail which he had not yet had a chance to look through. He didn't want to discourage Aidan from caring—it was an excellent sign that he should be taking action about someone else, moving beyond his old absorption in himself—but he had to be in court in an hour, and there was the mail and several phone calls and, oh god, half a dozen other things to do first. And all he could think about was Jess, racking his brains to see what he could do to help. Surely there was *something,* in his position? "And she was all right then," he added abstractedly. "Very cheerful, in fact."

"Something's wrong," Aidan insisted stubbornly. "We've been living together, remember? Now she's locked me out. She wouldn't do a thing like that for no reason at all."

David put down his letters and looked up at Aidan. He tried to

182

concentrate. "Of course not. But she's pregnant. Women do funny things when they're pregnant."

"Exactly."

"Well, yes. I agree, it's odd. And of course her father's coming out any minute now." He sighed. "No, you're right," he said, managing the switch at last. "We must do something. She mustn't be left alone." He opened his diary, and pulled a face. "Damn. I forgot this afternoon was full up too. It's impossible to see her today unless you think it's really urgent. I'd have to put several people off."

Aidan looked dubious. "Well, I suppose it's not that urgent. Her voice sounded all right when she talked to me. But it's not a normal thing to do, is it, to lock someone out like that? It's not as though we'd quarreled."

"I'd go tonight, but I've promised to see a family I'm working with. The father's run away, the daughter's just gone on the streets, and the mother's been beaten up by her lover." He laughed ironically. "At times I feel like chucking in the sponge. Some families are so bloody hopeless I'm not even sure I make the slightest bit of difference. Overall, I mean." He flipped the page over. "First thing tomorrow's all right. Do you think that'll be OK? I could put off seeing this family tonight if you really think . . ."

Aidan hesitated, then shook his head. "No, leave it until tomorrow. I'll go around again this morning and try to see her. If I think something's badly wrong, I'll call you."

Now he had cleared himself, David wondered if somehow he could find time after all. "Are you sure?"

"Of course I'm not sure," Aidan snapped. "I wouldn't be here if I were sure."

David turned back to his diary and ran his fingers over the appointments again. He had to ring Jess too, he was thinking, and sighed. Aidan, seeing the look on his face, felt almost sorry for him. What a life! "Don't worry," he said, thinking perhaps he was making too much fuss. "She'll probably be all right. I'll go over there now and check." He stood up and buttoned up his coat. "If she lets me in I'll ring you. Otherwise I'll see you at her place about nine tomorrow morning. OK?"

David nodded, looking relieved. If Carrie had been quite alone, he would have got to her somehow, but if Aidan was going to be there he couldn't see what could go wrong. Surely she'd let him in today, anyway. The boy had probably said something to upset her but didn't know it, that was all. He stood up and saw Aidan to the door, putting a friendly arm around his shoulders. "Tomorrow, then," he said, and opening the door beckoned to the first of the two clients who were waiting outside for him.

That day it was impossible for David to meet Jess—he couldn't even go to see her late at night as Adam would be there—but they managed to talk on the phone. She told him her new fears about Yvette; until now she had kept them to herself. David, who like her had lived in dread of exposure the first couple of weeks after Yvette caught them out, had eventually decided the girl wasn't going to do anything and had successfully put her out of his mind. He turned cold whenever he thought of her, but that was very rarely now—he had no time to brood and was too tired at night to do anything except fall asleep. He listened to Jess with growing horror.

"You don't honestly think she'd tell the police?" he asked.

"I don't know. She might. If she's still in England she's bound to read in the papers that the police want to see her. She'll go along just to clear herself. But once she's talking to them, if they ask her about me, don't you think she'll jump at the chance? Or . . . what really frightens me . . ." She couldn't say it.

"What? What is it? Are you crying? Jess, I've got to see you somehow. You need me."

There was a moment's pause, then her voice came over stronger. "No, no. I'm all right. What frightens me . . . is that she'll go to the papers with the pictures and sell them."

"Christ!" He was scarlet. "Christ!"

Neither said anything for a while. Then, "Do you think she might?" he asked, knowing the answer already.

"She might. That bitch is capable of anything."

"We've got to stop her."

"How? We don't even know where she lives. There's no way except to go to all the newspaper offices and say, please have you got any scandalous pictures of me and do be darlings and don't publish. That would really help, wouldn't it!"

"There must be something we can do."

"Well, if you can think of something, I can't. The only hope is that the pictures were useless—she can't have taken more than two in that time. Though she's a good photographer—she showed me some of her stuff the first day she was here, and she's talented, no doubt of it."

"I've an idea." He sounded more hopeful. "She'd probably go to the police first to clear herself, as you say. So I'll ask the Inspector to let me know if he hears from her. I'll cook up some excuse—there's no reason he'd suspect me of anything. Then I'll go and see her."

"Don't be mad. Even if you managed to track her down, the minute you involved yourself she'll know who you are. At the moment she's no idea. And no one is going to recognize you from the back of your head. At least *you're* safe. There's no point in you going down with me if you don't have to."

"Jess, I'm not thinking about myself. I'll do anything I can to help, even if it means . . ." He stopped. It was true. What was the point in risking his own career if it wouldn't help Jess? "I'm sorry," he said miserably. "I suppose you're right. It would be pointless." The minute he'd said it he so disliked himself he was forced to protest. "But I couldn't just stand by and keep quiet. How could I!"

"What good would it do? You'd lose your job straight away. They couldn't possibly keep you on after that sort of exposure. And how would that help me?" She paused, then added—she'd thought of it already—"It would be even worse for me if people knew who you were. It'll be bad enough if it comes out anyway, but to have been doing it with a *probation officer*! It would be the biggest joke in years." She had been in control of herself until then, but now she began to cry. "Oh David," she sobbed, "what a bloody, bloody mess! I feel so ashamed of myself. Not at what we actually did—that was nothing, nothing at all—but that such a sordid, *stupid* thing should be on my mind when nothing in the world should matter except Matthew . . ." She couldn't go on.

"I'm coming around. I've got to see you." He was already working out how he could arrange it.

"No. You can't—they're doing the reconstruction today." She pulled herself together. "And Adam may turn up at any time. He mustn't know anything about us if we can possibly avoid it. I've got to go now, anyway. I'll be all right. Don't worry. I've just been letting my imagination run away, that's all. It's not likely that even Yvette would do a thing like that. And if she did I don't think any paper would dare publish it." She paused, then said in a voice he had not heard before. "Listen, I really must go. Perhaps we can meet tomorrow. Ring me, anyway, will you? Just speaking to you helps."

He was aware it was the first time she had ever openly asked him to do anything for her. It confirmed his love for her, though the thought of the photographs destroyed any pleasure in it. When he put down the phone, he buried his head in his hands. He was seeing himself as front page news. How had he got mixed up in this? He knew it was craven of him, but he wished with all his heart he had never met Jess. This kind of life was not for him. To be involved with mess at second hand, through his clients, was one thing: to be involved with it personally was another.

Friday morning David kept his word. As soon as he saw Aidan's face he knew Carrie had not let him in the day before. They didn't say much but went straight upstairs to Carrie's flat.

Carrie had been half-expecting this to happen. She felt a little disappointed that Aidan had not trusted her, but she saw why. She would probably have done the same thing herself if she had been in his position. After all, how could he understand the truth of it? She let them bang on the door for a couple of minutes before she made up her mind what to do, then she turned on the radio in the living room where the baby was lying asleep. It was the first time she had switched it on since she brought him home. Then she went to the front door and opened it. With the chain on, it would not open more than three or four inches.

Aidan, who had tensed to throw himself at the door and force it open, saw the chain and held himself back. He stared at Carrie through the crack and instantly found it impossible to believe what was happening. She looked so normal. Happier, in fact, than he had seen her for several weeks.

It was David who spoke to Carrie first. He spoke soothingly, said he was a bit worried about her not coming to group and shutting Aidan out. Was it because of her father? Glowing, Carrie shook her head. No, she said, no, she was coming to terms with all that. All she asked was to be left alone for another day or two, then she promised she would let Aidan in again. She looked so fondly at Aidan, seemed so contented, that both men were puzzled rather than reassured. But she didn't seem to be in any kind of danger. She was properly dressed, the radio was playing, and as far as they could see the flat was clean and tidy. Nothing at all was out of the ordinary, except that it was clear she had no intention of letting them in.

Aidan found himself unable to talk in front of David. There was a lot he wanted to say to her, but the probation officer's presence inhibited him. He did once plead briefly with her, but she smiled so sweetly at him, shook her head so firmly, that he said nothing after that except to ask her to promise to let him in in a day or two. Happily she promised, then, smiling again at them both, firmly shut the door.

David and Aidan stood silently outside, looking at each other. Then David said that as far as he could see she was all right—she was a reserved sort of girl, and really it was quite understandable that she should want to be alone for a while. "Tomorrow's Saturday," he said, "I'm due in Northampton to give a lecture, but I'm coming back by the last train. If she hasn't let you in by then, give me a ring Sunday morning, and perhaps we can come back and have another try."

What could Aidan do but agree? To break down the door, a heavy one, would be extremely difficult, especially with the chain on, and what excuse did he have? It was her flat, after all, and she was an adult. No one could say she looked mad or anything like that. So they went down the stairs together. Aidan, after parting from David, went off to the public library for the rest of the morning for the sake of having something to do, though he never actually focused on a single word.

Next day, Saturday, he returned to her flat once more, knowing already she would not let him in. Sometimes rage at being treated like this surfaced, but love and anxiety for her always overcame his anger. Tomorrow, he said to himself when she did not answer his knocking, tomorrow is the last time I'll accept this. After that, somehow I'll break in, even if I get arrested for it.

The taxi drivers used by the BBC tend to be more than usually garrulous. They know all the names, have seen all the faces, and are full of stories of what the great said to them, and of what they said to the great. As they fetch and carry to the television studios or to Broadcasting House they entertain their current fares with stories of previous passengers, all well-known. Of their ordinary run-of-the-mill passengers never a word is said. Two sets of opinions only seem to interest them: those of the celebrities whose bottoms have graced the leather in their own back seats, and their own. They speak with authority: have they not expressed these same opinions to the Minister of this, the Chairman of that, to Lord whoever, as well as to more media "personalities" than they can remember—and rarely been spurned?

The thin nervous face of the taxi driver waiting to collect Jess looked familiar, and her heart sank. Tonight she did not want to speak to anyone, but it was obvious from the man's eagerness as he jumped out and opened the back door for her than he was alight with the prospect of communication.

"The wife and I were real sorry to hear about your little boy," he said in a concerned voice. As he drove away he went on talking. "That was terrible bad luck, that was. Have they come up with anything yet? ... Bloody fool!" he swore as a car shot the lights in front of him, "if he ends up a bowl of pulp I shall laugh." He reached back with his left hand and pushed wide open the sliding glass window separating him from Jess which she had surreptitiously half-closed. "No news yet then?"

Jess sighed and said no. She sat back and gave in to the flow. Usually she quite enjoyed chatting with the taxi drivers: a couple of weeks ago she'd even played with the idea of getting together a panel of them and letting them take over her own program for one evening. Vox populi let loose—they could hardly call that too intellectual. She'd discussed it with her producer, but he'd said—supposing it really works, takes off? Got moved to a Saturday night slot, God forbid, with panels of cleaning women, coal miners, bus drivers? Cartoons, canned laughter, the lot. It occurred to her then—but she didn't say it openly to him—what if the fever for that kind of success seized her? What price her integrity if bombarded long enough with leaping viewing figures? Mightn't she learn to beam and simper and welcome trash with the same sincerity she now welcomed the Warden of All Souls? She and the producer had looked at each other, and she knew the same thought had crossed his mind. They both shook their heads, but there had been a thoughtful look in their eyes.

Now, looking at the shaven back of the taxi driver's neck, she tried to think about work, but her mind refused to respond. She felt sick. She dredged up a deep sigh. And another. The driver talked on and politely she mumbled some reply, but she was not listening to him. She took out a hand-mirror and looked at herself. She looked awful—bags under her eyes, hair in a mess, skin gray. She shut her eyes and rested her head against the seat.

She tried to make her mind go blank, but there were too many things to think about, each worse than the other. Yet a month ago everyone had envied her.

That too! Not only Adam, and Matthew, and Yvette, but that too! To be pitied! What strength was left if pride was gone?

Someone no one wanted to be. Jess-of-no-account. *Poor old Jess.*

She shrank. All those years of work. Went on shrinking, backbone dissolving. Felt herself floating, a small wet blob floating on other people's pity. Tried to look inside herself for some trace of self and found nothing. Zooming headfirst into emptiness, her head spun with growing doubt that she existed—until nausea forced it down between her knees.

Sparks of color darting behind her closed lids, she breathed in the stench of crushed cigarettes. She retched, but only brought up the soured remnants of a brandy quickly swallowed before leaving the studios for home.

It was the taxi driver who rescued her. "You all right?" he called through the open window.

She forced herself back upright—some pride still, then, thank God—and said, "Dropped my lipstick, that's all." He shot her a quick glance in his mirror and went on talking.

At first she tried to listen, to take her mind off herself.

"I mean it," the man said, looking at her again in his driving mirror. "I don't intend any disrespect, you understand, but the truth is I don't think God meant women to take life that seriously. It don't feel right, having women staring at you from the box, going on about the wrongs of the world."

"What's God got to do with it?" she asked icily.

He shrugged his shoulders. "I only meant it as a figure of speech, as you might say. Women ought to be decorative, nice to look at—that's what it's all about. At least, that's what *I* think. And so do most men, if they're honest."

She ignored him. His voice drifted on and on. She looked out of the window, bored by him.

"Women newsreaders, now. Speaking for myself, I don't like it. It don't seem natural, somehow. They do all right, I suppose, but they're only reading other people's words. It's like I said earlier, it takes a *man* to think, so it stands to reason you've got to have a man running the really serious programs."

"Thanks," she muttered.

"No offense meant. I didn't mean nothing personal. The truth is I don't watch your programs much, they're too deep for me. But that don't make no difference to what I was saying."

Jess cut off. It would be too ludicrous to allow oneself to be needled by such a fool. It's all over, that stuff, all finished with.

Uninvited, an incident that had taken place a few weeks back slipped

189

into her mind. She had had a press invitation to an opening at the British Museum, and she had taken David along with her. It was a minor exhibition of coins and medals through the ages, and the rooms were not very full. Sipping glasses of sherry, she and David wandered around the display, stopping occasionally to examine a particular group more closely. To her surprise he showed excitement over a case of military medals. "I had that one," he said, triumph in his voice, the Welsh coming out strongly as it always did whenever he referred to his childhood. "I was very proud of myself getting hold of it—it was quite rare."

Jess turned to him, amused, but before she could reply an elderly man with a short white beard who had been standing alongside them looking at the same case said eagerly, "I should say it was. It took me months of searching to pick up one of those."

David's face lit up, and the two men entered into conversation. Jess recognized the tone of experts. Ignored, she melted inconspicuously into a mere female appendage, a creature of no opinion.

She had felt nothing but amusement. It had been positively enjoyable just for once to be outshone by David, to stand back and be ignored by the big clever men. She had savored the feeling, felt relaxed and easy in a deliciously reliant way; even looked at David with pride, and thought fond thoughts of him. Would—timorously!—have taken his hand (expecting nothing but an absent-minded squeeze) had there not been so many press people about.

Now, eyes closed wearily, head back against the taxi seat, her mind left David and wandered further back to a much earlier incident when she was seventeen or so. Her reactions had been very different then.

What had it all been about? She remembered her anger, her face scarlet with fury. She had been quite unable to control her words: they had poured out incoherent, badly organized, and he had laughed at her. Who had laughed? Some boy friend? They'd been debating something . . . or was it that she was talking about the career she planned for herself? Wasn't that it? Something right at the center of her pride. And he, whoever he was who owned that sneering voice that had never quite died, had laughed at what he called her pretensions and told her that women couldn't . . . couldn't what? Write? Organize? Achieve? Some nonsense or other. She wasn't so much angry at him—he only betrayed his own stupidity in talking like that—but at herself for reacting so because she knew she didn't believe a word of it. And yet, all the same, he had struck at

190

some remaining doubt in herself, a legacy from all the puttings-down of the past made personal to her through the books she had read, the considered words of wise men from Plato onward. The scorn, the accusations, the condescension apparent in almost everything she read—until now not even women writers had been quite free of it: they had followed the rules, spoke reverentially of their masters and pityingly of their sisters, most of them. That last had angered her most of all, that intelligent women should have been so brainwashed, or so servile: either was equally humiliating. And when that idiot boy, whoever he was, spoke with the old tyrant voice, she had reacted not as her father's daughter but as though she were the silly nitwit her mother wanted her to be, blushing and stammering—totally, hopelessly *incompetent*.

How long ago it all was. How boring now, all that.

Her thoughts drifted—she was tired, couldn't bear to think straight. Her mind wandered back to safer times. She played again with her father, watching every move he made, holding her shoulders tall and straight like him, learning to throw a ball straight like him, learning not to cry but to take it like a man when she got hurt.

But today nowhere was safe. For from somewhere deep inside her a voice cried to her father, "You castrated me!"

She was appalled. Shocked at the obscenity, shocked at the existence of this unknown intruder. It was not her, that was sure; some scrap of Freudian lore stored away with all the other detritus of her thirty-six years.

Whatever she had done, she had done of her own free will. She had become the person she had freely chosen to become.

She cut herself off from her thoughts, went back to listening to what the taxi driver was saying.

"Personally," his voice drifted back to her, "I wouldn't let my wife work." Then, unforgivably, "Apart from anything else, kids need their mums." She sprang forward, slammed home the sliding window dividing them, and crossed to the opposite end of the seat where he could no longer see her in his mirror. "Bastard, bastard, *bastard*," she intoned to herself until her grief had subsided.

Thoughts no longer drifted gently through her: accusations came roaring at her out of the dark, guided missiles making a strike every time.

Egoist! You put yourself before your children. Better if you'd been barren.

191

But only *I* am *me*! she defended herself. "There'll never be another *me* again. They'll have their own chance later." She wasn't convinced—somewhere there was a flaw.

If they live.

That wasn't fair. Hadn't she always . . . "It wasn't my fault."

Your priorities are all wrong. What can be more important than love?

Unfair. Unfair. Cheap phrases! Love. "I don't have to cook every mouthful, wipe every tear, to love them. I give them freedom to be themselves. Isn't that better?"

Free?

She had a terrible vision of Matthew shut up in a tiny prison, fighting the bars, his eyes wide and anguished.

She feared her control was going. Maybe, after all, she ought to take some pills?

Tears were running unnoticed down her face. The attacking voice left her, but she couldn't stop answering it. Defenses flowed. She'd have made a terrible full-time mother, Iris was far better with her children than she could ever have been. What could possibly be right about wasting her talents, her education? The children didn't lack for parents—wasn't she with them every morning, evenings as well whenever she could? Adam too, when he could spare the time.

Spare the time? Spare the time!

She had *made* time, however busy.

She too, then, had assumed a difference between her and Adam? Automatically accepted a special responsibility?

Why? Why should having an egg instead of sperm, womb instead of cock, make so much difference?

Feeling that old heaviness of full womb, physically she knew the fallacy in her argument. But still she continued to argue—she could not let it rest. Once the child was born, wasn't her duty done? Why shouldn't she be whole again, herself again, as Adam was? Why not? Didn't she have a natural right to be as dedicated to her work as he? As successful as he? Where was the justice that part of her should remain forever tethered? Adam had torn himself away to go to his mistress—it would never have crossed her mind to do the same.

Am I trapped, then? she asked herself bitterly. Am *I* no different from a million other women?

Unwelcome, unneeded, a terrible surge toward the lost being that—somewhere—was Matthew gathered itself together, then passed out of

192

her maiden body, leaving behind a wound raw as though torn open by explosives. Staring fiercely at her reflection in the darkened window she drove both her fists into her belly to stem the flow, but did not entirely succeed.

Jess had joined the human race, and didn't like it.

It seemed grossly unfair of fate that Jess should be faced with such an appalling evening when she had been made newly vulnerable.

As she let herself into the hall, took off her coat and flung it wearily onto the little Hepplewhite chair that used to be in her bedroom as a child, she rested a hand on its slender back, gathering strength from its permanence in her life. To Iris, hastening down the stairs to meet her, Jess looked the same as usual, though more tired. There were dark rings under her eyes, and a slight droop to her lips—otherwise she held herself straight as always, easily, without any suggestions of effort—chin up and ready to take on the world. That she had not bothered to hang up her coat and had merely run a hand over her hair without checking it in the mirror, Iris herself was too perturbed to notice.

"There's a policeman upstairs," Iris said urgently, her now permanently red-rimmed eyes wide with fright. "He insisted on waiting for you. He says he wants to ask you some questions. He's got a policewoman in uniform with him, I can't imagine what for. It's not that nice Inspector, I liked him, he was really friendly and nice. There's something about this one that makes me feel . . ." She pulled a face as though she'd smelled something nasty.

"Oh, God," Jess muttered, reluctantly beginning to climb the stairs to the living room, "what more can I tell them?" Her voice sharpened. "You're sure it's not bad news?"

Iris, behind her, shook her head. "I don't think so, they say there's nothing new. Oh, Jess, if only there was." A sob came into her voice. "I can't stand much more of it. I'll kill myself if anything's happened . . ."

"Do stop it," Jess interrupted her. "I've had enough too. It doesn't help, your going on. Couldn't you have sent them away? I feel so tired tonight."

Iris was devastated at her continual failure. Her voice was low and ashamed. "I told them you'd be tired, but they wouldn't go. They kept saying they had to see you."

Jess pushed open the living room door, feeling close to breaking point. She glared at the visitors, her face set and grim. "Yes?"

The woman constable, her severe uniform menacingly out of place in this elegant room, looked toward her colleague expectantly.

A spare, tall man with hollow eyes, dressed in sports jacket and gabardine trousers, stared at Jess with apparent distaste but rose from his chair politely enough. "I'm sorry to disturb you, madam, but there are a few points we are not quite clear about, and I'd be very grateful if you would come with us to the police station."

Iris gave a little gasp of horror. Stepping forward, she put her hand on her employer's arm in support. Jess ignored her. "Who are you?" she asked coldly. "Why isn't the usual Inspector here?"

"I'm Detective Sergeant Hoskins, madam. The case has been transferred from Hampstead, and you won't be seeing Detective Inspector Clifford any more."

"Why not? He seemed perfectly adequate." She suddenly regretted his absence: she hadn't much liked him, but he was infinitely better than this icy man.

"It wasn't a question of being adequate, madam. It was more convenient for us to take the case over."

"*Why?*"

"I don't think it's necessary to go into that, madam." He relented slightly. "Hampstead's already tied up with that Vale of Health murder and in addition two of their top men are on sick leave. We want to find your son as soon as possible, and it would help us greatly if you would cooperate, madam."

She went over to the cupboard to pour herself a drink. She had not intended to have anymore tonight: since Adam had walked out she'd been drinking too much. But she needed one now—God, she needed one. She wanted to normalize this terrible evening by going through the familiar motions of opening the cupboard door, selecting the glass, the bottle—the whole exercise as calming as the Japanese tea ceremony. But unexpectedly the woman constable, until then sitting with folded hands at the far end of the room, jumped up and came to her side. At the same time the sergeant crossed over to her, saying in a firm voice, "There isn't time for that, madam, I'm afraid."

"I wish you'd stop calling me 'madam,'" Jess said irritably, long-established obedience to authority making her hesitate all the same.

"I'm sorry, madam. But if you wouldn't mind coming with us now."

"I do mind," she snapped, her face reddening at the insult of being ordered around in her own house, "I mind intensely. I've told the police

194

everything I know. I've gone over and over it all, again and again. So has Iris. There's absolutely no more information we can give you." But still she hesitated, standing uncertainly in front of the cupboard. Yesterday she would have gone straight ahead and poured herself a drink: tonight she could not. What was happening to her?

"The Detective Chief Superintendent is very anxious to talk to you."

Titles always annoyed her. Instantly her hand was freed, and she opened the cupboard door. Inside delicate-stemmed glasses glittered against the dark rosewood lining. Their beauty, their orderliness reassured her—gave her back her dignity.

Uncertainly the policewoman looked at the sergeant for guidance. He put a light hand on Jess's arm. They stared at each other.

"He can come and see me tomorrow, then," Jess said, shaking his arm off and lifting out a bottle of brandy. The sergeant took it from her. "He's a very busy man, Madam. And he wants to see you tonight."

Jess gasped in outrage. "Give me back that bottle instantly! And *I'm* a very busy woman. If he can't come here, I'll call in tomorrow some time, but right now I'm very tired and I'm going to bed. There is absolutely no question of my going to the police station tonight."

The sergeant put the bottle back in the cupboard and shut the door. Then he turned the key. The sickness Jess had felt in the taxi returned. It wasn't more brandy she wanted after all, she thought, but coffee: a strong cup of good black coffee. She saw it in her mind's eye, steaming and consoling. She had to have that coffee right now. She turned away from the cupboard to go downstairs to the kitchen. She saw the two of them exchange glances. "I'll help you get your coat, madam," the policewoman said.

"I told you, I'm not going!" Jess said loudly, irritated now beyond politeness. She went firmly down the stairs, her long fingers running smoothly over the mahogany bannister.

"I'm afraid I must insist," the sergeant said calmly as though talking to a difficult child.

Jess stopped. "Are you arresting me?" she asked in disbelief. Her fingers tightened on the polished wood.

"We're only asking you to come along to the station, madam." He paused and added, "We feel it would be helpful if we spoke to you ourselves. We might pick up something that Inspector Clifford missed. I'm sure you want to do everything you can to help us find your son." He looked coldly at her, his deep eyes giving nothing away. "Now if you

195

wouldn't mind obliging us . . ." and he came down another step toward her, his hand out as though to take her arm. Jess drew away from him, then slowly turned and walked down the steps. She moved sluggishly, her normal spring gone. For the moment she was quite incapable of thought.

In the hall the woman constable saw Jess's coat flung across the chair and inwardly clucked with disapproval to see an expensive garment treated so carelessly. The dark brown suede felt like velvet to her appreciative hands as she picked it up and held it out, already opened, toward Jess.

Jess saw her expression, noted the short black hair curling up under her boxy hat and the brightly made-up red lips. A doll, Jess thought vaguely, a pretty little doll . . . She slipped without further protest into the proffered coat, aware of the girl's critical eye on her messy hair, her baggy eyes, obviously thinking that she looked a lot older than she did on the box. *That* she didn't mind—she was used to being gawped at, it was all part of the game—it was the hostility that emanated from these two strangers that undid her. *Why* were they hostile—it couldn't just be jealousy, surely? She longed as she never had before for a shoulder to cry on, a comforting pair of arms. Unaccustomed tears of despair rose to her eyes which, however, she hastily blinked away. Five days, and they knew no more than they did the first day. She had really believed what they had told her, that first time the Inspector came around.

"Wait," she said suddenly, "I must kiss my daughter goodbye."

The sergeant smiled, and nodded permission.

Why had she said "goodbye," not "good night"? she thought as she went back up the stairs to the nursery, the policewoman close behind her. As though she accepted that they actually were arresting her. Was guilty. Guilty? The policeman's smile came back to her. He had noted her slip.

Slip? What was the matter with her? She'd done nothing!

An instinct of self-preservation sharpened Jess's focus as she crouched to step into the back of the police car. With her head lowered and her knees bent, she felt she was making a deep curtsy to these expressionless representatives of the law. The policewoman, who had been holding the door open for her, followed quickly and sat beside her. Neatly she put her knees together and folded her hands on her lap. Were they taught to sit like that, Jess wondered, and considered what would happen if she tore open the door, jumped out, and ran.

I must think, she told herself urgently. There's something wrong. They haven't found Matthew dead, not that—it's not bad news or they'd have been pleasanter. Why hadn't she refused to go with them? They couldn't have forced her if she'd refused. Or could they? Not if they weren't arresting her. Arresting her! Absurd!

Over-tired, her mind fogged over. She was faintly conscious of driving some distance and of finally entering a police station and being taken to what someone referred to as the CID office. It was not until the door was shut and she found herself in a small room with only the policewoman that she was restored to something like her usual sharpness.

She looked around her. The room was small and neat. A scratched wooden desk stood in front of her and a gray-painted filing cabinet was at her side. Apart from three wooden chairs there was no other furniture. The one uncurtained window looked out onto a shopping street that had a faintly familiar air. The room was warm, so warm she wanted to take off her coat, but she decided not to as such an act would imply she expected to stay. Instead she took her handbag off her lap and hung it from its long strap on the back of her upright chair.

"I thought the Detective Chief Superintendent wanted to see me," she said finally to the woman sharing the room with her.

The constable looked up from an examination of her fingernails and said politely, "I expect he'll be along in a minute."

Jess calmly looked back at the girl. "I'd like a cup of coffee," she said pleasantly. "Is that possible?"

The girl nodded. "Yes, madam, in a minute. When someone comes in."

Jess looked at her oddly. "There's no reason for you to stay with me. I'm not a prisoner!"

"Of course not madam, but it's usual with . . ." she hesitated for a second, ". . . ladies for a policewoman to be present." She shrugged. "It's just one of those rules."

Jess laughed tiredly. "Oh God, I'm not going to accuse anyone of rape. I just need a cup of coffee. I'm so exhausted I can't think straight."

She hadn't noticed the door opening and was startled when a male voice behind her said, "I'm afraid we can't run to coffee, but I'll get Miss Collins here to fetch you a cup of tea in a minute."

Jess turned hopefully and saw the familiar face of the sergeant who had brought her in. His icy expression belied the social pleasantness of his words.

197

He said nothing further but went over to the filing cabinet and busied himself there for a minute or two, taking out files and putting them back again.

Finally he selected a file and brought it over to the desk. He pulled out the chair opposite Jess, coughed, sat down heavily, scraped the chair forward then spent some time opening the file and adjusting the positions of a heap of pencils and pens.

Jess watched him curiously. She knew the technique well enough—she had used it herself when she wanted to make someone nervous. But why? What were they after? It was impossible, surely it was impossible, but . . . they were behaving as if they suspected her of . . . *Matthew*? She must be imagining it. She sat back, crossing her legs, which she then made herself look down at with deliberate satisfaction. She had long legs that tapered gently to delicate ankles—in spite of their apparent fragility her feet were strong and she always wore high-heeled lightly-strapped shoes that intensified their elegance. Casually she swung a leg up and down, toe pointed, as though absent-mindedly beating time to some tune passing through her head. Out of the corner of her eyes she noted that the policewoman was watching her. She thought of her mother's old adage that you can always tell a lady by her shoes. Messy hair or not, Constable Collins envied her. She relaxed. Of course she had been imagining things.

Detective Sergeant Hoskins looked up. "Before the Chief Superintendent comes I'd like to clear up one or two points." He glanced down again at his papers as though reading something, but Jess could spot that ploy a mile off.

"Did you say you were still breast-feeding Matthew?" he asked. It was the last question she was expecting.

She stared him straight in the eye. "I never said. No one's asked me."

He stared back equally coolly. "Than I'm asking you now. Were you still breast-feeding Matthew?"

She shook her head. "No."

"Did you ever breast-feed him?"

"What on earth has that got to do with anything? It's totally irrelevant." She noted he had stopped calling her "madam."

As though he had read her thoughts he now used the word heavily—sarcastically, she thought. "All sorts of things are relevant, madam, in a case of this kind. Would you mind leaving it to us what is relevant and what is not?"

She stared at him angrily and did not reply.

"Well, did you ever breast-feed him?"

"I refuse to answer that question."

"I'm afraid I must insist."

She said nothing for a while, then decided to answer. He was just an officious fool—what was the point of arguing with him? "Then, no, I didn't."

"May I ask why not? Weren't you capable of feeding him yourself?"

Now she flushed in spite of herself. How dare he, she thought. His voice is the voice of a farmer confronted with a barren cow: useless—reject! exterminate! "This is a totally unnecessary line of questioning," she snapped. "Matthew was put on the bottle in the hospital, stayed on the bottle, and is still on the bottle. And thank God for it because whoever's taken him hasn't got to cope with an unweaned baby still hankering after a set of bursting tits."

That got him, she thought as she watched his mouth tighten. He'll be more polite now. But there came a memory of those first two or three days when her breasts were still tight with milk, so tight it had oozed out whenever she heard a baby cry—any baby at all—and she remembered the overwhelming sense of contentment when Matthew had been put to her breast to relieve her until the tablets had dried her up. She had even felt tempted as his mouth fastened on her to do the earth mother bit for a few months. She'd overcome it, though.

The sergeant consulted his papers silently. Then, pushing back his chair he crossed his legs and took out a cigarette. He did not offer her one. Looking not quite at her eyes but at an inch or so above them at some invisible spot on her forehead he said, "You've always had an *au pair* to look after your children—is that right?"

"A nanny. A trained nanny. I'd never dream of leaving a child of mine in the charge of an untrained *au pair*."

He consulted his notes again. "But you did have an *au pair*? A Miss Yvette Grüber?"

Ah, she thought, I was right then. Yvette is at the bottom of this. She longed to ask if the girl had turned up. She made herself nod casually. "For a week or two. Miss Grüber is a perfect example of why I would never leave a baby of mine with an *au pair*."

"Oh?"

"She was an irresponsible, self-centered, totally useless girl, which is why I sacked her. I take my responsibilities as a parent too highly to keep someone like that in the house." Her voice was stiff, dry.

199

"Were all your *au pairs* so hopeless?"

She saw she was putting herself in a bad light. "Of course not. I've had some excellent girls, and they've been fine for baby sitting and so on. But to take charge of the children while I'm working away from the house all day—sometimes for several days at a time—that's another matter altogether." Why was she defending herself? She had nothing to feel guilty about. She was responding as though she cared what this dreary man thought about her.

She was so tired. If only she could cry.

The sergeant picked up a piece of paper and held it in his hand, looking from it to her and back again. Finally he said, "Miss Grüber told us—and we do understand of course that someone who has been dismissed is likely to be unreliable—she told us among other things that you much preferred your daughter . ." he checked his notes, "your daughter, Emma, to Matthew."

She stared at him, shocked. She didn't take in the implications of what he was saying. Her only thought was that they had found Yvette.

Oh Christ, what had the girl told them? She relived that dreadful moment when she lay tethered to the bed, flashlights popping, blasting the scene forever into her mind.

Sergeant Hoskins examined her flushed face with interest and waited a few seconds before persisting. "Is there any truth in that?"

Jess pulled herself together. "Of course not. It's true that Matthew is much more like his father, while Emma's very like me. There's also the fact that she was my first-born. There's bound to be a special place for your first-born. But I love them both equally. Exactly the same."

"'He's much more like his father,'" the sergeant repeated musingly, and wrote in his notebook. Then he suddenly looked up and said sharply, "Your husband's left you, I understand?"

Jess, sickened, could only reply, "Yes." Such stupid little facts, but to a police mind . . . What did they add up to? If only she could think straight.

The man sat looking at his papers for a moment before pulling them together and rising. He looked briefly toward Jess as he went to the door, said abstractedly as though thinking of something else, "Excuse me a moment," then went out of the room, shutting the door firmly behind him.

This was a move Jess had not expected. She had been about to protest, to explain away, and he'd gone. She looked over to the policewoman, but she seemed totally absorbed in her fingernails and appeared to be taking no part in the proceedings at all.

Suddenly the door opened, and a short, plump man with a charming smile spread all over his face came bustling in. He hurried straight over to her, pumped her hand up and down enthusiastically several times, and told her how very delighted he was to meet her, how much he admired her programs and what a privilege to be able to talk to her in person. Jess felt like crying, she was so relieved to meet a civilized person, a real human being at last, instead of that frigid automaton Hopkins, Hoskins, whatever his name was. How mad to think that they suspected her.

Smiling up at the new policeman, who introduced himself as Inspector Clay, she asked him in her most melting voice if she could have a cup of coffee. "Or tea," she added quickly, "if there's no coffee available."

He beamed at her and nodded his head happily. "Of course, of course, my dear. You must be longing for one. But do you mind waiting for a few moments, because the rules, you know . . . they insist we mustn't ever be shut up with a lady, especially a delightful lady like yourself, without a woman constable being present. But Annie here will get you one when we've finished. You do understand, don't you? Of course you do. I'm so sorry you've been dragged out this time of the evening, but we do want to explore every possible avenue. Now you don't mind if I ask you a question or two?" He left her side reluctantly, sat down at the desk, and drew a notebook from his pocket in which he had apparently made some notes. Looking up he said in a warm chatty voice, more like a family doctor than a policeman, "It's all just routine stuff, nothing important at all, but you never know what might turn up. Now tell me, my dear, were you still breast-feeding Matthew when he was . . . taken?"

She felt as though she had been slapped on the face. She sat back, shutting her eyes. It had happened a thousand times before to other people as innocent as she was. Being Jess Bennett made no difference to the police—they had collected certain facts, and added together those facts suggested a possible conclusion. She ran them through in her mind, stupid little things—she hadn't breast-fed her children; she paid a nanny to look after them; Yvette said she preferred Emma; Adam had left her; Matthew looked like Adam. Was that all! She racked her brains—that first Inspector, he had implied she was cold, didn't care—she had sensed he mistrusted her. Was it he who had started them thinking in this way? Or was it Yvette? What had she said to them? What *could* she have said? Had she lied? Anger took her over, choked her so she couldn't even speak. *Yvette*!

The policeman was looking at her with grave concern. "It isn't important," he said, his expression assuring her of his warm concern for her, "It isn't important at all whether you were or not—I personally don't have any of these feelings about it being best for babies to be breast-fed—but we'd like to know just for the record. For the baby's sake, his present health and all that."

She reddened. Was he telling the truth? She felt herself losing touch with what was happening. Did they or didn't they suspect her? Was she going crazy to even think it? She looked at the man in front of her. She *was* mad. See how pleasantly he was looking at her. *Of course* they needed to know if Matthew was bottle-fed. It had been nothing personal at all, it was just she was so tired, so worn out, she misunderstood everything.

She tried to answer the man in her usual voice, but it came out shrewishly. "Your last interrogator has already asked me that. The answer is no. No, no, no—I didn't breast-feed him, I never breast-fed him, nor did I breast-feed Emma. All right?"

He smiled at her sweetly, nodding his head with satisfaction. "Thank you, Mrs. Bennett, that's very helpful of you. Now what sort of arrangements was it normal for you to make for the children when you were away working? You *were* away every day, weren't you? Or nearly every day?"

As the questions continued she felt her nerves being stretched to danger point. She began to stumble in her answers—she, Jess Bennett! She felt herself trapped, almost wanting to beg for mercy. She! I'm the victim, she wanted to shout, I'm the mother. What are you doing to me?

The Inspector had been with her for perhaps ten minutes, never once dropping his avuncular, flattering manner, when suddenly he rose, snapped his notebook shut, and in a quite different voice, curt and hard, said, "I'm not sure you've been telling us the entire truth, Mrs. Bennett. I must admit to some doubts about your story."

And without another word he walked out of the room, leaving Jess behind him speechless, her face drained of color.

Police Constable Collins followed Inspector Clay out. She did not return however with the expected cup of tea. Instead, a minute later a male constable in uniform arrived, apologized for inconveniencing Jess but explained in a chatty sort of way that a couple of suspects had just been brought in and the CID room was needed, so would she mind coming with him.

202

Jess had not yet recovered, but at the thought of action she instantly felt better. Presumably she was at last going to see the Chief Superintendent.

But when the constable opened the door of a small whitewashed room and led her inside she looked around in disbelief. There was nothing, nothing at all except a bunk bed built into the wall, a bed made of wooden planks like the fitted bunks in the officers' quarters of old sailing ships, but longer and wider. There was no mattress, no pillows, no furniture of any kind—not even a single chair. In the wall opposite the bunk, there was a small window, but it offered no comfort. Not only was it barred and covered with a wire grill, but it was also whitewashed over. Claustrophobia instantly grabbed her at the thought of being enclosed in this faceless room. "I'm not . . ." she started, but before she had chance to protest a voice called out from the other end of the corridor down which she had just been led. "Hey Charlie, not the detention room—I've got a young lad here. I'm bringing him up in a minute."

The constable nodded and turned amiably to Jess. "Sorry about that. We're not allowed to put juveniles in the cells, see, he'll have to go in here. A right busy night, tonight. Never mind, there's plenty of space." And pointing down a further corridor, he indicated that Jess should walk on.

What she saw then chilled her. Jutting out into the narrow artificially-lit corridor were two heavy iron barred doors. Black-painted, equipped with hefty locks and cylindrical bolts, they were the ancient, archetypal symbol of incarceration. Jess stopped immediately, drew her legs together, feet side by side, and clenched her hands.

"I refuse to go in there," she said, her voice tight with suppressed panic. "I was told I was going to see the Chief Superintendent. Why aren't I being taken to his office?"

The constable looked embarrassed. "He's in conference at the moment, madam. He'll be out shortly. And there's nowhere else left for you to wait. All the other rooms are in use."

"In conference? At this time of night!"

"He's talking to the Inspector. He'll be down in a minute. Now, if you don't mind, step along please, miss, I've got to get back to the desk. We're a bit short staffed and I can't leave you hanging around in the corridor."

Was the impatience that had crept into his previously amiable voice yet another ploy? she thought. Was every move of theirs deliberate?

What in Christ's name was she doing here?

Walking down the corridor toward the iron doors she made herself note the details. You never knew when inside information of this kind

203

would come in handy. At this thought she perked up. Program ideas began to buzz through her mind.

"What's that for?" she asked as they passed the first of the two iron doors, pointing toward a small white sheet like a cinema screen suspended from a roller against the end wall of the corridor. Underneath the sheet stood a chair, its back against the wall. Hanging from the ceiling above was a black box which she took at first to be an electric fire. "Dirty movies for the prisoners?" she joked, trying to inject a note of casual amusement into her voice.

The constable laughed. "That's right. We're real progressive here. No, it's for taking photographs for the CRO."

"CRO?"

"Criminal Record Office."

"Ah." She saw herself, haunted-eyed, glaring at the camera. "Very interesting. They sit on that chair, I suppose? And that," pointing to the black box overhead, "that's a special light?"

"That's right, miss. It's not very flattering, you might say, but it gets a good picture."

"Who takes the pictures?" she asked in her usual interviewing voice. It was out of the question to take all this seriously, to accept what seemed to be happening, but the constable would not be put off anymore.

"Would you come this way, please, through that door." He put a not-so-gentle hand on her arm to guide her in. She paused on the threshold of the second of the two iron doors, frozen. Her legs began to tremble, and briefly she leaned for support against the jamb of the door.

This was far worse than the detention room. Apart from the blanked-out window and the wooden bunk, that room could have been an ordinary one, small and mean as it was. But the corridor down which she had just walked was part of a cell block, she saw it now, and behind these iron doors were the cells.

They were putting her in the cells.

Why?

It made no sense!

She was the victim.

"Come along, please," said the voice at her side, firm, no longer amiable.

She considered refusing point-blank. She could march straight back to the reception desk and refuse to budge until the Chief Superintendent was free. Or she could simply walk out. But supposing—supposing they really thought that she'd done something . . . supposing they dropped the mask of civility and straightforwardly arrested her? Was it possible?

The policeman put gentle pressure on her arm. She looked up at him, then submitted. What else could she do? She stepped forward shakenly. Passed beyond the iron door.

She was in the middle of yet another corridor, this time a narrow very short one, running from the left to the right of her, like a connecting passage between two bedrooms in a hotel suite. On the opposite side of the passage, facing her, was a wall with two closed wooden doors let into it. Set into the middle of this wall, between the closed doors, was a wide recess into which was fitted what looked exactly like a pair of lavatory cisterns, complete with chains and water pipes, only underneath the cisterns there were no lavatory seats or pans. And instead of swinging loose, the dangling chains disappeared into the wall of the recess. At one end of the brief corridor, visible to any passerby, was a small washbasin with a new bar of soap and a couple of clean towels tucked behind the taps.

The policeman left her side and peered through an observation window in the door of the right-hand cell. He grunted to himself, then came back to her, his face grim. "This way," he said, and opened the left-hand door.

Hesitantly she walked inside. The constable stood holding the door open, watching her.

Jess turned back toward him. "I want to see my solicitor," she heard herself saying.

"No need for that, madam," he said with a return to his previous amiability. "We probably shan't be keeping you long."

She glared at him. "One minute is too long! I don't know what you're up to, but I insist on seeing my solicitor."

"We'll do our best, in due course, if it's really necessary. But like I said, you probably won't be staying long." He turned to go.

"Wait!" she said loudly and grabbed at his arm. "I know my rights. You can't treat me like this and refuse to let me see a solicitor. You've *got* to ring him for me. I'll make such a hell of a fuss afterward if you don't."

He gently removed her hand. "Certainly we'll ring him for you," he said soothingly, "as soon as someone can be spared to make the call. But you don't really want to bother your solicitor at this time of night, do you, when you'll probably be home in a couple of hours?"

She stared at him. "A couple of hours? You mean that?"

"Yes, yes, maybe even less." He spoke as to a child. "Someone will be along soon. I'm sorry about the accommodation, madam, but that's the way it is sometimes, when we're very busy." And then he was gone. As he passed through the door he kept his hand on it to slow its closing, apparently meaning to leave it on the latch, but immediately after he had gone the strength of the spring forced the door home. She heard a click as the automatic bolt shot into place. An accident? He didn't come back.

She looked around in disbelief. It was horrible, horrible. The atrocious neatness of this cell, its compactness—with no space anywhere for vision. A foul little box with nothing of the outside world in it. There were no windows, nothing open anywhere, not even a whitewashed, barred, eighteen-inch square. No air. Instantly her lungs choked up, and she felt sweat breaking out on her forehead and between her breasts. She spun around to the door with raised arm and was about to hammer it with her fist when she forced herself to stop, to think rationally. It was not possible there was no air. Of course there was air. They couldn't have prisoners dropping dead of suffocation, for God's sake.

She must look, search for air holes. She glanced quickly at the door. Yes, there it was, an observation window like the one through which the constable had observed the prisoner next door. (Who was he? What had he done—had he killed? The constable had looked grim.)

Beneath the observation window was a square opening half-closed by a steel grid. In relief she put her face to the gap, and though it wasn't big enough to put her head through she could see out through it into the corridor beyond. She breathed in deeply. At first she felt the relief of flinging open a window in a stuffy bedroom after returning to a closed-up home. Until she recognized that the air in the cell was the same as that outside. There must be more ventilation than that, she thought—the grid was obviously made to be closed.

At last, at the other end of the room she found two air vents let into the wall. She stood up by them, fighting panic again. They were appallingly small. How could they ventilate this whole room? She put her nose to them and filled her lungs, but it was no use, she was choking—she ran back to the door, through which she could at least see the outside.

She was an animal, trapped. She recalled the tigers at the zoo, walking up and down, up and down. She too began to walk, all the time keeping an eye on the opening, trying to wean herself further and further away from it.

Suddenly she stopped in the middle of the floor, stopped her pacing, ashamed.

What was it her father once said? In a crisis, take ten deep breaths, then
206

look calmly at the reality of what was happening. It is never that bad, he said, never so bad you can't take some palliative action. And once you're actually *doing* something, the worst is past.

She stood still, and breathed in. One—out. Two—out. Three—out. Already she felt calmer. Six—out. Seven—out. He'd never let her down yet. Nine—out. Ten—out.

Look around. Explore the cell. Look around, memorize it. You never know when an experience like this would be useful. No experience was ever wasted, that was another of his maxims.

The room was long and narrow. The bed was identical to the one in the detention room, shiny brown wood, tongue and groove planks fitted against the long wall to make a flat, wide bed, unsoftened by mattress or blanket. The bunk ran two thirds of the length of the room: the left hand end was fitted into the right angle of two walls, and the other end into a brick partition rising from floor to ceiling. Between the partition, which jutted out only a few inches beyond the bed and the far wall (she instantly saw what it was, felt sick—all those people—thieves, drunks, murderers! all squatting in there, then having to sleep with head right next to it. Her too? Jesus Christ, how could they!) was another flat built-in wooden surface at the same height as the bed, but this one had a round hole in the middle. A lavatory. Just like those smelly ones in old country cottages. No!

She went closer. Was reprieved. Beneath the wooden seat was not a stinking bucket but an ordinary-looking lavatory pan. But there was nothing to pull, no sign of any water-flushing system. She remembered the peculiar pair of cisterns outside in the recess in the corridor. She crossed to the wall opposite the lavatory that was the reverse of that recess. On the wall was a round knob, which appeared to lead to some mechanism on the other side of the wall. So that was it.

As she was puzzling over this, and picking at the knob without actually tugging it, she suddenly observed that close to the knob was a peephole. A peephole directly aimed at the loo. Oh Christ! One couldn't even do that without being observed. Not even shit!

She began to shudder. Feeling her legs on the point of giving way she crept back to the bunk and curled up on it, her face hidden in her hands. Quietly she wept. So distressed was she, she didn't even notice the hardness of the wooden boards.

When the shuddering died away Jess found her mood had changed. She felt physically weak, but calm, able to think. It was obvious a terrible

207

mistake had been made. Yes, it was clear now, somehow they thought it possible she was implicated in Matthew's disappearance—it was Yvette, she knew it was Yvette—and they were only treating her the way they treated all suspects. Better than. They wouldn't call a tart picked up off the street "madam," or be so polite toward a young lad taken in for assault and battery.

She sat up: they must not find her curled up so spinelessly. They were doing what they were doing for Matthew's sake. She had to remember that. She opened her handbag, took out comb and mirror and made some attempt at her hair. She wiped away a smudge of mascara and applied fresh. She considered whether or not to put on lipstick, and decided for it. Color was what she needed tonight.

But after that there was nothing else to do. She thought of David. What had she said to him about his world, that day they'd had that row? She was in his world now, all right. Knew what he was talking about from first hand. She wondered for a moment whether to ask to see him—he'd get her out of this mess at once—then rejected it out of hand. They'd take more notice of her, Jess Bennett, any day, than a probation officer. Then remembered Yvette. If David and Yvette turned up at the same time at the station! It never even crossed her mind to consider calling Adam for help.

Stronger now, she looked at her watch. Where on earth was the superintendent? It was grossly rude of him to keep her waiting like this. Then she recalled her present position, that in all probability all this making her hang around was quite deliberate. But she could wait now. She was herself again.

She began to think about Matthew, about Emma, whether she had lost anything by working. Tried to see herself as earth mother, dissolved in the egos of the young. Someone had once said to her, you shouldn't have children, not with your attitude—stick to your principles, be a man through and through. How trite that was. Men want children as much as women, but they don't consider being with their offspring day and night as a necessary part of the package.

She thought of some of her friends who tried to be everything. They gave up nothing, and in snatching all, lost—what? The satisfaction of total absorption in work as well as the peace of motherhood, going around with furrowed brows, half an ear cocked to the telephone that linked their two lives, endless "chore" lists rotting at the bottom of their handbags that never succeeded in being fully checked off. Guilt-ridden because an extra ounce on the scale for this one meant an ounce off the scale for the other.

That was no way to live. Compromise was not for her. She'd understood the necessity for choosing—and having chosen had accepted the inevitability of loss. That was her strength—she'd never grieved for what she had voluntarily discarded, never wasted emotion where it could give no return. And she had been right to do so. She had unquestionably succeeded. No one could deny it.

And now? Hadn't she the will power to get through even this terrible time? She only had to hang on to what she knew to be the right path for her, and soon, soon, everything would be normal again.

She was so lost in thought that she did not even hear footsteps outside her cell. When a stranger entered she looked up with genuine surprise.

"How do you do?" the stranger said, coming over to her with outstretched hand. "Chief Superintendent Parkinson. I hope you've not been too uncomfortable."

Jess looked at him in astonishment. "Uncomfortable! What do you think? It's hardly a suite at Brown's." He smiled, and she was aware instantly he had noted her instinctive choice for him of Brown's rather than the Savoy or the Ritz. A look of recognition passed between them. He wore the sort of well-cut tweedy suit, had the tall straight bearing, the healthy outdoor face, of the men she had been brought up among. All the same, how odd to think of Brown's Hotel here in this cell. She almost smiled at the memory of afternoon teas taken there as a child while her mother gossiped with visiting cousins.

But the temptation to smile put her on her guard. She was not being caught out again.

"The service isn't so hot, either," she said, putting on a pleasant, ironic voice. "I keep being promised a cup of coffee, but it never materializes. And I asked for my solicitor. Do you know if anyone has done anything about that?"

Superintendent Parkinson smiled back, not at all perturbed. "I do apologize." He turned to Sergeant Hoskins, who, together with Annie Collins, had followed him into the cell. "Mr. Hoskins, would you mind asking someone to bring a cup of tea for Mrs. Bennett? Better not send Annie." He turned back to Jess. "I'm sorry there's no coffee—the machine's broken down, and the canteen's closed."

He came over and sat next to Jess on the bench. Constable Collins

209

remained standing in the corner. "Now as to your solicitor, if you give me his name and telephone number we'll certainly ring him for you. But won't you wait a little? I am sure we can find out all we need to know within a few minutes. A solicitor really won't be necessary."

She gave him a sarcastic smile. "Would you mind telling me exactly why I've been locked in this cell? I've been in the station for well over an hour now, and I'm very tired. I've had an extremely busy day, and, as even the police must realize, this is a very distressing time for me."

He made a clucking noise of sympathy. She half expected him to pat her on the knee. "I'm extremely sorry they had to put you in a cell. And it was never intended to lock you in. Someone should have wedged open the door—they shut automatically, you know. It was purely a mistake, I do assure you." He looked at his watch. "I'll be as quick as I can," he said. "You understand that in a case of this nature we have to explore every possible angle. It's five days now since your son disappeared. As you know, the case has been transferred to us, and since you and I hadn't met I thought we ought to put that right. I realize the inconvenience to you."

"There must have been somewhere other than a cell."

"There was nowhere else free—we're awfully short of space, you know."

"I could have waited at the reception desk. And why are we here now, rather than in your office?"

He ignored this. "Ah, here's your tea. I expect you can do with it." He waited until she had sipped it, saying nothing when, after the first taste, she put it down on the floor with an expressive downturning of her lips. "Now as you probably know, we've had a lot of information from the public, but unfortunately it's come to nothing so far. There are still a few people we are trying to trace—we've several promising leads. Meanwhile, we're following up every single angle we can think of."

"And I'm one of those angles? Why don't you admit openly you suspect I've stolen my own child?" She hadn't meant to say it, but it slipped out. Appalled at what she was saying, she continued, "What am I supposed to have done with him? Murdered him and hidden . . . ?" She stopped, pale. That he might be dead was a thought she had until now steadfastly refused to entertain. She buried her head in her hands. All of a sudden, in this terrible place, it seemed only too possible that someone had done just that. She looked up with haggard eyes. "*Could* someone have . . . ?"

He looked at her curiously. "It's very unlikely. It happens that way very rarely."

She took control of herself. "Well, are you or aren't you accusing me?"

"No one has suggested that, Mrs. Bennett. You're only here for questioning."

She gave an impatient wave of her arm. "I'm not a fool. You'd never have put me in this cell if that were all. I know your methods. Ask your questions and have done with it." She hesitated. "I suppose it has something to do with Yvette Grüber?"

"I can't go into . . . But it's true that young lady gave us certain information. It doesn't follow we believe all she said."

"She told you I preferred Emma to Matthew, I think that was how Sergeant Hoskins put it. What else did she say?"

The Superintendent gave the sergeant a sharp look. To Jess he said, "There was some suggestion to that effect, yes. Is there any truth in it?"

"I explained all that to Sergeant Hoskins. Haven't you swapped notes?"

The Superintendent frowned. He began to look a little less friendly. "No, we haven't swapped notes, as you put it. Perhaps you would tell me yourself."

"You haven't cautioned me yet. Aren't you supposed to warn me that everything I say will be taken down and used in evidence and all that stuff?"

"You are not helping matters, Mrs. Bennett. You must know that we only do that if someone is being charged, and you are not being charged. Any notes that any of us take are only for our own use. Verbals are not admissible evidence. I would have thought a barrister's wife would have known that."

She gave in. Better get it over and done with. If Yvette had lied about her then they had to check her out. They were behaving correctly enough if that were so, even if the whole notion was so incredible she could hardly take it in. Thinking of Yvette made it impossible for her to meet the Superintendent's eyes. Had she talked about the photographs? She sighed wearily and tried to concentrate.

After two minutes Inspector Clay and, a moment later, another policeman—a huge bulky man with the surly frown of a dim-witted bouncer—came into the cell. After each newcomer the door closed itself again, and although she tried to keep her mind off the diminishing supply of air she could not stop herself taking deeper and deeper breaths. But even as her distress increased she could not help admiring their technique. If she had been guilty how could she have stood out against them?

Chief Superintendent Parkinson was talking about Adam, pressing her

211

to explain why she had torn up the photographs she had taken of him and Matthew. She had forgotten about that. But she'd never told the police she had torn them up! He had tricked her into admitting it, she suddenly realized. How had he guessed? Or had someone told him. Who? It was clear he found it very significant. Was it, tearing up pictures of her baby? She closed her eyes for a moment, feeling unsteady.

The Superintendent told her he had once been involved in a case in which Adam was prosecuting counsel—his respect for Adam and his calling was obvious. She became uncontrollably angry.

"Why don't you suspect *him*?" she cried. "He dotes on Matthew. Supposing *he's* stolen him? He knows he won't get him away from me any other way."

Everyone in the cell smiled, even Annie Collins. She was surrounded by widely smiling faces looking down at her. "A barrister?" said the Superintendent in amusement. "Steal his own child? Hardly likely."

"As likely as his own mother!" she shouted.

"Ah well, that's different. Mothers do very strange things sometimes. Under stress."

Suddenly—she couldn't help it—tears started pouring down her face. They've broken me, she thought. Soon I'll confess. Anything to get them all out of here before I suffocate. Gulping for air, she cried, "Have you no imagination? Can't you imagine what I've been going through?"

"Imagination is not our business," the Chief Superintendent said calmly. "We are here to play our part in seeing that justice is done. Law and order is what concerns us. We leave imagination to people like yourself."

Dully she shook her head. She felt herself detached now. She stopped listening to what they were saying. Vaguely she thought about the others who had sat like this in this cell, being broken down. Sinners.

This straight man patiently questioning her, how could he really understand about sin, when the possibility of committing it simply wasn't in him? Annie Collins was unnecessary. He'd never do anything out of line, he'd never make a sinner.

Nor a saint either. The mysterious unknown would never become known through men like him. Or Adam.

For the first and only time in her life Jess glimpsed a suggestion of that unknown, evanescent as the fringe of a sunlit cloud, and felt a momentary yearning to be different from what she was.

212

But never could be. With desolation she saw that. She was like them, of the same breed. Without people of their kind society would collapse. But it would never be lifted up, either. Mystery was not in their gift. They could not bring salvation. Only order.

And wasn't that enough!

DAY 6

When Jess, on this gray Sunday morning, opened the newspaper she had most dreaded, she was not really surprised at what she found.

She was already raw enough. The Chief Superintendent, having decided she was innocent and that Yvette had been lying, had personally driven her home the night before, full of apologies for so grossly inconveniencing her, but even so she had been too distressed to sleep until dawn.

Now she woke to find herself elected chief sinner of the week. The picture, spread all over the center-fold, had been carefully cut so that nothing was shown that would shock the children. As the blurb put it, their concern for public decency had prohibited them from printing the entirety of this disgusting illustration of the depths to which a woman would sink in her search for titillation. What was left was enough. The foreground was filled with David's naked shoulders and middle back. His head was bent down, continuing the curve of his spine. Fortunately for David he could have been any youngish Caucasian male with a full head of dark slightly curly hair. The same could not be said of Jess. She was instantly recognizable. Yvette had taken two photographs in rapid succession, bending further at the knees for the second. The picture they would have liked to have printed was the first, showing Jess's breasts reared up to presentable size by the backward stretching of her arms toward the bars of the bedhead to which her hands were tethered by chains. But it was decided to use the second when Yvette's focus had dropped so that Jess's nipples were obscured by David's shoulders (how they had pressed Yvette to reveal David's identity, not realizing that had she known who he was she would have sold his name to them as readily as she had told them her own).

So what was shown, item by item, was decent enough: Jess's face, horrified eyes wide open, mouth gaping (but whether with passion or protest it was impossible to judge); her bare shoulders and the nipplesless upper half of a pair of naked breasts; arms lifted back revealing a trim set of muscles—admittedly ending in hands tethered by chains to a bedhead, but maybe the kids could be persuaded she was doing her exercises; and David's anonymous back. It was a pity that his lower half, toes affectionately intertwined with Jess's leather straps, had had to be cut off; Yvette's talent for achieving instant composition had been at its best that day. But, as they had all reluctantly agreed, sitting around the editorial table examining the pictures with open pleasure—it simply couldn't be done.

The story line was clear enough. Shock, of course, that anyone so totally in the public eye should behave thus, intensified by the fact that she was not only female but a mother (not a randy middle-aged man, the more usual victim of such exposés), trebly intensified by the fact that this was the very woman for whom the nation's heart had been bleeding all week. Oh outrage! Oh horror! Oh shame! But after the expression of shock came laughter. Jess Bennett!! Heroine of the women's movement! The new New Woman, the future woman free of the bondage of man—famous symbol of woman's achievement. Queen Jess herself! In voluntary chains!

How they laughed. How they jeered. How they sympathized with poor Adam, driven from his home and bed by such outrageous goings-on (this last angle was partly due to a warning phone call from Adam himself the previous day to their lawyers, who then advised their clients that extreme caution would be necessary when writing about a barrister of Adam's ability. It had not been suggested that any punches need be pulled with regard to Jess, for it had never crossed Adam's mind that Jess was in any way vulnerable). Since scandalmongers like to believe it is only by suffering that a sinner can redeem himself, the editors saw no need to tread gently.

It could be argued they were doing Jess good; were giving her a chance of atonement and eventual redemption. Look at the victims of old scandals, such as Profume—would he have earned his soul's salvation by his *work in the East End if his sexual proclivities had not been so earnestly exposed? If some offenders against public morality, like Stephen Ward, choose to kill themselves in despair instead of thankfully seizing the chance of redemption offered them, that is their affair. And very selfish of them at that, for it denies the more sensitive reader the chance to rid himself of any slight residual guilt at sharing, however marginally, in the breaking of a man's life.*

S UNDAY morning the church bells began to ring. For a while Carrie enjoyed them, but today her mood was somber. Suddenly she jumped up and slammed the window shut. She picked up Matthew and rocked him quietly as she walked about the room. When he grew sleepy she laid him down on the floor, setting Aidan's blue sweater under his head.

Now she began to long for the bells to stop. Their incessant clanging ran like a hallucination inside her head. She tried to offset her growing distress by thinking about the pleasure Aidan would feel when she finally showed him their baby, but for some reason today she couldn't—it seemed unreal. She puzzled over this, lay down on the floor beside the baby, and rested her head beside his on the sweater. The familiar smell made her lips smile, and she rubbed her nose in the thick wool, but at the same time there was a kind of prickle in her mind, warning her off even this thought of Aidan.

After a bit she got up and went out to the kitchen to make herself a cup of coffee. These days the kitchen was kept spotless and tidy. Single-handedly St. Spock had installed in her a fear of dirt and respect for hygiene: the baby's bottles were boiled as clean as in any hospital ward. Suddenly she had such a passion of longing for Aidan she ran to the door, but stopped herself with her fingers on the lock. As though a hand had been laid on her shoulder, saying, "Not yet." Reluctantly she returned to the kitchen and took her coffee through into the living room where she sat once more in the chair by the window, vaguely looking out at the street without actually seeing anything.

The church bells had stopped ringing some time ago, but Carrie had not noticed. Matthew slept on, disturbed neither by noise nor silence. Sometimes he snuffled like an animal, and his limbs jerked as he dreamed, but Carrie did not leave her corner. She wondered whether to light the fire—she could do with the company—but decided against it.

Outside in the hall she heard the lid of the letter box thump shut. She

219

sat puzzling over this, it being a Sunday, until it occurred to her Aidan might have dropped a note through the box. He had posted half a dozen to her that way already, and though she had read and reread them and slept with them under her pillow she had answered none.

She leaped up and hurried into the hallway. There on the floor lay an official-looking letter, long and narrow in office manilla and typed address. Disappointed not to see Aidan's Italic hand, she almost did not bother with it. Some form or other delivered in error to a neighbor. It often happened. Idly she wandered to the door, picked up the envelope, and took it back with her to the living room, where she sat with it on her lap for some minutes before opening it.

She stared at the letter in her hand uncomprehendingly. At first all she could see were the words, "Home Office Prison Department—H.M. Prison Beckham" stamped across the top. Then her eyes read the typed words.

At the first reading they meant nothing. Her mind refused to take them in. She read them again. In brief official language they expressed their sincere regret that Gerald Warren, due to be released the following day, had taken his own life. He had "removed" a length of cord from the mail bag section in which he worked, and hung himself from the bars of his cell. They assured her—for their own sake more than hers—that he had shown no previous indication of disturbance, had given no hint of distress, and had in every way been a model prisoner. They were enclosing a note he had left on his bed, in which he explained his actions. And, finally, would she please be kind enough to contact them with regard to the disposal of his final remains. Sincerely.

The letter was addressed to Agatha.

Without believing what she was doing, Carrie peered inside the manilla envelope and found the note. It was torn out of a writing block, pale blue lines on cheap grayish paper. She examined the unknown handwriting. It had never occurred to her before that she had no idea what his writing looked like. There wasn't a single example of it anywhere in the flat.

It took her some time before she could read the note. Her gaze kept skittering off the page.

To whom it may concern.

I do not want anyone to feel themselves to blame for what I am about to do. It is true that at first my reception by the warders and the prisoners alike was not very friendly, but that is understandable, considering the nature of my crime. But the other prisoners in the isolation block with me and more lately the warders have been very forebearing, and some I would even call friends. I do not want any of these to feel they are in any way to blame.

The reason I have decided to take my life is that I have nothing to live for. I did not understand this until yesterday, when it became crystal clear to me that my life is only an embarrassment to other people. It is, I understand, very difficult to get a job without employers knowing I have been in prison. What am I to tell them if they ask? I could never tell them the truth. But I am not the kind of person to live happily on the dole.

My wife is dead. And I am dead to my daughter. I can understand that. Once I dared to hope that in the fullness of time she would learn to forgive me, and even write to me, but I can understand why she was not able to. I did not really expect her to thank me for the birthday and Christmas cards which I spent many happy days making for her. Not "thank," I didn't mean that, but sometimes I would daydream that she had come to understand that what I had done to her was done out of love. A little note from her would have lessened my—[a word was crossed out here and rendered quite illegible].

But I do not in any way blame her. She must never think that. There has not been a day when I have not thought constantly of her and—now that I am about to die—I can add without shame, thought constantly about her *with love*. She is a lovely girl, and inside myself my love for her has never seemed to me to be anything but of the purest. Though naturally other people could not be expected to see it like that.

I have nothing to leave her, except my father's pocketwatch, which the prison authorities hold, and the reproduction of the seascape by Turner, which she already has, but which I would like formally to bequeath to her. It was something we both loved to look at together when she was a child.

It seemed he could not end it. Two or three words had been crossed out, a new paragraph started and similarly abandoned. Finally, it was simply signed with his name, written, like the rest of the letter, in a crabbed half-educated hand, the bastard copperplate still taught in the schools when he was young.

That was all. The last will and testament of a man whose hands life had left empty.

Carrie raged. She shouted, "I wrote, I wrote! I sent you birthday cards and

221

Christmas cards, and it was you who never wrote! You bloody liar, you never sent anything, ever!"

Then wept, seeing her mother's treachery. His lovely days of happy work! And hers, to him. Destroyed.

Anger turned her wild. She cried for her mother to be alive so that she could kill her. Hate and despair sent her raging through the room, the note screwed up in her hand. Then seeing what she had done with it she knelt down in front of the sofa; laying the paper on the cushions she tried to smooth it out. Her tears spread the blue ink into overlapping waves. Later the note would dry cockled, the writing blurred, like an ancient document dragged into life from some dusty archive.

He was so innocent, her father, so tender. She held the paper to her cheek, kissed it with passion. This was all? Nothing else? How could he have done it to her!

She put the paper down and smoothed it again, fingers lingering. A stranger's hand. She hadn't even known that about him. Couldn't recall his voice. She knew *nothing*.

Not even who he was.

What kind of man was he? What might he have become if it had been otherwise? If he had not met Agatha. If she had not gone away to the hospital.

This was the worst moment of all. The awareness of total loss. All these years she had put him aside, pretended he no longer existed. But in her heart she had known that one day she'd see him again, and that part of her that had been frozen like some extinct creature would be taken from the ice and melted.

Then she'd be freed to move on.

But how, never. Her heart shriveled. She too was dead.

Matthew cried. He had started to whimper when Carrie first shouted. Now he let out a loud cry of outrage at her neglect. Carrie roused herself and went to him. Seeing her, Matthew instantly smiled. Blue-eyed against the blue sweater, his beam dazzled her. She saw in his face another, an amateurishly-tinted photograph of her father—smiling blue-eyed boy baby on blue cushion. Her grandmother had proudly bought a cheap paint box and touched in the sepia reproduction of her child's brightest feature, finishing up the brushful of paint on the cushion on which he lay. Until she died the photograph had always stood on a small table by her bedside.

Carrie as a child used to look at it, unable to believe her father could ever have been a small baby. It was many years since she had seen the photograph, but its presence now was so vivid that staring at Matthew she could no longer distinguish the one from the other. The two became blurred into one whole.

She stood looking until Matthew frowned, perhaps disturbed by something in her face. Then she bent and gathered the baby to her. Folding her arms around him she was engulfed in a tide of feeling that was neither joy nor sadness, but was of an intensity that surpassed both.

After a minute she knelt and gently laid the baby back on Aidan's sweater. Quietly she crooned to it, soothing them both. By the time Matthew's eyes had finally closed in sleep, the intensity had passed, leaving her drained but calm.

It was then that she saw who Matthew was. Or was not.

Saturday night while she lay awake Jess had grown more and more obsessed with the idea of suing Yvette for libel. She knew it would be a mad thing to do—she thought of Oscar Wilde—publicity would be her ruin. If Yvette had not already shown someone the photographs she would certainly bring out in court what she had seen. But Jess wanted vengeance. She could not visualize the unknown person who had stolen Matthew—it was Yvette's face, representing all the horror of these past five days, that floated clearly in front of her. She wanted to see that face suffer as she had suffered.

Sometimes Matthew came to her but the memory of that moment when she had imagined him dead was too powerful, and she put him out of her mind. She had to survive until the morning: there was a limit to what she could take. Strangely she didn't think at all of Adam.

But in the morning when she woke it was Adam who was on her mind. She thought of his betrayal. Those years of marriage, of trust, of—she had always thought—happiness: all thrown away. For what? Love? Was it love, what he felt for Fanny? What had he felt for *her* all those years, then? Hadn't that been love? Had he ever felt for her the kind of passion he obviously felt for Fanny, enough to risk everything? She knew the answer as soon as she asked the question, and also knew that she had never loved him that way either. She wondered if she were capable of that kind of love and sadly thought probably not.

Now it was day, though, she was able also to think of Matthew. A different kind of grief flowed through her, but unlike the night before in the taxi it was an accepting kind of grief. She saw she would never be the same again, that she was newly vulnerable. She considered this vulnerability (Emma was in her mind as well). It was as though she had moved into another dimension of experience. As she thought about it, painful as it was, she realized with surprise she was glad to be there.

When she heard the paper boy arrive she jumped out of bed, and throwing on her dressing-gown hurried downstairs. She went first to the paper she most feared. What she saw appalled her. She took it into the kitchen and while the coffee was filtering through she reread it. Her cheeks were flaming. The peace she had been arriving at while she lay thinking in bed disappeared. When her parents, Adam, his parents, her colleagues read it—oh God, oh God! She considered fleeing, getting into the car and driving off, but then thought of Matthew and knew she could not. She went to the phone and took it off the hook. Now she was alone in the house. Her parents were looking after Emma for the weekend, Iris was with her parents, and Adam had returned to his love nest. Fanny needed him, he had said: she too was being hounded by the press.

She drank the first cup of coffee too fast, scalding herself, but it steadied her. Though the thought of food made her sick, she forced herself to eat a slice of toast. She was glad she had, because afterward the sickness lessened and she became able to think. She poured out more coffee and took it into the living room, still in her dressing gown. Its orderliness calmed her; not quite everything was gone, not yet.

Her career was ruined, of course. She'd never be able to show her face on the box again. Journalism, possibly, but the BBC wouldn't have her, that was certain. Other channels, though—perhaps. She thought about Adam and felt bitterness. *He'd* get away with it all right. Trust Adam. Oh, he'd have to wait a couple of years or so before he became Bennett, Q.C. What's a couple of years? It crossed her mind that he'd be furious with her for dragging his name into the mud, as he'd put it. Never mind Fanny, that sort of thing happened, even to barristers; he'd live that down. But to get into the Sunday papers with that kind of dirt! How could she do it to him. She heard his voice, and suddenly his anger gave her pleasure. At least she'd done *that*, she thought, feeling as though she had slapped him really hard across the face.

She thought of ringing David, and wondered if he had already tried to phone her, though she doubted he took that particular Sunday paper. Should she call him? Seeing that photograph had made her feel a kind of shame. It was not because of what they had done, it was the knowledge of the thousands of sniggering smiles spread across the country that morning. It crossed her mind that though she didn't love David, she did feel affection for him. It wasn't just sex. But whatever she had felt, it had never remotely been worth all of this! She snatched the center page of the newspaper and crumpled it up between her hands, angrily squashing, smashing at the sheet until she had pounded it to a small ball.

Anger revived her, made her see how passive she had been this last week. From the beginning she had been stunned by Matthew's disappearance. Now, at last, there was some action she could take. For a start, there were the newspapers. She'd make them all so scared that none of Monday's papers would dare touch the story. And there must be some way she could get this disgusting rag for publishing the photograph. It came to her that she needed Adam's help. He'd pull out every stop, however mad he was, if only for his own sake. That was the first move. Then she'd ring all the editors, the television and radio news editors as well, warn them she'd sue anyone who left the slightest opening. She'd make such a stink. Energy flowed back, as when an ice block melts and the river flows free again. She jumped to her feet and ran out to the phone, breathing fast.

It was an extremely unpleasant phone call. Adam had not yet seen the papers, so she had to wait for him to bring them in and find the right page. While she waited she sipped her first brandy of the day. Adam's voice when he returned was unrecognizable. It was as though someone had hit him in the throat. At first she could not even distinguish the individual words. When his voice did clear she wished it had not.

"Whore!" he shouted. "Pervert! Where did you find him? Did you pick him off the streets? Did you pay him! Or did he pay you? Is that your kick too, to be paid!"

Jess held the phone away, too upset to reply. She had not expected this. He went on shouting for a minute or two, then stopped. "Jess," he said. "Jess?"

She considered cutting him off, but she needed his help. She forced herself to reply. "Have you finished?"

"No! I haven't started." He began again.

She was by the phone in the hall. She began to count the bannisters in the stairs, thought she'd miscounted and began again from the bottom. Suddenly she said loudly into the phone, cutting through his voice,

225

"You're a bloody hypocrite! All I've done is to go to bed a few times with someone, but you! You've walked out, left us all . . ."

He shouted obscenities back, too gross for her to take. She slammed the phone down but waited for him to call back. He did, instantly, as she had known he would. She let the phone ring a while before she picked it up.

"You'd better tell me exactly what happened," he said coldly. "How the hell did they get hold of the photograph? Were you being paid to pose, or did you do it for kicks?"

Her voice was slow, full of scorn. "You're disgusting. Next time I shan't pick up the phone."

"Well, who *did* take the photograph? What else am I to suppose?"

"Yvette took it. I thought she was out, but she wasn't."

"Christ. How many did she take?"

"I don't know. I think a couple."

"Why didn't you shut the door? What if Emma . . . ?"

"Emma was out, of course. What do you take me for?"

He told her. She was just about to replace the phone again when he stopped himself and asked her how many men she'd had.

"There were none until you . . . !" she cried in anguish.

"Hypocrite!" he shouted back. "All those times you were late, don't you think I knew! Those lunches, those weekends away, don't you think I knew what a whore you were!"

"Adam! I never, *never* . . ."

"You fucking hypocrite, you've lied all our marriage. Do you take me for a fool?"

They both fell silent. He realized what he had been saying. It had never occurred to him before to doubt her. Was what he had said true?

"Adam," she said at last. "I rang you as a lawyer. I want to know what to do now. We have to stop tomorrow's papers."

He groaned. He had not thought about the future, only of her and what she had so evidently done. When he spoke his voice was almost normal again—precise, careful, giving nothing away.

"Wait a minute. I'll look at it again. Hold on." Hearing a rustling of paper close to the phone, her cheeks burned. "I don't think there's any way we can get them," he said, apparently still looking at the picture. "The photograph's not exactly obscene. In fact, it's not obscene at all, I suppose. Though we could debate that—the definition of obscenity is pretty vague." He pulled himself up, stopped by the realization of what he was proposing to do. His temper rose again. "What have they cut? Eh? What else was happening?"

She couldn't answer. When he repeated himself she said dully, "Nothing. What else do you think?"

He began to shout about whips, black leather, chains, until she screeched at him to stop it. Stiffly, he apologized. For a minute or two they managed to talk like lawyer and client. There could be no question of suing for libel since what the photograph showed was so horribly, obviously true. She refused to tell him anything about what she had been doing, agreed only that yes, they had been making love; yes, that would presumably be absolutely clear in the untrimmed part of the photograph, and yes, if there were other photographs they would make it even clearer. What was shown was true: she had no choice but to admit it.

He was silent, then. She expected him to ask who the man was, but he didn't. He did say, almost casually, as though he no longer cared, "Are you in love with him?"

She couldn't judge his reaction when she said, "No."

They were discussing what line they would take with the rest of the media, for he had agreed, Sunday or no Sunday, to call all the newspaper editors himself, when suddenly he interrupted himself and asked in tones of amazement, "But how could you? You, of all people?"

She wanted to defend herself, to explain. "It was a moment's thing, that's all. I'd seen a film at BAFTA . . ." But the truth was too complicated.

He couldn't leave it alone. "What *else* were you doing?" He seemed in pain. It was not prurience, she could hear that; it was as though something fundamental to him had been damaged. She refused to answer, kept bringing the talk back to plans, but he couldn't let it go.

Finally, his voice so cold now, he said, "At least we can keep the other papers quiet until the excitement's died down. I'll see to that."

She hesitated. "Ought we to meet, to discuss it?"

His reply was instant. "I never want to set eyes on you again. Do you understand? Never."

She wanted to shout at the unfairness of it, that if it had not been for him she would never have bothered to look at another man, but she knew there was no point. He would not hear what she was saying.

"I'll ring you if there's anything unexpected," he said and put down the phone.

Jess dropped into the chair by the telephone, trembling. She sat for some minutes, trying to take hold of herself. It was quite a while before she was able to go into her study and start making a list of the television and radio people she needed to call. She had a sense of unreality and was not quite able to believe in what she was doing. After she had made this first move, what then? What action could she take after that?

She had almost completed the list when the phone rang. She stretched out a hand then hesitated. From now on every phone call was to be dreaded. Unless it were David. It might be David. Or the police about Matthew. She waited, then fearing what she might be missing she lowered her hand and picked up the receiver. It was an unknown voice at the other end, a woman's voice, slow and thick, as though heavy with drugs or drink.

An immense tiredness had overcome Carrie. That Matthew was not hers was a grief that seemed bottomless until she thought of what his true mother must be suffering. Then the remorse she felt for causing that woman's pain touched fibers so deep she doubted she could bear so much unhappiness.

She was standing quite still, hands hanging at her sides. She did not cry. Her eyes felt hot and swollen, but dried out. She was parched; empty; a huge chrysalid from which the living creature had departed, leaving behind brown paper-thin skin, and bone. It was the bone that kept her upright; that, and a last surviving shred of will power.

There was no madness left. She saw everything very clearly, sparing herself not at all. Of the real mother she could no longer think: at the thought of a grief perhaps greater than her own the bone began to disintegrate. She thought of Aidan, and of how in her craziness she had imagined making him a gift of "their" baby. She thought of her own dead child. Of her dead parents, and her guilt. Had she not killed them both? Young as she had been then, she had done what she had done, and as a result both had died. No use that she knew she was innocent: what difference could knowing that make in the face of their deaths?

She thought again of Aidan. She loved him. That was the true gift she had had to give him. Her love. There had been no need of anything else. Inside herself her love for him thrust against her chest like a live child; she put her hands there and felt it beating.

But she was too tired. Even if he forgave her what she had done, if somehow he came to understand, it would be too late. She was too tired. She couldn't take any more.

228

She thought, and saw what she had to do. Going into her bedroom she opened the top drawer of the white-painted chest of drawers and searched behind her handkerchiefs until she found the half-full bottle of sleeping pills stored away long ago. She looked at them for a while, then put the bottle down, unopened, on top of the chest. Picking up her keys she went out of the house, down to the telephone booth at the corner of the road. Carefully she looked around for Aidan before she left the house, but he was not in sight.

Everything happened exactly as she had anticipated. She dialed the police, told the voice that replied she had information about a stolen baby she would only give direct to the baby's mother. The man replying tried to delay her, but when she refused to tell her name and threatened to put down the phone he gave in and told her Jess's telephone number. There was something about the tense voice that convinced him this was no hoax. Carrie then dialed Jess, who answered with her usual crispness. Carrie had not imagined such a voice; had assumed tears, softness.

For a few moments Carrie was speechless. It was as though she had dropped out of warm stagnant air into a cold sea. She had been moving as a somnambulist moves, had already thought herself into the final sleep. The plan had come to her ready-made: it had needed no consideration. She would phone the baby's mother, hurry home and take the pills, then lock herself into her bedroom. With so many pills it would not take long.

The woman at the other end of the phone repeated her number, and asked impatiently who it was. Carrie heard herself saying the words she had planned on the brief walk to the telephone, finally adding the warning she had prepared. "You must not stop and look around," she said in a harsh voice. "Take the baby and go, or I can't be responsible for what might happen." From some old film the words and the tone came.

But even as she said them she was stirring into life. Until a moment ago there had been nothing left but guilt. The shock of this last hour had finally emptied her. But now? This woman's voice?

Very carefully she put down the phone and stood staring at it. That had not been a voice demolished by grief. A woman with that voice could survive anything. And anyway, there was nothing for her to survive any longer. She would have her baby back safely—she need not weep for *her*. Nor die for her.

Slowly Carrie walked out of the phone booth. She held the voice in her head and thought about the woman. About what her nature might be.

Wondered at such control, even if it were only surface. Compared the woman (about whom her intuition told her everything, she imagined) with herself.

On the way to the phone she had been blind, had seen nothing. Now, returning, she saw everything—a spike of grass pushing through a crack between the pavement and a garden wall, a child's marble gleaming in the gutter, the lovely shading of the heavy clouds above her—saw it all through eyes that a moment ago had assumed death. She heard, too; heard a plane unsighted overhead, an excited dog yapping, children shouting in play. She shivered. It came to her she had nearly sleepwalked into death.

She stopped and laid a hand on the low boundary wall cutting off the building from the pavement. The bricks were cold and rough to her touch. Behind the wall rubbish had collected, blown by the wind. She looked at it all with love. The scraps of discarded paper, empty packets, touched her to tears.

I've let it all happen to me, she said to herself, ever since I was twelve. I've just folded my arms over my head. She withdrew her hand and walked on. What could happen worse, she asked herself? So much, and yet I'm still alive. She touched the wall again. It was very solid. She felt the pavement under her feet as solid. Going to the phone, it had been as though she were walking through mist on soft rubber.

Entering her flat she saw it as though disconnected from it, saw it as a shabby depressing place that now she could leave. All that had happened to her until now she could leave. Except for Aidan, if he would still have her.

She took off her coat, and with a firm step set about preparing herself. First she went back to the front door and left it slightly ajar. She did not want the baby awakened by the doorbell when the mother arrived. Then she packed a few things in a small suitcase. Perhaps they wouldn't let her take anything with her to prison, but she might as well be ready. Halfway through the packing she noticed the bottle of sleeping pills and went and emptied them down the lavatory.

She looked at the baby only once. He was still asleep, lying on his back with one arm outstretched. She knelt beside him and, carefully lifting his head, freed Aidan's sweater. She stroked his hair gently for a few moments, then pulled the sweater on over her head. She was warmed by it, felt almost happy inside it. Finally she decided to light a last fire. There was only one firelighter left, so after setting a match to it she stretched out a sheet of newspaper over the front of the fire, propping it in place with a poker on one side and a toasting fork on the other. Even so, the fire would take some time to draw, she knew. She crouched in front of it, watching the paper for the first sign of browning. She felt endlessly patient. There was no rush. From now on there was all the time in the world.

Jess drove across North London with the controlled brilliance of a fireman on his way to an urgent call. Her horn served for the two-toned bell of the emergency services, though—fortunately for her and the public—since it was Sunday and a gray day at that, there were few cars about. She slowed at red lights but, horn blaring, continued through them, swerving neatly to avoid foolhardy drivers who ignored her warning. At a pedestrian crossing, where a taxi was waiting while an old lady hobbled over, she accelerated and roared past the traffic island on the wrong side of the road. Once, on a long straight stretch, the needle touched seventy. Always she had exulted in challenge. But privately. Excitement showed only in the brightness of her eyes and the controlled tightness at the corners of her mouth. The faster she went the cooler she appeared, though she burned inside. The intensity of her concentration lifted any remaining fears for Matthew. He was safe and well—in that at least she had believed the voice.

Rounding a corner her tires screeched. She saw the horrified face of a pedestrian leaping for safety, his mouth violent as he screeched abuse at her, and she laughed aloud. She overtook two ambling cars at sixty miles an hour, her hand never leaving the horn. In front a car, whose driver saw her coming in his mirror, careened wildly over the curb out of her path, brakes squealing like a terrified pig.

Once she glimpsed a shocked policeman spin around as she sped past him, but she was gone too fast for him to even note her number. There came into her mind a momentary desire for a victim, though when a dog ran across the road she automatically swerved to avoid it. It was this last that slowed her down: this, and the fact that she was coming to the end of her journey.

Turning off the main road into a small side street she skidded to a stop and consulted a town map. Quickly she memorized the route, and four minutes later drew up outside Carrie's flat. The entire journey had taken just under fifteen minutes.

The flat was silent. Matthew was sleeping deeply, curled up on his side with head sunk into circling arm. Carrie crouched in front of the fire,

231

watching the stretched paper. Through the closed windows no sound of outside traffic penetrated the still rooms.

A bluebottle, which had been crawling along the edge of a pool of spilt sweet tea on the kitchen table, suddenly rose, darted through the door into the living room and landed for a second on Matthew's cheek. The child twitched and the fly shot up to the ceiling where it circled, angrily buzzing for some seconds before hurling itself at the windows. Finding no exit it flew high and low, hitting the glass again and again but seeming to do itself no harm. Then it returned to the lake of tea where it settled once more.

Not even the sound of a slamming front door disturbed Carrie: she had passed into a state of meditative calm. Jess's arrival was momentarily incomprehensible to her though she had planned it. She became aware of footsteps hurrying through the flat, but even before she could bring herself to move there was a scuffling and the sound of Matthew being awakened unexpectedly—an objecting whimper, a half cry. Carrie turned and saw a woman on her knees gathering the child into her arms and kissing him wildly all over his face.

Jess was beside herself. The relief at finding Matthew unhurt released in her a force which Matthew instantly picked up, turned his cry into a wail of alarm. Until now Jess had stayed in control: with Matthew in her arms she broke.

It was now she became aware of Carrie's presence. Until that moment she had thought of nothing but Matthew; everything else was forgotten. As she looked up and saw Carrie it seemed to her this blond woman with large high breasts and clear eyes standing looking at her from the other side of the room was at the same time both the woman who had stolen Matthew and the hated Fanny.

There was nothing that woman had not done! she cried to herself, nothing she had not taken from her!

Jess's known world exploded in her face. All she had achieved, all she had worked for! She let out a sob of pure rage.

Carrie, hearing, misinterpreted the sound. She stepped forward, putting out a hand. It was a gesture of sorrow for what she had done, an asking for forgiveness—but in her wildness Jess took the movement to be one of attack. The last restraint disappeared. She became a vehicle of anger so fierce that conscious thought ceased. Laying Matthew down, she snatched up a pair of sharp pointed dressmaker's scissors from a low table and ran at Carrie, her face unrecognizable.

232

Carrie had known it all before. The same scissors, the same hate distorting a bitter face. She felt the old pain, the ripping, the stabbing. This time she would not endure it!

Her arms shot out, grappled with the stony figure; as in a dream she fought for herself. But she was fighting against someone inspired by outrage beyond her normal strength. She was forced to the present. The illusion of her mother faded: she knew where she was now. She hesitated; lost all desire to hurt this woman whom she had already so badly hurt.

Instantly Jess lifted the arm holding the scissors, reached back then drove them forward mercilessly. She pierced Carrie's chest as easily as if she had used a filleting knife. For a moment the two women stared at each other as a shock of pain ripped through Carrie. She tried to say something, but her head was bursting open in a soundless explosion. She dissolved in its incandescence, was gone.

Jess was standing looking down at the figure sprawled on its back on the floor. She wanted to run, to scream: instead she made herself drop to her knees, place a hand over the woman's heart.

It was beating.

When the relief had subsided, she cautiously touched the scissors, which stuck out a couple of inches above where she had lain her hand. Very little blood had formed around the entry, just a slight seepage that had already ceased. She shuddered and dropped her head between her knees as she accepted the knowledge that she had not chosen where to plunge in the knife—it had only needed to be a little lower, and then. . . ! She would have been a murderer. She crouched forward for what seemed endless time facing this thought—though no more than seconds passed—until suddenly she queried it, asked herself if this were really true, if she had not in fact at some level beyond thought chosen to stab high?

Now it seemed to her she was almost more to blame for wasting time than for the attack. Rousing herself she took Carrie's wrist and held it until she had satisfied herself the pulse was regular, strong. She left the scissors alone, fearful that blood might spurt out.

At this point her common sense took charge. Picking up Matthew, she hurried through the flat, searching for a phone. She found none and, running out of the flat, hammered on the doors of the two neighboring apartments. There was no reply from either. She wondered whether to run upstairs but what if they were out too, or without a phone? Better not risk it. She hurried down the stairs.

233

At the end of the street she could see a phone booth, but a gang of youths were occupying it. A couple of them standing outside turned and, seeing her, whistled out loud. Instinctively she leaped into her car. There would be another phone, a policeman, something, within a few yards.

Starting the engine and tucking Matthew into his carry cot seemed such normal functions, for the first time since she had taken that incredible phone call her mind regained its normal clarity. She saw what faced her. After what she had just done, after the scandal of the photograph, they'd never let her keep her children. Even if she were not jailed—she'd excuse enough, for God's sake—they'd deny she was a fit person to bring them up.

Then what would be left? No children, no job, no Adam.

She drove slowly, looking for a phone booth, but searched for three or four minutes before she found one. It was during those minutes—a time of pause in her life between one existence and another, for nothing now could ever be the same again—she made the discovery that all her life she had been under a complete misapprehension. Hadn't she been brought up to believe you could control life? that if you pressed the right buttons, did the right things, you got the right prizes. No one had ever told her life could, quite gratuitously, kick you in the belly for no reason at all, fuck up everything simply because life was like that—chaotic, unplanned, reasonless.

Why me? she had asked herself earlier, why me when I've always played fair, made the right choices? Now she saw into the pit and didn't know whether she could exist in a world where that sort of question is meaningless.

Seeing an empty phone booth she braked and drew up beside it. In the back Matthew was gurgling happily to himself—he always loved driving in cars, would talk to himself endlessly in contentment. She hesitated, her hand on the door. She could run. Go to her bank, draw out money, collect her jewelry and other inherited loot, put together enough to keep her and the children for a long time abroad.

But knew, even as she thought all that, that she would make the phone call, would not flee. That no, she wasn't free, she hadn't any choice. She would behave as she had been taught to behave, would face whatever was coming.

And after all, in a way, wasn't that a relief? Wasn't that very lack of

234

choice the only possible human answer to chaos? Wouldn't real freedom be more than anyone could bear?

The brown spot that Carrie had been waiting for appeared on the taut newspaper within half a minute of Jess slamming the front door behind her. First only the very center of the paper was singed. Then, as the flames grew and began to roar up the chimney, the paper was increasingly dragged inward until a patch a foot or more across was darkened. Soon the center turned black, started to crumble away, and suddenly burst open. Like a lion jumping through a circus hoop, flames leaped outward into the room. In a flash the entire newspaper was engulfed. Several scraps flew, blazing, up the chimney; others hovered delicately in the air before dropping harmlessly onto the hearth. The largest fragment, still burning, drifted away into the room; rising and dipping, it slowly floated toward the sofa. A few inches away, it fell onto the woollen carpet, twisting and curling in a final dance as the still unburned center slowly carbonized. But not before a final flare had reached out to the ancient horsehair sofa and licked the sacking at its base.

Immediately the sacking caught fire. Dried, full of dust, it flamed up and was consumed within seconds. But the damage was done. From under the sofa smoke began to drift, meager at first, no more than a harmless-seeming vapor. Then it thickened, took on a menacing solidity. Carrie, still in a deep faint, was unaware. She lay motionless, several feet away in the middle of the room.

Gradually the smoke thickened, poured out from under the sofa like thick cream. Undisturbed by any draft the smoke moved slowly, for Jess had closed the living room door behind her as well as the front door; earlier Carrie herself had shut the window against the Sunday morning bells. Soon the ceiling was totally obscured by rising smoke from which particles of soot dropped unnoticed onto the motionless body on the floor. Meanwhile the fire in the grate, without the newspaper to help it draw, went out.

Sunday mornings David always followed the same routine. Not even the occasional advent of girl friends disturbed it. Other days the morning papers were dropped early through the letter box, but on Sundays he liked to take a leisurely breakfast with properly made coffee instead of his usual tea-bag tea, preceded by a stroll in the fresh air down to the newsstand.

First he would rise at least an hour later than usual, then, after shaving, he would lay the table, slice the bread, and drop it all ready into the toaster, put a half-filled kettle onto the lit gas, turned as low as it would go, add whatever garment—coat or sweater—was necessary, and walk with none of his usual urgency the quarter-mile to the shops. There he would buy his favorite Sunday paper, and sometimes, if he felt especially self-indulgent, a small bar of candy for later. The walk back was usually slightly quicker, spurred on by the nearing prospect of breakfast, but if the sun were shining he tended to linger as he passed under trees or by a particularly attractive front garden. Back in his flat he would turn up the gas if the water were not yet boiling, spoon fresh coffee into the paper filter waiting in the coffee pot, press down the toaster, and pour the first drops of boiling water onto the coffee grains. By the time the last of the water was added, the toast would be nicely browned. Then he would sit down, butter his toast, spread it with honey or marmalade, and open the paper. Only if he were particularly hungry would he boil up an egg in the remaining water.

Today, as on all other days, he carried out this routine without any variation—though checking the headlines to see if there was any news of Matthew—except that he had bought a copy of every paper that was available. Not being hungry, he didn't bother with an egg and spread one slice of toast with honey, the other with marmalade. Pouring out his coffee, he breathed in the aroma with pleasure, slowly added milk and sugar, and stirred it with deliberation before putting the cup to his lips, conscious as always that this was his favorite moment in the day. When he turned to the papers he sighed: the pill was huge, reminding him of office work. He hesitated, then pushing the others away he began to read the front page of his usual paper. As he did so he took a bite of toast, a sip of coffee, another bite of toast, adjusted the paper so that he could read to the end of a column, and took more coffee.

But he couldn't settle. It was no good, the huge pile of papers nagged at him. He was certain they were innocent of what Jess feared, but he could not ignore them. With another sigh he pushed his toast and coffee to one side and settled down to skim through the heap. Rapidly he turned over page after page and, as he had expected, found nothing. Until he came to the last paper, the one, he knew afterward, he should have looked at first.

Perhaps it was its very reputation that had made him leave it until the end. Opening it at the center page he saw what he had not expected to find. At first he didn't even realize what he was looking at. In black and white reproduction the scene bore little relationship to how he had perceived what had been happening at the time the photograph was taken. Then he recognized what it was. He felt as though the pit of his stomach had caved in. A blush of shame traveled through his whole body, leaving him wet with sweat. He sat stunned for several minutes, looking again and again at the picture, reading and rereading what was written. He searched for any suggestion that he had been recognized. There was none, but he was horrified at what they had written about Jess.

Several times he started to go to the phone to ring Jess but turned away, assuming Adam would be there. Finally he could leave it no longer. He picked up the receiver and rapidly dialed Jess's number. The line was engaged. He tried twice more, but she seemed to be having a long call. Not knowing what to do with himself he poured out more coffee and sat drinking while he read again and again the copy accompanying the photograph. Then he looked carefully through all the other papers to check there was no mention of the affair in them. Finally he tried once more to phone Jess. This time he got the ringing tone, but there was no reply.

It was now that he remembered he had promised Aidan to meet him at Carrie's flat. He swore to himself, nearly decided not to go, but after unsuccessfully trying Jess's number several times more during the next quarter of an hour, he thought he would keep the appointment after all. It occurred to him as he cleaned his teeth that perhaps Jess was not taking any calls. At that he went back and after dialing again he sat listening to her phone ringing for five minutes or more, hoping that if she were in she might guess who it was and eventually pick up the receiver. When it was clear she wasn't going to, he debated whether or not to risk meeting Adam face to face and call at her house. He couldn't make up his mind how risky this was. In the end he decided he would meet Aidan, check that Carrie was all right, then phone Jess from a box somewhere. If she still didn't answer he would call around there. To hell with the risk. He couldn't leave her alone any longer on a day like this.

He met Aidan walking up the street from the Underground. He stopped and took him into the car though Carrie's flat was less than a couple of

237

hundred yards away. Aidan was looking haggard: the sight of him stirred David out of his own absorption. With the desire to help Aidan came a sudden intense wish that there were someone *he* could lean on, someone he could pour everything out to. He looked quickly at Aidan. The thought flashed through his mind that if Carrie still wouldn't let them in they could go together to some pub and swap miseries. Impossible though with a client.

Silently they walked together up the stairs. Climbing the last flight David became aware of the smell of smoke, but it was Aidan who darted forward and pushed up the flap of the letter box. He spun around, his face white.

"The flat's on fire!" he shouted.

"Can you see anything?" David cried, running the last few steps.

"No. There's a cover over the box." Years before Agatha had pinned a square of green baize over it in case of some peeping Tom: Aidan was already familiar with this hindrance—during the past week he had made many attempts to poke it aside. He began to hammer on the door but no one came.

David turned sideways and hurled himself at the door, but it did not budge. Aidan joined him in the next attempt, but it seemed useless. "There are two locks," Aidan said, "and then there's a chain, even if we do break it open."

David only grunted, and together they made another attempt.

"It's no use," Aidan said, "we'll never break it down in time." It was he who went and rang the bells of the other two flats, but the occupants were out.

"Perhaps there's a housekeeper with a key?" David suggested hopefully, and together the two men ran down the stairs to the ground floor. By the elevator there was a printed notice giving an address to be contacted in case of emergency. Neither of them knew the street. Aidan looked desperate.

"I saw a phone box on the corner. We'll get the fire brigade," David said.

"She'll be dead by the time they come," Aidan shouted and ran out to the front of the building. Looking up, he saw smoke pouring out of a narrow crack at the top of Carrie's window.

"I'll climb up and break in," he called back to David, "it's the only chance."

David hesitated. "You'll never make it, it's three floors up!"

Aidan felt furious with him. "What the hell are you waiting for! Go and ring the fire brigade!" He forgot David then, concentrated only on what was in front of him. He stared up at the window, searching out a route.

Aidan had always been terrified of heights. Until a moment ago the thumping of his heart had been purely for Carrie's safety. If he had succeeded in breaking down her front door, he would have crossed through flame, taken any risk, without thought for himself. But to climb up the outside of a house! Just looking over the parapet of a bridge left him quaking, while jumping from the lowest of diving boards, even climbing a tall ladder, were acts of fearful daring on his part. Yet he was thinking of doing something far worse.

He looked away, dragged his eyes from the stream of smoke. It couldn't be done, not even for Carrie's sake. But his eyes returned, plotting out how to do it even while he was fighting a desire to be sick.

There was an outside drainpipe that ran straight up the wall, passing close by the window from which the smoke was issuing. He forced himself forward and touched it. It was hopeless. The pipe was old, rusty. He saw himself halfway up and the pipe breaking away, creaking outward, himself hanging on like a monkey as the ground came up to meet him. He let out a choked groan and covered his face with his hands.

For another man, the terror would have been the climb's end: for Aidan a flaming room was a harbor in comparison. Then he thought he heard a cry—it was in his imagination, but it was enough—and instantly his hands reached out, grasped the drainpipe high up. It had not been painted in years: flakes of rust and the jagged edges of old peeling paint cut into his hands as with no more hesitation he began to haul himself up it. Eyes shut, remembering schoolboy attempts to pull himself up ropes, his legs knew what to do, how to take the strain with calf and thigh muscles while arms reached ever higher. As he climbed his palms, scraped and slashed by the flaking metal, began to bleed. Repeatedly he skinned his knuckles on the brick wall. A flapping TV aerial running alongside the drainpipe distracted him—once a loose staple attached to it snagged on his sleeve and he had to thrash his arm about before he could free himself. By the time his head had reached the level of the third floor window he doubted he could go any further.

He looked down. It was a nearly fatal move. The ground seemed an immense distance away. In panic he clung to the pipe, pressing his cheek

239

against it as a child clings to its mother. Upward, backward, either was appalling. Sickened, he forced himself on. Within seconds he had pulled himself up enough to stretch out his left foot toward the window ledge while his right foot had just sufficient purchase on a metal tie to temporarily support him. For a moment he rested, took breath. He overcame the almost irresistible temptation to look down again, reflected how odd it was he should at the same time both want and dread to do something so badly. Then he retracted his foot and once more began to climb. He was aware of pain, saw blood trickling down his wrists, but it was nothing compared with the terror in his head. With every inch gained the more his back crawled, as though hands were reaching out from the ground scrabbling at him, willing him to fall. And yet, even though he was pallid with fear, there was growing in him an excitement, a tentative sense of triumph. When he entangled himself once more, this time with a loose telephone wire, he found himself swearing loudly at it, and was surprised at the strength of his man's voice.

At Carrie's floor he faced the last terror. Somehow he must get from the drainpipe to her window ledge. Already, before he had reached the smoke layer, soot particles had spotted his face, his hands. Pulling himself up the last couple of feet thick smoke enveloped him, filling his throat, his eyes, burning him with its heat. He had not realized smoke could be so hot. Trying to duck below the worst of it, he crouched as low as he could while reaching out his left leg. The ledge was narrower than the one on the floor below. Luxury to a mountaineer or a goat, but terror, at that height, to Aidan. If there had been time for fear, for thought, he might never have risked it. But there was none. He stretched out his left hand and forced the tips of his fingers into the narrow gap where the sash window (made soon after the war of poor unseasoned wood) had warped so badly that Carrie rarely bothered to close it properly. Sweat running, he thrust downward until he had managed to get his hand through and grasp the frame firmly. Pressing his body against the window, he finally let go of the drainpipe and grabbed the other side of the frame with his freed right hand. This last action had been a sightless one—he was blinded and half-choked by the smoke that was pouring around him even more viciously now that he had increased the opening. Unable to see or breathe he gave a great tug with both hands to the window sash. To his relief it dropped—he would have smashed his way in headfirst had it not succumbed. He gave a last heave and, hauling himself over, fell gasping onto the floor inside the room.

For a foot or two at ground level the air was less smoky than higher up. He lay there for a few moments until he had his breath back. He became aware how much of him hurt, especially his face and eyes which had been scorched by the heat bursting into his face as he opened the window—but pain now was totally irrelevant. Coughing deeply, he rolled over and rising onto his knees but keeping his head below the canopy of smoke he looked for Carrie. At first he did not see her, then crawling forward he saw her lying stretched out on her back on the far side of the room.

He stopped, unable to believe what he saw—could not make sense of the jutting-out scissors. He looked around the once familiar room to orientate himself but could hardly recognize it. From beyond Carrie—he realized at once it was the unseen sofa that had caught fire—orangy-brown smoke poured upward. As it floated toward the window, dropping its burden of soot, it paled almost to cream. Carbon coated everything—the coffee table, the carpet, the body lying on the floor—and streaked the walls and ceilings with black stain. Smoke almost blotted out the entire room, filling it like a reverse sea-tide from the top downward—only the lowest level stayed comparatively clear, and soon even that would be gone and all within drowned.

Suddenly there was a flash. The sofa, only smoldering until now, burst into flame as fresh air from the window reached it. Aidan was on his feet in an instant. Without thinking he took a deep breath as he rose. Immediately the back of his throat and nose burned as though he had swallowed fire, while his lungs seemed filled with some terrible abrasive liquid that began to thicken within seconds, turn into solid concrete. His hair and eyebrows crinkled away even in that brief exposure, as if he had put his head too near an open furnace.

Eyes and nose streaming, he dropped back to his knees and crawled toward Carrie, stopping whenever his coughing became closer to retching. His chest felt as though enclosed by an ever-tightening steel band—he thought of medieval tortures and let his mind stay with the image; anything rather than face what appeared to have happened. In another moment he was by her. Sinking to his knees he laid his head low on her chest. It was an action without hope. He thought her dead. All color had left her face except for clownish rings of black carbon round her nostrils, her mouth, as though death had taken a black pencil and outlined her features as a macabre joke. Soot hung from her eyebrows and shrouded her hair like a veil. How could he imagine her alive?

241

He lifted his head to look at her face again, only able to open his streaming eyes for a second at a time. As he stared there came from her open mouth a heavy bubbling sound as she fought against the moisture draining into her lungs, and her eyelids moved as though she were trying to open them.

He had thought her dead, and she was alive! There was a moment when it seemed to him life within himself had ceased, that he had petrified, as though rather than risk false hope he would prefer himself dead. Then emotion broke through bringing with it power of action beyond what might otherwise have been left to him. He no longer paused, not even to consider how seriously hurt she was. Sitting behind her, head lowered to his chest, he stretched out his legs on either side of her, then pulling her head and shoulders onto his lap he humped them both toward the door by digging his heels into the carpet and levering himself backward. He dared not hold her any other way for fear of driving the scissors even further in. He did not think about who had stabbed her, or why, but only that somehow he had to get them both into the air. As he moved, sweating and coughing, streamers of blackened mucus swung from his nose like snot drooping from the muzzle of an old and rheumy dog.

When he reached the closed door he paused; remembered that sometimes rooms exploded into flame when doors were opened. But what choice was there? Leaving Carrie he rose and fumbling for the handle which was lost in the gloom of smoke he pulled the door open wide. The released smoke poured out harmlessly past his head—there was no explosion. Crouching now, he reached under Carrie's armpits and dragged her the last few yards, past the door and out to the hall.

Dimly he was conscious of the two-tone bells of fire engines and police cars. But she was nearly safe now. Coughing, he ran to open the front door, then pulled her out to safety. He squatted there on the floor and gathered her into his arms. He became aware of other voices, of people clapping him on the shoulders, but he ignored them, burying his face in Carrie's. When, within another minute, the ambulance men arrived with their stretchers and cannisters of oxygen he refused to let her go. In the end they had to tear her away from him.

DAY 7

The Press had a heyday.

AIDAN and David walked slowly up the drive to the main entrance of the hospital. Aidan was clutching a large bunch of daffodils to his chest. David, seeing his bandaged hands, had offered to carry the flowers for him, but Aidan shook his head. They were talking about Carrie.

"I blame myself," David said yet again. "I should have listened to you."

"It wasn't your fault," Aidan said. "What more could you have done? She looked all right when we saw her."

"*You* knew something was wrong."

"Yes, but I was in love with her. Am in love with her."

"I still can't believe it." David longed to admit his worst crime, leaving her in Village Row while he visited Jess. If it hadn't have been for him, none of this would have happened. "Her taking the baby. Jess . . . Bennett attacking her. It was all so out of character."

"What will happen to Carrie?" Aidan asked for the third time.

"Nothing. I keep telling you that, why don't you believe me? Not after what she's been through. There'll have to be a trial, but with her background and all that's happened, they'll keep her in the psychiatric wing for a while, then let her out on probation."

They walked on in silence.

"What about Jess Bennett?" Aidan asked as though penetrating David's thoughts. "I feel sorry for her in spite of what she did to Carrie."

David did not know how to answer. Jess, heavily sedated, was in the same hospital as Carrie. He could not make up his mind whether or not to try to see her: she'd made it clear enough when they'd spoken on the phone the other day that she didn't want his name linked with hers. Yet would it be cowardly not to visit her? He thought he wanted to, but even that he was not entirely sure of. He felt compassion, but did he feel love?

"I think they'll let her off on the grounds of a breakdown," he said at last, "mind temporarily disturbed, something like that. It was true enough, after all." He was desperate to talk about her, to discuss what he should do. How was he going to keep silent all his life about something like that?

Looking up he saw a familiar figure coming toward them, angrily waving his arms about his face as though trying to brush off a swarm of midges. It was Adam, come from visiting Jess, surrounded by pressmen. As they passed by each other the two men exchanged glances, but Adam did not stop or even nod. David turned red. He could not make out from Adam's expression what he had known. Or guessed.

The pressmen looked across at them. Hesitated as they recognized Aidan, the hero of the day—as yet they had not found out about his past. David sensed danger. If they photographed him and someone spotted the similarity! But the journalists were not interested in David. A group broke away from Adam and turned to follow Aidan, calling out to him to wait a bit, asking him if the daffodils were for Carrie. David, reprieved, dropped behind, keeping out of their way.

They ran up the steps in front of Aidan, forcing him to stop. Cameras flashed, someone thrust a microphone in front of his nose.

"What did you feel like after that climb when you saw she'd been stabbed?" a voice said. "Didn't you have any idea at all about the baby?" another shouted. "Will you stick by her?"

Aidan lifted his head and looked straight at them. "Fuck off!" he drawled deliberately and shoved his way through them.

"We're only doing our job," one protested, but Aidan was already pushing open the doors.